PRINCESS OF MERMAIDS

Fairy Tale Adventures Book Three

A.G. MARSHALL

D1714531

Avanell Publishing

For Aunt Cindy
And all my sisters
(in the mermaid sense of the word)

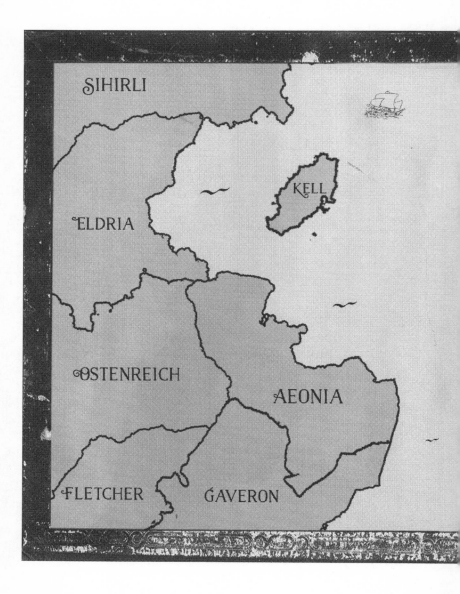

"Don't dawdle, Fiora."

The King of Kell pushed past his daughter and strode up the gangplank to his ship. Fiora glared at him. She hated the way his bright red beard flowed in the wind. It matched her own red hair perfectly, and that had ruined everything.

In spite of her father's warning, she stopped walking and turned for one last look at Aeonia. The royal castle glistened in the sunlight, showing no trace of the conflict that had just passed. No trace of goblins and shadows and rumors of war.

Fiora gritted her teeth. Blast them all, she had been so close! If they had followed the rules instead of letting an impostor waltz in and take the throne, she would be engaged to Prince Alaric right now.

She would be free.

"Get on the ship, Fiora! I won't ask again."

Something warm rolled down Fiora's cheek, and she hastily brushed it away. She wasn't the sort to cry. Blasted tear. Even her own eyes were turning against her.

She glanced around the dock to make sure no one had seen the treacherous tear and scowled when she realized someone had.

King Gustave of Montaigne watched her with concern in his gray eyes. Fiora glared to warn him away, but he approached her with a cautious smile.

"Are you well, Princess?"

"Fine. Wonderful."

Her accent was always stronger when she was upset, and it was positively lilting now. The strain of keeping her magic contained made the words shrill even to her own ears.

Fiora turned to walk away and tripped on a loose board. She stumbled, and King Gustave caught her arm with a steady hand. She looked up at him as he helped her regain her balance.

"Princess Fiora, I would be honored to assist you however I can."

His gentle eyes showed none of the contempt the other royals gave her. It was probably his youth. He was about her own age, although his neatly trimmed beard made it difficult to tell. Fiora suspected he had grown it for that very reason. He was young to be king, and the beard made him look more distinguished.

She met his compassionate gaze, and another tear rolled down her cheek. She jerked her arm away from him.

"I said I'm fine."

She couldn't afford to show weakness now. Fiora walked up the gangplank without looking back and went straight to her father's cabin. There was no point delaying the inevitable. He'd summon her there soon enough.

She paused outside the door to remove her shoe and pull a pearl ring off her toe. She could wear it normally again now that she didn't have to match all the other girls in the Princess Test. Fiora quickly shoved the ring onto her finger. She wiggled her toes, stretching them out and enjoying the freedom before she put her shoe back on. At least it fit properly now that she wasn't squeezing her pearl ring into it. At least she wouldn't have to fight every moment to keep from wincing or scowling from the pain.

Fiora had delayed long enough. She pushed open the door and

entered her father's study. King Fergal sat at his desk writing a letter. He didn't look up, so Fiora sank into a chair in the corner. She studied her ring while she waited. The pearl had lost some of its luster. Most of it, in fact. The luminous surface had gone dull.

This was bad.

The ship cast off, and the hateful land of Aeonia faded into the horizon. Fiora watched through a porthole, glad to be rid of the place that had so thoroughly rejected her.

When the mountains were nothing more than a thin line on the edge of the ocean, her father crumpled his letter around a rock, tied a piece of twine around it, and threw it out the port-hole. Then he turned to her.

"That was badly done, Fiora. You mangled things from start to finish."

"I would have won if they followed the rules of the Princess Test. I won the contests. Prince Alaric should have chosen me."

"A lot of good that does us now."

Her father's voice was calm, and that worried Fiora more than anything else that had happened so far. He should be yelling. He should be furious.

"There will be other Princess Tests, Father. I've mastered all the traditional skills. I'll win next time."

"We had a deal, Fiora. There won't be a next time."

Fiora fought the urge to shrink back and kept her head high.

"I was closer this time than ever. Give me one more chance."

"No more chances, Fiora. You agreed to the deal, and you'll keep your end of the bargain."

Blast. She had only made that bargain because she was certain she could win Prince Alaric's hand. Because she had devoted her every waking moment to practicing skills for the competition and was confident she would be the best.

"Look on the bright side. At least you won't have to embroider any more cushions."

"I like embroidery."

"Don't be ridiculous."

His tone said she was being unreasonable. Fiora bristled.

"I was the best, wasn't I? It's not fair! I won!"

"Fiora, it's time to face the fact that no one wants you. You've lost several Princess Tests in spite of your superior skills. Elspeth is of age now. Perhaps she'll have better luck wooing a king. Kell needs an ally, and our options are limited."

"How limited? Father what do you have planned?"

Instead of answering, King Fergal stood and gestured for Fiora to follow. She sulked a few steps behind him, delaying as much as she dared. Small acts of disobedience were all you could get away with around her father. She'd learned that the hard way.

The King of Kell stood on the deck of the ship, looking out at the open sea. In spite of herself, Fiora smiled a little as the sea breeze sweep over her face. She always felt free when sailing.

"An arranged match it is then," she said. "I agreed to let you choose for me if I couldn't secure a husband on my own, and I'll honor my word."

Her father glanced at her, and something gleamed in his eyes. Was that compassion? Fiora's heart beat faster. This was worse than she expected.

"Is he noble?" she asked. "You could at least tell me a little about him."

He stayed silent. The King of Kell never stayed silent. Fiora fought back the panic building in her chest and tried to sound calm.

"Is he old, then? I expect he's ancient, rich, and common. A wealthy ally would do as much good as a noble one."

Her father still wouldn't meet her gaze. Fiora swallowed and stared at the waves.

"What's wrong with him, Father? What's so wrong with him that he is willing to accept me?"

"I haven't chosen someone for you to marry, Fiora. No one

would have you. I said I would choose your next placement, not your next husband, and I've done that."

Something broke the surface of the water. Something sharp and black. King Fergal hummed a soft tune, and Fiora gasped.

"Father, no."

"Elspeth doesn't stand a chance with you around reminding everyone how very undesirable the royal family of Kell is considered. It's time for you to go home and get out of her way."

Fiora glanced down at her ring. The pearl was a blank white orb. All the luster had gone. Her breath caught in her throat as a sharp pain pierced her feet and traveled up her legs.

"Father, please don't send me away. I'll work harder. I'll do anything."

The King of Kell watched the boiling water with a stern expression. The hint of compassion in his eyes had disappeared.

"How could you? I'm your daughter as much as Elspeth is!"

A song echoed through the wind, and more fins pierced the waves. Fiora shoved her father aside and sprinted across the ship.

She wasn't fast enough. An enormous tentacle shot out from the water and wrapped around her waist.

Fiora screamed as it lifted her off the ship and pulled her beneath the waves.

❧ 2 ❧

A FEW WEEKS LATER...

"If I may say so, Your Majesty, that was an absolute disaster."

Marquis Corbeau held his long, white beard in place with one hand to keep it from blowing in the sea wind.

The other hand gestured to the wreckage that had once been the kingdom of Santelle's harbor and royal palace.

King Gustave of Montaigne wished he could disagree with his advisor, but Marquis Corbeau was right. Gustave had done his best to help Princess Carina and Prince Stefan save the day during the recent kraken attack, but things had not gone smoothly.

They sailed past the wreckage of the Onslaught, and Gustave winced. The kraken had swept away the mast and smashed holes in the sides. It would be a long time before Santelle's greatest ship was seaworthy again.

"I suppose it could have been worse," Gustave said. "At least the kraken didn't level the entire palace."

"I'm not talking about the kraken attack. I'm talking about Princess Carina!"

Gustave shrugged. The movement sent pain shooting down

his left arm, which had been injured in the recent fight. He winced, which made his head ache where a falling rock had hit it.

Both his head and arm were bandaged, but rather roughly. Santelle didn't believe in coddling people. The castle's doctor was a retired ship surgeon who had proclaimed Gustave's injuries nothing to be concerned about, wrapped him in bandages, and sent him on his way.

Gustave realized that Marquis Corbeau expected a reply.

"Carina's punishment was harsh, but I think she'll be happy with Stefan."

Marquis Corbeau narrowed his eyes.

"Stop deliberately misunderstanding me, Your Majesty. You were supposed to marry her yourself. Instead, she's sailing into the sunset with a hedgehog-haired second son of Aeonia."

Gustave smirked at this description of Stefan, and Marquis Corbeau's scowl deepened.

"This is not amusing, Your Majesty. Now I will have to start the search for a suitable wife for you all over again. There are only so many eligible young ladies available. You can't keep rejecting them out of hand if you want to be married by your birthday."

"I don't want to be married by my birthday."

Gustave turned away from the wreckage on the shore and looked to the open sea. To temporary freedom, if Marquis Corbeau would give him a moment's peace. As long as Kathelin and the mermaids upheld their end of the bargain, there would be no more kraken attacks.

But that didn't mean the damage from past ones would magically disappear. When they reached Montaigne, Gustave would be thrown back into the chaos of life as king. He wished Marquis Corbeau would let him have a few moments of peace before he began to rebuild the country and sort through the aftermath.

But the marquis wasn't finished.

"Your Majesty, marriage is an essential part of your responsibilities as king. Why are you being so stubborn?"

"I want to find my father before I marry. Before my duties as a suitor and husband take my focus away from the search, or my time spent searching takes me away from my future bride. Is that so bad?"

Marquis Corbeau clucked in disapproval.

"Your Majesty, this ill-conceived quest for your father must stop."

Gustave glared at his advisor and raised his ring to his lips.

"Find King Francois."

The magical ruby sparked to life and shone a light towards the horizon. The ring could track anyone that Gustave had personally met as long as they were alive. So if it tracked his father, King Francois must still be alive.

Except the light had led every search party it guided on a wild goose chase. Months of searching had yielded no results. His father had been missing for nearly a year, and Gustave had not found a single trace of him.

Marquis Corbeau gave up on Gustave and stalked over to question the ship's captain about their course. Captain Whist tilted his enormous hat at Gustave in a salute and proceeded to distract the marquis by pretending to implement his suggestions to speed their journey home.

Gustave pulled a small shell from his pocket and turned it over in his hand. Carina had given it to him after Kathelin the mermaid gave it to her. It must do something. Maybe something magical? It had a few markings carved into it, but as far as Gustave could tell, they were merely decorations.

He leaned over and stared into the water, hoping to see Kathelin and have her confirm that the kraken were under control now that the mermaids had the magic gem in their possession. The mermaids' behavior had been erratic. They had attacked and protected humans seemingly on a whim. Stolen from them and given gifts in return. Gustave wanted a chance to get to know them better. Perhaps they could become allies.

A flash of red caught Gustave's eye. He squinted at the water. Was something down there after all?

For a moment, he saw a mermaid shining in a sunbeam. Long, coppery hair billowed around her like a cloak.

Then a wave swept over her, and she disappeared into the depths.

3

"**M**adame Isla, that's a fork. Humans use them to eat."

Fiora crossed her arms over her scaly chest and reminded herself for the thousandth time that she wasn't naked. Mermaid bodies were covered in scales, and their hair floated over them like cloaks in the water. No one wore clothes.

She still felt naked.

Fiora sucked water through her gills and told herself that this was normal and she was fine. She had spent the first thirteen years of her life as a mermaid. She would adjust.

If only she actually believed that.

Madame Isla swished the fork through the water, creating a small trail of bubbles that floated up towards the ceiling.

"Don't be ridiculous, girl. This is obviously a human hair comb."

She ran the fork through her long, white tresses to prove her point.

"It's a fork," Fiora repeated. "Humans use them to put food in their mouths."

She mimed eating with a fork, not caring that this argument

was ridiculous. It just felt good to argue with someone. To be right and know the answer for once.

Madame Isla, the mermaid's top scholar of humans, was over-seeing the categorization of the unprecedented amount of human objects that littered the ocean floor as a result of the recent kraken attacks and subsequent shipwrecks.

Fiora had been assigned to help her after failing miserably at every other suggested position.

This one wasn't going any better.

"That's the most preposterous thing I've ever heard," Madame Isla said. "Why would humans need a tool to put food in their mouths when they have perfectly good hands?"

"Because human food is often hot. They cook it with fire."

Fiora wasn't sure Madame Isla knew what fire was. Judging from the way she blinked, she probably didn't. But the scholar was not used to being contradicted, and she wasn't about to admit weakness now.

"If food is too hot for hands, it is too hot for mouths," Madame Isla said as if that settled the matter. "Zoe, please take this rare human hair comb to Queen Gallerus. Perhaps Her Majesty would like to use it when preparing for the ceremony tonight."

Fiora's young cousin darted forward and retrieved the fork. She turned it over in her hands, studying it with wonder.

"It is very shiny, isn't it?"

Fiora sighed, sending a stream of bubbles towards the surface. Much like her mother Kathelin, Zoe was always cheerful and easily impressed. And much like her grandmother Madame Isla, she enjoyed discovering new objects on the ocean floor.

"Extremely shiny," Madame Isla agreed. "Humans love shiny things. Now take it to the queen like a good girl."

Zoe beamed at the praise and swam through an opening in the ceiling. Madame Isla watched her go with a smile, then turned back to Fiora with a scowl.

"Why can't you be pleasant and cooperative like your sister?"

Fiora fought the urge to argue that Zoe was her cousin, not her sister. To mermaids, every female relative was a sister. The merfolk had not been impressed when she tried to explain the human way of tracking relations.

"Because I'm not fifteen, and I actually know something. Because I am a human!"

Fiora's voice rose at this last statement, and the human quality she worked so hard to suppress crept into her tone. Water currents swirled around her, and she grimaced as they tangled her hair. Merfolk voices held power, which they controlled with emotions and song.

Or in Fiora's case, tried to control with mixed results.

She took a deep breath, and the swirling water calmed.

"You are half human," Madame Isla said. "And you only lived with humans for a short time. I can understand why you're confused about their customs. Meanwhile, I have studied human behavior my entire life. My field notes on the crew of the Seawolfe have revolutionized our understanding of human interaction."

"I lived with them for ten years! And stalking a merchant ship does not make you an expert on forks and combs. You've never even been on land. Never seen a human town."

"Haven't I?"

There was something in Madame Isla's tone beyond her usual arrogance. Something that caught Fiora's interest in spite of her annoyance.

"Have you been on land, Madame Isla?"

The mermaid nodded smugly, her white hair rippling as she moved.

"There are many ways to transform your shape if you are accomplished enough. Where do you think Kathelin and Althea learned the magic to make that ring?"

She gestured to the pearl ring that Fiora still wore. It was useless now that her father had given up on her, but she refused to part with it.

"You know how to transform a mermaid into a human?"

Fiora studied Madame Isla with new interest. Perhaps she had underestimated the mermaid. Her understanding of humans may be faulty, but apparently her enchantments were not.

"Among other things. Kathelin recently wrote a song to turn a human into a frog. Transformation magic is not particularly difficult if you know the songs and principles, Fiora. You would know that if you had stayed underwater and continued your education."

And there it was again. Any time Fiora did something wrong, Madame Isla was quick to remind her that she had abandoned her mermaid family for her human one.

The unspoken thought that followed was that her human family had abandoned her in return, and the mermaids were all she had left.

"Could you transform me into a human?"

"Not without the queen's permission, and you know how unlikely that is."

Fiora did know. Her grandmother had been furious when she ran away to live with her human father at age thirteen. Given how badly it had gone, Queen Gallerus was unlikely to give Fiora permission for a second attempt at humanity.

Zoe returned, dissolving the tension in the room with her bright smile.

"We're ready to rehearse, Fiora. Can you spare us, Madame Isla?"

"Yes, please go. My work will go faster without interruptions."

She gave Fiora a pointed look as she said this. Fiora scowled in return.

"Come on, Fiora!"

Zoe flipped in the water and snapped her tail. She darted forward in a burst of speed.

Fiora swam harder, trying to keep up. Zoe glided effortlessly ahead as if she belonged in the water.

Which she did.

Fiora was still struggling to find her sea legs. Or sea tail. She had never possessed whatever mermaid quality it was that made her family at home in the water. Not completely.

She pulled water through her gills and kicked even harder. She soared forward, her long red hair streaming behind her like a cape.

If she hadn't been trying to keep up with Zoe, she might have enjoyed the swim. As much as she hated to admit it, there was something magical about breathing underwater and swimming through the ocean. It was almost like flying.

She might have enjoyed the scenery as well if it didn't consist mostly of buildings and gardens wrecked by kraken. Judging from the reports she had heard, the kraken had also caused damage in the human world. They had sunk ships and knocked a few towers off a castle.

But the attacks had devastated the merfolk. Their capital city lay in ruins, as did the surrounding towns. The panicked evacuation had not exactly been a warm welcome back to the underwater world. Nor had the frantic search for safety. Zoe had somehow remained cheerful as she dragged Fiora from one hiding spot to another while Queen Gallerus and her most accomplished merfolk choirs fought to contain the rampaging monsters.

From what Fiora could piece together from overheard conversations, Kathelin and Althea had worked with the royal guard, stolen an enchanted sapphire from Santelle's treasury, and used it to subdue the dark creatures. The Kraken Heart had brought peace back to the water, but it would take time to rebuild.

A lot of time. Every mermaid and merman that could be spared was working on it now. Songs of building and repair echoed through the water. Graceful arches and domes of sand and rock grew each day, lining the horizon like a fanciful city built by a child during a day on the beach.

The castle in the mermaid's summer city had sustained the least damage. Probably because it was located near Montaigne and the kraken activity had centered around Santelle. So the queen and her court had moved to the summer city while the capital city was rebuilt.

Rehearsal was in the castle's highest tower. Zoe swam up the outside of the building, skipping the maze of tunnels that wound through the structure, and popped in through a large window. Fiora followed suit, thinking how unusual this behavior would be for a human. You would have to climb the walls to enter a land tower through a window. Much easier to simply take the stairs.

But in the water, it was as easy to go up as over. Mermaids did not worry about such things as gravity, and their lofty buildings showed it.

A pulsing blue light engulfed Fiora as she entered the room. Kathelin and Althea were already singing. Their voices wove together in a tight harmony laced with magic. An enormous sapphire pulsed in time with their rhythm, strengthening their enchantment and keeping the kraken in an enchanted sleep.

It was the first time Fiora had seen the Kraken Heart up close. It was mesmerizing. The sapphire was bigger than her fist and glowed with magic.

Santelle must be furious to have lost such a treasure.

"You're just in time," Kathelin signed. *"Let us finish this stanza, and then we'll begin."*

She made gestures with her hands to communicate the words. Mermaids created magic with their songs, so it was important to be able to communicate without interrupting the sound. Most mermaids learned sign language before they could speak.

Fiora leaned against a sloped wall and arranged her hair so it covered as much of her body as possible. Perhaps she should search Madame Isla's collection of human objects for a needle, thread, and fabric. It was likely that a sewing kit had washed overboard at some point. She would feel so much more comfortable underwater if she had clothes.

Zoe bounced up and down in excitement as the song progressed. Finally, Kathelin and Althea sang their final notes. The enchantment snapped into place and sent a small tremor through the water. The Kraken Heart brightened as it absorbed the magic.

"This is a rehearsal, but it will still affect the gem," Althea signed. *"Stay focused."*

It was difficult to tell if she meant this comment more for Fiora or Zoe. Both nodded, just in case. You didn't want to get on Althea's bad side. Unlike her cousin Kathelin, she was never happy and never impressed.

Kathelin and Althea looked at each other and established a tempo by waving their hands in unison. Then they drew water through their gills and began to sing.

The music was a lullaby meant to sooth the kraken. The song had been written specifically to be used with the Kraken Heart, and the gem responded as if it knew this. Its heartbeat pulse slowed and steadied as if the gem were falling asleep.

It was almost time for their part. Fiora shared a nervous glance with Zoe and breathed deeply. She was older than her cousin, but Zoe was a full-blood mermaid with a decade more training.

Kathelin gave the signal, and Fiora pushed her insecurities aside. The magic relied on emotion as much as the actual notes you sang. She couldn't afford to doubt herself.

She was prepared.

Kathelin nodded to signal her, and Fiora began to sing. She pulled the human part of her voice back, letting only the magical mermaid tones come through her song.

The mermaids wove four strands of melody together into one

enchantment. Fiora relaxed a little. It was going well! She had practiced hard to prepare for this quartet, and years of participating in Princess Tests had taught her how to perform under pressure. Finally, it was all paying off.

Maybe she could do this after all. She could find a place with the mermaids and finally belong. Perhaps with a little more training, she could join one of the choirs that wove magical songs through the sea and made the mermaid civilization thrive.

Then the Kraken Heart flashed purple, and the gem's pulse began to race. The mermaids shared alarmed looks and poured more magic into their voices. Fiora tried to remember everything she had ever learned about singing at once. Deep breathing. Even tone. Only use your mermaid voice.

The gem's pulse raced even faster. Althea motioned for Fiora and Zoe to stop singing. They did, and Kathelin and Althea returned to their original song. Slowly, the Kraken Heart's light settled back into a steady rhythm.

"What happened?" Zoe signed.

Althea scowled, and even Kathelin looked a little concerned.

"Something must have been wrong with the way our voices blended," Kathelin signed. *"Perhaps you girls should practice more before the concert tonight."*

"Review your notes," Althea signed. *"And if you want to test your magic, there is plenty of cleaning to be done in the gardens. We will continue singing to look for a flaw in the gem."*

Zoe and Fiora made the mermaid equivalent of a bow by curling their tails towards their heads and swam out the window. When they were a safe distance away, Zoe burst into a stream of chatter.

"I've never seen anything like that! Fiora, do you think I sang a wrong note? I thought I knew this song!"

Fiora shrugged. She was certain she had sung her part correctly, but she hadn't heard anyone else make a mistake either. Maybe the fault had been hers. Maybe she had let some of her human voice creep into the song. Or perhaps her magic wasn't strong enough to carry her part.

Or maybe, no matter how hard she worked, she just didn't belong here.

"We just need more practice," she said, refusing to acknowledge her doubts out loud. "It's a complicated enchantment."

Zoe nodded with enthusiasm.

"It's the hardest enchantment I've ever sung! Do you want to come to the library with me to go over the notes?"

"No, I'd rather practice on my own."

"Suit yourself, then. I'll see you tonight!"

Zoe turned a double flip and darted towards the library.

Fiora swam in the opposite direction. A knot had settled in the pit of her stomach, and she couldn't shake it. Usually it took an audible mistake in a song to ruin an enchantment. Fiora had studied singing with mermaids and humans. She was an accomplished musician.

If there had been any wrong notes in the performance, she hadn't heard them.

It was an honor to sing at this concert. The ceremony would dedicate the Kraken Heart and officially welcome Queen Gallerus to her new, temporary home. Every member of the royal family would participate.

Some would have only minor roles, singing in the enormous chorus at the end of the concert. But Fiora had been given a part in the opening quartet. That gave her equal standing with her aunts and cousin.

It officially acknowledged her place as one of the royal sisters. The queen's granddaughter and a princess of mermaids, if she put it into human terms.

Such responsibility was not to be taken lightly. It was Queen Gallerus's way of saying that she had accepted Fiora back and forgiven her for leaving. It was almost as good as being given a spot on the council.

And if she messed it up, Fiora would once again prove herself unworthy.

She shook her head. That line of thought would guarantee a bad performance. She may not have the most magical voice, but it was adequate for ensemble singing. She knew her notes. She would review them for the rest of the day to make sure she didn't make any mistakes.

She just needed some time alone to calm her nerves first.

Maybe she could find some embroidery supplies in a shipwreck. Sewing always soothed her anxiety.

Fiora kicked her tail and swam towards the open ocean, leaving the city behind her.

4

"But what about my ships?"

King Gustave of Montaigne rubbed his forehead. His injuries from the kraken attack in Santelle were healing as quickly as could be expected, but his head still ached when he was frustrated.

And right now, he was very frustrated.

He bit back the sharp reply he longed to unleash and took a deep breath instead. One word from him, and the guards would drag this man out and throw him into the street.

A king's words have power.

That had been one of his father's favorite sayings, and Gustave tried not to resent it. When your words had power, you had to carefully consider everything you said.

"Your Majesty?"

The merchant looked hopeful. As if Gustave's pause meant he had thought of a solution.

Gustave shook his head, feeling the weight of the crown as he did so.

"I am sorry for your loss, but I have no way to retrieve your ships from the bottom of the ocean."

"But I heard that you spoke with mermaids while visiting Santelle. Couldn't you ask them to help? They could at least look for the gold coins from the wrecks. Or the silverware. One ship was carrying several boxes of cutlery in a custom design. My client will be very upset."

It was actually a good idea, asking the mermaids to help recover sunken goods, but Gustave had no way to do it. His headache intensified, and he reached into his pocket and wrapped his hand around the small shell Kathelin had given them before she disappeared into the ocean. He had studied it thoroughly and searched the castle library for texts on mermaid magic.

But as far as he could tell, it did nothing at all.

Blasted mermaids.

"My apologies, sir, but I cannot help you. I have heard nothing from the mermaids since the kraken submerged."

"My entire fortune was on those ships."

The merchant looked ready to cry. Gustave sighed. He truly did feel sorry for the man. He wished he could help all of the merchants and sailors who had suffered damages in the attacks, but that was beyond his power as king. Even if he wanted to bankrupt the country to restore the merchant's fortune, his council wouldn't let him.

"And what of my daughters?" the man said, more to himself than Gustave. "How can I return to them empty-handed? This trip was meant to provide a dowry for my youngest."

Gustave tried to interject, but the merchant was lost in his misery and continued his mournful rant.

"She's a good girl. She only asked me to bring back a single rose. She could have asked for jewels or gowns, and she asked for a rose. I can't even give her that now. I don't even have money to buy a ticket home. All my things were on the *Royal Blaze* when it disappeared from port."

Fabric rustled to Gustave's right. Collette had entered the

throne room at some point and was trying to get his attention. Gustave caught his sister's gaze and signed to her.

"I can't do anything to help him. Marquis Corbeau won't let me set such a precedent."

Then Gustave rested his hands in his lap again and looked around the room. Everyone was too focused on the merchant's tragic monologue to have noticed his communication. He turned back to Collette, who nodded her understanding.

"The usual?" she signed.

Gustave bit back a grin and nodded. Collette returned the grin and waited for her cue. Gustave cleared his throat to stop the man's speech.

"As king, there is nothing I can do for you. I'm afraid you must-"

"Forgive me for interrupting, Your Majesty."

Collette stepped away from the wall and gave a graceful curtsy. Marquis Corbeau glared at her, but Gustave gestured for her to continue. Collette approached the merchant and smiled gently.

"What was your name, sir?"

"Dale, Your Highness. Dale Mercer of Eldria."

"Mr. Mercer, I'm sure your daughters will simply be happy that you are alive. Why don't I show you the castle gardens? We have lovely roses, and you can choose whatever you like to bring back for them."

Her offer shook Dale out of his misery. He took the hand she held out and looked at her like she was an angel of mercy.

"Truly? Thank you, Your Highness! You are most gracious."

Collette took the merchant's elbow and guided him out of the throne room, pausing only to wink at her brother on her way out. As soon as the door shut, Gustave nodded to the guard.

"Are there any more audience requests today?"

"No, Your Majesty."

"Thank goodness."

The guard smirked, and Gustave realized he had spoken aloud.

Blast.

He didn't mean to be callous, but the chaos of rebuilding Montaigne's harbor and sorting through the damage caused by kraken attacks was taking a toll. Being king was hard enough without magical creatures wreaking havoc on land and sea.

Gustave removed the crown and massaged his aching head. Maybe now he could have a few moments of peace and quiet.

Someone cleared his throat, shattering that hope. Gustave sighed and turned to the source of the sound.

"Would you like to request an audience, Marquis Corbeau?"

"Most humorous, Your Majesty. You know I cannot leave until the audiences are officially closed."

Gustave's headache intensified. The crown had pressed into his bruised skin, making it throb from the pressure.

"The audiences are obviously over."

"Not until the proper procedures have been observed."

"Very well. I make a motion to close the royal audience time. Do you second it, Marquis?"

"No, there is something we must discuss."

"But you said- Never mind. What do you wish to discuss?"

Gustave stayed slumped in his throne. Partly to annoy the marquis, partly because this was a rare moment where he didn't have to look like a king to impress anyone, and partly because he didn't have the energy to sit upright and be proper any longer.

"Your Majesty, if Princess Collette is going to adopt every stray that wanders through our doors, you must have the council approve the expense."

Gustave rubbed his pounding head. The last thing he wanted was an additional budget meeting with the council. Once a month was more than enough.

"Surely Princess Collette can help whomever she pleases without council approval. A flower from our gardens costs nothing."

"Perhaps not. But what about when she inevitably invites him to spend a night in the castle while she finds him passage on a ship home? As she has done for every other distressed foreigner to come through that door?"

"She is right to help where she can, Marquis Corbeau. We have plenty of empty rooms for her guests. If you truly object, we can deduct the expense from her pocket money."

Which Gustave would then need to find a way to pay back to her. Collette wouldn't mind, but it wasn't fair to have her shoulder the expense of their shared scheme to help those affected by the attacks.

Marquis Corbeau shook his head.

"If Your Majesty was fully king, you would have more control of the budget and could approve such spending without oversight. But as it is, you must make a motion before the council for the expense. I cannot allow this activity to continue any longer without the council's approval."

Gustave glared at the ceiling. As much as he wanted to order Marquis Corbeau out of the room, the man was right. Gustave was not permitted to make any budget decisions on his own until he married and assumed the full kingship.

A fact that Marquis Corbeau reminded him of many times each day.

"Perhaps we should reconsider hosting a Princess Test," Marquis Corbeau said. "It is a time-honored way for kings to find brides."

Gustave's eyes narrowed.

"You mean you don't enjoy having the power to approve all my decisions?"

"It creates a lot of extra paperwork, Your Majesty."

Gustave couldn't tell if the marquis was joking or not. Probably not. His council members weren't known for their senses of humor.

"And then there is the matter of your birthday gala," Corbeau said. "We may not have enough rooms for the invited guests if

Princess Collette keeps offering the castle's hospitality to strangers."

"How many guests are we expecting?"

"I have lost track, Your Majesty. Your grandmother recently added additional people to the guest list."

Gustave sat up in the throne.

"She can't! We've already finalized the list!"

"She can amend it with council approval, which she received this morning."

Gustave stared at his advisor. Was this the marquis's way of getting revenge for what had happened in Santelle? Or had his grandmother bullied the council until she got her way?

Either was possible.

"I make a motion to close the royal audience time," Gustave said. "Apparently I need to speak with my grandmother."

"I second the motion, Your Majesty. And I will add Princess Collette's hospitality budget to our next meeting's agenda."

Blast it all.

Gustave bowed to Marquis Corbeau and hurried from the throne room. His grandmother taking an interest in his birthday gala was a problem of kraken-esque proportions. He needed to make a plan.

5

Fiora swam until she reached the gardens on the outskirts of the city. She hadn't found a shipwreck to explore yet, but she needed a moment to catch her breath before she continued. She slowed her pace and circled over the gardens.

Mermaid gardens weren't anything like the ones humans made with plants lined into neat rows in the ground. They were more like enormous mosaics. Merfolk arranged beautiful shells and things that fell into the sea into intricate patterns on the ocean floor. Most gardens centered around a theme, and every mermaid had a different style of arranging the items.

Fiora drifted over a garden filled with mirrors arranged in a spiral pattern similar to the inside of a shell. The glass glistened like gems in the shifting underwater sunlight and reflected hundreds of versions of her as she swam.

She studied the reflections. From the outside, her mixed heritage wasn't obvious. She was a little smaller than the other mermaids. Her fins didn't spread quite as wide. But she looked like she belonged.

The water brushed her brilliant red hair over her shoulders, and Fiora sighed. The mermaid in the mirrors looked beautiful and serene and whole.

But the reflections were a lie.

She turned away from the mirrors and continued her swim. The next garden was one she remembered well from her childhood, and Fiora smiled when she saw it.

This garden was filled with statues that had fallen from ships. Fiora had visited it every summer when she was a young mermaid, floating around the stone carvings and pretending they were her human family.

The merfolk had added new statues in her absence, and the garden seemed to have escaped the kraken attacks mostly unscathed. A few statues had fallen to their sides, and some of them were covered in sand, but none were broken.

Fiora swam down to the garden. There was one statue in particular that she wanted to visit.

"What are you doing here, Fiora?"

Fiora twisted around and saw Leander. He swam towards the garden carrying a statue of an older man with long, flowing hair.

The craftsmanship was incredible. The artist had captured each strand of hair in the stone, and it seemed to move as Leander pulled it through the water.

This statue was made more recently than the others. None of the edges had eroded, and the man's clothes didn't look old fashioned. It must have fallen overboard during the recent attacks. He would make a fine addition to the garden.

"I asked you a question," Leander said, interrupting Fiora's musings.

"I'm practicing for the ceremony tonight."

Fiora's voice was defensive, and currents stirred around her when she spoke, lifting her hair towards the surface. She pulled her hair down to cover her body and reminded herself again that none of the merfolk cared that she was naked.

"Practicing? Here? Why aren't you singing with Zoe?"

Leander hummed a tune. Water swirled around the statue, lifting it from his hands and placing it in the garden. It also pulled his black hair away from his face, sweeping it neatly behind him.

"What are you doing here?" Fiora asked. "Shouldn't you be preparing for the ceremony tonight?"

"I don't have a singing role. Those are reserved for members of the royal family."

The scorn in his tone said she shouldn't have a singing role either. That he would do a much better job if given the chance.

Fiora had no doubt that was true, but family was important to merfolk. They stayed loyal to each other.

She had taken that for granted when she accepted her father's invitation to join him on land. She had assumed that human families felt the same loyalty and her half-sisters would welcome her as one of them. That had been a mistake.

"You're a captain of the guards. Surely you have some sort of responsibility tonight."

"Yes. Guarding. But for now I'm rebuilding gardens. Some of us know our roles well enough that we don't need to practice."

Fiora scowled at the merman. Leander met her gaze with anger in his hazel eyes.

"Go practice somewhere else, Fiora. I have work to do."

"I could help."

"I doubt it."

Something rumbled through the ocean floor. The statues trembled as if caught in an earthquake, but it almost sounded like laughter.

It stopped as suddenly as it began. Fiora looked at Leander, but the merman didn't seem concerned.

"I have work to do, and you're interfering, Fiora."

Leander sang. His voice crescendoed through the ocean, and an enormous whirlpool built in the center of the garden. It swept sand off the statues and pushed Fiora away. She tumbled through the water, catching glimpses of statues and her reflection in the mirrors.

Leander kept singing. Kept pushing her away until she was so far out in the open water that she no longer saw him, the gardens, or the mermaid city.

And she was covered in sand.

Fiora brushed herself off. Her hair was hopelessly tangled from the whirlpool. Maybe she should borrow a fork from Madame Isla to brush it out.

Something golden on the ocean floor caught her eye. Leander's song had swept more than Fiora away.

Maybe she'd be lucky and find a comb.

She swam to the ocean floor and pulled the gold object out of the sand.

It was a ball.

Fiora turned it over in her hands. What was this thing for? Gold seemed an impractical material for a toy.

She tossed it up in the water as if she were a child playing catch with herself. The ball drifted slowly up then sank towards the ocean floor. It slipped out of Fiora's hands when she tried to catch it.

She followed it down, trying and failing to grip the smooth metal. Finally, she swam under the golden ball and caught it against her chest.

The ocean around her dissolved in a flash of white as a strange vision overcame her senses.

Fiora saw herself floating in the ocean. Her hair was hopelessly tangled from the whirlpool. She held a golden ball and tossed it into the air.

THE VISION FADED, AND FIORA BLINKED AT THE SHIFTING light of the open ocean. What had just happened? She had experienced mermaid magic many times and human magic a few times in Kell, but this was something else entirely.

Was it meant to be some kind of mirror? Why had it showed her a vision of herself?

Fiora bit her lip and stared at the distorted reflection of her face in the gold sphere. It was dangerous to play with magic you didn't understand. She should probably put the ball back on the ocean floor and let the sand swallow it.

Instead, she pulled it to her chest. The ocean once again flashed white.

❧❦❧

"IT IS SO NICE TO MEET YOU ALL. MY NAME IS KATHELIN."

Fiora hovered in midair, slowing bobbing up and down. Kathelin floated in a bay near the shore, talking to humans who sat on land.

Humans that Fiora recognized. Princess Carina of Santelle and King Gustave of Montaigne sat on a blanket. They looked like they were having a romantic picnic by the sea. Fiora wouldn't have pictured them as a couple. But then again, Carina had been her nemesis at many Princess Tests and Gustave had ruined her chances with Prince Alaric by providing testimony to support Lina. Both had sabotaged her in Aeonia.

Maybe they were a good match after all.

A frog sat near Carina on the picnic blanket. Some kind of pet?

"Be careful," the frog said. "Don't get too close."

A talking frog? Or a transformed human? If what she was seeing was real, Fiora needed to search the library and find the transformation charms Madame Isla had mentioned. She tried to get a closer look at the frog, but the vision pulled her attention back to the mermaid.

Kathelin smiled and winked.

"I mean you no harm," she said. "I want to help you."

"By stealing ships?" Carina asked.

"*Those incidents have been beyond my control,*" Kathelin said. "*The kraken are restless. Far more so than usual.*"

The frog hopped onto Carina's shoulder and whispered something. Carina nodded.

"*You claim the kraken aren't under your control, but the one that attacked last night was summoned.*"

Kathelin sighed.

"*Yes, Leander is brash sometimes. He called the kraken to help him escape, and I apologize that it also took your ship.*"

❧

FIORA'S CONSCIOUSNESS RETURNED TO THE OCEAN IN A FLASH of white. She blinked, disoriented by the longer vision.

Was it real? Or had the ball shown her some kind of daydream?

If it wasn't real, it was oddly specific.

And if it was real, that meant Leander and Kathelin had interacted directly with humans in their quest to retrieve the Kraken Heart.

With Carina, Gustave, and a talking frog.

Fiora tried to sort it out, but the vision remained a tangle. She knew that Kathelin, Leander, and Althea had retrieved the Kraken Heart from Santelle, but she didn't know how. She had assumed they had stolen the gem without being discovered.

In the end, their method for obtaining the gem didn't matter. They had succeeded, and the kraken were sleeping again.

What mattered to Fiora was the frog. He was proof that the transformation magic Madame Isla had mentioned was possible. Fiora's ring was useless, but that didn't matter if there were other ways to transform.

She looked at the dull pearl and sighed.

Did Carina and Gustave realize how lucky they were to be fully human? To sit and have a picnic on the grass as if it were the most natural thing in the world? To not worry about being banished to the ocean if they failed to measure up?

Fiora blinked back tears. Crying underwater was a strange experience. Your tears simply floated away.

Maybe real mermaids didn't cry. Maybe that was another part of her human heritage.

Fiora had felt hollow and out of place since she returned to the ocean. Of course, she had often felt the same way when she was on land.

When you were part of two worlds, neither felt like home.

She brushed her tears into the ocean and swam up to the surface. It didn't take long. She must be close to shore.

Yes, she was. A strip of land was just visible on the horizon.

Blast it all, Leander had pushed her farther than she thought. It would take a long time to swim back to the city.

Fiora turned to the open ocean, then turned back to look at the land. The dedication ceremony would take place at sundown, and the sun was still high in the sky. She had time.

And she suddenly wanted very much to see humans.

Fiora dove under the water and swam towards the shore. She hummed as she went, creating a current that helped her swim faster. Soon the surface of the water was dotted with the shadows of ships. She must be near a city with a bustling port.

Fiora didn't dare look above the surface with so many ships around. She swam along the coast until she found a quiet cove. When she peeked into the air, she found a castle looming above her.

That must be the royal castle of Montaigne. Fiora had never visited that kingdom. As a human, she had only traveled away from Kell for Princess Tests, and Montaigne hadn't hosted one in her lifetime. She studied the castle with a critical eye.

There wasn't much to criticize. Montaigne had a reputation for making beautiful things, and it seemed that reputation was well deserved. The castle emerged from the hillside in an elegant wave of marble spires and balconies. The silvery stone sparkled against the mountains and pine forests behind it.

It was surrounded by human gardens filled with flowers and shrubs. From what Fiora could see, pathways led from the castle through the gardens to the ocean. Sandy beaches stretched on either side of the estate. They were empty, unlike the bustling port. Maybe they were part of the castle grounds.

Instead of making her feel better, seeing the castle made her even more homesick for land. Fiora ducked under the water and glared at the golden ball. This was all its fault. The vision of human life had reminded her of all that she had lost.

She lifted it towards her chest, then shook her head and pulled it away. Whatever else it could show her, she didn't want to see. It was simply a painful reminder that she was trapped under the ocean.

As the dull pearl was a constant reminder that she had failed. Even her father found her useless as a human. So she would have to make the best of her life as a mermaid.

Fiora resurfaced and sang softly, practicing her part for the ceremony and letting magic seep into her voice until waves swirled around her. She reviewed the more difficult passages in the song a few times, checking to make sure she was breathing in the right spots and perfectly in tune.

She was. Perhaps whatever had gone wrong earlier wasn't her fault after all. Fiora knew her notes. She had control of her magic.

She would perform tonight as she had performed at countless Princess Tests. Hopefully with better results.

She should swim back. The ceremony began at sundown, and she needed time to get ready.

Fiora studied the castle a moment longer, drinking in the sights of the human world before she submerged. A man stood on a balcony looking down at the water. He was too far away for her to see more than his silhouette, which hopefully meant he was too far above the water to see her. The last thing she needed was to break mermaid law by interacting with a human.

Fiora dove beneath the waves and swam away from the shore. When she was a safe distance from land, she sang with her full voice. She pushed as much magic as she could into the melody, creating a current in the water to carry her back to the summer city.

❧ 6 ❧

Gustave walked through the castle to his office, taking the long way around to avoid running into anyone who might want his input on anything. He wanted to deal with the problem of his birthday gala before he got swept up in the rest of his duties for the day. He just needed a few minutes of quiet to regroup and strategize before he faced his grandmother.

But when he flung open his office door, the room was already occupied. Gustave paused in the doorway, wondering how Marquis Corbeau had managed to get there before him.

"What is that?"

The marquis stood next to a dressmaker's mannequin wrapped in billowing, white fabric. Gustave blinked in confusion, and Marquis Corbeau shook his head in a patronizing way.

"This is a wedding dress, Your Majesty. Placed on a dressmaker's form to show it off to best advantage."

"Yes, but why is it in my study?"

"It is for your bride, of course. Did you sleep well? You're a little slow this morning."

Gustave took a deep breath and let it out in a soft sigh. As a matter of fact, he hadn't slept well. Not that anyone actually cared.

"Marquis Corbeau, I have told you this more times than I can count. I am not getting married until we find my father. Not to mention we are in a time of crisis as we rebuild the harbor. In spite of your impressive efforts, I have not found a bride in the short time I have been back in Montaigne, and I have no intention of doing so."

The marquis shrugged.

"You'll never find a bride with that attitude, Your Majesty. We had Princess Carina's marriage contract practically signed, and you managed to mangle that. I'm taking precautions to make sure it doesn't happen again."

"And how will a wedding dress help? You don't even know that this will fit the woman I choose. It might be out of fashion by then."

Marquis Corbeau smirked.

"When you do find the right woman, there will be no need to delay to plan the wedding. I'm arranging all the details now to make sure we are ready. The designers assure me this classic silhouette will stand the test of time and flatter any figure. They've made the gown in a number of sizes just to be safe, and the fit can be altered in a matter of minutes."

"Minutes?"

Marquis Corbeau was ever an optimist and strategist. In different circumstances, it was admirable.

Right now, it was beyond annoying.

Was this his revenge for Gustave's refusing to marry Carina?

Or perhaps punishment for the way he kept going behind the marquis's back to help merchants?

If not, that certainly hadn't helped matters.

Gustave studied the dress. It was elegant, but that wasn't a surprise. Montaigne was known for its good taste in fashion and everything else. The white satin was trimmed with pearl beads and embroidered patterns of seashells. The full skirt and trim waist would flatter most figures. Marquis Corbeau had even set white shoes decorated with matching pearls beside the dress. Doubtless those were available in a variety of sizes as well.

"Your Majesty must marry sometime," Marquis Corbeau said. "Why not sooner rather than later? Think how nice it will be to be fully king. To be able to make decisions without the approval of the council. The budget meeting I scheduled this afternoon to discuss Princess Collette's hospitality would be completely unnecessary."

"This afternoon?"

Yes, this was definitely revenge. Blast it all.

Gustave was so frustrated that he considered the marquis's proposal for a moment. Given how often he disagreed with the council, it would be nice to have the power to decide matters without their oversight.

All he had to do was find a bride.

Gustave tried to imagine the woman who would wear the gown. When he did marry, Marquis Corbeau was stubborn enough to insist that his bride wear this exact dress.

Gustave's mind remained stubbornly blank whenever he thought of his wedding. He tried to replace the wooden mannequin's features with those of a living, breathing woman, but nothing stuck. Even in his imagination, his future bride remained far out of reach. She was something to consider when he found his father and figured out how to balance his duties as king with the attention his love would deserve.

Right now, Gustave couldn't even find the time to breathe.

A breeze from the open window teased the fabric, making it dance around the mannequin. Music floated on the wind, and Gustave walked out on his balcony to look for the source of the song. Someone was singing. A woman.

He searched the shoreline but couldn't see anyone. Her voice seemed to come from the ocean itself.

"It will move beautifully at your first dance," Marquis Corbeau said. "Won't that be nice? You and your bride twirling around the dance floor. Your arm wrapped around her waist. Her eyes sparkling as she smiles up at you, silently asking for a kiss."

The singing grew and filled Gustave's senses. For a moment, he could see it. The daydream swept him away, and he pictured himself hand in hand with a woman on the beach. He still didn't know what she looked like, but he knew her voice. She sang as they danced, providing the music since they were alone.

The singing stopped, and Gustave came to his senses. He glared at Marquis Corbeau.

"You're trying to tempt me into marriage with talk of kisses? That's low even for you."

"I will do whatever is necessary to ensure the future of Montaigne."

"I don't doubt that."

The men stared at each other, neither willing to look away and admit defeat. The marquis looked decidedly unashamed for resorting to underhanded tactics.

"Gustave, are you in there?"

Collette danced through the door. Her smile faded when she saw Marquis Corbeau.

"Forgive me, I didn't realize you were in council. I just wanted to let you know that I decided to give the merchant a room for the night. He had nowhere else to go. Is that alright?"

Marquis Corbeau gave Gustave a knowing look before turning to Collette.

"I'm sure that's perfectly fine, Princess. I'll see you in the budget meeting this afternoon, King Gustave."

"Fine. Please take this dress with you when you go, Marquis."

"I think not, Your Majesty. The council and I recently decided to redecorate the castle, and we are starting with your office."

"That's-"

"Completely within our power until you marry and assume the full responsibilities of the kingship. The dress stays. Good day, Your Majesty."

Collette bit back a smile as the marquis bowed and left the room. Gustave raised an eyebrow at her.

"Sorry, but he must be desperate if he's resorting to fashion and decorating to persuade you to marry."

"I appreciate his efforts to secure the future of Montaigne, but this is getting ridiculous."

Gustave grimaced and looked around his study. The room was made from marble and trimmed with blue tile. Several large windows provided a view of the sea and Montaigne's harbor. Apart from the floor to ceiling bookshelves lined with ancient texts, the room had few decorations. The swirled marble was decorative enough.

It wouldn't be nearly as nice when Marquis Corbeau was finished with it.

Gustave realized he had wrapped his arm around the mannequin's waist at some point and hastily let go. Blast Corbeau, the fabric was soft. It would be fun to dance with a woman wearing it.

"That's a nice dress," Collette said. "Does this mean you've chosen a bride?"

"No. You'll be stuck with your responsibilities as lady of the house a while longer."

"Grandmother takes care of most of those."

"Yes, I heard she's taken an interest in my birthday gala."

"With a vengeance, and she's recruited Marquis Corbeau to help. I expect the guest list will consist largely of eligible young ladies."

Gustave groaned, and Collette's eyes twinkled.

"If you're truly desperate to escape, you could tell everyone you're heartbroken over your failed engagement to Princess

Carina and pay a state visit to Aeonia. You might be able to win her away from Prince Stefan if you're extra charming."

"I think it's best if I stay away from Carina and Stefan for the time being. For many reasons."

Most of them being his sanity. Gustave appreciated Carina's cleverness and Stefan's... well... he didn't quite have the words to describe Stefan. But their recent adventure in Santelle would make him think twice before visiting the pair in Aeonia. Even if that visit would get him out of his birthday gala.

Collette grinned.

"I'm joking, of course. I never thought you and Carina would be a good match. But Grandmother and the marquis won't give up, you know. Everyone in this castle is determined to see you married."

"Even you?"

Collette tried to look innocent.

"Of course not, Gustave! You'll find the right lady in your own time."

"Blast it all, Collette. You have someone in mind, don't you?"

She shrugged.

"Maybe. Was I that obvious?"

"Let's just say you're no Carina."

"Fine, I invited someone to your gala that I think you'll like. Maybe you'll do better with a normal girl than whatever crazy political match Marquis Corbeau dreams up next."

Gustave realized he was playing with the pearls on the wedding gown sleeve and stepped away from it. Blasted dress.

"You know I can't think about marriage, Collette. Not while Father is out there."

He stared out the window where the ocean stretched to the sky. The song had faded, leaving only the sound of wind and waves. His sister stood beside him and leaned her head on his shoulder.

"But you could, Gustave. You can move forward with your life without giving up on Father."

"No, I can't."

"Gustave, what if he isn't out there? What if the ring is wrong?"

"Don't tell me you refuse to believe in magic now. After the Princess Test and the kraken?"

"Of course I believe in magic, but you have been looking for almost a year. Father wouldn't want you to waste your life obsessing over magic we don't fully understand."

"This charm finds people, Collette. It only points light towards people who are still living."

"You shouldn't pin all your hopes on a magical light."

But he should pin them on a single woman?

Gustave raised his hand and stared at the signet ring his father had given him before he disappeared. It had an enchanted ruby set in a gold band marked with the royal crest of Montaigne. Dwarf made. The ruby gleamed in the sunlight.

Gustave raised the ring to his lips and whispered to the enchanted gem.

"Find King Francois."

A red light shot out from the ruby and pointed towards the sea. Gustave pulled a compass from his pocket and checked the direction. It hadn't changed since the last time he looked.

It hadn't changed in months. That should have meant his father was in the same place, but their searches had led to nothing.

"Maybe the mermaids have seen him," Gustave said. "I should have asked them about it when I had the chance. Maybe they turned him into a frog like Prince Stefan."

"I hope not. I don't think Father would do well as a frog."

Someone knocked on the door. Gustave opened it and did his best not to frown at the servant, who bowed low before delivering his message.

"Begging your pardon, Your Majesty, but there is an urgent matter of state that requires your attention. Marquis Corbeau requests your presence in the throne room immediately."

Gustave sighed and hurried away to the throne room. Apparently his few moments of peace and quiet would have to wait.

❧ 7 ❧

Zoe was still practicing in the library when Fiora returned. The young mermaid stared so intently at the seashell carved with her notes for the ceremony song that she didn't notice Fiora swim in.

Fiora circled the library as she looked for a place to hide the golden ball. The room was round like a sphere and lined with shells of every shape, color, and size imaginable. Light filtered in through artistically carved gaps in the structure and gleamed off the shells, creating a magical effect that Fiora had always loved.

It had been a shock the first time she visited a human library. All those straight lines filled with paper books felt so static and artificial. And why did the books all look the same when they contained different information?

Underwater libraries were organic, like something grown rather than made. The merfolk carved stories and songs onto shells in curving lines of text that followed the shell's shape rather than trying to make everything uniform.

Fiora found a large clam shell carved with a record of Madame Isla's observations of the *Seawolfe*. That should be a safe enough hiding place. Nobody but Madame Isla was interested in the work

43

habits of a merchant ship, and Madame Isla would be too busy sorting through the kraken wreckage to read this for a while.

Fiora hid the golden ball under the shell and pushed it into the sand to make sure it stayed. She wished she could carry the ball with her, but she had nowhere to store it. None of this would be necessary if mermaids had pockets.

Or clothes.

She sighed, sending a stream of bubbles floating towards the top of the library. They gleamed like jewels in the light and caught Zoe's attention. The young mermaid turned away from her shell and waved to Fiora.

"How did your practice go? I've reviewed my notes so many times I feel like I wrote them!"

Zoe hummed, creating a current that carried the shell she had been studying back to a crevice near the top of the room.

"I feel ready for tonight."

At least, as ready as she would ever be. Zoe beamed.

"It is exciting, isn't it? Our first time performing with our royal sisters!"

If Fiora had been the same age as Zoe, she had no doubt this evening would have been the highlight of her young life. As it was, this concert was simply something she had to do. Another step on the journey to prove she belonged under the sea.

The vision of King Gustave and Carina at the picnic flashed through Fiora's memory. Maybe she wouldn't have to prove she belonged with merfolk if she could return to the humans.

"Zoe, have you ever studied transformation magic?"

Zoe's eyes darted up to a section of the library that held large conch shells. Fiora followed her cousin's gaze and mentally marked the spot.

"I learned a few of the songs, but I've never performed them. Why do you ask?"

Fiora shrugged, trying to sound casual.

"I overheard someone mention turning a human into a frog."

Zoe giggled.

"Kathelin did that to Prince Stefan while she was trying to retrieve the Kraken Heart. Althea was going to kill him otherwise."

Fiora wasn't surprised. Althea could be rather intense and didn't like anyone standing in her way. Not to mention that Prince Stefan was so annoying Fiora had been tempted to kill him herself a few times.

"How exactly do the transformations work?" Fiora asked. "Do you sing them as you would any other enchantment?"

Zoe's face fell.

"You want to leave again? Fiora, you just got back."

"No, I don't want to leave!" Fiora lied. "I'm just curious about the magic. I was thinking about how my ring works and wondering if there are ways to accomplish the same thing through songs."

She twisted her ring around her finger, frowning at the useless, dull pearl. Zoe glanced at the ring, then back at the conch shells.

"I don't think it's the same. Your ring relies on human affection, doesn't it?"

"Yes. It uses the love of a human man to transform the mermaid wearing it into a human."

How exactly it did that, Fiora couldn't say. As far as she knew, her ring was the only one of its kind.

Maybe because human emotions were fickle, and it was safer to rely on the magic in your voice than someone's feelings.

"Althea made the ring," Fiora said. "Do you think she made other transformation enchantments?"

Zoe shook her head.

"Althea doesn't do that sort of magic anymore, but Madame Isla uses it to help her studies sometimes. She wrote the song Leander used to transform into a human when they were looking for the Kraken Heart."

"Leander transformed into a human?"

Zoe looked up to the conch shells again and frowned, as if realizing she had said too much.

"We should go, Fiora. We need to get ready for the ceremony."

Fiora resisted the urge to look at the space that held the transformation songs and followed Zoe out of the library instead. She would return later to see if the shells held any useful information.

Although if everything went well tonight, she might not need it. If she could prove that she belonged here, maybe she wouldn't feel so eager to leave.

The entire city bustled with activity as everyone prepared for the ceremony. Merfolk swam loops around each other, and a strange chorus of unrelated yet harmonious songs floated through the water. Fiora looked for Leander, hoping to find an opportunity to ask about the enchantment that had made him human, but whatever he was doing, he was doing it somewhere else.

"You're late," Althea said as they swam into the castle.

She was already prepared for the ceremony. Her hair was filled with decorative shells and rocks tied and braided into the strands. She wore eight oysters clipped onto her tail, marking her status as a member of the royal family.

Fiora's plans to ask Althea about the transformation magic withered and died when she saw her aunt's expression. That conversation would have to wait until Althea was in a better mood.

Which meant it would be waiting a very long time.

"Eat something first, girls," Kathelin said.

She gestured to a flat rock covered with what passed for food in the underwater world. Zoe smiled and darted over to it. Fiora gagged.

Since they were underwater, mermaids could not cook as humans did. There was no fire. No spices.

Instead, they mashed ingredients together into thick blobs the consistency of mud. The blobs on the rock were an unappetizing gray-brown color and had crab legs sticking out of them.

Zoe picked one up and munched it with obvious enjoyment. Tiny clouds of black floated away from her mouth as she crunched a crab leg.

"Squid ink," Althea said with a scowl. "I told Chef to make something that wouldn't make a mess, and he sends this!"

"But they're delicious!" Zoe said.

"Don't talk with your mouth full," Kathelin said. "Fiora, are you going to eat, or should I do your hair now?"

"I already ate."

Fiora would rather go hungry than eat anything on that rock. The squid ink floated through the water in dark lines. Althea was right. It was a mess.

Before she had experienced life as a human, Fiora had found the merfolk food tolerable. Now it was unbearable. Just another reminder of the life she had fought for and lost.

Kathelin swam around Fiora and tied shells into her hair. Althea hummed a tune to gather all the squid ink Zoe had spread into the water into a single dark cloud. She pushed it out an opening in the wall then joined her sister in helping Fiora prepare for the ceremony.

On land, wearing this many ornaments in her hair would have weighed it down and given Fiora a headache. But underwater, everything simply floated. She would notice a little more drag when she swam, but nothing else.

"Beautiful," Kathelin said. "The blue shells look lovely with your red hair."

Fiora rolled her eyes. Her hair color had caused her nothing but trouble.

"She looks like Nyssa," Althea said softly.

Fiora wasn't sure which surprised her more: the emotion in her aunt's voice or the fact that she had mentioned Fiora's mother.

"She's Nyssa's daughter," Kathelin said gently. "A royal sister. I've always thought she looks like her."

Fiora stared up at her aunts. She had only ever heard that she looked like her father, but perhaps that was because she had his hair.

Althea studied Fiora from head to tail, then nodded.

"You do look like Nyssa. I don't know why I haven't seen it before."

"And you act like her to," Kathelin said. "She was always getting into trouble."

"And we'd get her out of it."

"Like when you made the ring?"

Fiora couldn't help asking. Althea scowled, but not as deeply as Fiora had thought she might.

"Have we never told you the story?"

Fiora shook her head, causing the shells tied in her hair to bob in the water.

"You never talk about her at all."

She was pushing her luck, but she had never seen the royal sisters so receptive to talking about her mother. Maybe she could get new information while they were feeling sentimental.

Althea sighed.

"You've probably guessed most of it. Nyssa visited land and fell in love with your father. She was never happy in the water after that, so we made the ring for her."

"We?"

"I helped," Kathelin said. "It took months and every bit of magic we had."

"And it uses the love of a human man to transform a mermaid into a human?"

Althea nodded. Fiora ran her thumb over the pearl's lifeless surface. She had tried not to think too hard about it since she returned to the ocean, but the evidence was too overwhelming to ignore any longer.

If the ring had lost its magic, then her father no longer loved her.

Fiora hated that her eyes filled with tears when she admitted that to herself. It shouldn't hurt so badly. Why should one person's opinion matter so much?

Because she had given up her entire world to live with her father. Because she had dedicated her life to marrying well and making an alliance for Kell when he asked.

Because, no matter how hard she tried, she had still lost him in the end. To the stepmother who never approved and the stepsister who never failed.

Elspeth.

Fiora gritted her teeth as she remembered her father's words. Fiora had been sent away to give Elspeth a better chance.

A hand settled on her shoulder, and Fiora flinched. Kathelin gave her a sad smile.

"That's enough reminiscing, I think. Let's put the oysters on Fiora's tail so we can start Zoe's hair."

Perhaps this was why the mermaids never wanted to talk about their younger sister. Kathelin looked less cheerful than usual, and Althea looked capable of murder.

She pulled eight oysters out of a large clamshell basket and swam down to Fiora's tail fin. Kathelin hummed a tune to open the shell, and Althea clipped it onto her tail.

"Ouch!"

Fiora jerked her tail away as pain shot through her fin. The emotion in her voice created a small whirlpool that spiraled through the water. It knocked the blobs of food off the rock and sent them flying across the room.

Where they crashed into Queen Gallerus.

Dark clouds of squid ink spread slowly through the water, leaving blotches of black on the queen's long, white hair. Everyone in the room stared at Fiora.

She stared back in horror, watching helplessly as the squid ink spread.

The other mermaids regained their composure and hummed

to create magical currents in the water. They pushed the squid ink away and pulled crab legs out of the queen's hair.

The dark spots remained. Apparently squid ink was an effective hair dye.

Queen Gallerus didn't say anything. She simply looked at Fiora for a moment, then shifted her gaze to Althea and Kathelin, sending them a clear message.

Fix this.

The queen backed out of the room and swam away. As soon as she was gone, the room sprang into motion.

"What was that?" Althea asked. "Why did you scream?"

"It hurts!" Fiora said, pulling at the shell. "It's ripping my fin!"

"Fiora, the oysters are harmless."

Kathelin grabbed Fiora's tail and clipped the rest of the shells on in quick succession.

Tears filled Fiora's eyes. She clamped her mouth shut, not daring to speak for fear that she would create currents strong enough to wreck the room.

When they had finished, she floated to a dark corner of the room and tried to focus on anything but the pain shooting through her tail. At least it was a distraction from the ache in her heart.

The mermaids ignored her while they cleaned the room and finished getting ready. Fiora flexed her fin, trying to stretch away the pain, but nothing helped.

Zoe swam over when her hair was finished and oysters had been clipped to her tail.

"I know it pinches, but you get used to it."

She smiled sympathetically, and Fiora glared. Pinch? That was the understatement of the century.

Zoe's eyes widened when she realized Fiora was in genuine distress, and she sang a soft song. It was one Fiora recognized from her childhood. A song of healing and comfort.

The sharp pain in her tail eased into a dull throbbing. She relaxed a little.

"Thank you, Zoe."

"That's what sisters are for!"

The mermaid beamed, making Fiora think she should probably be nice to her more often. The youngster meant well.

"Getting dressed up is always uncomfortable," Zoe said. "Do humans wear decorations?"

Fiora nodded, not quite sure how to explain earrings and corsets and high-heeled shoes and the various other human clothing meant for formal events. The heels had been uncomfortable, but nothing like this.

"It's time," Althea announced. "Is everyone ready?"

She glared at Fiora and Zoe as she said it. Both mermaids nodded.

"We're ready, Althea," Zoe said.

"Then let's begin. Everyone follow me."

The rest of the mermaids followed Althea and the royal sisters in a single file line. They sang a solemn tune and moved slowly since this was a formal procession. Thank goodness for that. The oysters pulled at Fiora's fin every time she moved her tail.

She watched the other mermaids for signs of discomfort, but none of them seemed to be in pain. Maybe Fiora's fin hurt more because she was half human. Because the fish part of her was a little less fishy than everyone else.

Lucky her.

They reached the site of the ceremony, and Fiora did her best to push the pain out of her head. She needed to focus.

If she wanted to find her place as a mermaid, then she needed to sing perfectly.

8

Gustave stared at the tables covered with flower arrangements. They filled the ballroom in a riot of color and perfume. Ribbons in complementary colors and vases of various shapes and sizes took up the rest of the space.

When Marquis Corbeau said he was planning the wedding, he meant it.

Gustave wished there had actually been an urgent matter of state to deal with. Anything was preferable to this.

"Surely this can be decided without my input."

Marquis Corbeau shook his head.

"Your Majesty is well aware that you cannot delegate important decisions until you claim the full kingship. We must work together."

Gustave massaged his forehead. That law of partial kingship was designed to help young rulers learn the basics of ruling in a supportive environment. A sort of apprenticeship if they took the throne before they came of age, and a way to make sure they had time to figure out life and find a suitable bride before taking on too much responsibility.

"I doubt my forefathers had flowers in mind when drafting

that particular piece of legislation. You are deliberately misinter-preting the law."

Marquis Corbeau shrugged.

"The florist had to come anyway to deliver the arrangements for your birthday gala. It seemed efficient to select flowers for your wedding as well."

The florist dropped a vase of roses when Marquis Corbeau mentioned the wedding. His assistant rushed to pick them up while the florist turned his full attention to Gustave.

"Your Majesty has chosen a bride?"

Why did everyone light up when discussing his marriage? The florist was absolutely beaming.

"He has not decided quite yet," Marquis Corbeau said, "But we would do well to be prepared."

"Of course. These lilies are popular wedding flowers and will be in bloom a few more weeks."

"Weeks?" Gustave said.

"How many do you have available?" Marquis Corbeau said.

A servant ran into the room, and Gustave looked up at him hopefully. Maybe something important had happened that required his attention. At this point, another kraken attack would be a welcome distraction.

"Begging your pardon, Your Majesty, but the Dowager Queen would like to see you."

Gustave's hope for a distraction flickered and died.

"I am rather busy at the moment with important state business-"

"It's not that important," Marquis Corbeau said. "I can finish here without your help."

He turned back to the florist.

"Tell me more about the wedding lilies. How many could you provide on short notice?"

Gustave gritted his teeth and walked through the castle to his grandmother's sitting room. This was becoming unbearable.

He knocked on the door even though he knew his grandmother wouldn't be able to hear it. Someone would tell her, and then–

"Come in!"

Dowager Queen Bernadine's voice rang through the chamber, and the door swung open. Thomas, her interpreter, held the door for Gustave then reclaimed his seat by the dowager queen's side. Gustave hurried to greet his grandmother, who sat in her wheelchair as regally as if she still held the throne.

"How are you today, Grandmother?"

He spoke the words and made signs with his hands at the same time to make sure she understood him. Dowager Queen Bernadine had been deaf since Gustave's childhood, but that didn't stop her from taking an active role in both official and personal affairs. Gustave, Collette, and a few members of the castle staff had learned sign language so they could better communicate with her. The rest of the time, Thomas translated.

"I'm busy," Dowager Queen Bernadine replied. "Far too busy."

The gleam in her eyes said this was how she preferred things. It was how Gustave preferred things as well. The dowager queen had less time to interfere with his life when she was occupied with affairs of state.

"Rebuilding the harbor?" he signed.

"Of course not. There are far more important things to do at the moment. I've been revising the guest list for your birthday gala."

Gustave swallowed.

"Grandmother–"

Bernadine waved her hand to stop him.

"Please step out to the hallway, Thomas. I'd like a moment of privacy with my grandson."

Thomas bowed and left the room. His translation wasn't necessary since Gustave knew sign language, but he rarely left Bernadine's side. This wasn't good.

As soon as the door closed, the dowager queen pinned Gustave in place with sharp eyes that had once caused even the most sea-hardened admirals to quake in their boots.

They still would, if she hadn't given up control of the navy to focus her attention on her grandchildren. The entire navy had breathed a sigh of relief when she announced her retirement.

"I've been looking over the guest list, Gustave. I'd like to make some changes."

"The council and I approved that list months ago, Grandmother."

"I understand that, but you neglected to consult me at the time. It isn't every day my grandson has a birthday. I'd like to invite some of my friends to celebrate with me."

"Your friends?"

Gustave had no problem with Queen Bernadine inviting friends, but the gleam in her eyes made him nervous

"Yes, my friends. Don't give me that look, Gustave. Suspicion is unbecoming in a king."

"What kind of friends?"

"Oh, members of my embroidery club, former ladies-in-waiting, that kind of thing."

"And I suppose they'll bring their granddaughters?"

He raised an eyebrow as he signed the words. Dowager Queen Bernadine gave him an innocent smile.

"Perhaps. They might even send them in their place if they are too busy to come themselves."

"Dealing with the last suggested bride almost killed me, Grandmother. I'm not ready for another so soon."

She chuckled.

"I told Marquis Corbeau that courting Princess Carina was a bad idea. My guests will be nice, local girls. Nothing like those ruffian princesses from Santelle."

Gustave slumped into his chair, not caring that it was improper for a king to slump. Dowager Queen Bernadine's eyes grew even sharper.

"Why are you so opposed to this, Gustave?"

"I don't want to rush into a marriage."

"I'm not asking you to rush. Just to dance with some girls at a party and see if you like them. But you're reluctant even to do that. Why?"

Gustave's hands hovered in the air for a moment as he considered his words.

"I don't want to give up my search for Father," he finally signed. *"And I don't want to take a bride when I can't give her my full attention. If I become fully king and have a wife, I won't be able to devote time to the search. And what happens when Father returns, but I've claimed the full kingship? He won't be legally allowed to take it back."*

Meaning Gustave would be stuck with the responsibility for the rest of his life. He had always known he would be king. He just hadn't expected it to happen so soon.

Dowager Queen Bernadine's gaze softened.

"You've been searching for almost a year, Gustave."

"I'm not giving up."

"I'm not saying you should. Do you think I want to admit my son is dead? Do you think I'm not clinging to hope just as tightly as you are?"

Gustave sat up straighter.

"Then why push me to become king before we find him?"

"You can't stop living because of tragedy, Gustave. Your father is missing, and of course you want to find him. But you also need to think about the future. Your future and the kingdom's. Montaigne needs a king. You need a wife."

"I can rule without being married. The council and I have made it this far."

"Not happily."

Gustave sighed.

"You don't have to worry about me, Grandmother. I'm fine. Please stop plotting."

"Is it plotting to want my only grandson happily married and the future of my country secured?"

"Yes."

A sly grin spread across Bernadine's face.

"I've taught you well, Gustave. You're clever for all that you're quiet and too polite sometimes."

Gustave bit his lip, resisting the urge to point out that his grandmother was the one who had insisted he mind his manners as a boy.

"Let's make a deal then," Dowager Queen Bernadine said. "I'll convince the council to devote extra resources to searching for your father."

"And in return?"

"Nothing at all. Just let me add a few friends to the guest list."

Gustave considered this. He had no doubt that, given free rein, his grandmother would invite every eligible young lady in the kingdom to his birthday gala. That would be unbearable, but it was only one night.

And it would be useful to have additional support in the search.

Besides, Dowager Queen Bernadine would find a way to invite the girls no matter what he did. Gustave might as well get something out of the exchange.

"Deal," Gustave signed.

He would dance with the girls. Maybe it wouldn't be so bad. Maybe he would find someone he liked.

If only it was that simple. Finding love meant losing the last bit of freedom he had. It meant spending the rest of his life in budget meetings.

And it meant scaling back the search for his father while he stepped into his new responsibilities.

As usual, Dowager Queen Bernadine seemed to read his thoughts.

"I'm not giving up on your father, Gustave. There's no need to look so resigned."

"You never give up on anything."

"Not when I think there's a chance. And there is still a chance, isn't there?"

She nodded to his ring. Gustave held the ruby to his lips and whispered, "Find King Francois."

A red beam of light shot out from the enchanted gem and glittered against the wall. Gustave blinked at it.

"It's changed directions."

"What did you say? Don't mumble, Gustave."

He had not signed the words, and Dowager Queen Bernadine waited for him to remedy this. Instead, Gustave pulled the compass from his pocket and checked the light's direction.

"Why the blazes are you carrying a compass around, Gustave?"

In case this happened. In case whoever was holding his father captive moved him.

"The light has moved, Grandmother. Father has moved. I need to go."

Dowager Queen Bernadine raised an eyebrow.

"You can't just rush off to sea, Gustave. What about your meetings this afternoon? What about preparations for the gala?"

He shook his head.

"I'm taking the Delphinette to look for Father. Consider it part of our deal. If you smooth things over with the council, I'll give you control of the guest list. You can invite as many ladies as you want."

He didn't wait for his grandmother to respond. The gleam in her eyes was answer enough. Gustave stuffed the compass into his pocket and ran out the door.

9

The procession of merfolk swam out of the city and over the gardens, finally stopping at a large ravine near the Montaigne shoreline. Fiora followed her sisters as they wove through a crowd of merfolk gathered above an enormous crevice. The Kraken Heart sat on a coral pedestal at the edge of the ravine, and Queen Gallerus floated beside it.

Fiora swallowed. Her grandmother's long white hair was still stained from the squid ink. The queen met Fiora's gaze for a moment. Her expression remained serene, showing no signs of the displeasure and disappointment she doubtless felt.

The royal merfolk took their places floating above the Kraken Heart. Althea and Kathelin used sign language to adjust everyone's position, moving them so the song would be balanced. Above them, the rest of the merfolk formed a large dome so they could watch the performance and join the song when it was their time.

Fiora followed Althea's directions and took her place beside Zoe. Then she studied the sleeping kraken while Althea turned her attention to everyone else.

Fiora had seen the dark creatures from a distance when they

attacked the capital, but she had never been this close to one. The kraken's body was silvery purple and filled the entire ravine. If you counted the tentacles stretched along the ocean floor, the sea monster was longer than the width of the mermaid's summer city.

Its enormous eyes were closed, and its beaked mouth fluttered open and shut. The sleek body expanded and contracted as the creature breathed in a rhythm that matched Kraken Heart's pulsing light.

"A small one," Zoe signed to Fiora.

Fiora raised an eyebrow. This was a small one?

Althea glared at them and signed, *"Focus, girls."*

Fiora and Zoe nodded back to her.

"Is everyone ready?" Kathelin signed.

Fiora nodded, as did the merfolk around her. Then they all turned to Queen Gallerus. The queen swam to the center of the crowd so everyone could see her.

"This is a joyous moment for all merfolk," the queen signed. *"The Kraken Heart has returned to the sea, and we are safe from dark creatures once again. I would like to thank the merfolk who made this possible."*

She gestured to Kathelin, Althea, and Leander. They bowed, curling their tales towards their chests. Merfolk applauded in sign language, fluttering their fingers in the water.

"The Kraken Heart relies on the magic of our voices to direct it. The royal sisters will begin the song, as is our tradition, then each of you will join in turn. I thank you all for your bravery, and I dedicate this gem to what we lost in the attacks. May we sing with honesty and courage so we never suffer such a loss again."

The crowd silently applauded the queen. She nodded to Kathelin and Althea and swam back to take her place amongst her royal guard.

Kathelin and Althea nodded to each other and tapped a beat in the air. Then they sang, their voices rising and falling in a soothing duet. The light of the Kraken Heart pulsed to match their music, growing brighter as their voices swelled with song.

Fiora pulled water through her gills and watched for the signal. It was almost time. Her chance to prove she belonged here. Until she found more information about the transformation enchantments, this was the only home she had.

And she knew her part. All she had to do was sing.

As the magic of the mermaid's song filled the water, the oysters clinging to Fiora's tale began to tighten and loosen in time with the music. Perhaps there was a little darkness in those blasted creatures as well.

Fiora gritted her teeth and tried to ignore the pain. She could do this.

She had to do this.

Fiora was so focused on her tail that she missed her cue. Althea scowled as she took a hurried breath and started singing a beat too late. Her voice wobbled, out of tune with the rest of the mermaids.

She listened to the music around her and quickly adjusted her pitch. Zoe caught her eye and winked. The young mermaid was confident now and singing at full volume. She seemed to be having fun.

Fiora poured magic into her voice as the quartet crescendoed. Her sound expanded as some of the human quality crept into her song. Althea frowned and motioned for her to sing more quietly. Fiora listened for a moment, then nodded. Althea was right. Her voice was sticking out.

The royal sisters, like most mermaids, had voices as clear and pure as flutes. Contrasted again them, Fiora's was more of a bassoon. Darker and more nasal than it ought to be.

Another downside of being part human.

Fiora listened and tried to match the sisters' tone. She pulled back, sang at half volume, and rounded her vowels to soften the nasal quality. There. Her voice blended now. She was doing it!

Queen Gallerus smiled as the quartet continued. Even Leander and the other guards looked more relaxed than normal as they stood watch beside her. The Kraken Heart's blue light filled the ocean with a gentle heartbeat. The song was nearly finished. Kathelin and Althea waved their arms to get the rest of the merfolks' attention and establish a beat. Soon everyone would join together to sing and complete the enchantment.

The ground rumbled, and Fiora glanced down at the kraken. Was it snoring?

Althea and Kathelin shared a look, then shrugged and kept singing.

Something cast a shadow overhead. Fiora's heartbeat quickened until she realized it was only a ship. Not a dark creature or anything dangerous.

The ship traveled in slow circles on the surface above them. Were the sailors curious about the light? Could they hear the mermaid's song?

"Focus, Fiora," Althea signed.

"Sorry."

Kathelin gave the signal, and the rest of the merfolk joined the song. Fiora took a deep breath and poured magic into her voice. The other merfolk did the same, and music filled the ocean with a beautiful harmony.

Then the ground rumbled again, and the kraken's eye opened.

A few merfolk lost focus and gasped in alarm. The rest tried to ignore the eye and stay focused on their song.

The eye opened wider. It glowed yellow, mixing with the blue light of the Kraken Heart until the water was tinted green. Fully opened, the eye was bigger than any of the mermaids. Bigger than the ship that floated above them.

"Switch songs," Althea signed. *"Sing Teuthida Somnum Statim on my signal."*

The merfolk nodded. Althea and Kathelin breathed in unison and waved their hands to conduct the song. The merfolk began a slow, gentle chorus, filling their voices with magic. Fiora followed their lead, pushing everything she had into the lullaby.

The kraken's eyelid drooped for a moment. Then the rumbling grew louder, and both eyes shot open. An enormous tentacle lifted from the ground and swiped at the crowd.

The song dissolved into screaming as merfolk scattered to dodge the tentacle. Fiora darted backward. Zoe swam down and grabbed the Kraken Heart before the tentacle smashed into the coral pedestal.

"Keep singing!" Althea screamed above the chaos.

She and Kathelin sang a frantic duet as they swooped down to rescue Zoe.

"Teuthida somnum statim."

A new voice rang above the crowd. Queen Gallerus. The queen had the most powerful voice of all the mermaids. Surely she could subdue the dark creature.

The kraken swayed as the queen's magic swept over it. Then it pushed off the ocean floor and shot towards the surface.

Towards the ship.

The kraken's sudden movement sent a shock wave through the water and scattered the merfolk. Leander and the other guards formed a ring around the queen and urged her to swim away to safety. Most of the merfolk followed suit and fled. Those with the strongest voices stayed behind. They grouped together into ensembles and abandoned the lullaby for an intricate song performed at top volume. A song of attack.

Strands of music wove together, creating a counterpoint meant to confuse and subdue the creature.

The kraken ignored them and rammed against the ship, accenting the merfolk's song with the percussive crack of splintering wood.

❦ I O ❦

"Did you hear that?"

Gustave leaned over the ship's railing. The sea wind rushing past him carried a faint trace of music.

"Your Majesty will fall overboard if you lean any further."

Captain Whist pulled Gustave back with one hand while using the other to secure his enormous hat against a sudden gust.

"But there's something out there."

Around him, the crew shared nervous glances, but Gustave ignored them. This was the best lead he'd had since his father disappeared. He wasn't going to let anyone stop him from following it.

"Find King Francois," he whispered to his ring.

The red light shot towards the horizon.

"We're still on course," Captain Whist said. "As we were when you checked five minutes ago."

Another gust of wind swept over the ship. This time the song it carried was unmistakable. Captain Whist's eyes widened.

"Who could possibly be singing out here?"

"It could be mermaids."

"Perhaps we should go back to shore," Captain Whist said.

"The last time I heard a mermaid sing, she seized my ship with a kraken."

"If you're afraid, I suppose we have no choice but to turn back."

Gustave's words had the desired effect. Captain Whist and every sailor within earshot stood taller and glared at him.

"We're not afraid."

"Then we keep going?"

Captain Whist nodded to the sailors, and the *Delphinette* continued on its course.

The singing grew louder, filling the wind and dancing across the waves. Gustave couldn't quite make out the words, but they reminded him of the ancient language that Kathelin and Althea had used to control the kraken and activate the Kraken Heart.

"Find King Francois."

The red light shone behind him, stretching past the ship towards Montaigne. Gustave grabbed Captain Whist's arm.

"Turn around! We passed him!"

"That's not possible."

The captain and Gustave sprinted to the stern of the ship and stared at the open sea.

"There's nothing there," Captain Whist said. "How could we have passed him?"

The mermaid song swelled around them, and the water glowed green. The captain swallowed nervously.

"We should leave, Your Majesty."

"But my father is here."

"If he is, he's under the waves. We can't do anything about that at the moment."

Gustave pulled Kathelin's seashell from his pocket, tossed it into the air, and caught it in his palm. That was how Princess Carina had activated her golden ball. Perhaps it would work with mermaid magic as well.

"Kathelin, are you there? Kathelin? Althea?"

Something rippled under the water. Gustave stuffed the shell into his pocket and leaned over the edge of the ship to get a better look. Had a mermaid finally heard him and decided to talk?

"Your Majesty, be careful!"

Captain Whist was too busy turning the ship around to pull him back, so Gustave ignored the warning. The *Delphinette* circled slowly as it changed course. The setting sun added red to the green glow of the ocean, creating an otherworldly atmosphere. The light under the water flickered against the waves, and a group of shadows scattered, moving away from it. Mermaids? Or simply a school of fish?

Gustave leaned further still. The answers were under the sea. His father was there.

One of the shadows broke away from the rest and moved rapidly towards the surface. It grew larger and larger. Closer and closer.

"Kathelin, it's me! King Gustave!"

Something large and silver shot out of the water. A tentacle. It smashed against the *Delphinette*, and Gustave tumbled overboard.

He heard Captain Whist cry out in alarm, then Gustave plunged into the water and heard only chaos. Screams mixed with a choir singing at full volume. The music faded when his head broke through the surface. He gasped for air.

"Your Majesty!"

Captain Whist's voice was faint. Gustave kicked and turned until he found the ship. Somehow, the *Delphinette* had floated away from him. Its sails were limp, but it was quickly fading into the horizon.

"Wait! I'm here!"

Gustave waved his arms, but the ship was already too far away for him to see the people on the deck. That meant they couldn't see him.

A wave knocked him under the water, and he heard the

singing again. It was stronger now. An unworldly harmony laced with magic and desperation.

The sea churned as another kraken tentacle broke through the waves. It crashed into Gustave and knocked his breath away.

He gasped for air and got salt water instead. The cut on his head stung as the wound reopened. As he sputtered, a solo voice emerged from the choir. It was more piercing than the others. More powerful somehow.

If his men couldn't save him, maybe a mermaid could.

The next time a wave pushed him under, Gustave screamed for help as loud as he could. The sound dissolved into the water, lost in the mermaid's song.

He tried to swim back to the surface, but where was it? Panic built in his chest as it occurred to him that he might not make it out of this alive.

No, he couldn't die here. He wouldn't.

Gustave forced his eyes open and swam as hard as he could towards the brilliant red light of the sunset. He broke the surface of the water and gasped for air. It came mixed with salt spray, and he sputtered.

Something shot past him. Another tentacle?

Gustave kicked to avoid it, and his foot connected to something solid. Pain shot up his leg. It was like kicking a rock.

The rock turned and crashed on top of Gustave. The mermaid song grew louder as he sank deep into the water. Then something crashed into his head, and everything went silent.

❧ 11 ❧

Kathelin swam closer to the surface and pushed the ship to safety with a magical current. Zoe and Althea held the Kraken Heart and desperately sang a lullaby. The rest of the merfolk continued their song of attack.

Queen Gallerus and her guards floated a distance away, out of tentacle reach but still close enough to contribute to the song.

None of it did any good.

The queen sang a high sustained note. The oysters clipped to Fiora's tail shuddered and let go.

Fiora revised her thought. The magic had done some good, but it hadn't stopped the kraken.

She shook out her tail and gritted her teeth. Surely she could do something to help. She didn't know the song of attack, but at this point the music was chaos anyway.

Fiora pulled water through her gills and sang a single note as loudly as she could. She didn't worry about blending in or not sounding human. She simply poured everything she could into a pitch that was more of a scream than a song.

When she had released her frustration, she transitioned the

note into a more aggressive form of the lullaby, commanding the kraken to go to sleep rather than coaxing it.

The kraken's eyelids drooped, and it sank towards the ravine.

"Gather around it!" Althea ordered. "Follow my lead."

Fiora turned to swim towards her aunt, but something on the surface caught her eye. Splintered wood from the ship cast dark shadows against the waves, but there was something else.

Clouds cleared, and the last rays of the setting sun showed the silhouette of a human floating in the waves.

He must have fallen overboard, and Kathelin's song had pulled the ship away before they could retrieve him.

Below Fiora, the kraken wriggled in the ravine as it fought sleep. The mermaids had regrouped into a dome over the creature. Under Althea's direction, they were weaving the attack song and the lullaby together in a more organized fashion, creating a coherent enchantment that seemed to be working.

They didn't need her help. Fiora turned away from the choir and swam as fast as she could towards the human.

He slipped beneath the waves as Fiora raced to meet him. Was she too late? Please, don't be too late. She reached the man, wrapped her arms around his torso, and pulled him back to the surface. He was unconscious, but he gasped for air when they broke through the waves.

Thank goodness.

His ship was nowhere in sight. Kathelin must have sent it back to shore.

Something rumbled beneath them, and Fiora dragged the man through the water. It would be best to put some distance between them and the kraken just in case it woke up again.

He sputtered as she squeezed a little too tightly. Fiora adjusted her grip so she could see his face. She almost dropped him in surprise.

"King Gustave?"

The king did not respond.

A.G. MARSHALL

Fiora wrapped her arms around him and swam harder. She tried not to think about the resentment she felt towards this man, but she couldn't shake it. King Gustave had ruined her chances at the Princess Test by presenting evidence for Lina.

"I would be married by now if not for you," she whispered. "I would be human."

King Gustave did not respond. His face was limp, and he looked more pathetic than aggravating at the moment. Blood from a cut on his head trickled down his face and into his beard.

Fiora pushed away her anger about the Princess Test and focused on swimming. King Gustave wasn't particularly heavy since he was floating, but it was hard to keep his head above water and move with any kind of speed. His clothes added to his bulk and dragged in the water.

So this was why mermaids didn't wear clothing. Fiora considered removing some of the king's clothes to make swimming easier, but that would be difficult to do while keeping his head above water.

Not to mention how awkward it would be if he woke up while she was doing it.

She gritted her teeth and kept pulling the king towards shore. The mermaid's song faded into silence as she swam. Fiora swallowed the guilt she felt for leaving them. They had a full choir. One voice wouldn't make a difference.

The cut on Gustave's head left a trail of blood in the water. Hopefully that wouldn't attract sharks or other predators.

Fiora stopped to rest and grimaced at the dark patch that formed around them. The king was losing a lot of blood.

He was still alive, wasn't he? His skin was cold from being in the water. Was he breathing?

Please still be alive.

The water behind her flashed green then changed to a pulsing blue glow. Did that mean the merfolk had finally put the kraken back to sleep?

Why had it woken up in the first place?

Fiora swallowed. She was the only singer who had made a mistake. She had entered late and out of tune and allowed her human voice mix into the song.

Had that disturbed the music enough to wake the monster?

If so, that made her responsible for King Gustave's death if he didn't survive.

He had to survive.

Fiora sang the song of healing that Zoe had used to ease the pain from the oysters. Thank goodness those hateful shells had fallen off during the chaos of the attack. Tradition or not, she refused to wear them again.

Magic traveled through her voice and settled on Gustave's wounds. The bleeding slowed as the cut healed. Fiora sang until the skin knit itself back together and closed the wound. There was still an enormous bruise on his head, but at least he wouldn't lose any more blood.

King Gustave stirred and opened his eyes but didn't seem to see her. He stared at the sky, not focusing on anything in particular. Moonlight shimmered on the waves around them, and stars twinkled overhead.

Fiora changed her song to a lullaby. Gustave closed his eyes and relaxed in her arms. As soon as he fell asleep, she kicked her tail, eager to reach land and put him back where he belonged. She swam towards the same beach she had visited earlier that day. It was close enough to Montaigne's castle that she could fetch help for Gustave once he was safely on dry land.

She kept singing the lullaby, and he didn't wake up again. Finally they reached the beach. Fiora pushed King Gustave as far as she could onto the sand.

It wasn't far enough. His legs were still in the water. He would end up chilled that way and might be pulled to sea by a large wave.

Fiora pulled herself onto the sand, crawling on her belly in a truly undignified manner. She felt a sudden burst of sympathy for every fish she had ever seen flopping around on dry land.

When she had made it far enough up the beach, she grabbed King Gustave's shoulders and pulled him towards her. He was much heavier now that he was out of the water. Fiora dug her tail into the sand to brace against his weight, but she still couldn't drag him far enough. She sang a song and created a small wave to pull the king up the beach. When the water receded, he was safely out of the ocean.

Fiora sighed in relief and leaned over him to check for further injuries. The king's eyes fluttered open. Fiora froze, as if he wouldn't see her if she stayed perfectly still. What would she do if King Gustave recognized her as a mermaid?

But the king's eyes held no recognition. He seemed dazed as he stared at her, his gray eyes unfocused. When he tried to sit up, his face contorted in pain.

"Stay down," Fiora said.

The king obeyed, and Fiora sang again. There was no point in dragging His Majesty halfway through the ocean only to leave him on the beach in agony.

She was by no means an accomplished healer, but her singing seemed to make Gustave feel better. His eyes closed, and his features relaxed.

"Hello?"

Fiora looked up. Someone had emerged from the trees and was running towards them. She pushed away from King Gustave and rolled down the beach. She hit the water with a splash and dove under the waves. Then she hid behind a rock and watched.

A woman ran to the injured king. She wore a black cloak and hood that hid her face from Fiora's view. She knelt over Gustave and seemed to be speaking to him. Fiora frowned as the woman pulled something from her cloak. What if she harmed King Gustave? Fiora still felt responsible for him.

King Gustave woke up and said something in response, but

Fiora couldn't quite make out the words. She leaned further around the rock, trying to see what was happening.

Voices rang out from further up the beach, and flickering torches lit the darkness. Someone was coming from the castle. Fiora swam down the shore, following the sound. When she was as close as she could get without leaving the water, she picked up a rock and threw it at a tree.

"Did you hear that?" someone called.

The voices drew nearer. Fiora threw more rocks, leading the search party down the beach towards Gustave.

"Gustave, are you there?"

The speaker came around the corner and gasped.

"Oh, I've found him! Everyone, I found him!"

Fiora recognized Gustave's sister, Collette, and sighed in relief. The princess would take care of her brother. Fiora hid behind a rock and watched a small crowd gather around Gustave.

The woman in the cloak had disappeared.

King Gustave recovered consciousness and stammered a reply to the multitude of questions being hurled at him. Judging from the crowd's responses, he wasn't making much sense. Collette took control and directed the guards to carry her brother back to the castle. Satisfied that Gustave was safe, Fiora dove beneath the waves and swam into the open ocean.

12

There was singing. A woman's voice coming from all directions at once. It sounded familiar, but Gustave couldn't remember where he had heard it before. Her song surrounded him and filled his senses. He opened his eyes, but water blurred his vision.

Liquid copper floated around him. He reached for it but found he couldn't move. Someone held him tight.

Gustave struggled against the arms that restrained him, and his vision blurred again. He closed his eyes and focused on the singing. There was healing in the music. It settled on the places the kraken had bruised and eased the pain.

The kraken. He had been attacked by a kraken.

In a cave in Santelle, and it had knocked a rock loose that cut his head. But the throbbing from that wound faded as he listened to the singing.

And that wasn't quite right. He had been attacked by a kraken again, recently. There had been music and light and a chaotic ocean.

Something solid pressed against Gustave's back. Solid and dry.

He reached down and dug his fingers into sand.

The singing stopped as hands clasped his shoulders and dragged him further the beach. Gustave opened his eyes and saw two sapphires framed by a starry sky.

No, they were eyes. Bright, beautiful blue eyes in a woman's face. She seemed familiar somehow. Brilliant red strands of hair blew in the wind, obscuring the woman so Gustave couldn't see her well enough to distinguish her features.

He tried to sit up for a better look, but the world blurred as he moved.

"Stay down."

Gustave obeyed, and she started singing again. The music banished the dark spots in his vision and eased the throbbing in his head.

"Hello?" a new voice called out.

The woman's blue eyes widened in surprise, and she disappeared from his view. Gustave heard a splash, then footsteps. Then the angel was back, her hair more golden than red now that it was dry.

How had she dried it so fast? Had her eyes always had that tint of green?

She held a sparkling golden gem over Gustave's heart. It glowed as she whispered words he couldn't quite make out, and his chest filled with warmth like a newly kindled fire. He smiled at the woman.

"I love you."

Why had he said that? He didn't even know her.

But he meant it from the bottom of his heart. She had saved him. She must be a good person. The warmth in his chest grew hotter, as if confirming his love.

"Good."

She sounded bored with the whole thing. What had Gustave done to upset her? That would never do. He couldn't let his lady be upset. He squinted, trying to make out her face, but the night was dark and the woman wore a hood. When had she put on that cloak? Was she cold?

If she was cold, it was his fault. He should have offered her his coat.

He wasn't wearing a coat, and he was cold and wet himself. How had that happened? He tried to remember, but the warmth in his chest distracted him.

He loved her.

Voices rang through the night, and the woman disappeared into the darkness. Gustave struggled to sit up, but a wave of dizziness forced him back to the sand. He coughed up a bit of sea water and stared at the sky. The warmth in his chest turned heavy and held him down as it settled into his skin and slowly spread through his body.

"Gustave, are you there?"

This was a different voice, but one he knew well. Why did he know that voice?

"Oh, I've found him! Everyone, I found him!"

Collette. The name floated into his mind, although he couldn't quite remember why he knew it. He tried to focus, but the warmth in his chest had spread to his head. It wrapped his thoughts in a lovely warm cloud, reminding him that only his love mattered.

Where had she gone? He had finally found the right woman, and now she had gone. He needed to find her again so he could propose and set a wedding date.

Then Collette's face appeared over him, and Gustave remembered she was his sister. His mind cleared, and memories rushed back as she hugged him. Tears of joy streamed down her face, and Gustave smiled weakly.

"I'm fine."

"Captain Whist returned without you. He said you'd been attacked by a kraken. Oh, Gustave!"

Kraken. That was why he was wet. He had been attacked by a kraken.

And someone had saved him by singing to him.

And whoever she was, he loved her.

A crowd of soldiers, courtiers, and sailors surrounded him, and Gustave lost Collette in a blur of people and questions. Then two soldiers picked him up and carried him off the beach, ignoring his protests as he searched the dark woods for his mysterious savior.

When they reached the castle, Dowager Queen Bernadine took one look at her grandson and ordered him to bed. Gustave made a token protest as the doctor checked him over and tucked him in, but he fell asleep as soon as they left him alone.

He dreamed of a song with words he didn't understand. It was cool and refreshing like summer rain, and strands of copper floated around him. Then a warm fire built in his chest, and the rain evaporated to golden mist.

❧ 13 ☙

Sunlight woke Fiora. Not the full, golden sun of land. This was underwater light dancing in silvery beams refracted by waves, and it pulled her back to consciousness gradually. She slid out from the grotto and stretched. Her tail was stiff from sleeping curled up in a ball, and she checked the edge of her fin. The oysters had left dark bruises, but the pain was mostly gone.

Thank goodness for that at least.

Memories of yesterday floated slowly into Fiora's mind like bubbles rising to the ocean's surface. The choir. The kraken. King Gustave. She had been too tired to swim all the way back to the city last night, so she had slept in the statue garden instead.

Ugh. She regretted that decision as she massaged the tension out of her neck. She had spent several nights there as a child, but she had apparently outgrown this particular nook while she was away.

Fiora ducked back into the grotto and peeked out to make sure the statue garden was empty. It was. Well, empty of mermaids, at least. There were plenty of stone humans to keep her company.

Fiora swam up to her favorite statue. This garden felt safe and familiar. Mostly because of him.

The statue was a human boy, about ten years old. He had fallen from a ship when she was the same age, and she had helped Kathelin place him above the grotto in the garden that summer.

He looked ordinary, and that was Fiora's favorite thing about him. Amid the glitz and sparkle of the mermaid gardens, he seemed real. He wore simple clothes and held something in his hand. Whatever it was, it had broken off when he fell from the ship and never been recovered. His expression was open and friendly, ready to listen even if he couldn't answer.

Fiora pulled water through her gills in a deep breath and smiled at the statue.

"I'm glad you survived the kraken attacks."

He smiled back at her.

"We were supposed to be safe now that we have the Kraken Heart, but one woke up and attacked last night. It think- I think I might have caused it."

Why couldn't she have paid attention? Her late entry and out of tune note had been the only flaw in the performance.

Perhaps the problem wasn't her voice or her human heritage. Maybe it was just her in general.

"I don't belong here."

She had always known that deep down, but saying it out loud made it real. It brought back memories of terrified screams and waving tentacles. King Gustave's pale face. He could have died. Others on the ship might have been injured.

Had any merfolk been hurt?

Fiora closed her eyes to push away the thought. Then she opened them and studied the statue to distract herself. Talking to him had been comforting when she was a child. When she became human and joined her father, she had searched every crowd for his face, certain that they would be friends in real life if they ever met.

But she had never found him, and the boy that had once seemed like a friend now looked like a mere child. She had changed, and he had not.

"I'm not that different," Fiora muttered.

He seemed to agree. It was somewhat comforting, which made Fiora feel even more pathetic.

She hummed a tune, tentatively at first, then with more confidence when her magic responded normally and nothing exploded.

Water swirled around the statue, brushing sand off the stone until he gleamed in the silvery light. She swished her tail and curtsied, feeling a little better now that she had put something in order.

"I don't suppose you did anything interesting while I was away?"

Of course he didn't answer. Fiora sighed.

"I didn't do much either. I trained to be a princess then went to parties and tried to catch a husband. I needed love to stay human, but I couldn't find it. You might be the only human that actually likes me."

The boy simply smiled back at her. Fiora pushed water out of her gills in a sigh. This had been much more comforting when she was young. Now she just felt crazy for talking to a rock.

The kraken attack had kicked up a lot of debris, covering the statues in a thin layer of white sand that almost looked like snow. Fiora swam through the garden, singing softly and brushing the statues clean. She told herself she wasn't delaying her return to the summer city. She was setting things right as best she could.

The statue Leander had delivered yesterday had fallen to its side, as had several other new additions. Fiora chose the nearest one and pushed it upright. Once it was secure, she hummed and created a current to pull sand from the statue's intricate beard. The hair seemed to ripple in the water. For a moment, it seemed the statue was alive and looking at her.

Fiora blinked, and the moment passed. She should probably

stop talking to statues if she was going to imagine things. She studied the man's face. His expression was sad and resigned. A strange thing to carve, but the craftsmanship was incredible. His beard was just as detailed as the statue she had noticed Leander moving yesterday. Perhaps they had been carved by the same artist?

"Stop being pathetic," Fiora muttered to herself.

How desperate did you have to be to procrastinate facing your family by studying a statue's beard?

The ground rumbled, and Fiora dove back into the grotto. Perhaps she had been stupid to sing again. What if she had awoken another kraken?

When the ground stopped shaking, Fiora peeked out from the grotto. Nothing seemed damaged, and there was no sign of kraken.

What was causing the tremors then?

Whatever it was, she didn't want to stick around to find out. Fiora hummed a tune to speed her journey back to the city. Her red hair glistened in the morning sun as she swam. She darted behind buildings on her way to the castle, not eager to face any more merfolk than she had to. She swam up the side of the castle and ducked into an opening that led directly to the throne room.

"There's no sign of her," Madame Isla was saying. "You must admit it looks-"

She clamped her mouth shut when Fiora entered. Fiora swam down through the room and settled next to Zoe. Her cousin gave her a tentative smile.

"Was anyone hurt last night?" Fiora signed.

Zoe shook her head, and Fiora relaxed a little.

"And the kraken?"

"Asleep," Zoe answered.

Fiora relaxed a little further. Everything was alright then.

So why was everyone on the royal council looking at her like that?

"Fiora, where have you been?" Queen Gallerus asked.

Fiora winced at the accusation in her grandmother's voice. The words carried just a trace of magic, and the merfolks' hair stirred in the current it created.

"A human fell overboard during the attack. I took him to shore and was too tired to swim all the way back. I spent the night in the statue garden."

Kathelin and Zoe sighed with relief. Althea and Queen Gallerus remained stoic. Madame Isla and Leander looked like they didn't believe a word she said.

"What happened to your singing yesterday, Fiora?" Kathelin said.

Fiora winced. So they were just going to jump right in then. She should have expected this. Mermaids tended to be more direct than humans.

"I got distracted. I'm sorry."

"Distracted?" Leander said. "You accidentally woke a kraken because you got distracted?"

The disbelief in his tone made Fiora stiffen.

"Yes, I was distracted. The oysters were pinching my fin, and there was a lot going on."

"I see. You were distracted by oysters. The same oysters everyone else was wearing."

"Fiora's magic isn't very strong," Zoe said.

Fiora turned to her cousin in surprise, and Zoe smiled as if she had said something helpful. Queen Gallerus considered Fiora for a moment before turning to her sister.

"Madame Isla, what do you think?"

The human scholar looked distinctly uncomfortable.

"It seems unlikely that a few out of tune notes from a weak singer would completely cancel the Kraken Heart's enchantment. However, if they were carefully planned-"

"Wait. Do you think I woke the kraken on purpose?"

Leander swam forward, putting himself between Fiora and

Queen Gallerus.

"Your Majesty, Princess Fiora has spent the last ten years among humans. It is possible that she was sent back to the ocean to spy on us and sabotage us however she could."

Fiora gasped.

"You think I tried to sabotage you?"

"The kraken attacks started when you arrived."

Leander's face was calm, and his hazel eyes remained serious. Fiora looked at the other mermaids, hoping to see her own disbelief mirrored in their expressions.

Kathelin and Zoe looked bewildered, but Althea, Madame Isla, and Queen Gallerus seemed to be considering the idea.

Fiora's tail flicked in irritation, making her float a little higher than the rest of the merfolk. Leander swam higher as well, keeping himself between Fiora and the queen.

"That's ridiculous! That's the most ridiculous thing I've ever heard. I would never sabotage you! Even if I wanted to, my voice isn't strong enough to control a kraken!"

Leander turned to Madame Isla.

"Kell is one of the more magical human kingdoms, is it not?"

"They do have their own style of magic, and it seems unaffected by whatever caused the rest of the human kingdoms to give up the art of enchantment."

"Don't lecture me about Kell's magic!" Fiora said. "I lived there for ten years!"

"Then you know it," Leander said.

Fiora sputtered, too angry to speak. As a matter of fact, she didn't. Her stepmother had declared her too old to learn magic and shut her out of the rooms where such things were studied.

But if the merfolk believed she was capable of waking dark creatures to rampage through their cities, they would certainly believe she was capable of lying about her magical education.

Queen Gallerus turned to Althea and Kathelin.

"What are your thoughts on this matter?"

"Fiora would never do such a thing!" Zoe said.

"Quiet, dear," Kathelin said. "Of course she wouldn't. Queen Gallerus, Fiora is family. Our royal sister. Nyssa's daughter would never attack us in the way Leander suggests."

"But she's also the daughter of the human responsible for Nyssa's death," Althea said.

"What did you say?"

Althea's face stiffened until it seemed made of stone. Fiora clenched her fists, desperately trying to keep her voice under control.

"What do you mean that my father is responsible for my mother's death? What are you saying?"

She looked around the gathering, hoping to see something in their faces that would refute the statement.

Instead, the mermaids refused to meet her gaze.

"That can't be true."

"We don't believe he did it on purpose," Kathelin said gently.

"So you think he killed her by accident? And you didn't bother to tell me?"

"That is not the matter we are discussing," Queen Gallerus said. "The past can be sorted out later. Right now, the important question is the matter of Fiora's voice. If it is at all possible that she woke the kraken-"

"I didn't wake the kraken!"

Magic rippled through the water as Fiora yelled the words. She swallowed and tried to calm herself.

"I didn't wake the kraken," she whispered, desperately trying to keep the emotion out of her voice. "How can you think that? Since I returned, I have worked as hard as I can to help. I have studied every song. Given my best to every assignment."

"I certainly hope that wasn't your best," Madame Isla said.

She pulled a fork from behind her ear and combed her hair. Fiora clenched her fists.

"I'm trying! Why can't anyone see that I'm trying?"

Her words rumbled through the throne room, pushing the merfolk away.

"Perhaps it would be best to imprison her until we can evaluate her magic and investigate her ties to the human world," Leander said.

"No!"

This time, Fiora unleashed her magic on purpose. She pushed the merfolk against the walls while she swam through a hole in the ceiling. She raced towards the first building she saw.

The library.

She would rather wear oysters on her tail again than let them put her in prison. If neither of her families wanted her, she would escape and make her own way.

She didn't need them.

What had Althea meant, saying that her father was responsible for her mother's death?

Fiora didn't know exactly how her mother had died. Only that it had been a complication from the magic that had allowed her to live as a human and be with the man she loved.

In her darker moments, Fiora had thought perhaps her mother's death had been related to giving birth to her. That perhaps she had been the cause, and that was why no one would ever discuss it with her.

But apparently that was not the case.

Why hadn't they told her?

Why didn't they trust her?

Fiora wiped angry tears away and ducked into the library. She swam towards the shelf that contained transformation charms and grabbed the largest conch. That seemed a good place to start. She read the first lines of the elegant script that wound around the shell.

"An enchantment for transformation into a human."

"Fiora?"

Fiora clutched the shell to her chest and spun around. Zoe

floated slowly towards her, shaking her head when Fiora tensed to swim away.

"I'm here to help," she whispered. "Fiora, I know you didn't wake the kraken. If anything, I probably sang a wrong note. I'm sure it was my fault."

Zoe looked like she truly believed that.

"No, you didn't, Zoe. I'm the one who sang off-key, but it wasn't on purpose."

Zoe frowned at the conch shell in Fiora's hands.

"You're not planning to run again?"

"What choice do I have?"

"Talk to them. Explain."

"They won't listen. They never listen! It's why I ran away the last time!"

The emotion in her voice swept water through the room, knocking shells out of their places. It pulled the clamshell off the golden ball Fiora had hidden. The metal glinted in the light, distracting Zoe for a moment. Then the young mermaid shook her head and turned back to Fiora.

"Then let me talk to them. I can convince them."

Only Zoe would believe that was possible, but Fiora couldn't bear to extinguish the hope in her cousin's eyes.

"I'll hide in the statue garden while I practice the transformation song. Come alone and sing the healing song as a sign if they change their minds."

Zoe nodded and darted through the library ceiling. Fiora swam through the hole nearest the floor. She moved slowly through the city, staying in shadows so the sunlight on her red hair wouldn't give her away.

Her hair always gave her away. She would need to do something about that.

Fiora changed course and swam to the kitchens. She ducked in and grabbed a bottle of squid ink before she left the summer city.

❧ 14 ❧

Gustave woke up to darkness. He untangled himself from blankets and sat up. Where was he?

His heart rate settled into a steady rhythm as his eyes adjusted and he realized he was in his room. Familiar sounds washed over him. Bird songs. Wind in the trees. People bustling through the hallways.

Normally Gustave slept with the curtains open so he would wake with the sun, but someone had pulled the thick velvet drapes closed last night. Probably trying to ensure he would sleep in.

Gustave swung his legs over the edge of the bed and groaned. His whole body was stiff, and his head ached. What had happened?

Right. Kraken.

Blasted dark magic.

He stood and stretched out the stiffness in his muscles. All things considered, he felt better than expected. He opened the curtains and blinked in the sunlight. It was still fairly early. He could make it to breakfast if he hurried.

Meals were the one time he could count on his family and council being in the same place and relatively undistracted. If he wanted to arrange another search party for his father, breakfast would be the best place to start the conversation.

Gustave pulled on a robe and opened his door. It crashed into a servant standing outside his room.

"Oh! Good morning, Your Majesty!"

Gustave's eyes narrowed.

"Did they station you here to watch me?"

The servant bowed.

"Dowager Queen Bernadine gave orders that you should sleep in as late as you could and were not to be disturbed. I'm to summon Doctor Batiste as soon as you wake."

"That won't be necessary. I feel fine."

"Her Highness's orders, Your Majesty."

Gustave considered this for a moment, then shrugged in surrender. As partial king, his orders should take precedence over the dowager queen's. In reality, servants were much more likely to listen to her. He could probably convince the servant to ignore orders, but not without a great deal of effort. And then he would have to explain to his grandmother why he had refused to see the doctor.

Gustave didn't feel like fighting that battle today.

He returned to his room and dressed for the day. Then he passed the time reviewing the enormous stack of paperwork on his desk. Marquis Corbeau wasn't wrong when he said that the partial kingship created a lot of extra work. Multiple people had to approve and sign each edict.

Gustave read and signed several building permits for repairs to the harbor, then picked up Marquis Corbeau's proposed gala budget.

Or rather, a request for more funds for the gala.

The event was in three days. How could the marquis have incurred so many extra expenses at the last minute?

Gustave looked closer at the itemized list in the report. Ten formal gowns. White shoes in every size available. A deposit on lilies, with the balance to be paid on delivery.

The marquis was sneaking wedding expenses into the gala budget.

Blast it all.

Someone knocked on the door, and Gustave pushed the report away, grateful for the distraction. The fight could wait until the next budget meeting. Perhaps it would give him some leverage when arguing that Collette should be allowed to spend whatever she liked to host those affected by the kraken attacks.

"Your Majesty should not be working!"

Doctor Batiste's bushy, white eyebrows rose in alarm when he saw Gustave hunched over his desk. Gustave shrugged.

"The kingdom won't run itself, Doctor."

"And your body won't heal without rest. Now tell me what happened."

Gustave left the desk and sat on his bed so that Doctor Batiste could examine him. The doctor was a short, portly man, and it was easier for Gustave to sit than for the doctor to stand on a chair.

"Your Majesty seems to attract trouble lately," the doctor scolded as he pushed Gustave's hair aside and checked his head. "Two kraken attacks are too many for a lifetime, let alone a few weeks."

Gustave shrugged. What could he say?

Doctor Batiste continued his examination, checking Gustave's old wounds and looking for new ones. He clucked to himself as he worked, creating a strange rhythm of vocal sounds that always made Gustave nervous.

The doctor ruffled through Gustave's hair one last time, then stepped back and met his king's gaze.

"How exactly did Your Majesty get back to shore?"

Gustave tried to remember, but thinking back made his head ache. He rubbed his forehead.

"I'm not sure. I remember falling off the ship and waking up in the sand. The rest is a blur."

Doctor Batiste clucked to himself again. He seemed to be weighing his words carefully, deciding how much information to share with his patient.

That made Gustave even more nervous.

"Apart from the memory loss, Your Majesty seems to be in excellent health."

"You don't sound happy about that."

The doctor swallowed.

"If I'm honest, your health is a little too good. Not only have you suffered no ill effects from a kraken attack and an evening floating in the ocean, but your wounds from the last attack have healed completely."

"What?"

Gustave hurried to a mirror and pushed back his hair. A thin scar was barely visible under his hairline. It looked like it had healed years ago, but yesterday it had been an open wound.

Doctor Batiste shook his head at Gustave's questioning look.

"My best guess is that Your Majesty came into contact with some sort of magic. It seems to have had a positive effect, but our understanding of such things is incomplete. It would be best if you spent the day in bed and avoided unnecessary exertion."

"No, I need to go to breakfast."

Now more than ever. If someone had helped him with magic, maybe they would be willing to aid the search for his father. He just needed to find the person who had rescued him.

"Your Majesty, there is no need. I've already arranged for a tray to be brought for you."

As if on cue, a servant entered carrying a tray of food. Gustave shook his head.

"I appreciate your concern, Doctor Batiste, but I have an important matter to discuss with my council."

He hurried out the door before the doctor could express further objections. Gustave understood the doctor's reasons, but he felt fine.

Better than fine.

Now if he could just remember why.

Gustave passed an open window, and a breeze swept over him. It carried the scent of the sea, and Gustave's head cleared for a moment.

There had been a woman and a song.

He froze as the memory washed against him like waves on the shore.

Her voice. It had felt like magic.

Based on his quick recovery, it probably had been.

Had she healed him somehow? Had the singer been responsible for delivering him safely to shore?

Or perhaps that had been the mermaids.

If they had saved his life, why weren't they willing to speak with him? They were the only hope Gustave had of searching for his father in the ocean.

He needed to go back to that place. Kraken or not, Gustave needed to contact the mermaids.

He sprinted through the castle and burst into the dining room just as the waiters finished serving the first course.

The usual people were there. Collette and Dowager Queen Bernadine sat at the head of the table. Thomas sat nearby, translating for the dowager queen.

Marquis Corbeau and Marchioness Rouge sat at the other end. Gustave had hoped to find more council members present, but those two were senior enough to approve a motion if they agreed on it. Although they rarely agreed on anything, so that could be difficult.

But there were extra guests at the table. Three young ladies sat in the seats usually reserved for the rest of the council. They blinked at him with wide, expectant eyes.

Gustave blinked back. Maybe he should have taken breakfast in bed after all. He hadn't expected Grandmother to start match-making so quickly.

He blinked at the ladies again and fought the urge to retreat to his room. It was too late for that now.

❧ 15 ❧

Fiora ducked into her grotto and studied the shell. As Madame Isla had said, the transformation song wasn't particularly complicated. It was rather long, but no more difficult than the kraken lullaby.

The kraken.

How could they accuse her of waking it on purpose? Did they honestly think she would do such a thing?

Or that she was capable of doing it?

Only Zoe had believed her, and Zoe believed the best of everyone.

Fiora finished reading the shell and frowned. It contained the song to transform a mermaid to a human, but the song to reverse the enchantment was carved on another conch because this one had run out of space. The last line of text was a warning not to complete the enchantment without memorizing the counter charm and understanding the magic behind it.

Perhaps this was a bad idea. If she didn't know the other song, Fiora would be stuck as a human. And she had no idea what the potential consequences of the transformation would be.

But being human had been her goal all along. She had been

willing to marry any man that would have her to achieve it with her ring.

Now she could achieve it on her own. Why would she want to return to the sea when her own family didn't trust her?

Because if she left for good, she would never know the truth about her mother.

Fiora shook her head. As much as she wanted the truth, that knowledge wasn't worth risking imprisonment. If Althea truly believed she was responsible for waking the kraken, there was no telling what the mermaid would do.

She should go now. She should run while she still could.

Before Fiora could act, the ground rumbled. It shook so badly that the statue of the boy toppled over. Fiora gasped as he crashed onto the rocks beneath the grotto. He fell slower in water that he would have on land, but the impact was still enough to chip his head and crack his arm.

"Are you alright?" Fiora asked, not caring that it sounded ridiculous.

She reached for the statue, but the rumbling turned into deep laughter that shook the ground. Fiora darted back into the grotto and curled around the shell and bottle of squid ink. The statue's cracked face stared at the surface, shaking as the earth quaked.

The laughter became a voice.

"Well, fish boy, you've made a mess of things."

It rumbled and shook the grotto as if the ground itself were speaking. Fiora pushed deeper into the shadows and held her breath. Who was that?

Whoever it was, she didn't want to face him.

"I can hardly be blamed for this."

Fiora's eyes widened as she recognized Leander's voice. Why was he talking to a stranger all the way out here?

"No? Well, you can't exactly be thanked for it either."

This was a new voice. Soft and cold and feminine. Fiora

resisted the urge to peek around the edge of the grotto to see who Leander was speaking with.

"It can be fixed," Leander said.

"I'll deal with things on land," the female voice said. "I trust you can take care of one little mermaid?"

Were they threatening Zoe? If her cousin was in danger—

"Don't worry about it. I'll take care of Fiora. The royal family agrees with me that something must be done."

Fiora shivered and pushed further back into the grotto. Rough stone pressed against her back as she flattened against it.

"Are you sure you can handle her?" the deep voice rumbled.

"She's been nothing but trouble since she arrived. Everyone will be glad to be rid of her."

Fiora pulled water slowly through her gills, breathing as quietly as possible. That sounded more serious than imprisonment. Did Leander truly want to kill her? Did her family find her that much of a nuisance?

"We'll talk again when you have something worthwhile to say," the female voice said.

The rumbling laughter erupted again, then faded into silence. Fiora stayed hidden, listening to the muffled echoes of open water. Her heart pounded in her chest until she was sure that Leander would hear it and find her.

But the ocean stayed quiet. When nothing interrupted the silence for some time, Fiora pushed her way past the broken statue that now seemed her only friend and peered into the garden.

There was no sign of Leander or his mysterious companions. Just toppled statues and sunlight gleaming on mirrors. This was her chance to escape.

It didn't seem right to leave the statue toppled on the ground. Fiora tried to lift him back onto the grotto, but the stone crumbled as he moved. She lowered him to the ocean floor instead. He stared up at the sparkling surface with stone eyes that seemed to understand her pain.

"Goodbye. I'm sorry."

Fiora curled her tail to her heart in a bow, then clutched the conch shell and squid ink to her chest as she raced towards the shore.

16

"Gustave, we didn't expect you out of bed so soon," Dowager Queen Bernadine said.

"Doctor Batiste said you would need at least a day of rest," Collette said.

"Doctor Batiste just finished examining me. He said I'm fine."

That wasn't exactly the truth, but it was close enough. No one questioned him further. Marchioness Rouge recovered her composure first. She waved at a servant and gestured to an empty place at the table. The waiters hurried to pull out a chair for Gustave.

He sat, and they set a plate of food in front of him.

"Was anyone else hurt in the attack?" Gustave asked.

Collette shook her head.

"A rogue current pushed the ship to shore. The *Delphinette* needs repairs, but the crew is fine."

Gustave smiled in relief. Unfortunately, he was facing one of the girls when he did it. She smiled back, looking pleased at the attention.

Blast.

Collette caught the exchange and grinned.

"Gustave, you remember my friend Kara. She spent several summers with us when we were younger."

Gustave vaguely remembered a giggling crowd of girls gathering around Collette every summer. He had been too busy horseback riding and studying to spend much time with them. He looked at Kara again and tried to remember her face in the crowd. She had light brown hair and dark brown eyes. Not particularly memorable. Gustave's head began to ache when he tried to picture Collette's childhood friends. Maybe he wasn't completely recovered after all.

"Of course I remember," he lied. "Welcome back to the castle, Kara."

Kara flushed bright red and became very interested in her plate of food. Gustave raised an eyebrow. It was a shame that Collette was going to the trouble to introduce him to her friend when his heart was already taken.

The thought caught him by surprise. He wasn't in love with anyone. Why had he thought he was for a moment?

He stared at his plate until he realized his grandmother was trying to get his attention.

"Elaine is the granddaughter of Jeanine, a very dear friend of mine," Dowager Queen Bernadine said.

Elaine wore her blond hair pulled into a tight bun that enhanced her unpleasant expression and piercing brown eyes. She scowled at Gustave, then seemed to remember she should look pleasant and tried to smile instead. Her face contorted into a sort of sneer before settling into indifference.

"It was very kind of Dowager Queen Bernadine to invite me to the castle," Elaine said. "I do hope you don't find my presence intrusive."

Her tone said she found *his* presence intrusive, and Gustave bit back a sarcastic response. She was visiting his home. If she didn't want to see him, why had she come?

Kara blushed even brighter, seeming horrified at the idea that

Gustave would find their presence intrusive. Of course it was intrusive. Three strange women had appeared at his breakfast table, and he was in love with someone else.

No, that wasn't right. Gustave pushed the thought out of his head. He wasn't in love. He wasn't looking for love until he had found his father and had more time to consider the decision and properly woo his lady.

"Not at all intrusive," he lied again. "I am delighted to have visitors."

He would have said he was delighted to meet her, but he had no idea if they had met before or not. She didn't look familiar, but that didn't mean much. Again, his mind became hazy when he tried to think back to parties she might have attended.

"And of course Your Majesty remembers *Lady* Annabelle," Marquis Corbeau said.

He emphasized Annabelle's title with a self-satisfied grin. There weren't many noble families in Montaigne, so having a title meant significant wealth, power, and social standing. Which meant Gustave had likely met Lady Annabelle before, although she didn't look any more familiar than the other two. She had hazel eyes and curly black hair that cascaded around her shoulders like thick smoke.

"Of course."

All this lying was exhausting. Gustave would have to ask Collette about the girls later to make sure he didn't say anything stupid to them.

Except Kara was clearly Collette's choice for his future bride, and it would be extremely rude to admit that he did not remember her and was not interested in getting to know her better. Gustave looked out a window, watching the ocean waves crash against the shore. He was used to having Collette on his side, but this time it seemed they had different goals.

Lady Annabelle giggled and fluttered a fan. It was too early in the day to be hot, so she seemed to have brought the fan just so she could flutter it flirtatiously.

"It is such an honor to be invited to stay at the castle," she said. "I have attended every ball here since I came of age, but I've never stayed for more than a day. Of course I danced with His Majesty often on each visit."

This last comment was directed at Kara and Elaine. Kara flushed even redder, which Gustave had not thought possible. Elaine met Annabelle's gaze with a steady one of her own. Accepting the challenge? Or ignoring it completely?

"You will all have plenty of opportunities to dance with His Majesty at his birthday gala," Marquis Corbeau said.

This was getting out of hand. He couldn't let this continue when he was in love with someone else. Gustave cleared his throat.

"Actually, I won't be dancing with them at the gala."

"No?" Lady Annabelle asked, fluttering her eyelashes. "Why not, Your Majesty?"

"Because I've already found the woman I want to marry."

Everyone in the room gasped. Gustave nearly gasped himself. What was he thinking, making such an announcement without discussing it with his council first?

The council seemed to have similar thoughts. Marchioness Rouge pressed her lips together in a thin line and shared a questioning look with Collette, who shook her head slightly. Lady Annabelle looked murderous. Elaine looked relieved. Kara looked ready to cry.

Dowager Queen Bernadine and Marquis Corbeau didn't look as pleased by the news as Gustave thought they would be.

"What do you mean you've already found someone?" Bernadine asked. "Yesterday you were completely opposed to the idea of marriage."

"Yesterday I hadn't met the love of my life."

They all stared at him. Was it really so hard to understand?

The doubt in their expressions gave Gustave second thoughts. Maybe it was crazy.

A fog wrapped around his thoughts and whispered that he wasn't crazy at all. Didn't love always feel a little crazy at first?

"A woman rescued me on the beach yesterday. She's the one I want to marry."

A warm glow built in Gustave's chest as he said the words. It seemed to agree with him.

"Gustave, there wasn't anyone else on the beach with you yesterday. You were alone."

Collette's gentle voice was full of concern. Gustave scowled.

"She was there until you scared her away. She has red hair and blue eyes and the most beautiful voice in the world. I'm going to marry her."

Kara sniffed into a napkin. Was she crying? Lady Annabelle snapped her fan shut.

"You could have found her a day earlier and saved me the trip," Elaine muttered.

Queen Bernadine and Marquis Corbeau shared a look. The warmth in Gustave's chest flared to anger.

"You're the ones who have been pushing me to get married. You should be happy that I've found someone!"

"Of course we're happy," Collette said. "But we're also surprised. Gustave, you've been through a lot. Perhaps you should go back to bed and rest."

"You don't believe me! Why don't you believe me?"

Why was he yelling? He never yelled. Especially not at Collette.

But she didn't understand. She had never been in love, and she didn't understand.

"But what about us?" Lady Annabelle asked.

Gustave shrugged.

"What about you?"

"Gustave, mind your manners," Dowager Queen Bernadine said.

"Your Majesty, be reasonable," Marquis Corbeau said. "You cannot ignore your guests so callously. These ladies have traveled a long way to meet you."

"I'm not the one who invited them."

A small, sensible corner of Gustave's mind said he was being rude. The rest filled with fog and said everyone at the breakfast table was trying to separate him from the love of his life.

Frustration built until Gustave knew only two things. He was in love, and he would say something he regretted if he stayed in this room a moment longer.

"Please, excuse me."

Gustave hurried through the castle and ran through the gardens towards the beach. He was desperate to get away.

Desperate to find the woman he loved.

He tried to remember exactly what she had looked like, but the memory was hazy. Red hair. Was there gold in it or not?

Blue eyes.

Or maybe they were green?

The only thing that he clearly remembered was her voice. He would know her at once if he heard her sing again.

Gustave reached the beach and looked out at the ocean. The tide and wind had erased any footprints from last night, so there was no way to track where his love had gone. He half expected to see her standing there waiting for him, but the beach was empty.

No matter. He would find her again if he had to turn the whole kingdom upside down.

❧ 17 ❧

Fiora stayed close to the ocean floor, ducking behind rocks and reefs as often as possible to avoid detection. When a ship sailed over her, Fiora swam to the surface so she could hide in its shadow. Wherever it was going, she would go as well. It was the long way around, but it was safer than swimming in open water. She couldn't risk being found when the merfolk wanted her dead.

Taking the long way around took a long time. The ship sailed at a leisurely pace until it reached a harbor far too busy to accommodate her transformation. Fiora swam along the coast, dodging piers until she found a secluded stretch of shoreline. She studied the underwater terrain one last time to make sure she hadn't been followed by merfolk. Then she slipped her head above the surface and checked the land for humans.

The ocean waves crashed against an empty beach. A forest stretched along the rugged coast, and large rocks jutted out from the shallow water, creating the perfect hiding place for her to work her magic. The royal castle of Montaigne sat on a hill in the distance. It was close enough that people would think twice about swimming on the beach, but far enough away that Fiora wasn't likely to be bothered by royals.

In fact, this might be the same beach she had brought Gustave to after rescuing him last night. Fiora hesitated. There had been people on the beach then. Gustave's family and the woman in the cloak.

She swam a little further away from the castle just to be safe. Fiora found an outcropping of rocks to hide behind and set the squid ink on a small ledge. Best to wait on that in case the magic from the transformation affected the dye. It would be just her luck to turn her hair green by accident.

"Squawk?"

A seagull landed on the rock and studied the bottle with interest. Fiora waved her hands at it.

"Shoo! Go away!"

The seagull tilted his head and hopped closer. He pecked at the bottle and tipped it over. More gulls landed on the rock, studying Fiora and the ink with greedy eyes.

"Bad birds! Bad!"

Fiora grabbed the bottle before it spilled and set it on a lower ledge where she could guard it more easily. The seagull squawked at her again and flew to a higher perch to watch. The rest of the gulls left to search for an easier target.

Blasted birds. She'd better do this quickly before they caused more trouble.

Fiora slipped her pearl ring off her finger and set it beside the bottle of ink. She doubted the ring would affect the enchantment, but there was no point taking that chance.

She studied the shell and signed the notes to the song in a silent rehearsal. She really should have grabbed the second shell and read the rest of the details about the spell.

But there was no time for that now.

Fiora took a deep breath and sang. She kept her vowels round and only let the mermaid part of her voice into the song. Please, let her magic be enough!

Her throat tickled when she reached the final phrase. Then the tickle turned into a burning that swept through her lungs. Fiora gasped for air, and her song became an otherworldly scream that scattered the seagulls perched nearby. Then the scream faded into silence so sudden that it seemed deafening.

The burning in her throat spread through her body and settled in her fin. The pain grew stronger until it felt like a thousand knives were stabbing and slicing her tail. Fiora writhed on the rock and nearly fell into the water. She tried to stop singing and reverse the enchantment, but it was far too late for that.

The shell hadn't mentioned that the transformation was torture. Maybe it wasn't for full-blooded mermaids. Maybe this was like the oysters but a thousand times worse.

Or maybe the pain was described on the second shell.

Tears streamed down Fiora's cheeks as the stabbing spread from her bones to her skin. She had once seen a chef scrape the scales off a fish with a knife. It felt like someone was doing that to her now, but they hadn't had the decency to cut her head off first.

Fiora sank into the water and stared at the sky, willing the screaming in her head to stop. Another burst of agony spread across her neck. Fiora tried to massage it away and realized her gills had disappeared. She breathed deeply through her mouth, and the air eased the burning in her lungs.

The stabbing sensation in her bones slowly faded away. Her skin felt raw, but the worst of the pain had gone. Fiora clung to the rock and lifted her right foot out of the water. Her skin was smooth and clear. It showed no sign of damage from the magic and searing pain.

Fiora wiggled her toes and tried to stand, but her legs shook too badly to hold her weight. A wave pushed her against the rock, and Fiora clung to it to avoid being swept out into the open water as the wave receded. She would drown if she fell into the sea before she recovered her strength enough to swim.

The seagull hopped down and pecked at the ink again. Fiora yelled at it, but no sound came out.

That wasn't good.

Fiora screamed, but only managed to produce a soft burst of air. She tried to sing. To speak. To hum.

Silence.

Had the magic taken her voice?

She hoped that was the last surprise from the enchantment.

Fiora straightened her legs and swatted the bird away. She stood still, panting, as her legs steadied and the ringing in her ears settled. Fiora dug her toes into the sand and grinned. Even if they were shaky, she had legs again.

She was human again!

And she was naked.

Of course the mermaids hadn't bothered to mention that the charm didn't include clothes. They never wore them.

Fiora shook away the mental image of Madame Isla walking naked into a human town and declaring that she had come to study them.

It was entirely possible that had happened at some point, but that was the least of Fiora's worries.

She lowered herself into the water and arranged her hair over her shoulders. At least it was long enough to cover her chest.

There was nothing she could do about clothes now. She would have to stay in the water until nightfall then sneak to a farmhouse and steal something from a laundry line.

The thought of creeping through someone's farm naked made Fiora's face burn with embarrassment, but what choice did she have? She would find some clothes and mark the place so she could repay them later.

Repay them with what? She had nothing. Fiora tried to sigh,

but it came out as a small puff of air. She hummed, testing her voice again.

Nothing happened.

She tried to speak, but her lungs began to burn. She pressed her lips together in a grim line.

So, the enchantment took her voice.

At least she still had her life.

Fiora poured squid ink into her hands and worked it through her hair. A seagull dove for the bottle, and Fiora slapped him away. The ink on her fingers left black spots on his feathers. The seagull craned his head, trying to eat the ink off his back, but he couldn't reach.

It served him right.

Fiora silently giggled at his antics as she continued dying her hair. She decided to call him Spot since he was now spotted with ink stains. If he was going to keep her company while she sat naked in the water, he should have a name.

The hair treatment was a messy business, but Fiora grinned when she finally finished and looked at her reflection in the sea. She barely recognized herself without her bright red hair. If she was discovered, it was unlikely that anyone would know her by her face alone.

Her hair had always been her most distinguishing feature. The only thing about her anyone remembered.

Her stomach growled, and Fiora glared up at the castle. They were probably eating breakfast right now and marveling at King Gustave's lucky escape.

She'd have to find a way to get food once she had clothes. She could find work somewhere. Perhaps offer her sewing services to a local seamstress in exchange for a meal.

She was so hungry. Fiora tried to drink the remainder of the squid ink and gagged on it. She'd rather go hungry than finish that.

Spot squawked hopefully, so Fiora poured the rest of the ink on a rock for him. He pecked at it, dying his beak black in the process, then began to groom himself. This streaked even more dye through his feathers. More seagulls landed on the rock. Most of the birds looked the same, but Spot stood out now with his unusual markings.

Fiora scrubbed the ink off her hands and put her pearl ring back on her finger. Then she glared at the sun. It was just rising above the horizon. This was going to be a long day.

She leaned against the rock, making herself as comfortable as she could. As impatient and hungry and thirsty as she was, she had no choice but to stay put. It would still be risky, but there far was less chance of being caught if she waited until dark.

The last thing she wanted was to try explaining why she was wandering around Montaigne naked.

That would be difficult enough with words. It would be impossible without them.

❧ 18 ❧

"Your Majesty, where are you?"

The voices were faint, but they were getting closer. The soldier's deep shouts mixed with high-pitched squeals that suggested some of the women had come looking for him as well.

Gustave groaned. The sea air had cleared his head, and he realized he had been horribly inconsiderate. He needed to apologize to everyone. That was the mature, responsible, kingly thing to do.

"He's going to dance with me," Lady Annabelle said, her defiant voice carried on the wind. "I don't care if he thinks he's in love with someone else, he's going to dance with me!"

Then again, perhaps apologizing could wait a little longer. Gustave turned away from the castle and walked further down the beach. He rounded a corner so that trees would hide him from view and stopped to examine his surroundings.

Large rocks jutted out from the water, looking like small mountainous islands just off the shore. Waves crashed against them, and seagulls perched on the jagged surfaces while they waited for something edible to float their way.

A seagull streaked with black flew over to Gustave to beg for food. He ignored the bird until it gave up hope and flew back to one of the boulders in the water. It seemed very interested in that particular rock.

More birds had landed on the rock and watched something with interest. It was probably just a dead fish, but Gustave's curiosity got the better of him. He left the cover of the trees and walked towards the water to get a better look.

His head pounded as the wind roared in his ears. Maybe he should have listened to Doctor Batiste and stayed in bed.

Then Gustave saw a hand clinging to the rock and completely forgot about his headache.

He ran to the water's edge and squinted into the sun, trying to see. A wave swept over the rock, and the hand disappeared. Water lapped at the toes of Gustave's boots as he leaned closer.

"Hello? Is someone there?"

Another wave washed against the stone, and the water receded a little. Just enough for Gustave to see the outline of someone's head.

"Hello?"

Whoever it was didn't answer. She clung to the stone and stayed very still. Gustave moved closer, hardly noticing that he was ankle-deep in the ocean.

The woman slid back, trying to hide behind the rock.

Maybe it was *her*. A wisp of smoke wrapped around his thoughts, reminding him he was in love and looking for the woman who had disappeared

Then a wave filled Gustave's boots with water, and the smoke cleared.

It was definitely a woman. The outstretched arm clinging to the rock was decidedly feminine. But she was in shadows, so he couldn't tell much more than that.

"Are you in trouble?"

Gustave's heart raced. What if there had been another shipwreck or kraken attack? Why else would a human be clinging to a rock in the ocean?

Or maybe it was a mermaid?

"Kathelin, is that you?"

Silence.

"Do you need help?"

Still nothing.

If it was Kathelin, surely she would have spoken by now. It could be a different mermaid. Perhaps Althea? Gustave wasn't particularly eager to speak with her, but at this point he would take whatever contact with the mermaids he could get. They knew something about his father. They had to.

He waded deeper into the ocean, not caring that it would ruin his trousers. The woman slid further around the rock, still trying to hide.

Why wouldn't she speak?

"My name is Gustave. You can trust me."

The water was well past Gustave's knees now. He stopped wading and wiped sweat from his brow. What if this was a trap? What if whoever had taken his father was after him as well?

A large wave swept the water up to Gustave's thighs and pushed the woman higher against the rock. Then it retreated, exposing the woman's shoulders. Her skin was white and smooth with no sign of scales.

She ducked down and cast a nervous glance in his direction.

Gustave stepped back. She was human after all. And naked. No wonder she was hiding from him. She was trying to have a peaceful morning swim, and he was yelling at her about mermaids.

"I am so sorry, miss. I didn't mean to disturb you."

Gustave covered his eyes to show he meant her no harm, then turned away and walked back to shore. He searched the beach for her clothes but saw nothing. Had someone stolen them? Had a current pushed her further down the beach than she planned to swim?

He glanced in her direction. She peered at him from behind the rock. Dark hair clung to her skin, and her enormous blue eyes were wide with alarm.

"I'm going to take off my cloak and leave it for you," Gustave said. "You can come to shore and put it on. I'll turn around until you tell me you're ready."

He removed his cloak, spread it on the sand, and turned to stare into the forest. Would she take his offer? Was she moving? He listened, but whatever sound she made was lost in the waves and wind.

How had she ended up naked on a rock in the ocean? This beach wasn't exactly his property, but most locals treated it as part of the castle grounds. They certainly didn't swim here.

Someone called his name in the distance, and Gustave flushed. If they found him now, it would be very difficult to explain what he was doing on the beach with a naked woman. His grandmother would have plenty to say about it, not to mention everyone else.

Gustave narrowed his eyes. Was this part of some scheme to see him married? What exactly would happen if he was discovered right now? Would they insist he marry the girl to save her honor?

He fought the urge to turn around and closed his eyes instead. They couldn't force him to do anything if he didn't see anything. What was taking her so long? What if she didn't want the cloak and was still hiding behind the rock? How could he know if she didn't tell him?

Someone touched Gustave's shoulder, and he whirled around, ready to run for his life if necessary. He meant to keep his eyes closed, but they opened as his defenses kicked in.

The girl stared at him with enormous blue eyes. She had wrapped his cloak around herself, and her long, dark hair fell over her shoulders. A few wet strands clung to her face, contrasting with her pale skin.

Her expression relieved Gustave's suspicions. She didn't look like she was part of a scheme. She looked terrified and cold and alone. Her blue eyes held something familiar, but he couldn't quite place it.

"Are you in trouble?"

Something in the back of Gustave's mind warned him that he would be the one in trouble if he wasn't careful. He was in love with someone else. He shouldn't be chatting with naked women on beaches.

Gustave pushed the thought aside. For all he knew, this was the love of his life. Her face was familiar, and her blue eyes fit what he remembered. Her hair was the wrong color though.

The fog swept through his mind, filling it with memories of red hair and a sweet song.

The song. Gustave didn't trust his memories of his love's appearance since it had been dark, but he remembered her voice. The woman watched him with a wary expression and said nothing.

"Can you speak?" Gustave asked.

Irritation flashed through the woman's eyes, and she shook her head.

Gustave tried not to let his disappointment show. If she couldn't speak, then she wasn't the one he was looking for. Her irritated expression reminded him of someone, but the fog clouded his head when he tried to remember who.

"Have we met before?"

Was it Gustave's imagination, or did she hesitate before she shook her head? He squinted, trying to get a better look at her face. She ducked her head as if embarrassed, and Gustave looked away as well. It was rude to stare, even under such circumstances.

Especially under such circumstances.

Voices echoed down the beach, and the woman shifted as if she meant to run.

"Don't go," Gustave said. "I can help you."

She smiled at him. A tiny, half smile that disappeared in a moment. She met his eyes again, then looked quickly away.

Gustave looked down at the sand and realized that his cloak only covered her to her knees. He pulled his eyes away when he realized he was staring at her ankles and bare feet. Blast it all, where was he supposed to look? He stared at the sky for a few moments before turning his gaze back to the woman's face. Her mouth quirked upward, and her eyes crinkled.

Did she find his distress amusing?

"I don't live far from here. I'm sure my sister has a dress you can borrow."

She frowned at that. Why?

"Or if you live nearby, I can escort you home."

She shook her head. Was she saying she didn't live nearby? Or that she didn't want to go home?

"You're sure you can't speak?"

Her scowl deepened, and she raised an eyebrow. Gustave swallowed, feeling like an idiot.

"I'm so sorry. It would just be easier if you could."

Her expression said she was well aware of that fact. Honestly, she had the most expressive eyes.

But the lack of voice meant she wasn't the one. It meant he couldn't even learn her name.

Names. Other than yelling at her from across the beach, he hadn't introduced himself.

"Oh, forgive my lack of manners. I'm Gustave."

He offered his hand, realized she would have to let go of the cloak to take it, and quickly pulled it away. Her mouth quirked upwards again. Blast it all, she was laughing at him!

"Your Majesty, are you there?"

Lady Annabelle's voice cut through the air, and Gustave groaned. He should have known she would find him eventually.

"I'm King Gustave, actually. Of Montaigne."

He might as well get the royal title out of the way. There would be no hiding it once the mob found him.

She didn't look surprised. Perhaps she was local after all and had already recognized him.

There was no point in delaying his inevitable discovery. His only other alternative was to run and hide in the woods with the naked woman, which would definitely not help his plans to avoid romantic entanglements until he found his father.

Collette and Lady Annabelle rounded the corner first. They stopped in their tracks and stared at Gustave and the girl. A group of guards followed them and did the same.

"I found her in the water," Gustave said. "I think she's in some sort of trouble."

They all blinked at him. Collette recovered first.

"Are you well, miss? What happened to you?"

The naked woman ducked her head. Was she frightened of Collette? That made no sense.

"She can't speak," Gustave said.

"Of course she can speak! She is simply preying on Your Highness's compassion," Lady Annabelle said.

Her shrill voice made Gustave grit his teeth. The dark-haired girl drew the cloak tighter around her shoulders and glared at Annabelle. She seemed more offended by this accusation than the comment warranted.

"We'll take her back to the castle and get her settled," Gustave said. "We can sort out the details once she's comfortable."

"Gustave, is that wise?" Collette asked. "We don't know anything about her."

He blinked at his sister.

"I thought you of all people would be eager to help," he signed.

"Respectable ladies don't show up naked on beaches. This seems suspicious."

Collette's face said she considered the matter settled. Gustave did as well. Just in the opposite direction.

"She's coming back to the castle with us. The least we can do is give her a dress."

He would have helped the girl anyway, but the outraged expressions on Lady Annabelle's face made it doubly worth it.

"Perhaps she doesn't want to come," Lady Annabelle said. "I'm sure her clothes are here somewhere."

She gestured vaguely to the beach as if this would make clothes appear. The woman smirked and shook her head. Then she shifted her grip on the cloak so she could hold it with one hand and offered the other to Gustave. He held out his arm, and she rested her hand lightly against it.

They walked up the pathway together. The woman stumbled on a rock, and Gustave caught her arm as she fell. She stared at him with enormous blue eyes, and a memory tried to surface.

"I've met you before, haven't I?"

She shook her head. Gustave looked down to hide his confusion and noticed that her feet were leaving drops of blood on the jagged rocks.

"Oh, forgive me. You're injured."

He pulled off his boots and offered them to her.

Her eyes crinkled in amusement again. Gustave looked from the shoes to the woman's feet. Right. She was almost his height, but her feet were much smaller. Not to mention his boots were soaked from sea water.

"They will still be better than walking barefoot on the rocks."

He didn't mean to sound gruff as he said it, but his irritation only seemed to amuse the woman further. She nodded to the ground, and Gustave set the boots down. She slipped her feet into them and continued to walk towards the castle.

The boots clomped against the rocks as she walked. Rocks stabbed Gustave's stockinged feet, but he ignored the discomfort. His thick socks gave him more protection than her bare skin had.

She stumbled again, and Gustave helped her stand upright. He took her hand to help her up the stairs to the garden and noticed she wore a pearl ring.

Was it some kind of clue to her identity?

Then she looked up at him with those enormous blue eyes, and he forgot about her jewelry.

He had seen those eyes before. He knew it.

"Some women will do anything to catch a man," Lady Annabelle whispered loudly enough for everyone to hear.

The woman's blue eyes sparked with fury. She pulled her arm away from Gustave and walked the rest of the way to the castle by herself.

F iora's feet stung as she climbed the hill towards the castle. Every so often, a stabbing pain shot through her skin, as if she had stepped on a knife. She hoped it was because the rocks had cut her feet and not a lingering effect of the enchantment.

Whatever the cause, there was nothing she could do about it now. A fresh wave of pain swept through her legs, but she gritted her teeth and kept going. King Gustave's boots helped a little. At least she wasn't stepping on stones and knives at the same time. Hopefully her body would adjust to the transformation enchantment soon.

She really should have grabbed the second shell and read more about how the enchantment worked. Without that information, she had no way of knowing if this pain was part of the magic or not.

Blast it all!

At least she was human and clothed now. It was better than being human and naked.

Except she had somehow ended up with the only humans in Montaigne who knew her as Princess Fiora. What would they do if they recognized her?

Should she try to break away from the group and find her own way now that she was somewhat covered? She could still steal clothes from a farm and look for work.

Fiora glanced back and groaned silently to herself. Everyone in the group was staring at her. There was no way she could escape them.

Not yet, anyway.

Not only had King Gustave ruined the Princess Test in Aeonia, he had effectively kidnapped her.

Maybe this was for the best. The castle was as good a place as any to hide from Leander and the other merfolk.

Unless someone recognized her.

Gustave had found her familiar but didn't seem able to place her. That was fair. They had only spoken once before.

But what about Collette? Fiora had spent time with her at several Princess Tests. Of everyone in Montaigne, Collette seemed the most likely to see past Fiora's disguise.

But she hadn't yet, had she?

Fiora scowled. Collette had been less welcoming than Gustave, but surely she would have said something if she had recognized Fiora.

So unless someone had recognized her and was keeping it secret for now, Fiora was safe. But what exactly would happen if they realized who she was?

Most likely they would send her back to Kell. Fiora felt a small burst of hope at the idea of going home, then brushed it aside. Kell wasn't home. Not anymore. Her father didn't love her and had sent her away to give Elspeth a chance.

Fiora gripped the cloak tighter around herself. Humans were nothing but trouble. Mermaids weren't much better, but at least Zoe had done what she could to help. The only help Elspeth had ever offered was flirting advice that inevitably backfired whenever Fiora tried it.

She just needed to lie low and spend as little time as possible with Gustave and Collette until she could escape the castle and find work.

The guards at the gate raised their eyebrows when they saw Fiora walking towards them. She glared until they looked away in embarrassment. Collette ran ahead, and the guards hurried to let her in.

"We found him!"

A small crowd had gathered in the hallway. Fiora recognized Marquis Corbeau from a few state functions she had attended. A woman with a stern expression stood beside him. Another council member? The older woman in the wheelchair must be Montaigne's dowager queen. A young man stood by her side. Probably some sort of attendant. Maybe it was his job to push the wheelchair.

Two young women stood near the queen. Not servants, if their clothes and attitudes were any indication. Perhaps the lady who chased Gustave down the beach had some competition?

Whoever they were, everyone was so focused on Gustave that they didn't notice Fiora. She edged towards the door. Seeing this many people made her rethink her strategy to hide in the castle. It would be far safer to hide in the woods or a small village.

Fiora's stomach growled, and she hesitated. There was food in the castle. Human food cooked with fire and seasoned with spices. Who knew what she would find in the woods? If she found anything at all.

"Gustave, you must stop running off!" the dowager queen said.

Her voice boomed through the hallway. It was stronger than Fiora would have suspected from looking at her. The dowager queen's body may be weak, but her voice was not.

"I needed to clear my head," Gustave said.

He waved his hands while he said it. Was he signing? Fiora moved a little closer, trying to see. All mermaids learned sign language, but she had never known any humans who communicated that way.

"That is no excuse for insulting guests."

The woman who had chased Gustave down the beach sniffed loudly. She must have been the one he insulted. Fiora couldn't blame Gustave for that. If she had her voice, she would have insulted the woman several times by now.

Gustave bowed.

"On this point we agree. Lady Annabelle, Kara, Elaine, please accept my apology. I had not recovered from my injury, and it clouded my judgment. I am sorry if I caused offense."

The two young women standing beside the queen nodded their heads in acceptance. Lady Annabelle sniffed.

"So you're not in love with the girl who rescued you on the beach? And you'll dance with me at your birthday gala?"

Fiora's hands went slack with surprise. The cloak slipped off her shoulders, and she quickly adjusted it to cover herself again.

Gustave was in love with the woman who rescued him?

That was impossible.

She glanced at her ring, but the pearl was as gray as ever.

Then why would he claim to be in love with her?

She stepped closer so she could see the king's face. Gustave looked embarrassed, but he didn't deny the accusation. When he realized everyone was waiting for an answer, he bowed and said, "I would be honored to dance with you at my birthday gala, Lady Annabelle. With all of you."

He bowed to Kara and Elaine in turn. They curtsied and looked gracious. Annabelle looked annoyed. Probably because he hadn't answered the part about being in love with his rescuer.

The young man standing beside the dowager queen signed a translation of Gustave's words for her. Fiora edged a little closer so she could see his hands.

Yes, it was sign language, and very similar to what the mermaids used. Perhaps mermaids had taught humans how to sign at some point?

"And who are you?" the dowager queen said.

If Bernadine was surprised to find a wet, mostly naked woman dripping on her marble floor, she showed it only with a small twitch of her eyebrow.

Fiora blinked. She had come too close and drawn attention to herself. Everyone gaped at her.

So much for escaping.

"What is that?" Marquis Corbeau said.

"I believe that is a woman, Marquis. We can see quite enough of her to feel confident in that assessment."

The dowager queen fixed Fiora with a fierce stare as if she could pin her in place with her gaze alone.

Fiora considered answering in sign language, but what could she say? Besides, her hands were busy holding the cloak in place.

Perhaps it would be easier if they thought she had no way to communicate with them.

So rather than attempting to answer, Fiora glared at the marquis. It had only been a few hours, but she missed her voice. No matter how expressive your eyes were, they could only convey so much scorn.

"Where did you come from?" the dowager queen said. "What is your name?"

"She can't speak," Gustave said. "Miss, this is my grandmother, Dowager Queen Bernadine."

He hurried to Fiora's side, then stepped away so he stood a respectable distance apart from her. Fiora smirked in spite of everything. What was he so afraid of?

"You know this woman?" Marquis Corbeau asked.

"I found her in the water. She can't speak. I believe she's in some sort of trouble."

King Gustave made signs with his hands as he spoke. The dowager queen watched him to read the signs, but they did not help her confusion.

"Or she was causing trouble," Marquis Corbeau said. "Decent young women do not swim naked in the ocean."

"They certainly do not!" Lady Annabelle added.

Fiora glared at her. Oh, how she wished she had her voice. She wanted to give that woman a piece of her mind.

"We're going to help her," Gustave said.

"Are we indeed?" Dowager Queen Bernadine said.

She looked from Gustave to Fiora with a curious expression. Fiora scowled at the dowager queen's silent implication. She had failed to catch a man's interest too many times to think this would be any different.

"Your Majesty cannot be responsible for the care of a loose woman," Marquis Corbeau said.

Loose woman? Fiora stuck her tongue out at the marquis. With voice gone and her hands occupied holding the cloak, it was the only method of retaliation available to her.

The marquis and Lady Annabelle gasped. Gustave's eyes grew wide with surprise.

The dowager queen chuckled.

"Perhaps Gustave is right. We should help those in need."

She looked to Collette as if she expected some response to this. An answer to an unasked question.

But Collette remained silent. She was staring at Fiora with eyes that, while not quite hostile, were certainly not friendly.

"Out of the question," the marquis said. "The hospitality budget-"

"This young lady will stay as my personal guest," Dowager Queen Bernadine said. "I have been given free rein to invite friends to the gala, and I'm inviting her."

Fiora wasn't sure if she should be annoyed to be thrust back into the world of royal politics or amused at Marquis Corbeau's face. He looked absolutely horrified.

And speechless, which left him unable to protest.

Fiora sneezed. It barely made any sound, but the motion was enough for everyone to notice. It was cooler in the castle than it had been in the sun, and she was still soaked.

"We're not throwing her onto the street in this condition," Gustave said.

"She might not be comfortable staying in the castle," Collette said.

"Take this young lady to a guest bedroom and find her some appropriate clothing," Dowager Queen Bernadine said.

She waved her hand, and a servant moved towards Fiora. Fiora blinked. This was all happening rather fast. If she officially became a guest, it would be even more difficult to escape.

"If you'll come with me, miss?" the servant said.

As if she could refuse now. Fiora looked at the crowd of people. How had she gotten into such a mess? She had only been human for a few hours, and she was already in a difficult situation.

Gustave mistook her hesitation for nervousness.

"It will be alright, miss. We only want to help."

He smiled at her, and Fiora couldn't help smiling back. In spite of everything, there was something reassuring about King Gustave.

When he wasn't ruining your life, that was.

"The rest of you report to the Council Chamber," the dowager queen said. "Those of you that are on the council, that is. We have things to discuss."

"Like the hospitality budget," Marquis Corbeau said.

Gustave made a face, then flushed with embarrassment when he realized Fiora had seen. She winked at him and turned to follow the servant.

And realized she was still wearing Gustave's boots, while he was barefoot. She stepped out of the shoes and nudged them towards the king with her foot.

She wanted to make a comment about how they were ruined from seawater, and he might not want them back after all.

But she had to settle for a small shrug. Gustave smiled as if he understood and was saying it was all right.

Of course it was all right. He was a king. He had other boots.

Still, Fiora couldn't help giving him a small smile in return. He had given them to her as if it were the obvious thing to do. Even though his feet were likely now scraped from walking barefoot up the rocky path.

Neither of her families had ever treated her with such kindness.

"Come along, Gustave."

The dowager queen nodded to her attendant, who pushed her wheelchair down the hall.

She gave Fiora a shrewd glance before turning her attention back to her grandson. Fiora swallowed. Perhaps Princess Collette wasn't the person she needed to worry about most after all.

❧ 20 ❧

"Well, let's hear it," Dowager Queen Bernadine said. "How exactly did you come to be in the company of a naked woman on the beach?"

She sat at the head of the council chamber. Technically, there wasn't a head place. The chamber was a round room with chairs around the wall, designed to encourage the idea that everyone's input was equal and welcome. But Bernadine still managed to look like she was sitting at the head of the room.

Gustave swallowed. Skipping breakfast after surviving a kraken attack was making it hard to focus. Not to mention he hadn't had time to change. He was still barefoot, and his clothes were soaked with seawater. The last thing he wanted was to do battle with his grandmother.

"There's not much to tell. I walked to the beach to clear my head and found the young woman in the water. She clearly needed help, so I offered it to her."

He was so agitated that he forgot to sign. Thomas quickly translated his words for the dowager queen.

"It is an outrage!" Marquis Corbeau said. "We arranged for lovely eligible ladies to travel to the castle so you could meet

126

them before the gala, and you insulted them by ranting about how you're in love with some mystery girl you met on the beach. Then you further insult them by bringing a naked woman home. Your Majesty, this behavior cannot continue."

"Not to mention you nearly drowned in a kraken attack yesterday," Marchioness Rouge said. "You have faced death far more times than any king should. Let alone one without an heir.

The rest of the council murmured their agreement.

"I was looking for my father! I certainly didn't plan on being attacked by a kraken!"

Gustave looked to his grandmother for help. She had promised to support his search. She nodded at him.

"Gustave discussed the expedition with me beforehand and could not have predicted the kraken attack. We thought the mermaids had them under control, but apparently they don't. We will have to be more careful."

"Which is exactly why we should not welcome a mysterious young woman of questionable morals into the castle. Especially when she comes from the sea," Marquis Corbeau said.

"You think she has something to do with the mermaids?" Collette said.

Her calm voice dissolved the tension in the room. She looked to Gustave for an answer.

"You have the most experience with mermaids. Do you think it's a possibility?"

"She looks nothing like a mermaid, but I don't understand enough about them to say anything for sure. If she is somehow connected to the mermaids, that would be useful."

"She can be useful elsewhere," Marquis Corbeau said. "We're already housing a suite full of misfortunates, some of whom are taking long-term advantage of our hospitality. That merchant is still here."

"Dale received word that one of his ships may have survived the attack," Collette said. "I told him he could stay until he learned its whereabouts. And you can't ask him to cross the sea when kraken are attacking again."

"But we could ask him to get his own room in the city," Marquis Corbeau said.

"He doesn't have any money."

"Enough," Dowager Queen Bernadine said. "We have too much to do to waste time arguing about this. The sea girl will stay as my personal guest until further notice. As for the merchant, I trust we are not being bankrupted by Princess Collette's generosity?"

This question was directed to the royal treasurer, who shook her head.

"No, Your Highness. It costs nothing for someone to sleep in a bed that would have otherwise been empty, and we always have extra food at meals. The hospitality expenses are minimal. Especially when compared to the cost of the birthday gala, which has once again exceeded its budget."

Collette shot a triumphant look at Marquis Corbeau, then smiled at Gustave. Gustave nodded in an absentminded way. He was trying to pay attention, but he was also thinking about the woman. How had she ended up naked on the beach? There had been no sign of a shipwreck. If she was simply a local village girl who had gone for a swim, she could have told them that somehow. She could have agreed to be escorted home.

He knew her from somewhere. Those eyes-

He realized he had closed his own eyes and forced them open. No matter what else had happened, he refused to fall asleep in a council meeting.

Gustave glanced around the room. Most of the council hadn't noticed his lapse, but his grandmother had.

Blast it all.

"If we have concluded our business, then I suggest we conclude the meeting," Marquis Corbeau said. "I am still busy finalizing details for the gala."

"Details that weren't part of the approved budget," Marchioness Rouge said. "Perhaps you would like to enlighten us about that?"

"His Majesty is tired and should not be bored with such trivial matters."

Marchioness Rouge leaned forward, her eyes glittering. Gustave slumped back in his chair. He knew that look. This meeting was about to escalate into a war.

"I have something to say," Dowager Queen Bernadine said.

Marquis Corbeau looked relieved at the interruption. Marchioness Rouge looked disappointed.

"I believe we have been unfair to Gustave. I would like to remedy that situation."

Gustave sat up a little straighter as everyone turned their attention to him. Had they realized he was daydreaming about mysterious blue eyes instead of focusing on the meeting?

No, that was impossible.

So what did his grandmother want to say?

"We have asked Gustave to learn the duties of king and run the country while he searches for both his father and for a bride. It is too much. Especially since he has now twice been injured by kraken and is still recovering."

"No one asked him to search for his father," Marquis Corbeau said. "That quest has proved deadly and pointless and should be discontinued."

"But Father moved yesterday, and the light changed directions while we were sailing, as if we had passed him," Gustave said. "It seems too much of a coincidence that a kraken also happened to be guarding that particular place in the ocean. This is the best lead we've had since he disappeared. I think it is possible that the mermaids are holding him underwater."

"Be that as it may, the search must be postponed until after your gala, Gustave," Dowager Queen Bernadine said. "You cannot risk yourself again in such a manner. You must focus on hosting your guests and finding a bride. At the very least you should get to know the young ladies who have been invited to the castle."

Gustave narrowed his eyes, and his thoughts strayed to the woman from the beach. He wouldn't mind spending more time with her. Maybe he could learn her name somehow or remember where he had seen her before.

A golden fog wrapped around his mind, teasing his memories and reminding him that he was already in love with someone.

"I know who I will marry," he said. "I just have to find the woman who rescued me."

The council members shared nervous looks but did not comment.

"Your Majesty, there is no need to obsess over mystery women," Marquis Corbeau said. "I have arranged for many suitable young ladies to attend the gala."

"I certainly hope they are more suitable than Lady Annabelle," Dowager Queen Bernadine said.

Marquis Corbeau glowered.

"Any of the young ladies I have suggested would make excellent brides. But since King Gustave has proved himself unreasonably picky, I have widened the net, so to speak."

"Aren't you worried about the expense of housing so many guests?" Gustave said.

He winked at Collette. She giggled, and Marquis Corbeau scowled.

"We are getting off-topic," Dowager Queen Bernadine said. "As I began to say, we have asked too much of Gustave. We must lighten his load so that he can focus on finding a bride and recovering from his injuries. I propose we relieve him of his administrative duties until after the gala."

Gustave stared at his grandmother.

"I have put my whole heart into ruling this kingdom. Are you saying it's not enough?"

"Calm down, Gustave. I am saying that it is too much. You cannot rule with your whole heart while also looking for love."

"I do not intend to marry until I find Father."

"And you cannot be a proper king until you do."

She was giving him a look. The one that made him feel like he was a child again and had done something disappointing.

"Someone must rule," Marquis Corbeau said. "You cannot expect the council to cover for His Majesty. The extra paperwork alone–"

"I propose that we name Princess Collette co-regent until after the gala. She can review and approve any decrees that need royal approval."

Collette gasped.

"Oh, I couldn't, Grandmother. Gustave is doing just fine. I could never take his place."

She looked at Gustave, her eyes full of apology. He shook his head and smiled at her.

"No one accused you of that, Collette. Do you truly think I'm incompetent, Grandmother?"

He watched Thomas translate and scolded himself for being inconsiderate and not signing the words himself. Having an overwhelming day was no reason to be rude.

If he was honest, he wouldn't mind a few days off. He just didn't want to spend them searching for a bride when the options presented were Kara, Elaine, and Lady Annabelle.

And the mysterious woman from the beach.

But none of that mattered, because he was in love with the woman who had rescued him.

Gustave rubbed his temples, trying to fend off his building headache. This was all a bit much.

Maybe his grandmother was right.

Dowager Queen Bernadine watched him in silence for a moment, as if his actions had confirmed her theories.

"You're more than capable, Gustave, but you are also injured and distracted. Your birthday gala is more than a family party or a chance to find a bride. It is an affair of state. You need to be well-rested to greet diplomats and any royal families that visit."

"There will be several," Marquis Corbeau said. "Princesses of–"

"Perhaps I should clarify my proposal," Bernadine interrupted. "We will empower Collette to handle the administrative matters of Montaigne for a short time. Gustave will continue to handle diplomatic responsibilities. Does anyone have any objections?"

She looked around the room, daring anyone to object.

No one did.

Gustave studied his sister, trying to read the truth behind her guarded expression.

"Do you object, Collette?"

She shook her head.

"I'm happy to help however I can, but how will it look? I don't want anyone to think that you're incapable or that I'm trying to overshadow you."

"If anyone is to be given more power, it should be the council," Marquis Corbeau said. "I suppose I could take on extra duties if necessary. Or perhaps I could instruct Marchioness Rouge in how to complete the necessary tasks."

Marchioness Rouge sniffed.

"I hardly need your instructions to run a kingdom, Marquis. Besides, I thought you were too busy with gala preparations to take on extra duties."

"You truly don't object, Gustave?" Collette asked.

"It is a temporary measure that will help the gala go more smoothly. I don't see any harm in it."

Although, given the way his grandmother's eyes twinkled, perhaps he should.

Well, too late to turn back now. Maybe if he ended this meeting, he could finally eat something and change into dry clothes.

"I make a motion for Princess Collette to be given administrative authority until after the gala," Gustave said.

"I second it," Marchioness Rouge said. "Meet with me later, Princess. I will show you what needs to be done over the next few days."

She gave Marquis Corbeau a look as she said this, daring him to interfere or offer help.

The marquis was too busy watching Gustave to notice.

"You still have diplomatic duties to complete this afternoon, Your Majesty. You have received birthday gifts from royal families and need to open them and write thank you notes."

Gustave swallowed a sigh. His father was somewhere under the ocean, his true love was somewhere on the edge of it, and he was spending his time opening presents.

"Is there any other business before we adjourn?" Dowager Queen Bernadine said.

Everyone shook their heads.

"Then please excuse me while I check on my guests. I invited the young ladies to my parlor for tea and sewing. Will you join us before you begin your training, Collette?"

Collette nodded. Dowager Queen Bernadine gestured for Thomas to push her chair out of the room.

Gustave stood to follow her. A ladies' sewing circle was not his preferred way to spend an afternoon, but he should check on the woman from the ocean to make sure she had recovered from her ordeal. It was only polite.

Marquis Corbeau ducked in front of him before he could walk through the door.

"Your Majesty, we will need to complete some paperwork to make Princess Collette's appointment official."

Gustave sighed. More paperwork. He truly did want to help his country, but why did the tasks involved in ruling have to be so very tedious?

Perhaps once this paperwork was done and Collette was helping with administrative duties, he would have a break from those tasks and be able to convince Captain Whist to sail back to look for his father.

Which would be a more exciting prospect if he had any idea what to do once they were there. If his father was under the sea, Gustave needed mermaids to retrieve him. And except for the mysterious gift of a shell, the mermaids had offered no help at all.

It was all extremely frustrating.

The fog in his head amplified his frustration and agreed that the search was a hopeless matter. He needed to be out on the beach looking for the girl he loved, not sailing the ocean in a pointless quest for his father.

Gustave pushed the thought aside as he stood to follow Marquis Corbeau to his office. When he finished this paperwork, he would have more time to focus on what mattered.

If only he knew what that was.

❧ 21 ❧

Now that she was dressed, Fiora felt more nervous than ever about being in the castle. The squid ink dye held fast to her hair when she bathed, but would it be enough of a disguise to fool the royal family?

She studied her reflection in the mirror as a servant helped her dress. She certainly looked different without her red hair, but her face was still her own. It was only a matter of time before someone recognized her. She needed to leave before that happened.

Fiora glanced around the room, searching for anything valuable that was small enough to hide in her skirts when she escaped. She felt a twinge of guilt at the idea of stealing from people who had been so kind to her but pushed it aside. They wouldn't miss whatever she took. If they did, she could repay them once she had found work.

"I'll need to take your measurements so we can tailor something for you, miss," the servant said.

Fiora gave up her search and returned to studying her reflection in the mirror. The dark green dress she wore was not a perfect fit, but it was surprisingly close since the servants had been given so little time.

The hems were decorated with an embroidered pattern of silver seashells, and the fabric was far nicer than anything her father had ever provided for her. This was an expensive gown.

Perhaps she didn't need to steal after all. They had given her the dress. If she sold it, it was valuable enough to provide for her needs until she found work.

Maybe she should stay a little longer. If they tailored more dresses for her, she could keep one and take the extras to sell when she made her escape.

Fiora frowned at her reflection. It was slightly less blatant theft but still dishonest.

Well, she was on her own now. She would have to do whatever was necessary to survive.

The servant finished taking her measurements and stepped away. Fiora twirled in front of the mirror, admiring how the fabric moved through the air. Almost like the way her hair floated through water when she was a mermaid.

Pain shot through her feet, and Fiora stumbled. She grabbed a chair to catch her balance and leaned against it until the pain subsided.

"Are you injured, miss?"

Fiora sat and looked at the bottom of her feet. They were a little scratched from walking on the rocks, but nothing too serious. Nothing that would have caused a burst of pain like that.

That could be a problem. If she was going to run, it would be best to have her feet in good condition.

Her pearl ring had not caused any side effects when it transformed her into a human, so Fiora had not expected any from this enchantment. But it seemed that had been a mistake. First her lost voice, now pain in her feet. What else could go wrong?

She didn't want to know the answer to that question.

Fiora turned her attention back to the room. There were

several silver candlesticks that were small enough to take if she needed to limp away before the dresses were ready.

It wasn't much of a plan, but it was something.

Fiora walked over to the window and looked at the scenery below. Her room was on the third floor and provided a panoramic view of the gardens and the ocean. She half expected to see a kraken or an army of merfolk coming after her, but the water was calm. Just endless waves with ships sailing over them. No clues about what was happening under the surface.

Whatever it was, that was no longer her concern.

She felt a bad for leaving without saying goodbye to Zoe, but what else could she have done? Her family wanted her locked up.

Or dead, if they supported Leander's plan.

Fiora wiped a tear away. She wasn't enough. No matter how hard she tried, she was never good enough. She understood that the merfolk had felt betrayed when she left them to join her father, but what choice did she have? He had promised her a place to belong, and she had no reason not to believe him.

Maybe if her aunts had shared their suspicions about his role in her mother's death, she would have acted differently.

What had they meant by that?

Fiora ignored the voice in the back of her head that said she probably would not have listened if Kathelin and Althea had told her the story. She had idolized her father when she was young. Been devoted to her entire human family.

Until she'd come to know them better.

Fiora wiped away more tears of frustration. These thoughts were not helpful. The past was the past, and she needed a plan for the future.

She was human again, and this time her humanity didn't depend on anyone but her.

She had exactly what she had always wanted. Time to move forward.

The servant tactfully ignored the tears and presented a selection of shoes in various sizes. Fiora slipped her feet into a stylish pair of silver heels that matched the embroidery on her gown.

Another burst of pain rushed through her feet when she stood. Fiora collapsed onto the bed and glared at the shoes. Heels had never been comfortable, but they had never been torture either.

This was not how this was supposed to go.

"Should I call the doctor, miss?"

Fiora shook her head. Someone knocked on the door before the servant could ask further questions. Fiora tried to call out and tell them to go away, but her voice made no sound. They kept knocking. She gestured to the servant to open the door.

A well-dressed woman with streaks of gray in her auburn hair stood on the other side. Fiora recognized her from the crowd that had gathered in the hallway when she arrived. She kicked off the shoes and curtsied, wobbling a little as her legs shook.

The woman nodded in response and waved her hand to dismiss the servant, who curtsied to Fiora and hurried out the door.

"Forgive my disturbing you. I am Marchioness Rouge, a member of His Majesty's royal council. I wanted to check on you and personally welcome you to the castle. Did the servants see to your needs?"

Fiora nodded. She was as well as could be expected under the circumstances. She would be even better if she could find some food, but she wasn't quite sure how to communicate that.

Marchioness Rouge looked pleased but did not smile.

"You have been invited to take refreshments with the Dowager Queen Bernadine and join her sewing circle for the afternoon. Do you feel well enough to do so?"

Fiora considered this. On one hand, spending more time with the royal family was risky.

On the other hand, food would be most welcome.

As would sewing. Embroidery always cleared her head.

"It is a great honor," Marchioness Rouge said. "And it would be polite to accept the invitation as you are the personal guest of the dowager queen."

Fiora nodded. It would look suspicious if she refused their hospitality, and without her voice, she didn't have the means to make up a convincing excuse.

"I see you are nearly ready," the marchioness said. "Once you put your shoes on, I will personally escort you to the sewing room."

She stated this as if it also were a great honor. It probably was. A servant should be responsible for such a task. Not a marchioness.

If the marchioness knew that Fiora was a princess, she might feel differently about who was bestowing an honor.

Fiora scowled. She was trying to stay unnoticed and undiscovered. The last thing she needed was for anyone to realize she was important.

She selected the most sensible shoes available in her size, a pair of blue slippers that didn't match the dress, and nodded to the woman.

The marchioness eyed Fiora up and down, doubtless debating if she should comment that the slippers were hardly appropriate for paying a call to the dowager queen.

She must have decided against it, because she led Fiora down the hall without saying a word.

Fiora followed, doing her best not to show discomfort. Her feet burned. She looked down several times, sure that they must be bleeding through the thin shoes.

But whatever was causing the pain must be internal and related to the enchantment. The scratches on her feet weren't deep enough to cause it, and there was no other sign of injury.

Blast.

The marchioness noticed her slow pace and matched it without comment. She led Fiora to a spacious parlor with a balcony overlooking the ocean. Sunshine and a fresh sea breeze streamed through the open windows. Five ladies sat in a circle near the window. Dowager Queen Bernadine, Princess Collette, and Lady Annabelle were sewing. Kara was knitting. Elaine was reading a book. The translator sat by the dowager queen's side.

"Your guest, Dowager Queen Bernadine," Marchioness Rouge said. "I will see you in a few hours to review the budget, Princess Collette."

The marchioness curtsied and left the room. Fiora stood awkwardly in the doorway, not sure where to sit. There were a few seats in the circle, but also some in the corner of the room. Perhaps that would be safer.

"Come and sit down, girl," the dowager queen said in her booming voice. "Take the chair by me."

Fiora curtsied in response. The shift in balance sent a wave of pain up her leg, and she stumbled. The dowager queen did not comment on her lack of balance, but Lady Annabelle sniffed in derision.

Fiora took the offered seat with her head held high and her nose tilted slightly up. Lady Annabelle scowled at her, then sniffed again and turned back to her sewing.

"And what shall we call you, miss?" Dowager Queen Bernadine said.

"Grandmother, she can't speak. You know that."

Collette made gestures with her hands as she spoke. The young man did the same, although the double translation seemed unnecessary. Fiora watched them with interest. Yes, the signs were very similar to the mermaid sign language. The main difference seemed to be that the humans used smaller gestures. Almost as if they were whispering.

Fiora supposed it made sense. The humans were using the sign language to communicate in close, intimate settings. The mermaids often communicated across larger distances while singing enchantments.

"There's a difference between not speaking and being unable to speak," Dowager Queen Bernadine said. "Are we sure she can't?"

She gave Fiora a very sharp stare. Fiora clasped her hands in her lap and tried to look humble. Best not to antagonize the dowager queen.

"She's our guest, grandmother. Be kind," Collette signed.

Bernadine gave Fiora another piercing look and returned to her sewing. Fiora leaned over to see what she was working on. It was a pattern of seashells and water lilies sewn in various shades of blue and green. Lovely.

She tried to say that, but no sound came out. Fiora grimaced. Being mute was beyond annoying.

"I believe you met Lady Annabelle this morning," Collette said. "And these are my friends Kara and Elaine. They are attending Gustave's birthday gala and came a few days early."

Collette had picked up her sewing and was no longer signing since she wasn't addressing her grandmother directly. The young man at the queen's side took this over, translating the conversation for the dowager queen.

Fiora nodded towards him.

"Oh, forgive my manners. This is Thomas. He translates for my grandmother since she has difficulty hearing."

Thomas nodded at Fiora and flushed a little. Apparently he was used to staying in the background.

That was the role Fiora needed to play. Maybe she could watch Thomas for some ideas on how to avoid notice.

"So what should we call her?" Lady Annabelle said. "And how long will she be staying?"

Fiora recognized that tone. It was the voice of a woman who

smelled competition and didn't like it. Lady Annabelle, Kara, and Elaine had doubtless been invited to the castle early to be presented as marriage prospects for King Gustave. It seemed even when she wasn't a princess, Fiora found herself in a sort of Princess Test.

She met Lady Annabelle's challenging gaze and shrugged, doing her best to look innocent. As she intended, this only irritated Lady Annabelle further.

"Lady Annabelle, will you please pass me another skein of yarn?" Kara asked.

Lady Annabelle did so, and Fiora took advantage of the distraction to slip off her shoes and kick them under her chair. Even while she was sitting, they pinched and made her feet ache. She pressed her feet against the marble floor. The cold stone soothed the pain, and she relaxed a little.

Servants carried trays of food into the room, and Fiora gratefully accepted a plate. Conversation slowed while the ladies ate, and Fiora studied the room.

She couldn't help comparing it to the castle in Kell. While her father's castle was made of thick stone that created a dark, damp atmosphere, the Montaigne castle was all elegant marble and open windows. It seems to be made of sunlight and fresh air.

The food was the same. Kellish cuisine was heavy and dark. Better than mermaid food but not by much. The Montaigne luncheon was the best thing Fiora had ever eaten. She had sampled the cuisine of many nations while participating in Princess Tests but never had anything this good.

"I've never seen a lady eat so much," Lady Annabelle said. "Then again, they do say that sea air works up an appetite, and you've had plenty of that recently."

Fiora simply smiled and took another sandwich from a silver tray. She knew Lady Annabelle's game. She was the master of that game. No way was she letting this jealous harpy ruin her day. She wasn't competing, so nothing Lady Annabelle said mattered.

It wouldn't have mattered anyway.

Servants cleared away the lunch trays, and the ladies returned to their tasks. Elaine was deeply engrossed in her book and ignored everyone else in the room. Kara's knitting began to take the shape of a sock. Collette picked up a sewing basket and offered it to Fiora.

"Would you like to sew?"

Lady Annabelle, who was embroidering a pattern of seashells that was a blatant copy of Dowager Queen Bernadine's, sniffed derisively.

"You really think some wild girl from the ocean is well-versed in the refined arts? Honestly, Princess Collette. You'll only make her feel bad about her lack of accomplishments."

Fiora smiled innocently at Lady Annabelle and took the basket. She chose a square of white linen, secured it in an embroidery hoop, and threaded her needle with crimson thread. Then she ignored everyone and lost herself in her work. As always, the repetitive stabbing motion soothed her nerves. She finished a rose in the center of the fabric and changed to green thread to make a decorative border of leaves around it.

When Fiora finally did look up, Lady Annabelle's scowl had deepened. Her own project was moving slowly, hampered by knots and uneven stitches. Fiora's was perfect.

Never challenge a woman to a sewing competition when that woman had learned to sew as if her life depended on it.

Her life had depended on it. Fiora had studied all the traditional skills for the Princess Test hoping they would help her win a prince's affection and power the pearl ring so she could remain human.

But it hadn't been enough.

She rested the embroidery hoop on her lap and looked out the window. A breeze blew spray off the waves and carried the scent of saltwater into the room.

Why did it smell like home? She had spent her entire life

trying to escape the ocean. Now even the scent of it made her miss the underwater world.

Fiora gritted her teeth and turned back to her embroidery. Maybe stabbing the fabric a few hundred more times would make her feel better.

❦ 22 ❦

"I'm sorry, Your Majesty. The *Delphinette* needs repairs. I can't take it out again until they're finished."

Gustave bit back the frustrated words he longed to unleash. It wasn't Captain Whist's fault that kraken had attacked and damaged his ship.

Or that his father was still missing.

But now that he had finished the paperwork to let Collette take over administrative duties, Gustave wanted to take advantage of his extra time before he was pushed into something else.

"Surely there's another ship that could be spared."

"Perhaps there is. If you can convince the council to risk it."

"That's not likely. The council wants me to focus my full attention on finding a bride."

"So that's why you're hiding in my office?"

Gustave laughed.

"We're discussing official business. Not accomplishing anything, but at least we're trying. Isn't there anything you can do? We were so close to finding him."

The captain rubbed his forehead.

"The navy is already taxed to capacity. I've asked every

merchant ship in port to watch for mermaids or anything unusual, but I can't dedicate another ship to the search without council approval."

Gustave crossed his arms, then uncrossed them. Then crossed them again. Captain Whist's reasoning made sense, but that didn't make it any less frustrating.

"We can't just leave him out there," Gustave said. "Find King Francois."

He checked the light's direction with his compass. It remained the same, which meant the mermaids hadn't moved his father. It wasn't much comfort, but it was something.

Now all Gustave needed was a ship and a way to contact the mermaids.

He pulled the shell out of his pocket and handed it to his friend. He hadn't showed Kathelin's shell to anyone yet, but maybe a sea captain would have an idea what to do with it.

"What do you make of this?"

Captain Whist took the shell with raised eyebrows.

"Collecting seashells is a peaceful hobby and harmless enough. If it helps relieve the stress of running a kingdom, then I wish you luck."

Gustave glared.

"A mermaid gave that to me. Well, she gave it to Princess Carina, who gave it to me. Have you ever seen anything like it?"

Captain Whist whistled and looked closer at the shell.

"There are decorative markings carved on the surface, but I expect you've already noticed that. They don't seem to mean anything."

"You don't recognize them?"

Captain Whist shook his head. Gustave took the shell back and tucked it into his pocket.

"It's the only connection I have to the mermaids. I thought perhaps it was a communication charm, but instead it seems to be a useless trinket. Do you know anyone who might know something about mermaid magic?"

"Maybe you should ask your new guest. I heard she has a connection to the sea."

Captain Whist winked, and Gustave groaned.

"Has news really traveled so fast?"

"The king finding a naked woman on the beach and bringing her home is pretty newsworthy."

"It's nothing like that. I'm just trying to help her."

"And you also need a bride. Whoever she is, she's bound to be better than the mess your family rounded up."

"Lady Annabelle, Kara, and Elaine are perfectly respectable young ladies."

"I'm not even going to dignify that with a response."

Gustave pictured Kathelin and tried to find similarities between her and the woman from the beach. They both had enormous blue eyes. Did that mean anything? Was that why he thought she looked familiar?

The longer he thought about the woman, the more his head ached. Then a golden haze washed the pain away, and Gustave remembered that he was already in love. Why did he keep forgetting that?

"It doesn't matter how many girls they invite here. I know who I want to marry."

"Since when? Is it Princess Serafina? You seemed to get along well with her when we were in Santelle."

"What? No, it's not Serafina. She's a little too intense. Besides, she is crown princess of Santelle. She can't marry a king from another kingdom."

"Technically she could, but I see your point. It would make things politically complicated. So who are you marrying?"

Gustave rubbed his head, trying to banish the headache that kept building.

"A woman saved me on the beach after the wreck. I'm going to find her and marry her."

Captain Whist raised an eyebrow.

"I suppose that's one way to go about it, but what if she doesn't want you? Maybe she was just helping a stranger because she's a decent person."

At least he hadn't called Gustave crazy and said the woman didn't exist. It bothered Gustave that Captain Whist's argument sounded reasonable. What if his lady didn't want him? You didn't automatically fall in love with someone just because you saved their life.

The fog wrapped around that thought and pulled the doubt away. Of course the woman loved him. Why wouldn't she?

A knock interrupted Gustave's thoughts. Captain Whist looked to the king, checking to see if their meeting was finished. Unfortunately it was. The search for his father remained as fruitless as ever. Gustave nodded, and Captain Whist called, "Come in!"

Dale Mercer peeked through the door. The merchant had been given new clothes at some point and looked less depressed than he had in the throne room. His face lit up when he saw Gustave.

"Oh, Your Majesty! I was hoping to ask Captain Whist if he has received any news of my surviving ship. What luck to find you here as well! I have several questions about mermaids for you."

Gustave swallowed.

"Unfortunately, I'm late for an engagement with my grandmother, but I'm sure Captain Whist will be happy to answer your questions as best he can. Please excuse me."

He bowed and hurried from the room, ignoring Captain Whist's exasperated look at the merchant's hopeful gaze.

❦ 23 ❦

"That's lovely. You are quite talented with the needle," Collette said.

Fiora looked down at her handiwork. She had finished the leafy border around the rose and started to edge the fabric with a pattern inspired by the etchings mermaids used to record their enchanted songs. In fact, she had unintentionally notated part of the kraken lullaby.

She shrugged, brushing off Collette's compliment. The design was pretty, but certainly not her best work. She was simply passing the time.

And she hadn't meant to draw attention to herself.

Lady Annabelle leaned forward to get a better look at the fabric and scowled.

"I suppose every commoner knows how to sew. It's necessary if you don't have servants to make your clothes for you."

Fiora wanted to say that Lady Annabelle must have an army of servants to sew for her since her own embroidery project had turned out so badly. If she had been able to speak, the words would have flown out without a moment's thought.

Since she couldn't, she settled for a scornful look at Lady Annabelle before turning back to her own project.

"Let me see it," Dowager Queen Bernadine said.

She set her own sewing aside and reached for Fiora's. After a moment's hesitation, Fiora handed it to her. What else could she do?

Bernadine studied the sewing, turning the hoop over to look at the back of the fabric.

"Nicely done," she said. "It takes real character and discipline to keep your stitches uniform and make the back of your embroidery as neat as the front. Not a single knot or tangle. And you've used an interesting mixture of sewing techniques. Most accomplished."

Lady Annabelle sputtered, and the dowager queen winked at Fiora. Fiora grinned at her. It seemed she wasn't the only one who recognized Lady Annabelle's game for what it was.

Then Fiora remembered she was trying not to attract attention and looked away. She didn't need friends. She had never needed friends.

As if responding to that thought and determined to prove her wrong, a seagull flew through the open window and landed on Fiora's chair. If she'd had her voice, she would have shrieked in surprise.

The seagull's feathers were streaked with black stains.

Spot.

Fiora tried to shoo him away, but Spot shuffled from side to side to avoid her hands. He squawked and studied a crust of bread on her plate with interest.

Fiora picked it up and held it towards him. Perhaps food would make him go away.

Spot tilted his head, and Fiora realized he had something in his beak. He dropped whatever it was into her lap, grabbed the crust, and flew out the window.

Everyone in the room stared at Fiora with wide eyes. She

shrugged at them as if to say she had no idea what that was about and slowly moved her hand to cover the object that Spot had dropped. Her fingers closed over it, and she struggled to keep a neutral expression as she realized what it was.

A shell.

Fiora ran her thumb over it. The shell's surface was rough with carvings. It was possible Spot had found this on the beach, but not likely.

Had someone used the seagull to send her a message? That meant the mermaids knew where she was. They had found her already.

She hadn't been able to hide for even a single day.

Fiora blinked and realized everyone was still staring at her. Lady Annabelle's jaw moved up and down as if she were trying to think of a clever insult but couldn't quite manage it.

"Am I interrupting something?"

Gustave entered the room and studied everyone's surprised looks with amusement.

"Your guest is some sort of witch," Lady Annabelle said.

She said the words 'guest' and 'witch' as if they were the worst insults she could think of.

They probably were. Lady Annabelle had spirit but lacked imagination.

Fiora tightened her grip on the shell, desperate to read it. But there was no way to do so with so much attention focused on her.

"She fed a hungry bird," Elaine said, looking up from her book for a moment. "That's no sign of magic."

Gustave looked to his grandmother for an explanation. The dowager queen chuckled.

"You should pull things from the ocean more often, Gustave. This young lady is full of surprises."

She gave Fiora an approving smile. Fiora blinked in surprise. No one had ever approved of her so quickly or easily before.

She wasn't sure anyone had ever approved her in general.

Whatever people expected from her, she usually managed to do the opposite and cause a scene.

She had still done that, but Dowager Queen Bernadine seemed to be enjoying the scene very much.

Gustave looked from Fiora to his grandmother. He looked equally surprised at the praise. Fiora guessed the dowager queen was not easily impressed.

"What happened, Grandmother?" Gustave signed.

He didn't say the words out loud. Doubtless this was meant to be a private conversation.

"Nothing of consequence. We're simply sewing. How did your meeting with Marquis Corbeau go?"

Dowager Queen Bernadine looked a little smug as she signed.

Lady Annabelle, Kara, and Elaine watched the exchange for a moment then lost interest. Apparently they didn't understand sign language. Some gestures were slightly different from the mermaids' version, but Fiora was able to follow the conversation without difficulty.

"It's rude not to speak aloud," Collette signed silently. *"Our guests will think you're gossiping about them."*

"As if there was anything worth gossiping about there," Dowager Queen Bernadine signed. *"Elaine cares more about her book than any of us. Kara is too shy to contribute, and Annabelle is trying to prove herself a lady through gross incompetence in both needlework and conversation."*

Fiora snorted at this description. This didn't require her voice, so it made a sound.

An extremely unladylike sound that filled the entire room.

Everyone turned to look at her. She froze.

"Do you understand sign language, girl?" Bernadine signed.

Fiora tried to keep her expression blank, but the dowager queen's eyes gleamed with the joy of discovery.

"Where did you learn? Certainly not from your seagull friends. They don't have hands."

Fiora couldn't help the flash of amusement in her eyes at the dowager queen's words.

Blast it all.

"So you do understand?" Gustave spoke out loud in his enthusiasm. "You know sign language? That's marvelous! Now you can tell us about yourself."

Thomas resumed his translating duties for the dowager queen, who nodded her agreement.

"What's your name?" Gustave continued. "Where do you come from?"

Fiora set down her sewing and raised shaky hands to answer. But what could she say? No lie would sufficiently explain how she came to be naked in the ocean on castle grounds.

The truth was equally improbable and even more dangerous.

"What's going on?" Lady Annabelle asked. "Are you saying she can communicate with us but has chosen not to?"

Her voice sounded innocent, but her expression was predatory. She may not completely understand the situation, but Fiora's discomfort was obvious. Annabelle had gained the upper hand over Fiora, and she knew it. They both knew it.

"I-"

Fiora signed the single word, and everyone leaned towards her waiting for the next.

There was nothing she could say that would help. Her thoughts were too scattered to even give them a fake name.

Fiora grabbed the shell from her lap and bolted from the room. Pain shot through her feet, and she realized too late that she had left her shoes hidden under her chair.

She ducked into the first empty hallway she found and paused to read the shell. As she had suspected, it was carved with a song. Zoe's part from their royal quartet.

Such an enchantment was unlikely to have washed up on the beach. This was a message.

From Zoe?

Or was it a trap?

Fiora took a few deep breaths, trying to calm her racing heart. Someone knew she was here.

She could run further inland, but they had tracked her here so easily that they would doubtless find her again. And even if they didn't, she would always be looking over her shoulder, waiting until they did. She needed to face whoever had sent the shell on her own terms instead of letting them ambush her.

If it was Zoe, meeting her was probably safe enough.

Unless her cousin had told others.

There was only one way to find out.

Blast it all.

Fiora ran through the castle, ducking into corridors to avoid the guards, servants, and nobles that meandered through the halls. Finally, she found the door to the garden and hurried outside. Beds of flowers and manicured hedges gave way to sandy beaches at the garden's edge.

Fiora ducked around a corner, hoping she was out of sight of the doorway by now. Something rustled in a nearby tree, and Fiora ducked down to avoid being detected.

"Squawk?"

Spot the seagull looked down at her.

"You."

Fiora spoke the word even though it made no sound. Then she signed it for good measure. Spot hopped on the ground and pecked for crumbs.

Fiora held the shell towards the bird, hoping he might lead her to the place he had found it. But he had discovered an apple core under a bush and was no longer interested in Fiora.

Something splashed in the water.

A wave? Or something more?

Fiora followed the sound, ducking under trellises whenever possible to stay out of view from the castle windows overhead. Finally she reached a bench hidden by a wrought iron arch covered with climbing ivy. She sat on it, glad to give her feet a break, and dug her toes into the sand. She was close enough to the water to see anything unusual that happened, but not close enough that anyone could catch her by surprise.

Spot landed on the sand beside Fiora's feet. A soft song drifted through the air, and a fish washed up on the beach. The seagull grabbed it and flew away.

Before Fiora could react, Zoe emerged from the water. The young mermaid beamed when she saw Fiora.

"Oh good, the bird found you."

Fiora nodded and tossed the shell back to her cousin. Zoe caught it and tied it in her hair.

"They're searching the ocean for you. I've almost convinced Grandmother that you didn't wake the kraken on purpose. I told her that I lost focus and sang a wrong note."

"Zoe, you shouldn't have done that."

"But maybe it's true. What else could explain the kraken waking?"

"I didn't do it on purpose, but I did sing a few notes out of tune. You can't take the blame for this. You'll ruin your chances of joining a choir."

"I'd rather have you home than sing in a choir. I told you I would fix everything. Why did you leave before I could?"

To Fiora's surprise, Zoe's eyes filled with tears. It seemed mermaids could cry after all.

Fiora swallowed. She hated to involve Zoe further, but if the mermaid was determined to interfere, she should know what she was dealing with.

"While I was hiding in the statue garden, I overheard Leander plotting with someone to kill me."

Zoe gasped. When she tried to speak, her questions ran into each other and came out as sputtering.

"I don't know who it was. There was a lady and someone with a deep voice that made the ground rumble."

"Like it did before the kraken woke up? Do you think Leander was responsible for that?"

"Why would Leander wake a kraken?"

Zoe frowned.

"I'm sure there could be a reason," she said after clearly failing to think of one.

Fiora wished she had any idea what that reason could be, but Leander was a trusted member of the royal guard.

"If Leander truly believes I woke the kraken on purpose, he might see it as his duty to eliminate me to protect the queen."

"That's ridiculous," Zoe said. "I'll keep an eye on him. Maybe I can find something useful."

"Zoe, no. That's dangerous."

"I'll be careful."

Fiora sighed silently. She doubted Zoe was capable of being careful. Maybe if she had another mission to distract her, she would forget about following Leander.

"Zoe, could you do something for me?"

"Of course!"

"I used an enchantment on a conch shell to transform myself into a human. There's a second shell with more information about the song in the library. Could you bring it to me?"

"So you didn't use your pearl ring?"

Fiora held out her hand to show the dull pearl. The young mermaid brightened.

"You said it was a conch shell? I can find it and bring it to you tomorrow. Unless you find love before then and don't need it."

"I'm unlikely to find love so quickly, Zoe. That isn't how it works."

"Are you sure? I've been using that golden ball you hid in the library to learn more about the human world. The princess and the frog fell in love rather quickly."

Fiora had no idea what Zoe was talking about, and she had too much on her mind to ask further questions.

"So you'll bring the shell tomorrow?"

Zoe nodded.

"I'll give your pet seagull a message for you when I'm here."

"He's not a pet. He's a pest."

A sound interrupted them. Footsteps coming closer.

"Hello?" Gustave's voice called. "Are you there, miss?"

"You should go. He'll find us soon."

Zoe ducked lower in the water.

"Is that a human man? Are you trying to win his love so you can use the pearl ring instead of the enchantment?"

Fiora raised an eyebrow. Of all the escape plans she had considered, winning Gustave's affection was not one of them.

"No, I'm not trying to make him love me."

"Do you love him?"

"No."

Zoe smiled.

"Then you should return to the ocean as soon as possible. I miss you, Fiora."

The young mermaid dove beneath the waves and didn't resurface. Fiora stared at the water, unsure what to feel. No one had ever wanted her before. No one had ever missed her when she left.

Or maybe they had, and she had simply failed to notice.

⚜ 24 ⚜

Gustave sprinted through the castle, cursing himself for not following the woman the moment she fled. He had been too surprised to react when she bolted from the room, and now he had lost her.

Servants pointed down the hallways when they saw him. He assumed this meant that the lady had passed that way. There was no time to stop for questions.

After a few false trails, he found himself outside. Gustave stood in the doorway and searched the garden. No sign of the woman. No sign of anything out of the ordinary except a rather dirty seagull eating a fish on the shore.

Well, it was a start.

Gustave walked slowly through the garden, checking likely hiding spots as he made his way towards the water.

Why did everything always come back to the sea?

He heard voices. A woman speaking. His heart raced. Could she speak after all? What if she was the one who had saved him and was simply too shy to say so?

"Hello? Are you there, miss?"

Silence.

Gustave jogged towards the place he had heard the voice. Maybe it was someone else. But if that was the case, perhaps she had seen the woman.

He reached a trellis and rounded the corner slowly, hoping not to scare whoever was hiding behind the ivy.

The woman sat on the bench staring at the ocean. She flinched when she saw Gustave but didn't run. She didn't look like she had the energy to go any further.

"I'm sorry," Gustave said

Then he signed the words for good measure. Maybe she was deaf as well?

She stared at him for a long moment. Gustave stood as still as he could, trying not to scare her further. He didn't want her to run again.

Finally, she sighed and relaxed a little.

"I understand speech and sign language," she signed.

"Why did you run when we asked you about it?"

They were beyond the bounds of propriety at this point. He might as well just ask.

Instead of answering, the woman limped to the edge of the beach and sat on a low seawall. She pulled her skirt up to her knees and dangled her bare feet in the water. Some of the tension in her face eased. Gustave watched her for a moment, then kicked his shoes off, rolled up his trousers to his ankles, and joined her. There was something soothing about waves lapping against your skin. It cleared his head until he almost remembered where he had seen her before.

Questions hadn't helped, so Gustave remained silent. The woman seemed deep in thought and content to simply sit there. Gustave took a deep breath and closed his eyes. He couldn't remember the last time he sat on the beach and enjoyed the warmth of the sun.

When he opened his eyes, the woman was watching him. She raised her hands as if to sign something then lowered them again.

"You're sure you can't speak?" Gustave said. "I thought I heard someone speaking a moment ago."

She glared at him, not needing words or signs to communicate that she found his question extremely stupid.

"Sorry. I'm so sorry. It's just, I'm looking for someone who sings. I heard a voice in the garden and thought it might be you."

"I'm sure Lady Annabelle would be happy to sing for you. All you need to do is ask."

Gustave winced, then noticed the gleam in her eyes.

"You're mocking me."

She shrugged.

"There are hundreds of people in your kingdom who could sing for you. Why are you so determined to find this particular woman? Who is she?"

Gustave considered the question a moment, trying to form the story in a way that wouldn't sound crazy.

"I was in a shipwreck yesterday and washed up on the beach. Someone dragged me out of the water and sang to me. I'd like to thank her for saving my life."

I love her. The words almost came out on their own, but Gustave managed to hold them in. He had a lifetime of practice keeping his thoughts to himself. It was only in the past few days that he had become careless and unpredictable in what he said.

He searched her eyes for doubt or disbelief but found only curiosity. He traced the faint scar in his hairline and continued the story.

"My ship was attacked by kraken. I was washed overboard and somehow floated to shore. I don't remember much of that. Just a voice and a woman."

And magic.

"Why were you sailing? Where were you going?"

She pulled her feet out of the water, stared at them for a moment, then submerged them again.

Maybe it was because she was using sign language, but Gustave felt no judgment from her question. It had been a long time since someone simply asked him something without any sort of accusation or expectation accompanying their words.

"My father went missing almost a year ago. This magic ring is supposed to track him. I thought I could use it to find him, but it led me to the middle of the ocean instead. Then kraken attacked."

"I'm sorry about your father."

And she did look sorry. She met Gustave's gaze with a sort of sad understanding in her eyes.

"You've lost someone?"

She nodded.

"My mother died when I was young. No one has ever told me exactly what happened to her. I think not knowing is worse than anything the truth could be."

Her expression darkened at whatever memories thoughts of her mother brought up. Gustave studied her face, desperate to know more about her.

"I understand the sentiment. If I knew my father was dead, I could move on. I could grieve and heal. But I can't leave him alone to an unknown fate."

The woman placed her hand over his and squeezed his fingers.

"Of course you can't."

She had to let go of his hand to make the signs, and Gustave wished she didn't. He wanted to return the gesture and take her hand to comfort her, but that would leave her effectively mute. Instead, he placed his hand near her on the wall. Just in case she wanted to hold his hand again.

Sadly, she didn't.

"Your mother died when you were young?" she signed. *"I think I remember hearing that."*

Gustave nodded and made a mental note that she must not be from Montaigne. Any citizen would know for certain when the queen had died and how it had happened.

"What about your father?" Gustave asked. "The rest of your family?"

The woman pursed her lips together.

"They want nothing to do with me."

"Why not?"

She shook her head and stared at the ocean.

Gustave couldn't help wondering if her family had treated her badly because she was mute. But surely a father wouldn't abandon his daughter simply because she couldn't speak. Someone had taught her sign language. Someone had taken her in.

And then someone had left her in the ocean with literally nothing.

There was something so familiar about her. Some mystery he felt the need to solve.

Maybe she was cursed. Under some magical influence less obvious than being transformed into a talking frog. Could a curse steal someone's voice?

Or their clothes or memories?

He thought back to his misadventures with Stefan and Carina. Prince Stefan's curse had come with a set of rules. Things he couldn't talk about without severe consequences.

Perhaps this girl's curse meant she couldn't talk at all. Or that she couldn't answer certain questions. Even with sign language.

Gustave had researched curses as thoroughly as he could when his father disappeared. Their effects and conditions varied, but most didn't allow the person under the enchantment to admit they were cursed.

So it would be pointless to ask her. She might run again if he tried to pry.

Or he would look extremely insensitive for assuming that a physical disability must be the work of dark magic. Perhaps she was simply mute.

But if it was magic...

There were as many ways to break curses as there were curses themselves. Princess Carina had set Prince Stefan free with a kiss and recommended that Gustave do the same if he ever needed to break an enchantment.

Gustave's eyes settled on the woman's lips. She had a nice mouth. Even if it was scowling at him in confusion right now.

He flushed. It would be beyond inappropriate to lean over and kiss her right now. Curse or not, definitely inappropriate.

Tempting, but inappropriate.

"I should go," she signed.

"Where is your home?"

She shrugged and didn't answer. Apparently that subject was also off-limits.

"Perhaps I'll travel inland. I've always lived by the sea. A change might be nice."

"Do you have someone to stay with? Any friends or family?"

She shook her head, but her eyes were defiant. As if daring him to say that she needed those things to survive.

That was exactly what Gustave had been going to say, but her expression stopped him. Instead, he pulled his feet out of the ocean and turned to face her.

"I wonder if you could do me a favor?"

Her expression became suspicious. Gustave smiled, trying to relieve her fear.

"I'm supposed to spend the afternoon opening birthday presents from royal families and writing thank you notes. It will be dull, but you could join me if you like. It would annoy Marquis Corbeau immensely."

She grinned at him. Then her grin broadened into a silent laugh. Gustave joined her, his laughter echoing over the waves and mixing with the cries of seagulls. When was the last time he had laughed like that? Sometime before his father had disappeared, that was certain.

"Not to brag, but I have a history of annoying people. I'd be happy to help annoy your marquis."

"Perfect."

Gustave hopped up and held out his hand. She took it, and he helped her to her feet. The hem of her skirt was damp, and the back of her dress was covered in sand. She stumbled, and Gustave offered his arm. The woman hesitated, then took it with a trembling hand. She kept her grip light. As if she might run away at any moment.

Halfway back to the castle, Gustave realized he had left his shoes on the shore. He would need to send someone to fetch them later.

If he had been walking with anyone else, he would have turned back to fetch them and saved a servant the effort. But something in the way the girl walked suggested that she was in pain. She didn't limp, but her steps were cautious. As if the ground might give way beneath her.

She met his gaze and smiled a little, and Gustave forgot all about his shoes.

❧ 25 ❧

"Why is she here?"

Marquis Corbeau looked every bit as annoyed at the woman's presence as Gustave had hoped he would. It was probably immature to take so much pleasure in that, but the marquis had thwarted attempts to rescue Father and tried to force Gustave into marriage. He deserved a little discomfort.

That was an unkingly thought, but Gustave reminded himself that he wasn't fully king yet.

"She is our guest and wanted to see more of the castle."

"Send her away to tour the kitchens with a servant then."

"He does realize I can hear him, doesn't he?"

Gustave bit back a grin as the woman signed. Marquis Corbeau scowled.

"So, she can communicate after all? What did she say?"

"She said that she needs a translator, and Collette and my grandmother were busy. The rest of the servants who know sign language are preparing for the gala."

"Hmm."

The marquis looked at the woman like he might look at a

wilted flower arrangement. She returned his glare, equally unimpressed. Gustave stepped between them.

"I believe we have things to do, Marquis? Where are the gifts?"

"There were too many for your office, so I sent them to the library. You'll work from there today."

The marquis bustled ahead towards the library, eager to get started. Gustave hurried after him, then noticed the woman had fallen behind. She wasn't limping exactly. It was more like she was trying not to look like she was limping.

He walked back to her and offered his arm.

"I'm not a weakling. I don't need help."

"I didn't say you were. It's common courtesy."

He signed the words so that Marquis Corbeau wouldn't overhear and demand a translation of the conversation.

She looked suspicious but took his arm. At first, her hand barely rested on his sleeve. As if she were accepting his gesture but also determined to make her point. Her entire body was stiff.

Gustave didn't comment. He simply walked beside her at a comfortable pace. So slowly that he hardly noticed it was happening, her hand rested more weight on his arm and her shoulders loosened. Her face relaxed.

"What is taking you so long?" Marquis Corbeau said.

She tensed again and gritted her teeth as if biting back a response.

"Please forgive his eagerness," Gustave said. "He gets a little carried away with gala preparations."

"Only a little?"

The words were innocent, but the smirk that accompanied her signs was far from it.

She had to let go of his arm to make the gestures. Gustave was pleased when she took it again.

His satisfied feeling disappeared when he entered the library. The enormous room was full of gifts. Brightly wrapped boxes were organized into stacks that reached to the top of the lofted ceilings and leaned against bookshelves. It would take hours to go through them all and be impossible to reach any of the books until they had been removed. The woman stared with wide eyes, just as surprised as Gustave.

Marquis Corbeau was already commanding a small army of servants and scribes.

"You there. You will bring the gifts to His Majesty. You will record his impressions. You will take down his official messages of thanks."

Collette's taking over the administrative duties was supposed to give Gustave more time, but opening so many gifts would leave no time to search for his father or the mystery girl. He was no better off than before.

"You'll need to build another castle to fit all these."

Gustave smiled.

"What did she say?" Marquis Corbeau said.

"She said everyone is extremely generous to give me so many gifts."

She gave him a look. Gustave shrugged. There was no point upsetting the marquis with an accurate translation.

"Please, what should I call you?" he signed. *"What is your name?"*

She had grown more comfortable, but the question set her on edge again. She crossed her arms and looked away from him.

Perhaps she wasn't able to tell him because of the conditions of her curse.

Or maybe she just didn't want to.

The servants had placed a chair near the scribe's desk for Gustave. He pulled another one beside it so the woman could sit with him.

"We'll start with gifts from royal families," Marquis Corbeau said. "It is important that you send a heartfelt message of thanks for each one to help strengthen our relationships."

Gustave looked at the mountains of boxes and bit back a sigh. Yes, this was an important diplomatic task.

And he wished he didn't have to do it.

"From the royal family of Aeonia," a servant said, offering a package.

The woman stiffened. Gustave studied her from the corner of his eye, looking for a clue. Did she have some connection to Aeonia?

The box was wrapped in silver paper with golden illustrations of goats painted on it.

"Do you think they sent you a goat?" she signed.

"What did she say?" Marquis Corbeau demanded.

"She said the wrapping paper is very shiny. She likes shiny things because they're pretty."

He didn't try to keep the sarcasm from his tone. This time it was the woman who bit back a grin. She raised her hand to cover her smile, and Marquis Corbeau looked at the two of them suspiciously. Gustave did his best to keep an innocent expression as he tore open the wrapping paper and pulled out the gift.

It was a sweater. Cashmere from the feel of it.

And it was the ugliest thing Gustave had ever seen.

The fabric, while soft, was bright red with yellow and orange stripes of seagulls flying across it. Each gull had a jeweled eye that sparkled and reflected color through the room as the fabric moved.

Gustave turned to his companion, but she was too surprised to comment. She stared at the sweater with her mouth hanging open.

"They included a note," Marquis Corbeau said.

He pulled a small piece of parchment from the remains of the wrapping paper and read aloud.

"Prince Stefan and Princess Carina offer their good wishes for His Majesty King Gustave's birthday and hope he enjoys this sweater designed by Bastien, Head Tailor and Royal Designer of Aeonia. The designer calls it A Study of Cashmere and Sunset."

Marquis Corbeau took the sweater from the stunned Gustave and handed it to a servant. The jewels sent even more flashes of light around the library as she folded the sweater and tucked it into a box.

"We need to record your thoughts, Your Majesty," the scribe said. "What thanks would you like to send the royal family of Aeonia for this generous gift?"

Generous did not begin to cover it. Blast Stefan and Carina.

Gustave looked around the room trying to think of something appropriate to say.

"Will they expect you to wear that?" the woman signed. *"Tell Marquis Corbeau that I think you should wear the sweater to your birthday gala as a sign of diplomatic goodwill towards Aeonia."*

Gustave glared at her. He couldn't picture a single occasion that would be appropriate for him to wear that monstrosity.

"What did she say?" Marquis Corbeau said. "Honestly, Your Majesty, it will take ages to open these gifts if she keeps interrupting."

The woman stuck her tongue out at the marquis. Fortunately, he was looking at Gustave and didn't notice. Gustave gave her a sideways glance.

"She said that the sweater is beautiful because it is so shiny, and she wishes she had one like it. I would like to offer it to her as a way to welcome her to Montaigne. Perhaps she would honor me by wearing it to the gala?"

She crossed her arms and glared at Gustave. Marquis Corbeau looked horrified.

"Your Majesty can't offer a birthday gift from the royal family of Aeonia to someone else!"

"Ha! You're stuck with it."

The scribe sitting at the desk cleared his throat.

"What message would Your Majesty like to send to Aeonia?"

Gustave swallowed. What on earth could he say about the sweater that would not start a war? Diplomacy had never been so difficult.

"Tell them it left you speechless."

It was better than anything he could think of. Gustave nodded.

"Tell the royal family of Aeonia that their generous gift was so unique that it left me speechless. I literally do not have words to express my feelings of thanks."

Marquis Corbeau nodded his approval. Gustave sighed and leaned back in his chair. Surely the gifts couldn't get any worse than that.

"This one is from Lord Panais," Marquis Corbeau said.

"Lady Annabelle's father," Gustave signed to explain the concerned face he was making.

He eyed the box suspiciously. It was rectangular and flat and wrapped in a crimson cloth. Probably not a sweater.

"Any guesses?" he asked the woman.

She studied the gift.

"Art?"

"Perhaps."

Marquis Corbeau rolled his eyes and did not request a translation. Gustave untied the ribbon and pulled the red cloth away.

He saw a gilded gold frame first. Then he saw the painting and forgot all about the frame.

A portrait of a naked woman stared back at him. She was tastefully covered by carefully draped hair and flowing fabric, but the overall effect was undeniably seductive. Gustave blinked at the portrait and felt his face go red.

"Your Majesty, what is the- oh dear."

Marquis Corbeau stared at the portrait, just as shocked as Gustave. Gustave heard rustling and turned. The woman bent over to pick up a note that had fallen to the ground. She read it and began shaking with silent laughter.

"It isn't funny," Gustave said.

She was laughing too hard to reply and handed him the note instead. Gustave read it aloud.

"Your Majesty, please accept this recently commissioned portrait of my daughter, Lady Annabelle, as-"

Gustave stopped reading the note. He handed the portrait to Marquis Corbeau who handed it to a servant. He hadn't paid much attention to the portrait's face before, but he looked at it now.

Yes, it was Lady Annabelle.

"What a unique gift," Marquis Corbeau said in a choked voice.

The woman was laughing so hard that she was in danger of falling out of her seat.

"Unique indeed," she signed. *"If it makes any difference, she is supposed to represent an ancient goddess. It said so in the note."*

"Is that so?" Gustave said. "Marquis, please tell me that the rest of the suitable local ladies you've invited to the gala have not also sent gifts."

"Perhaps she'll come to the gala like that. If she does, you can offer her the Aeonian sweater to wear. I almost hope she does. Someone should get use out of that monstrosity."

"You're one to talk about going places unclothed."

Gustave signed the words before thinking. The moment his hands made the gestures, he wished he could take them back. The woman's face fell, and all traces of laughter left her eyes.

Stupid. This was why he always thought before he spoke. A king couldn't afford careless comments!

"Forgive me," Gustave whispered. "I did not mean it like that."

"What are you two talking about?" Marquis Corbeau said.

"She suggested that I offer Lady Annabelle the Aeonian sweater as cover."

Was it Gustave's imagination, or did a flicker of amusement cross Marquis Corbeau's face?

"What message of thanks would Your Majesty like to send?" the scribe asked.

Good grief. What could he possibly say in such a situation?

"You could say that you appreciate the effort she has put into catching your attention by throwing herself at you naked, but that another lady beat her to it."

The woman had a dangerous gleam in her eyes. Gustave swallowed, unsure what to do. She studied him for a moment, then shrugged.

"I know you meant no offense," she signed, offering a small smile.

Gustave let out a breath he didn't realize he had been holding. He hadn't offended her with his careless comment. Thank goodness for that.

"Your message?" the scribe prompted again.

"Perhaps a simple thank you and a complement to the artist would suffice," Marquis Corbeau suggested.

Gustave nodded.

"Yes, that will do very well."

"And where would your Majesty like the painting to be displayed?" a servant asked.

"Somewhere my grandmother won't see it," Gustave said.

"Perhaps your private chamber?"

The woman's blue eyes twinkled with amusement. Gustave shook his head.

"She's not my type."

Out loud he said, "We'll leave it in the library with the other gifts for now. Put it by the sweater."

❧ 26 ❧

F iora didn't try to hide her amusement as the servant tucked the nude portrait of Lady Annabelle under the sweater. It seemed the people of Montaigne were even more desperate to marry off King Gustave than she had been to catch a husband in a Princess Test.

Although, she had never tried sending such a portrait ahead of time. Maybe it would have been effective.

Maybe Lina had done that to catch Alaric.

As much as Fiora wanted to believe the worst about them, she didn't think that was the case. Alaric had not responded well to Fiora's flirting. Or anyone's flirting. He probably would have been just as scandalized to receive the portrait as King Gustave was now.

Fiora glanced at Gustave, and her grin widened. He was still bright red and trying to recover his composure. Was he truly that shy? Or perhaps just unsure how to respond as a gentleman? He had been equally flustered yet considerate when he found her on the beach.

She blushed. If she had been trying to catch King Gustave's attention, that would have been a bold move. And possibly an effective one, since she had somehow ended up as his personal guest in the castle.

But she wasn't trying, and it had been an accident. She didn't care about Gustave. Staying in the castle was simply the best hiding place at the moment.

Although Zoe had found her in a single day, so perhaps it wasn't such a good hiding place after all.

The servants brought another gift to Gustave. Another painting judging from the shape of it, but this one was much bigger. The package was nearly as tall as Fiora.

It was wrapped in thick, brown paper likely chosen for durability rather than appearance. The gift was far less attractive than the rest of the brightly colored parcels and considerably more disheveled.

"It looks like it had a long journey," Fiora commented.

Gustave nodded.

"Who sent this one?" he asked.

"Princess Elspeth of Kell."

Fiora flinched at the mention of her sister's name. Gustave looked concerned. It was unlikely that he knew Elspeth, so he was probably imagining another scandalous portrait.

Would Elspeth try such a thing? She had never needed such tactics before. Her sweet smile and soft voice were usually enough to get her way with whatever man she needed to manipulate at the moment.

Fiora shifted in her chair as Gustave unwrapped the present. He had some trouble tearing it open, but eventually managed to free a corner. A silver frame peeked out from under the paper. Gustave swallowed, and Fiora leaned forward to get a better look.

A servant offered Gustave a small knife, which he used to cut away the rest of the wrapping. Then he pulled it back to reveal a floor-length mirror.

Gustave sighed in relief, and Fiora sank into her seat. She

wasn't sure what she had expected, but this wasn't it. A mirror seemed a strange gift to give a king for his birthday.

Although it was better than that hideous sweater.

"It's a mirror," Marquis Corbeau said.

He seemed disappointed. What had he been hoping to see?

"It's nice," Gustave said.

He also sounded a little confused.

"Is that what Your Majesty would like to send in the thank you note?" the scribe asked.

"Of course not. Give me a moment to think."

He sat down next to Fiora and looked at her. Was he asking for a suggestion?

"It will be helpful for trimming your beard," she signed.

"That's all? No witty comment about Princess Elspeth and how the gift reflects her?"

Fiora's expression darkened at the mention of her sister. Gustave leaned forward.

"Please tell me I haven't offended you again. I usually think more before I speak. I just-"

"Don't concern yourself about it. I often bring out the worst in people."

"Don't be ridiculous."

He didn't seem to realize he had spoken aloud.

"Your Majesty, if that woman's presence is upsetting, I am sure we can find another place for her to spend the afternoon," Marquis Corbeau said.

Fiora stiffened. She had done it again. Said too much and been too much herself and brought out the worst in a situation. She had even managed to shake King Gustave's calm demeanor. Maybe it would be better if she left.

But Gustave shook his head.

"The lady will stay here as long as she wants. I find her presence quite refreshing."

He gave Fiora a bright smile. She returned it with a small one of her own. She had no idea why Gustave enjoyed her company, but she wouldn't ask too many questions since she needed a place to stay.

"So what message of thanks would you like to send Princess Elspeth?" the scribe said.

Gustave turned to Fiora and raised his eyebrow in a challenge.

Oh, it was like that, was it? Fiora considered the mirror. It was nice, as mirrors went. The glass was smooth and clear without flaws. The frame was elegant and would suit a variety of rooms.

It looked nothing like the rest of the decorations in the castle at Kell. The tiny mirror in Fiora's room had been framed in wood with bubbles in the glass. They must have imported it from somewhere. Perhaps sent someone on a shopping mission to find a suitable gift for the King of Montaigne.

But why go to all that trouble? Perhaps Elspeth had set her sights on King Gustave and hoped to catch his attention and marry him.

But that seemed unlikely. If they had never met, there was no reason for Elspeth to choose Gustave as the object of her affection.

And if they had met, there was no need to win him over with a gift.

It seemed more likely that the gift actually came from their father. King Fergal was always looking for allies. Perhaps this gift was a way to open communications with Montaigne and eventually seek their aid.

But if that was the case, why send the gift in Elspeth's name?

Perhaps this was the match her father had in mind for Elspeth. The opportunity he had decided not to squander on his unmarriageable older daughter.

Fiora realized she was scowling at the memory and tried to push thoughts of her family out of her mind. They were done with her, so she was done with them. It would do no good to dwell on the past.

She wished the hurt would go away so easily.

"The polite response is to thank her for such a practical gift and say it will suit the décor in your castle perfectly, as no doubt she intended."

Gustave gestured for her to go on. Fiora grinned.

"The more tempting response is to compliment her on knowing you so well. Not everyone would realize that you find your own face vastly superior to anything a so-called master could paint."

Gustave snorted in surprise. The servants stared in wonder as their king doubled over with laughter. Marquis Corbeau glared at Fiora, and she gave him the most innocent smile she could manage.

"Perhaps we should take a break from opening gifts," Marquis Corbeau said. "It seems Your Majesty is unable to form reasonable messages of thanks at the moment. It will take months to finish at this rate."

"My apologies, Marquis," Gustave said when he regained his composure.

But he didn't sound sorry at all. Marquis Corbeau's scowl deepened.

"Leave the presents here in the library," he instructed the servants. "King Gustave will finish opening them when he is in a more suitable frame of mind. Perhaps we should all prepare for dinner now."

The servants nodded and returned the gifts they held to the enormous stacks of boxes. They leaned the mirror against the wall beside the sweater and painting of Lady Annabelle.

"Your message of thanks for the mirror?" the scribe prompted.

"I thank Princess Elspeth for a gift that is as practical as it is elegant," Gustave said.

The scribe nodded and began to write. Gustave stood and offered his arm to Fiora. She hesitated only a moment this time before taking it.

❧ 27 ❧

Gustave escorted Fiora back to her room and bowed when she released his arm.

"I'm afraid we annoyed the marquis so much that he let us go well before dinner. You have a few hours to spend as you wish."

She nodded, not quite sure what to say to that. Or what to say to Gustave in general. She escaped into her room and sighed with relief. If no one had recognized her so far, surely she was safe in her disguise. She could spend the night in the castle and meet with Zoe in the morning to retrieve the shell and figure out what was wrong with her enchantment.

Fiora considered looking for a productive way to pass the time, but decided to nap instead. It had been a trying day, to say the least.

She slipped out of her dress and collapsed onto the bed. Her head sank into the feather pillow, and she sighed in silent content-ment. She had missed human beds. They were so much better than the rocky ledges that mermaids slept on.

She awoke to the sound of knocking. Fiora tried to call to whoever was at her door. Her lips moved but made no sound.

She cursed silently. Not having a voice was horrendous. How

many times had she called for someone to enter a room without thinking twice about it?

Not nearly as often as she had yelled for them to stay out and go away.

Fiora crawled out of bed, wrapped a robe around herself, and stumbled to the door. She pulled it open and blinked at the servant who smiled at her.

The servant curtsied.

"I'm to help you get ready for dinner, miss."

"*A-n-d I k-n-o-w s-i-g-n-s.*"

She spelled each word slowly

"At least, I know the alphabet," she said with a cheerful smile. "You can spell words to me if you need to."

"*V-e-r-y w-e-l-l.*"

Fiora signed each letter as slowly as the servant had. The girl nodded her understanding.

"We put a few gowns tailored to your size in the wardrobe. Do you have a preference on what you wear?"

Fiora raised her hands to say no, then stopped herself. She might as well see what was available. If something happened, and she needed to run away, she should make sure she was wearing an expensive dress.

All the gowns in the wardrobe looked expensive. Fiora blinked, taking in the array of fine fabrics and beautiful embroidery. How had they assembled such a wardrobe so quickly?

A pink silk gown caught her eye. She pulled it out to study the embroidery on the sleeves. It was a different style than the patterns she had learned in Kell. More delicate and intricate.

"Very good, miss," the servant said. "The pink fabric will look lovely with your hair."

Fiora blinked. What was the girl talking about? The color wouldn't suit her red hair at all.

Then she remembered her hair was black now. She could wear any color she wanted without worrying about how it might clash.

She pulled the pink gown out of the wardrobe, and the servant helped her into it. Then she twisted Fiora's hair into a simple but elegant style.

That seemed to be Montaigne's motto. Simple but elegant.

"You look lovely, miss."

And she did. If Fiora's feet didn't ache so much, she would have twirled in front of the mirror when she finished dressing. Instead, she nodded her approval.

"T-h-a-n-k y-o-u."

"Oh, it's my pleasure. Now which shoes would you like?"

Fiora limped back to the wardrobe and tried to convince herself that the pain in her feet was not so bad. That she could take advantage of the lovely things the royal family had provided and wear something that suited her gown.

Her slippers were still under a chair in the dowager queen's sewing room, so those were not an option. That left several pairs of fashionable heels in her size. Fiora selected an elegant white pair decorated with tiny pearls.

Pain shot up her legs as soon as she put them on, and Fiora grabbed the servant's arm to catch her balance. She kicked off the shoes and sank onto a nearby chair. Sweat beaded on her forehead.

"Are you well, miss?"

Blast it all, why did her feet hurt so much? It was the oysters all over again. Pain for the sake of beauty.

Well, they could keep it. Her best efforts to be beautiful had never done Fiora any good anyway.

"N-o s-h-o-e-s," Fiora signed.

The servant looked concerned but didn't protest. Instead, she pulled a pair of elegant silk stockings from a drawer and helped Fiora put them on.

"We'll see how clean the maids are keeping the floor," she said. "Yesterday one of them told me you could walk through this castle in your stockinged feet without encountering a speck of dust."

She smiled, and Fiora tried to smile back. Hopefully the royal family would not banish her from the palace for not wearing appropriate footwear. She was willing to spend the night in the woods, but she didn't particularly want to.

She stood and relaxed a little when the intense pain did not return. It seemed she would be fine as long as she went barefoot.

Besides, the pink gown had a long, full skirt. Maybe no one would notice.

৩৯৩

"WHY AREN'T YOU WEARING ANY SHOES?"

Lady Annabelle said this as if she were scolding a young child who ought to know better.

Fiora glared at her and adjusted her skirt to cover her feet. This was not a good start.

"I suppose we should be glad you're wearing any clothes at all."

She was one to talk. Fiora wanted to make a snide comment about the painting, but that was impossible without her voice. She had to settle for a raised eyebrow instead.

Lady Annabelle giggled and looked around the room, clearly expecting everyone to laugh along with her joke.

To Fiora's relief, the other guests either hadn't heard the comment or were pretending they hadn't. An assortment of council members, castle staff, and guests milled around the parlor talking and sipping drinks before the meal began. Not one of them laughed.

"You look lovely, dear," Dowager Queen Bernadine said as Thomas rolled her chair towards them. "That shade of pink suits you nicely."

Fiora gave a little curtsy as thanks.

"Dowager Queen Bernadine, thank goodness you are here,"

Lady Annabelle said. "I feel rude not addressing your guest by her name, but since I don't understand sign language I haven't been able to ask her what she calls herself."

Fiora shot a dirty look at Lady Annabelle, who batted her eyes, all innocence. Thomas translated Lady Annabelle's words for the dowager queen.

"*I don't know who she thinks she's fooling with all that simpering,*" Dowager Queen Bernadine signed. "*I've seen cows with better acting skills.*"

Her face remained neutral, as if she were commenting on the weather. Fiora's eyes widened in surprise, and she pressed her lips together to hide a grin. Lady Annabelle watched their interaction with a deepening scowl.

"*But we should call you something,*" the dowager queen continued. "*What do you prefer?*"

"What are you saying?" Annabelle asked.

"Her Highness asked the young lady what she would prefer to be called," Thomas said, reversing his role to translate sign language into speech.

Fiora noticed he didn't mention the cow comment. It was probably wise to side with the dowager queen over Lady Annabelle.

"If she won't tell us her name, we'll have to make something up," Lady Annabelle said. "Perhaps Sandy since she was found on the beach."

She giggled, once again laughing at her own joke.

"*Oh merciful heavens,*" Dowager Queen Bernadine signed.

Lady Annabelle scowled.

"You can speak out loud, Your Majesty. She does seem capable of understanding speech."

"If you wanted to be included in every conversation, you should have bothered to learn sign language," Dowager Queen Bernadine said. "Sometimes my voice gets tired, and it is easier for me to sign."

She winked at Fiora, who fought back an ever widening smile. No one with ears would believe that Dowager Queen Bernadine's voice was tired. She was always the loudest person in the room.

Lady Annabelle blinked, and Dowager Queen Bernadine turned back to Fiora.

"Well, what do you think? Would you like to be called Sandy after the beach you were found on?"

Lady Annabelle glared at Fiora as if it were her fault that the dowager queen was choosing to leave her out of the conversation.

"Perhaps Mer?" Gustave suggested.

Both Fiora and Lady Annabelle jumped. Neither had realized that Gustave was nearby or paying attention to their conversation. Fiora shifted her weight to the balls of her feet, ready to run if necessary. Why had he suggested such a name? Had he guessed that she was a mermaid?

"That's a bit short," Dowager Queen Bernadine said after Thomas translated. "Perhaps Lady Mer?"

"She isn't a lady," Lady Annabelle said. "You can't just walk around giving people royal titles."

Dowager Queen Bernadine cackled.

"That is literally one of my jobs. To give royal titles to people who deserve them."

"But she doesn't deserve it," Annabelle said. "She hasn't done anything to earn a title."

"It's a nickname," Dowager Queen Bernadine said. "Don't be so literal."

"Why Mer?" Fiora signed to Gustave.

For that matter, why add a title to it? If they had guessed her true identity, she would rather know now instead of dancing around the matter.

"Mer means sea," Gustave said. "It seems appropriate."

"It's better than Sandy, but not by much," Dowager Queen Bernadine said.

She gave her grandson a critical look. He shrugged, and the dowager queen turned her attention back to Fiora.

"Are you sure you can't tell us your real name? I think it would save a great deal of trouble down the road."

She gave Fiora a searching look, and something glittered in her eyes. Understanding? Recognition? Fiora tried to remember if she had ever met Dowager Queen Bernadine. Surely not. She would definitely remember that encounter.

But if Dowager Queen Bernadine hadn't guessed her true identity, what was she trying to accomplish with her antics?

Maybe she just wanted to annoy Lady Annabelle. Fiora understood the feeling.

Or maybe Dowager Queen Bernadine was just the kind of person who was always up to something.

That seemed likely. Fiora relaxed a little. Maybe it wouldn't be necessary to run after all. Lady Mer was an innocent enough nickname so long as they hadn't actually made the connection to her true identity.

"You may call me Lady Mer if you like."

"Lady Mer it is then," Dowager Queen Bernadine said. "Because you are a true lady of the sea."

It was closer to the truth than Fiora would have liked, and the sparkle in the dowager queen's eyes set off warning bells in her head. Bernadine may not know the truth exactly, but she seemed to know something.

"I believe they're ready for us to go to the dining room," Lady Annabelle said.

She batted her eyes at Gustave, making it clear that she expected him to escort her to the table and sit beside her.

Kara hurried forward.

"Your Majesty, I was hoping I could ask your opinion about something tonight."

It was the most Fiora had ever heard Kara speak, and Kara also seemed to think it was a bit much. She whispered an apology for interrupting and ducked back into the crowd to stand beside Princess Collette. Lady Annabelle's eyes followed her, as if daring her to try that again.

They were worse than vultures. Fiora searched the room for Elaine but didn't see her. The other marriage prospect was either not as desperate as the rest or was playing hard to get.

Gustave's eyes darted around the room. He seemed well aware that he was the center of attention. Fiora felt a pang of sympathy for all the princes she had met while competing in Princess Tests. She had never considered how uncomfortable it would be to have your every move analyzed while so many women vied for your attention.

"Lady Mer, will you walk with me to dinner?"

Fiora blinked in surprise. Why would he choose her when he had so many ladies competing for his affection?

Maybe because she wasn't competing or even a viable option. Young ladies fished out of the sea did not wed kings.

Gustave offered his arm, and Fiora took it. She tried not to look smug, but she couldn't resist a backwards glance at Lady Annabelle. It served her right to be snubbed. Lady Annabelle stared back, meeting Fiora's gaze with an expression that said this was far from over.

Then she rushed over to Kara, who was staring at the floor to hide her disappointment.

"Why did he choose her?" Lady Annabelle hissed. "She isn't even wearing shoes!"

❧ 28 ❧

Gustave hadn't expected his choice of dinner companion to cause such a stir. In retrospect, he should have expected it to cause more of a stir. He was supposed to be choosing a bride, and he had ignored the ladies hand-picked by his family and council in favor of one literally pulled from the sea.

He didn't regret the choice. In spite of the jealous looks and frantic whispers, he was glad to have Lady Mer by his side. He helped her into her seat and noted the way she studied the place setting.

"Are you familiar with formal dining etiquette? I am happy to show you which forks to use if needed."

He signed the words so she wouldn't be embarrassed to accept his help. She raised an eyebrow and tapped the forks in the order they would be used. Gustave flushed. He shouldn't have assumed she would have unrefined table manners because she came from the sea.

Blast it all, that was a perfectly normal thing to assume. Who was she?

He needed better ways to gather information about her. No matter if she was shy or cursed, the result was the same. She refused to say anything about herself. If she was shy, maybe it was just a matter of winning her trust over time. A curse would be more difficult, but Prince Stefan had managed to drop hints when he was cursed to be a frog. Surely Lady Mer could do the same.

Maybe she was already dropping hints. Maybe Gustave had missed them.

Waiters placed bowls of soup on the table in a movement so synchronized that it looked like a dance. Lady Mer watched Dowager Queen Bernadine, waiting to pick up her spoon until the hostess began to eat.

Perhaps giving her a title wasn't such a stretch after all. She clearly knew how to behave in polite company.

Had she confessed something about her identity to his grandmother? Or maybe they had met before. Was that why the dowager queen had invited Lady Mer to stay and suggested the title?

"Begging your pardon, Princess, but which of these do I use first?"

The question came from down the table. Dale had been invited to dinner with the rest of the gala guests, and he stared at the collection of silverware in front of him as if it were an array of torture devices. Collette showed him, and the merchant began to eat. Marquis Corbeau looked exasperated by his presence. Especially when Dale's spoon slipped from his fingers and landed in his soup with a splash.

"Sorry. I'm not used to such fine company. My ships transport luxury wares, but I've never used them myself. What would my daughters say if they could see me now?"

Princess Collette hurriedly apologized to Dale for not instructing him on how to use the spoon beforehand. They apologized back and forth to each other until Dowager Queen Bernadine told them to stop talking and eat their soup before it got cold.

Lady Mer caught Gustave's eye and raised an eyebrow. The

gesture asked her question as effectively as words could have. Maybe more so, since it was discrete.

"Dale Mercer. He's a merchant whose ships were destroyed in a kraken attack. Well, most of them were. One may have survived, and he came here to investigate the report. We invited him to stay until he can learn the ship's whereabouts and find passage home."

Gustave answered in sign language so Dale wouldn't overhear. Lady Mer raised her other eyebrow.

"You weren't responsible for the destruction of his ship. Why go to such trouble to help him?"

"Why not help him when it is within our power to do so?"

She blinked in surprise, as if she had never considered the possibility of helping someone for its own sake.

Given the circumstances Gustave had found her in, she probably wasn't used to random kindness.

Blast it all, why had she been in the ocean? No matter how hard Gustave thought, he couldn't come up with a single scenario that involved a respectable young lady naked and alone on the beach. What had happened?

He raised his hands to sign the question, then lowered them. He could ask her, but what if she ran away again? Even asking her name had upset her enough to make her flee.

If she was cursed, revealing information must come with serious consequences.

If magic wasn't at work, had someone mistreated her in the past? Was that why she didn't trust them with her true identity? Was she running from someone?

"Do you like the soup, Your Majesty?" Kara asked from the other side of the table.

"What? Oh, yes, it's very good."

Kara smiled at him and blushed bright red.

"I love soup," Lady Annabelle said. "The castle chef always makes the best soup every time I visit. I've had his soup before, but this recipe is new."

Gustave gave her a strained smile. Thank goodness he only had to endure this for a few more days. They would go home after his birthday gala.

Wouldn't they? Surely they would.

Only, if he wasn't engaged by then, they might be asked to stay.

That alone could be enough reason to pick a random lady at the ball and propose.

Lady Mer was trying not to laugh. Gustave frowned at her.

"You find this funny?"

She nodded.

"I had pumpkin soup the last time I visited," Lady Annabelle said. "Do you remember that, Your Majesty? Do you like pumpkin soup?"

Lady Mer's smile widened.

"What do you find so funny about soup?" Gustave signed.

She shook her head.

"It isn't about the soup. They're trying to engage you in conversation by asking about things you like. You said you liked the soup, so they're trying to use that to catch your interest. Say you like something else and see what happens."

"I understand that Your Majesty wants to make your guest feel welcome," Marquis Corbeau said, "But you should not exclude everyone else from the conversation. Perhaps Thomas could translate the young lady's words so everyone can have the privilege of her comments?"

Gustave bowed his head.

"My apologies. I was just telling Lady Mer how intriguing I found the seagull that visited her in the sewing room today."

"Wasn't it charming?" Lady Annabelle said. "I adore seagulls."

Gustave gave Lady Mer a surprised look. She nodded her head, clearly saying "I told you so."

"Lady Mer?" Marquis Corbeau said. "So you discovered her identity? That's marvelous! Where is your family's estate, lady?"

He sounded as enthusiastic about calling her by a title as he would have been to learn that Princess Collette had invited more guests to the castle.

Lady Mer's eyes grew wide with panic at Marquis Corbeau's question. Gustave stared into them, noticing again how blue they were. They looked so familiar, but surely he would remember those eyes if he had seen them before.

"It's only a nickname," Lady Annabelle said. "She isn't really a lady."

Marquis Corbeau relaxed a little.

"That is a little strange, don't you think? Giving her a title as a nickname?"

"We have to call her something," Dowager Queen Bernadine said.

"Do we?" Marquis Corbeau said. "Why not simply address her as miss?"

"Or madam," Lady Annabelle said. "Perhaps she's married. She is wearing a ring."

All eyes turned to Lady Mer. She ducked her head and looked like she was seriously considering climbing under the table. Gustave searched for something to say to keep her from running away again.

"Are you married?"

Stupid! Why did he always say whatever he was thinking around her? It was no wonder she had run away. No matter how much he wanted to know, she clearly didn't want to answer questions about herself.

Lady Mer met his gaze.

"No, I'm not married."

"She said she's not married," Dowager Queen Bernadine translated loudly for everyone.

Gustave relaxed, although he didn't know why. Why did he care if she was married?

He shouldn't care. He was in love with someone else. This girl's fate meant nothing to him.

The thought was accompanied by the memory of a song. That sweet voice that had healed him on the beach.

"I understand Your Majesty opened birthday gifts this afternoon," Kara said. "Did you receive anything interesting?"

It was a perfectly innocent question, but it made Gustave choke on his soup and sent Lady Mer into a fit of silent laughter. The scene was distracting enough that everyone at the table noticed. Kara frowned.

"Have I said something wrong?"

She looked to Collette for help, but Collette simply shrugged in confusion.

"I take it some of the gifts were very interesting," Elaine commented.

She had been so quiet throughout the evening that Gustave had almost forgotten she was there. He nodded.

"Excessively interesting."

"Indeed?" Lady Annabelle said.

She leaned forward, her eyes taking on a predatory gleam that made Gustave's throat go dry.

"Are you going to tell her you've already opened it?" Lady Mer signed.

Gustave shook his head. He had no idea how that conversation would go, but it was not one he wanted to have. Especially at the dinner table.

"Best to talk about the sweater then. Thomas, please tell everyone that I said that King Gustave received a most interesting sweater from the Aeonian royal family."

Thomas relayed the message. Lady Annabelle looked disappointed, but quickly rallied.

"A sweater? How interesting. Made from cashmere, of course. I adore Aeonian cashmere."

"I'd like to see it sometime," Kara said. "The royal tailor of

Aeonia is known for his bold designs. I'm sure his knitwear is quite unique."

Unlike Lady Annabelle, her interest in the sweater seemed genuine. Gustave vaguely remembered that she had been knitting at his grandmother's sewing circle.

"Unique is one word for it," he said. "One of the librarians could show it to you any time you like."

"Oh. Thank you."

Kara sounded disappointed. Gustave couldn't imagine why. He had offered her exactly what she wanted.

"She wanted you to show it to her," Lady Mer signed.

Oh. Now Gustave felt like an idiot. However genuine Kara's interest in knitting may be, she was apparently more interested in him.

No wonder the council had chosen to relieve him of administrative duties so he could focus on finding a bride. He was rather bad at wooing ladies.

But then, he wasn't trying to woo any of these ladies.

Still, Gustave wasn't sure things would have gone much better if he had been making a genuine effort.

In fact, they might have gone worse.

Lady Mer ate her soup with an innocent expression, but merriment twinkled in her eyes.

"You find this amusing."

Gustave signed the accusation. Lady Mer took another bite and did not deny it.

"Princess Collette did well today," Marchioness Rouge said, filling in the awkward silence that had spread through the dining room. "She is settling into her temporary duties very well."

"Tell me all about it," Gustave said, eager to move the focus to someone else.

Collette's eyes sparkled as she told the assembled guests about her first day of administration. It had mostly involved training with Marchioness Rouge and the royal treasurer, but she had still enjoyed it.

Other than the gleam in Lady Annabelle's eyes when she learned that Princess Collette was now helping with administrative responsibilities so that Gustave could focus on the gala, the rest of the dinner passed without incident.

❧ 29 ❧

Fiora woke up to the sound of tapping. The silvery glow of moonlight made her think she was underwater again.

Until she pushed off her bed, expecting to float towards the ceiling, and crashed onto the floor instead.

Fiora stayed on the floor for a moment, recovering her breath and trying to remember where she was.

Montaigne. In the castle. She was a guest of the royal family.

And something was tapping on her window.

She pulled herself up, wondering why she had ever missed being on land. Balancing on feet was much harder than floating through water.

Especially when those feet hurt more with every step she took.

But never mind that. What on earth was tapping on her window? She was on the third floor. That was quite a climb.

Fiora stumbled over and pushed it open. Something flew through past her in a blur of feathers and landed on her bed.

"Squawk."

Spot dropped a seashell onto her pillow and looked at her with expectant eyes.

Fiora sighed. She didn't have any food. But even if she could speak and tell him that, the bird wouldn't understand her.

She held her hands out, palms open, so Spot could see they were empty.

"Squawk."

He ruffled his feathers indignantly and flew out the window. Fiora picked up the shell and held it to the moonlight to study the carvings.

It was Zoe's again.

This must mean her cousin was waiting to meet her. Probably in the same place along the shoreline.

And hopefully she had brought the second conch shell with her so that Fiora could figure out why her feet were hurting so much.

Fiora wished Zoe had waited until morning. It would have been easier to get to the garden in daylight.

But if her cousin was waiting, Fiora would just have to find a way to get to the beach.

She wrapped a robe around herself and sighed, missing the satisfaction of making a sound as she did so. Strangely, she also missed the stream of bubbles that would have accompanied the sigh if she had been a mermaid.

Fiora crept across the room and turned the latch slowly. It clicked, and the sound echoed through the empty hallway. Those elegant marble floors amplified every sound in the castle.

She left the door slightly open, not willing to risk another latch click, and walked along the edge of the hallway, hoping to be mistaken for a servant if she was seen at all.

The castle was empty. Apparently everyone was already in bed.

Now, which way was the garden?

Fiora should have paid more attention when following people around the castle. She had only a vague sense of where she was, and everything looked different at night.

After ten minutes of wandering through hallways, Fiora had to admit she was lost. Her castle in Kell had been small and easy to navigate. Mermaid dwellings were so open that you could always see where you were going through the numerous holes in the walls and ceilings.

The Montaigne castle was an elegant marble maze.

Fiora fought back the panic building in her chest. Not only did she not know the way to the gardens, but she wasn't sure she could make it back to her room either.

That would be difficult to explain to whoever found her.

Fiora flattened against the wall as a sound filled the hallway. She listened for a moment, then relaxed.

Somewhere in the castle, someone was singing. The sound echoed against the marble, making it impossible to decipher the words. The singer was female, but the music echoed too much for Fiora to say more than that.

There was a trace of magic in that voice. Had Zoe somehow come into the castle to look for Fiora?

Only one way to find out. Even if it wasn't Zoe, the singer might know the way to the garden.

Fiora turned slowly in a circle, trying to find the direction the sound was coming from. She picked the hallway where it seemed the loudest and began to walk.

The feeling of magic intensified as Fiora moved through the castle towards the music. The voice became a little clearer. It definitely wasn't Zoe singing, and it didn't feel quite like mermaid magic.

Fiora had never heard a human weave magic with singing before. Usually they just spoke enchantments to magical gems.

The song seemed vaguely familiar, but the echoing against the marble distorted the melody and voice, so she couldn't quite place them.

She swallowed. Maybe it would be better not to disturb the singer. What if they reported her to the royal family or insisted on taking her back to her room rather than showing her to the garden? It would probably be better to keep searching on her own.

Fiora turned away from the music to retrace her steps and ran into something warm and solid.

Rather, someone.

She screamed. Or at least she tried. It came out as a sort of raspy cough that faded into silence.

The man stepped back, just as surprised as she was, and Fiora recognized King Gustave.

She leaned against the wall as her heart pounded in her chest. Gustave blinked, looking confused. Had he been sleep walking?

"Lady Mer?" he finally said.

Fiora nodded and stepped into a patch of moonlight streaming through a window so Gustave could see her more clearly.

"I- That is- Are you alright?"

Gustave looked around the hallway, and Fiora felt she should be asking him if he was alright. He still seemed a little dazed.

"I'm fine."

She turned to walk away. The last thing she needed was to linger alone with the king in the middle of the night. Fiora would leave those sorts of strategies to Lady Annabelle. She was done trying to win the hearts of men.

"Don't go."

Desperation tinged Gustave's voice. He grabbed her hand as he said it, and Fiora pulled away as if she had been stung by a jellyfish. Gustave retracted his hand just as quickly.

"I'm sorry! I didn't mean to hurt you. I just- I didn't want to be alone."

He still looked confused. Fiora knew from recent experience how alarming it was to wake up and not know where you were. Who would have guessed the King of Montaigne was a sleep walker?

She crossed her arms over her chest but stayed where she was. Gustave stared at her face, then down at the floor.

"I mean- That is-"

Fiora smiled in spite of everything. His awkwardness was rather endearing.

"It's alright, Your Majesty."

He didn't see her signs because he was still staring at the floor. She tapped his arm to get his attention, which caused him to jump in surprise. She repeated the signs, and he relaxed a little.

"I dreamed I heard a voice," he said. "I thought it might be the woman who saved me on the beach, and I was trying to find her."

Fiora pressed her lips together to keep from smiling. That was more ironic than Gustave knew, but she couldn't tell him why. He misinterpreted her expression for disapproval.

"I just want to thank her. I-"

The singing, which Fiora had not realized had stopped, suddenly began again. They looked towards the sound, then to each other. Gustave blinked.

"I love her," he said.

Fiora stepped back.

"What do you mean?"

"She saved my life, and I love her."

Fiora swallowed. Surely that wasn't true. No one fell in love that easily. Especially not with her.

"Your Majesty is still half-asleep."

"No, it's true," Gustave insisted.

Fiora glanced down at her pearl ring. The gem was as dull as ever. If Gustave actually loved her, it would glisten with magic again.

She shook her head. It would do no good arguing with him. She had her own problems to worry about.

"I should go."

"Where? What are you doing up so late?"

He was more awake now. Aware enough to be suspicious.

Fiora bit her lip. She could say she wanted fresh air and a stroll in the garden, but what normal guest sneaked out of their room for a midnight walk along the beach?

King Gustave was probably too polite to question the statement, but Fiora couldn't afford to raise suspicions. Besides, he might insist on accompanying her on her walk. What would happen if he saw Zoe?

"I couldn't sleep. I wanted to borrow a book from the library, but I lost my way."

"Allow me to escort you."

Gustave offered his arm. Fiora said a silent apology to Zoe as she took it. She hated to leave her cousin waiting by the shore, but what else could she do?

"These hallways do all look the same. Especially at night. The best way to keep track of where you are is to watch the artwork. Each wing of the castle contains different collections. We're still in the bedroom wing, which contains family portraits. That one is my grandmother at her coronation."

The painting showed a woman in her thirties. Bernadine looked fierce in spite of the artist's efforts to portray her as a serene figure. Fiora smiled.

"And her wedding portrait," Gustave said, leading Fiora to a painting further down the hall. "Familiarize yourself with these, and it will be easier to find your way back to your room."

Fiora nodded, nearly laughing at how dissimilar Bernadine and her husband looked in the wedding portrait. The king was a round, jolly sort of man, while Bernadine was all angles and intensity.

Perhaps opposites really did attract.

She studied the portraits as they walked, doing her best to memorize them so she could find her way back down the hallway again. She would need to sneak out later if she couldn't find a way to escape King Gustave and meet Zoe.

As Gustave had said, this wing contained family portraits. Fiora wondered if everyone was actually as happy as they looked in the paintings. If so, the royal family of Montaigne must be one of the most contented in Myora. The royal family of Kell never looked or acted this happy. Her stepmother's face was always pinched as she expressed disapproval about anything unlucky enough to cross her path. Her father yelled at everyone. Even Elspeth on occasion, and she was his pride and joy.

Gustave paused in front of a painting of a man with an enormous wavy beard. His eyes were kind and somehow familiar. Fiora blinked as she realized they were the same as Gustave's.

"Your father?"

Gustave nodded.

"Lady Mer, meet King Francois of Montaigne. I know he would enjoy your company if he were here to welcome you."

Tears sparkled in Gustave's eyes. Fiora couldn't imagine missing anyone that much. Let alone her father. She curtsied to the painting.

"It will be my honor to meet you someday, Your Majesty."

She signed to the painting, and Gustave smiled at her. Then he raised his hand to his mouth and whispered, "Find King Francois," to his ring.

A red light shone out the window towards the sea. Gustave pulled a compass from his pocket and checked the direction.

"He still hasn't moved, which means he must still be underwater. I think the mermaids must be holding him prisoner under the sea."

Fiora blinked. If the mermaids had any human prisoners, she knew nothing about it. It seemed unlikely, but she couldn't tell Gustave that without explaining why she knew it.

And she was not willing to do that.

"They were singing when I was there," he said. "Mermaids were singing underwater, and then a kraken attacked. I need to go back there to investigate. There has to be a way."

He studied Fiora for a moment, as if deciding how much to trust her.

"A mermaid named Kathelin gave me this shell," he whispered, pulling a small shell from his pocket and handing it to Fiora. "I thought perhaps it was magic. A way to contact them. But it doesn't seem to do anything."

Fiora took the shell and turned it over in her hand to study it. It was carved with a song. A transformation enchantment. Perhaps Kathelin had given this to Gustave, expecting that he would be able to read it, transform himself, and come speak with her.

Although, it didn't exactly seem a practical plan, since the enchantment would turn Gustave into a frog.

Fiora thought back to the vision she had seen in the golden ball. Perhaps this was the enchantment that had been used to transform the talking frog she had seen in the vision. Interesting, but it didn't help at all with her problem.

She handed the shell back to Gustave and shrugged.

"The carvings are pretty," she signed.

Gustave nodded. He looked so disappointed, that Fiora couldn't resist adding, *"I grew up by the sea. A sailor once told me that mermaids carve enchanted songs onto shells. Perhaps it is a spell?"*

Gustave's eyes brightened.

"You think it's an enchantment I need to perform?"

"Perhaps."

He looked so hopeful that Fiora regretted saying anything. Even if he did manage to turn himself into a frog or contact Kathelin, it wouldn't help him find his father. Queen Gallerus had not trusted humans since Fiora's mother died. She certainly wouldn't help one human search for another.

"The singing stopped," Gustave said.

Fiora listened, but heard only the familiar sounds of land at night. A combination of crickets, night birds, and wind rustling through the trees. This mixed with the sounds of the ocean. Waves and seagulls.

"It is late," she signed. *"I can do without a book if you would rather go back to bed."*

Gustave shook his head.

"I don't think I could fall asleep now. I might open a few more birthday gifts and write thank you notes. I only have a few royal duties right now. I shouldn't shirk my responsibilities."

So much for ditching King Gustave. But if Fiora remembered correctly, the library was not far from the garden door. Maybe she could sneak away once he was distracted by the presents.

She took his arm, and they continued walking through the hallway. Fiora watched the portraits, noting each time King Francois appeared in them. The king's face made her feel she knew him. Was it because he reminded her of Gustave, or had she met him in person at some state event? It was certainly possible that he had attended a Princess Test she had competed in.

They rounded a corner, and Fiora froze. Gustave kept walking. His arm slipped from her fingers, but she didn't notice. She was too busy staring at the portrait on the wall.

It was him.

She walked towards the painting as if in a trance, wondering if it was simply a trick of the moonlight.

But no, it was him.

It was a painting of her statue. The boy above the grotto.

He wore the same clothes, although they looked different in color than in stone. He had the same friendly expression. The same eyes that had always invited her to talk while he listened.

The only difference was that the boy in the painting held a scepter in his hand. So that was what had broken off the statue.

How? How was he here?

Fiora ran her fingertips along the golden frame, searching the boy's face for answers. Then she looked down at the nameplate and gasped.

Gustave.

The statue in her mermaid garden was King Gustave.

But that was impossible.

She looked from the painting to the real Gustave, who was watching her with confusion.

"Yes, that's me," he said, laughing awkwardly as Fiora looked from the painting back to him again. "Grandmother commissioned that from an artist in Eldria to celebrate my father officially naming me his heir. There was a statue as well, but it fell overboard in a storm and was never recovered."

Fiora nodded slowly, too stunned to say anything.

King Gustave was her statue. The boy she had looked for all those years.

Well, the man now. Humans changed when statues didn't.

Perhaps it wasn't so surprising. The mermaid's summer home was close to Montaigne. Royalty were more likely to be carved into statues than common folk.

"Is something wrong, Lady Mer?"

Fiora tried to regain her composure. A normal person would not react so strongly to a simple portrait. She tore her eyes away from the painting and focused on King Gustave, trying to make out a resemblance to the statue that had been her only friend in childhood. Now that she knew it was him, she did see a resemblance in the eyes. Or maybe that was wishful thinking. She stared so hard that Gustave flushed with embarrassment.

"Shall we continue to the library? There are other paintings of me we can look at along the way. And some of Collette."

He offered his arm. Fiora nodded slowly and took it. She held onto him a little too tightly as they walked, reluctant to let him go now that she had found him.

✿ 30 ✿

By the time they reached the library, Lady Mer had regained her composure. Gustave resisted the urge to stare at her and forced himself to act as if everything was normal.

Why had his childhood portrait fascinated her so much? She hadn't found any of the other portraits as interesting.

Just that one painting of him as a boy.

It had caught her interest even before she knew it was him. It was all very strange. Another mystery.

Lady Mer let go of his arm and walked, not to the shelves of books, but to the window. She stared at the moonlit ocean, searching for something Gustave could only guess at.

He had nothing but guesses where Lady Mer was concerned. Half-formed questions with no answers.

Gustave surveyed the library, half expecting to find the woman from the beach there. Surely that had been her voice echoing through the halls. And it hadn't been a dream. Lady Mer had heard it as well.

But he saw no one. The singing made no more sense than Lady Mer's fascination with his portrait. How would the woman from the beach get into the castle? Why would she sing in the middle of the night?

Maybe she lived here. Maybe she was a servant in the castle, and that was why she was afraid to show her face. Perhaps she had been taking a break from her duties that day and didn't want the royal family to know.

It made as much sense as anything else he could think of.

But why would she sing to summon him and then run away? Why was she so afraid of everyone but Gustave?

Gustave turned from the window to face the mountain of presents piled against the wall. If he opened enough of these tonight, maybe he would have time tomorrow to strategize with Captain Whist about forming another expedition to search for his father. He picked a small package from the pile and carried it over to the scribe's desk. Motion in the corner of the room reflected in the mirror and caught his eye.

He turned to see what the mirror was reflecting, but there was nothing there. Lady Mer sat on the windowsill staring at the ocean. The rest of the library was empty except for moonlight and shadows.

Gustave rubbed his eyes. All those blows to the head had not done him any favors. It was not like him to be jumpy and imagine things.

He read the label on the box he had selected. This was a gift from the royal family of Fletcher. Hopefully something more typical than the rest of the gifts he had received so far.

Gustave tore the paper and pulled aside velvet fabric to reveal a small golden arrow pin. He turned it over in his hands, admiring the way it gleamed in the moonlight. Now this was a normal birthday gift. He could wear it pinned to his cloak the next time he visited Fletcher or entertained their diplomats. They would see that he appreciated their gift, and he would be reminded that their arrows were the best in Myora. Both nations would benefit.

Gustave expected a note from King Richard or his heir,

Princess Marian, but instead found one from the king's younger brother, Prince John.

"I admire Your Majesty's dedication to excellence and trust you will do the same when you see excellence exhibited in the government of Fletcher in the future. Many happy wishes on your birthday. May you have a long and prosperous reign."

Gustave shrugged. The message was a little strange, but perhaps King Richard and Princess Marian were busy running their country and had delegated the gift giving to Prince John. He could understand that.

He dipped the quill into the inkwell and wrote, "I thank you for the beautiful pin and kind birthday wishes. I look forward to our countries' continued relationship."

Gustave signed his name, set the note aside so the ink could dry, and eyed the mountain of gifts. Which to open next?

He turned back to Lady Mer, who was still staring at the ocean. She had pulled her feet onto the windowsill and wrapped her arms around her legs as if she were trying to make herself as small as possible. Her dark hair hung loose over her shoulders like a cloak, and her enormous blue eyes glittered with moonlight and unshed tears.

Perhaps he could do something to cheer her.

"Would you like to choose the next gift to be opened, Lady Mer?"

She jumped in surprise, as if she had forgotten he was there. She cast one more look at the ocean, then nodded and walked towards the pile of gifts. Lady Mer looked from the presents to Gustave, making a show of choosing just the right one. Finally, she settled on a bright red package wrapped in silver ribbon. She picked it up and turned to the desk.

A low rumble shook the castle. An earthquake? As the shaking grew worse, Lady Mer dropped the box and put her arms out to steady herself. She stumbled backwards and crashed into the mountain of gifts. The pile wavered precariously, and another deep rumble echoed through the room. It almost sounded like laughter. Gustave saw a shadow move out of the corner of his eye. A violent jolt rocked the castle as he turned to search the room. Something crashed behind him.

Gustave whirled around just in time to see Lady Mer's terrified expression as the mountain of gifts fell over and buried her. She didn't scream. Of course she didn't. She made no sound as she disappeared beneath the boxes.

"Lady Mer!"

Gustave ran forward, dodging books that flew from the shelves as the earthquake continued. A good number of them landed on the avalanche of presents, further trapping Lady Mer. Gustave hoped that none of the presents were heavy. If anyone had sent gems or statues or coins, they could seriously injure Lady Mer. The pile of books wouldn't help matters.

"Lady Mer, I'm coming. Stay calm."

Not taking his own advice, Gustave's heart pounded as he frantically tried to uncover her. He grabbed boxes and tossed them across the room, not caring that he was abusing royal gifts. Something glass shattered when a bright purple box crashed into the scribe's desk. Probably some kind of priceless vase, but Gustave didn't stop.

If only Lady Mer could speak! If only she could call out so he would know where to dig.

This incident removed any suspicions Gustave had that Lady Mer could speak and was choosing not to. If she had a voice, surely she would call out for help now.

Unless she was dead.

Gustave shoved the thought from his mind. She was alive. She had to be!

He doubled his pace, throwing priceless books and gifts across the room with abandon. He shouted when he uncovered a hand in the debris. He grabbed it, and it grabbed back. Gustave let out a sigh of relief. She was alive.

"Just a moment more, and I'll have you out."

Lady Mer squeezed his hand before letting go so he could continue to dig. Gustave dug down until he freed her arm. She began grabbing boxes and throwing them aside as soon as she was able to move. Together, they worked until he found Lady Mer's face. She smiled with relief when she saw him. She had a scratch across her forehead and a bruise on her cheek, but looked like she hadn't been seriously injured.

Before he quite knew what he was doing, Gustave leaned forward and kissed her. Lady Mer wrapped her free arm around his shoulders, pulled him closer, and kissed him back.

The ground rumbled again. A book flew off a shelf and hit Gustave on the shoulder, bringing him back to his senses. He pulled away and stared at Lady Mer in horror. What had he done? Taken advantage of her helpless state and kissed her while she was trapped? No matter how happy he was to see her, such behavior was unthinkable.

"Please forgive me! I should not have- That is- I meant-"

Lady Mer's eyes flashed with annoyance, and Gustave felt his face go red. She couldn't answer him through sign language with one arm trapped. He would have to free the rest of her before she could give him the scolding he deserved.

He continued to dig her out, avoiding eye contact and being careful not to touch her as he removed the boxes. What had possessed him to kiss her?

Finally Lady Mer was uncovered enough for Gustave to pull her out. He wrapped his arms around her waist and pulled her free. Gifts and books tumbled down around her, and Gustave held her steady until she found her balance. They looked into each other's eyes, both searching and neither finding answers.

"Are you injured?" Gustave asked.

He let go of Lady Mer and pulled a chair over for her to sit in. She collapsed into it.

"Nothing serious. What happened?"

"An earthquake, I think."

Her expression darkened.

"Are those common here?"

Gustave shook his head. They were common enough that sailors knew to watch for large waves afterward, but earthquakes seldom happened in Montaigne.

This would affect sailing routes for a few days. He wouldn't be able to take a ship and look for his father until the sailors decided the risk of tidal waves had passed.

Blast it all.

The thought made him scowl. Lady Mer noticed his dark expression and hung her head. Gustave flushed. What was wrong with him this evening? Thinking about earthquakes when he needed to apologize for his atrocious behavior.

"I- I'm sorry I kissed you."

Her head shot up, and she stared at him with fire in her eyes.

"Say no more about it. It doesn't matter."

"But it does! That was an extremely inappropriate thing for me to do. I don't know what came over me."

"You were simply glad to find me alive. And now you regret it. There's no harm done."

Only Gustave didn't regret it, and her expression said there was certainly harm done. He tried to think of something he could say to make it better. Some way to apologize.

Some way to politely bring up the fact that she had kissed him back. To ask... To ask what exactly?

Before he could find the right words, Marchioness Rouge burst into the library.

"There you are, Your Highness! Thank goodness you're alright."

She turned back to the hallway and called out, "He's in the library! I found him!"

Then she returned to the library and surveyed Gustave, Lady Mer, and the debris strewn about the room.

"I was working late," Gustave said. "Lady Mer couldn't sleep and was looking for a book to read."

If Marchioness Rouge suspected anything else had happened, she didn't show it.

"We were checking on everyone after the earthquake and panicked when you weren't in your room. Your Majesty-"

A crowd of servants, soldiers, and courtiers burst into the room, interrupting whatever she had planned to say. They surrounded Gustave, cutting off his view of Lady Mer. Doctor Batiste pushed his way through them to examine the king.

"I'm fine," Gustave said. "Please, take care of Lady Mer. The pile of gifts fell on her and may have injured her."

But when the crowd parted to make way for the doctor, Lady Mer's chair was empty.

❧ 31 ❧

The incoming crowd provided the perfect opportunity for Fiora to escape the library. She ran from the room and down the hallway while everyone focused on King Gustave.

Well, she limped as quickly as she could. The bruises from falling boxes combined with the pain in her feet slowed her pace.

She was lucky. Her injuries could have been far worse. It was a good thing King Gustave had been there to dig her out.

And then to kiss her. Fiora frowned. It didn't matter what she felt, because Gustave clearly regretted his actions. He hadn't meant to kiss her, and she had kissed him back like the idiot she was.

What kind of man kissed someone accidentally? It was nonsense.

This was what she got for letting her guard down. For daring to think, for even just one moment, that someone could possibly want her.

Fiora leaned against the wall and took a deep breath as a wave of pain that had nothing to do with bruises and magic washed through her. When would she learn to stop hoping for such things?

Dwelling on it would do no good. She pushed Gustave out of her mind and instead thought about the rumbling and the earthquake. The noise that had preceded the shaking was far too similar to the one that accompanied the kraken attack to be a coincidence. Was something causing the earthquakes? Or someone?

Perhaps that deep rumbling voice that had communicated with Leander. The one that wanted her dead.

Had this been a deliberate attack on her?

Fiora reached the shore long before she developed any theories that made sense. She tried to call out to Zoe and scowled when she remembered she couldn't. Instead, she picked up rocks from the garden and threw them into the water. Hopefully that was enough to catch her cousin's attention if Zoe was still waiting. The edge of the ocean was already tinged pink from the impending sunrise.

"Ouch!"

One of Fiora's rocks hit Zoe's head as the mermaid emerged. Fiora dropped the rest.

"Sorry."

Zoe's expression turned from annoyance to concern as she looked at Fiora.

"Fiora, what happened? Did you get in a fight?"

Fiora shook her head.

"The earthquake knocked a few things on top of me. I'm fine."

"Earthquake?"

Before Fiora could further explain what had happened, Zoe swallowed nervously.

"Fiora, I can explain."

"Explain what?"

The water around Zoe rippled, and Kathelin and Althea burst through the waves. Fiora backed away from the shore.

"Don't be silly, Fiora," Kathelin said. "We're not going to hurt you. What happened to your hair?"

Althea said nothing. She simply held up a large conch shell. It was more effective than any words, and Fiora froze.

"I got worried when you took so long to meet me," Zoe said. "And they were looking for me and found me here. They're your sisters, Fiora. They can help."

"Help me into a jail cell, perhaps."

Althea frowned.

"So what Zoe said is true. You used the transformation song."

"Obviously. Was it supposed to take my voice?"

Althea nodded.

"And cause pain in my feet?"

"No, that isn't supposed to happen. I suspect it's because you're half human and your magic isn't as strong as a full-blooded mermaid. This is why you shouldn't experiment with enchantments that you don't fully understand."

"As if I had a choice. You want me in prison, and Leander wants me dead."

"What's this about Leander?" Kathelin said.

Fiora rolled her eyes and explained what she had overheard in the garden. Her aunts stared at her.

"That's a serious accusation," Althea said.

"It's the truth. And I heard the rumbling again just before a stack of boxes fell on me in the human castle. It might have been a deliberate attack."

Although Fiora hoped not. That would mean Leander had allies on the shore. Allies that knew who and where she was.

"If it helps, we no longer suspect you of waking the kraken," Althea said. "There have been more rumblings since you left. It seems the earthquakes weaken the effectiveness of the Kraken Heart. We have adjusted our songs, and the kraken are once again sleeping soundly. It was simply a matter of unfortunate timing."

Or was it? Fiora was beginning to suspect there was more going on here than met the eye. Before she could comment on the situation, Althea tossed the conch shell at her. Fiora caught it and hugged it to her chest.

"That transformation charm is only meant to last a short time," Althea said. "Three days at the most. You need to change back to a mermaid."

Fiora looked to Kathelin, who nodded in agreement.

"It is worrying that the enchantment is causing you pain. Perhaps we should have considered sooner that being half human would affect your magic and tried to discover exactly how it did."

Perhaps, but they were a decade too late for that. Fiora had spent most of the time she was underwater trying to pretend her human side didn't exist.

Just like she tried to pretend her mermaid side didn't exist when she was human.

Maybe that hadn't been the best strategy.

Fiora lifted the conch shell and read it. The counter charm was a complicated cacophony of extremely high notes. More of a scream than a song. She would have to focus her voice and push her magic to the limits to break through the enchantment that made her mute and human.

Out of a sense of morbid curiosity, Fiora read through the cautions for the charm. The details of the enchantment were just as Althea had said. The song was not meant to last more than three days, and it was not supposed to be painful.

"You're sure I'll be safe if I come with you? This isn't some sort of trap?"

"Of course not," Althea said.

"Would we tell you if it was?" Kathelin said.

That probably shouldn't have been reassuring, but somehow it was. The royal sisters were as straightforward as ever.

"I won't let anyone hurt you, Fiora," Zoe said fiercely. "Not even them."

Fiora wasn't confident that Zoe would be much good in a fight against Kathelin and Althea, but she nodded her thanks. The pain in her feet was growing worse, and perhaps it would be best not to return to the castle. Then she wouldn't have to face Gustave again after the kiss he so clearly regretted.

It seemed she wouldn't be able to run from the sea forever.

She stepped into the water. Waves washed over her feet and eased her pain. She pulled the pearl ring off her finger and set it on a rock. No point in taking a risk that the magic would interfere.

She looked at the conch shell as she sang to make sure she knew her notes. The song would be easy to get wrong, and who knew what would happen then? Fiora opened her mouth and screamed.

Nothing happened. No sound. No sudden burst of magic. No relief for her aching feet.

Fiora screamed louder. Tried harder. Reached into that place in her soul where the magic resided.

But the magic was gone.

She collapsed, landing in the shallow water with a splash. The salt water stung her cuts and made her eyes burn. The mermaids swam as close as they could.

"*I can't do it,*" Fiora signed.

Zoe and Kathelin shared a concerned look. Althea's brows knit together.

"I was afraid of that. It takes a powerful burst of song to reverse the enchantment. Your voice isn't strong enough."

"What are you saying, Althea?" Kathelin said.

Althea didn't answer. They all knew what she was saying.

"The enchantment is meant to last three days," Zoe said. "What happens at the end of those three days?"

"It won't come to that," Althea said. "I couldn't save your mother, Fiora, but I will save you."

There was something reassuring about the fiercely protective look in her eyes. Terrifying, but also reassuring.

"*What happened to her?*" Fiora signed. "*Before I left, you said some-*

thing about my father being responsible for her death. What exactly did you mean by that?"

Kathelin and Althea shared a look that made Fiora's heart sink. Whatever they had to say, it wasn't good.

"I suppose she should know," Kathelin said.

Althea nodded.

"Perhaps we should have told you before. Fiora, you know that your mother broke our laws and formed a friendship with a human. With your father."

"Obviously."

"Nyssa was always fascinated by humans," Kathelin said. "She was always getting into trouble underwater and thought she would do better on land. She loved listening to Madame Isla's stories about her research trips."

Fiora could only imagine how those stories had warped her mother's view of humanity.

"When she befriended your father, we helped her keep it a secret," Althea said. "But then she fell in love with him and swore she would never be happy without him. That's why we made the pearl ring. It was forbidden magic, but Kathelin and I were accomplished enough to create it."

Fiora wondered why her aunts had known forbidden magic in the first place, but didn't want to interrupt the story to ask.

"We thought it would make her happy," Kathelin said. "And for a time it did. She lived in a tiny cottage on the shore with your father. We thought he was a fisherman."

"But he wasn't," Althea said. "He was a prince. And when his older brother died, he became heir to the throne. His parents were not pleased to discover he had already chosen a bride. They ordered him to leave her so he could marry the girl of their choice and strengthen political alliances."

Fiora clenched her fists in the sand. She knew this part of the story. Well, her father's version of it.

"He told me she died before he remarried. Are you saying he abandoned her?"

Althea's face was grim.

"Not entirely, but he was conflicted. And that was enough to weaken the charm and turn Nyssa back into a mermaid."

"It takes strong magic to create a permanent transformation," Kathelin said. "When we made the ring, we designed it so his love would let him share his life with her and make her human. But he had to love her enough to forsake his mother and father and all else in the world. And in the end, he didn't. The charm failed, and Nyssa came back to the sea. She rallied a little when she had you, but she couldn't pull through."

"I confronted him," Althea said. "I told him about his daughter, hoping it would convince him to abdicate his throne and return to Nyssa. But it still wasn't enough. All that accomplished was to cause him to look for you years later and take you away from us."

"So my mother died from a broken heart?"

Althea snorted.

"Nyssa was stronger than that. She died from side effects of the magic. There's a reason such charms are forbidden. The day King Fergal married someone else, she dissolved into sea foam."

"That won't happen to Fiora, will it?" Zoe asked. "She used the ring to become human, and then her father stopped loving her."

Althea shook her head.

"If it was going to happen, it would have by now. We believe the magic worked differently because Fiora is half human and was transformed by the love of her father rather than a husband. His love wasn't as strong, but she also didn't need quite as much help to change her form."

Fiora glared at the ring. Were it not for that enchantment, her mother would still be alive.

And she wouldn't exist.

She didn't know what to feel.

"Surely he didn't know it would kill her," Fiora signed.

"Of course not," Kathelin said a little too quickly.

"Probably not," Althea said. "We don't know how much Nyssa told him about the magic. It is possible that he had no idea his love was keeping her human."

Her tone said it was possible, but not likely.

"But he did love her then," Zoe said. "He loved her enough to power the ring."

Althea nodded.

"Love is a powerful magic, useful in breaking curses and sometimes in causing them. But the hearts of men are unpredictable. More fickle than I realized when I created the enchantment. He was torn between his love for Nyssa and his duty to his country."

Althea picked the ring up and turned it over in her hand. Then she blinked and looked from the pearl to Fiora. Her expression was so alarmed that Fiora slid deeper into the water to look at the pearl herself. She gasped.

When her father had disowned her, the pearl had lost its sheen and turned a dull gray. It had stayed that way in the days that followed.

But some of the luster had returned. A tiny stripe of pink and blue danced across the gem.

"Someone loves you," Althea said "At least they're beginning to."

"Really?" Zoe squealed.

She slid forward on the sand to look at the ring.

"That's impossible," Fiora signed.

She squirmed under the mermaids' questioning gazes.

"This could solve the problem of Fiora not being able to break the enchantment with the song," Kathelin said.

"Absolutely not," Althea said. "This ring is too dangerous to use again. I only let her keep it because I thought the magic was gone."

"Does Fiora need to love the human man in return?" Zoe asked.

Althea and Kathelin turned back to Fiora.

"Are you falling in love with someone?" Kathelin asked.

Fiora blushed, remembering her kiss with Gustave.

"Of course not. I've only been on land for a day."

Althea and Kathelin shared a look that said they didn't believe her, and Zoe squealed again.

"But the ring is dangerous. It killed my mother."

Althea considered this.

"It didn't turn you to sea foam when your father abandoned you. Perhaps it affects you differently because you are half human. It might be worth a try."

"She means it's our only option," Kathelin said. "If you can win a man's love and turn human with the ring, you'll regain your voice. Then you could sing the counter charm and become a mermaid again."

"See, Fiora. I knew it would all work out," Zoe said.

Except for the part where she had to win a human man's love in two days, possibly come to love him in return, and then abandon him so that she wouldn't die if he abandoned her. There were so many impossibilities in that scenario that it was difficult to choose which to criticize first.

"There must be another way," Fiora signed.

"I will look for one," Althea said. "But I can't guarantee that I will find anything. And you only have two days until the enchantment runs out."

"What happens then?"

"You'll die."

Althea's face was grim. Far grimmer than usual. Fiora swallowed.

"At least try to win his heart," Kathelin said. "It would be such a nice solution, and you already have made progress."

She handed the ring back to Fiora. Fiora took it and glared at the treacherous streak of color.

"Lady Mer? Are you there?"

Gustave's voice rang through the garden. The mermaids pushed backwards into deeper water to hide.

"He sounds cute," Kathelin said.

She winked and disappeared into the water.

"Be careful," Althea said. "I'll do what I can, but two days is not much time to create a new enchantment. Using the ring is your best chance."

Fiora raised her hands to ask Althea what she should do about Leander and the attacks, but the mermaid was already gone.

"I'll check on you as soon as I can," Zoe said. "And I'll find some ways to help you win the man's heart so you can return to the ocean."

She hummed the song of healing, and the pain from Fiora's bruises faded away. Then she disappeared before Fiora could tell Zoe that she definitely didn't want the mermaids' help courting King Gustave.

"Lady Mer? Are you there?"

Gustave hurried through the garden searching for her. Perhaps he should have checked her room first, but every time Lady Mer disappeared, she ended up by the sea.

She wasn't on the bench where he had found her before. Gustave scanned the shoreline. His heart stopped when he saw a woman with long dark hair sitting in the water.

"Lady Mer!"

He ran towards her. How had she fallen into the ocean? Was she hurt further?

What if she had drowned?

Lady Mer turned to look at him, and Gustave's heart began to beat again. She was alive.

Her feet and legs were completely submerged in the water. Waves lapped at her waist, soaking the fabric of her robe. She turned away from Gustave and slipped a ring onto her finger.

"Are you well?"

He stood at the edge of the water panting for breath. It wasn't the question he really wanted to ask, but he had a feeling that

Lady Mer would not appreciate being asked why she was sitting in the water.

Why was she sitting in the water? Why did she always end up by the ocean?

Perhaps it was part of the curse.

Gustave blinked. He had kissed her. If Lady Mer was under a curse, that kiss might have broken it. For a moment, he thought perhaps it had. Perhaps she had come down here to gather her thoughts and decide what to say now that she had a voice.

But Lady Mer didn't speak when she finally looked up at him. Her eyes were as sad as ever. Possibly even more haunted than they had been before. Gustave didn't know what to say, so he simply reached down and offered his hand. Lady Mer took it without hesitation and let him pull her out of the water.

Her wet robe clung to her legs, and she shivered in the ocean wind. Gustave pulled off his coat and wrapped it around her shoulders. It wasn't long enough to cover her legs, but at least it would give her a little warmth.

The sun rose, casting a warm glow over the garden as they walked back to the castle. Lady Mer stopped for a moment to retrieve a large conch shell that sat on the shore. This was a strange time to collect seashells, but Gustave didn't comment. If it made her feel better, he would search the beach and fill her room with shells.

He almost said that, but he didn't want to sound overbearing.

"Doctor Batiste will tend to your cuts and bruises," Gustave said instead. "Do you have any other injuries he should look at?"

Lady Mer shook her head. It seemed impossible for her to come out of such an accident uninjured, but apparently she had been very lucky. The cut on her forehead had stopped bleeding. In fact, it had almost disappeared. Gustave had thought the bruise on her cheek looked rather serious when he saw it in the library, but it was faint now and would probably fade by tomorrow.

Maybe he would have been more observant if he had focused on helping her instead of kissing her.

Blast it all.

They walked through the garden in silence. She may not be bruised, but Lady Mer was limping worse than before. Gustave would tell the doctor to check her feet thoroughly. Perhaps there was something that could ease her pain.

"I am sorry. I-"

He meant to apologize for the kiss again, but she silenced him with a fierce look from her brilliant blue eyes. They stared at each other for a moment, and Gustave fought the urge to kiss her again. The rising sun shone behind them, bathing Lady Mer in a warm glow that made her look more beautiful than ever.

What in the world was wrong with him? He had never behaved so rashly before. Gustave turned away before he did something he would regret.

Marchioness Rouge met them at the castle door. Her expression was carefully neutral as she looked from Gustave to Lady Mer.

"I'll escort Lady Mer to her room so Doctor Batiste can attend to her, Your Majesty."

Gustave started to protest. He didn't want to let Lady Mer out of his sight, but Marchioness Rouge shook her head.

"She needs to rest, Your Majesty. Come with me, Lady Mer."

The marchioness held out her hand. Was it Gustave's imagination, or did Lady Mer tighten her grip on his arm a little before she released it? She met his gaze, then pulled the conch shell to her chest and limped after the marchioness.

Yes, her limping was definitely worse than before. Was it from the accident? Had it aggravated a previous injury?

He would check in with Doctor Batiste later to get his opinion. But for now, Marchioness Rouge was right. Lady Mer needed rest more than his company.

Gustave paced the hallway for a bit, then decided he was

being ridiculous and should do something productive. Perhaps he could check in with Captain Whist to see if any of the incoming merchant ships had brought news of mermaids. He peeked through the doorway of the captain's office and grimaced when he saw Dale was there studying shipping charts. Captain Whist noticed his expression and shrugged in amusement. Gustave couldn't blame the merchant for trying to locate his lost ship, but there was unlikely to be new information after a single day.

He took a deep breath and entered the room.

"No luck," Captain Whist said. "I submitted a request, but the council refused. And now-"

"Tidal waves?" Gustave said.

The captain nodded.

"All unnecessary voyages will be postponed until we can assess the effect the earthquake will have on the sea. We're clearing the harbor just in case."

"But surely it won't be that bad," Dale said. "The last word we received about my ship-"

He looked hopefully at Gustave.

"I haven't heard any news of your ship," Gustave said.

He backed into the hallway and closed the door before Dale could ask more questions. Captain Whist was far more qualified to give news on ships and sailing routes. Why did everyone expect Gustave to have all the answers simply because he was king?

His head pounded, reminding him that he had not slept much that night. Or the previous few nights.

Or the past few months.

Gustave stepped aside to let a servant pass, but the young man stopped and bowed.

"Your Majesty, Marquis Corbeau asked me to remind you that royal guests are arriving today. You will be responsible for greeting them."

The servant cast a significant look at Gustave. He took the hint. He looked nowhere near ready to receive royalty.

"I understand."

"And there are still gifts to open. It would be best to finish that before the gala so you can thank everyone in person. The marquis is supervising the cleanup in the library and looks forward to seeing you there when you are presentable."

Gustave swallowed his frustration and bowed instead.

"I will get dressed and meet the marquis as soon as possible."

"I will relay the message."

The servant hurried away, and Gustave walked slowly to his room. Doubtless these were important parts of his duties as king, but right now they felt like a waste of time. He should be out looking for his father and trying to contact mermaids.

Or making sure Lady Mer was well.

He shook his head. Doctor Batiste was far more qualified to take care of Lady Mer. Gustave needed to pull himself together and fulfill his duties as king.

❦ 33 ❧

"You're sure you have no other injuries?" Doctor Batiste asked.

Fiora nodded. The doctor looked skeptical, but he couldn't deny the evidence in front of him. Thanks to Zoe's song of healing, Fiora was fine.

Other than the curse that would kill her in two days if she didn't win a man's love, but that didn't seem like something the doctor would know how to heal.

Unless he was desperately looking for love and willing to give up everything for her?

Unlikely.

Fiora realized she was scowling at Doctor Batiste and looked away. This wasn't his fault.

"Truly, I'm fine. Just a few minor bruises."

Thomas, who had been sent by Dowager Queen Bernadine to assist, translated this for the doctor.

"You were very lucky, then. I saw the aftermath of the earthquake in the library. That was a sizable stack of presents."

Fiora shrugged.

"Even if you haven't sustained any injuries, I think some rest would do you good."

"Dowager Queen Bernadine invited you to join her sewing circle again today," Thomas said, "But I can convey your regrets."

"I would like to attend."

If she only had two days left to live, she might as well spend them doing something she enjoyed. And she couldn't spend time with Gustave and win his love if she was stuck in her room. Thomas translated, and Doctor Batiste shook his head.

"I must insist that you rest, Lady Mer. Dowager Queen Bernadine will understand."

Fiora resisted the urge to stick her tongue out at the doctor and nodded instead. She just wanted him to go away and leave her alone.

Doctor Batiste smiled.

"You'll feel better after you get some sleep. Ring this bell if you need anything. I'll instruct the servants to listen for it."

He set a brass bell beside the conch shell on her nightstand. Both he and Thomas had cast curious glances at the shell throughout the visit, but neither had commented.

Fiora nodded, doing her best to look sweet and compliant. Doctor Batiste and Thomas bowed and left the room. As soon as the door closed, she collapsed into bed and grabbed the conch shell.

It would be disastrous to transform into a mermaid while lying on a human bed, but Fiora tried anyway. She read the notes of the counter-charm and screamed them in her head as loudly as she could.

Nothing happened. She remained as human as ever.

As cursed as ever.

Fiora set the shell back on the nightstand. Three days, and she was already well into the second. She sighed in silent frustration.

Blast it all.

She twisted the ring on her finger and watched the pearly streak dance across the otherwise dull gem. She had spent years trying to win a man's love so she could use the pearl to stay human. It had seemed simple enough.

Now it seemed even that had been in vain. Based on Althea's story, she needed someone to love her completely. Not just enough to marry her for political gain.

And even if she somehow managed to win a man's heart, it wasn't a guarantee. She would dissolve into sea foam if that man ever found himself conflicted about his love for her and his duty to something else.

If he abandoned her, as her father had abandoned her mother, she would meet the same fate.

Fiora gritted her teeth How could she have been foolish enough to trust her father? To run away from the merfolk and put her faith in him and the human world?

Perhaps it was a family trait. Her mother had made the same mistake and paid for it with her life.

Would that be her fate as well?

Fiora squeezed her eyes shut and let tears run down her cheeks. Her heart ached worse than her feet. Her mother was dead, and her father had betrayed both of them.

And she had separated herself from the sea and the only family that still cared about her. Possibly forever.

Unless she could win a man's love and break the curse.

The mermaids would do what they could to save her. Fiora had no doubt of that now. But would it be enough? They must not have much faith in their ability to find a solution if they wanted her to use the forbidden magic that had killed her mother.

Based on what Althea had told her, Fiora had never had a chance of becoming permanently human. All her years spent training for the Princess Tests had been in vain.

And yet, that stubborn streak of color on the pearl said otherwise. Somehow, she had begun to win someone's affection.

Had it appeared when Gustave kissed her?

Fiora squeezed her eyes shut even tighter. Why had he kissed her if he was going to regret it and make things so awkward between them? Why did he look at her with love in his eyes then apologize for doing so?

It was even further proof that human hearts were fickle. Men could not be trusted.

Fiora sighed again, wishing she was underwater so the sigh would send bubbles streaming up towards the surface. It made the gesture so much more satisfying.

She stared at the ceiling, trying to make sense of it all. As ceilings went, it was a nice one. The light blue plaster was decorated with swirling silver vines around the edges. Leave it to Montaigne to turn a ceiling into a work of art.

The vines blurred as tears filled Fiora's eyes again.

She didn't want to die. She had felt a moment of panic when the boxes crashed down on her. That was as close to dying as she wanted to get any time soon.

She thought of Gustave's face when he had uncovered her. His gentle kiss.

And then his regret.

Blast it all!

She stared at the ring again. Even if he regretted kissing her, he felt something. He cared a little, if the streak of pink and blue was any indication.

Maybe the ring was mistaken. Maybe Gustave was not in love with her, but with the woman who saved his life. He had admitted that much when he was half asleep and willing to speak more freely.

And he didn't know they were the same person. How could he? He only remembered the song from that day on the beach, and Fiora was currently mute.

What if Gustave only loved the woman on the beach because she had saved his life? What if that love faded when he learned that woman was Fiora and came to know her better?

Fiora wiped away her tears. This whole situation had a lot of uncertainty, but it was her best hope of survival. If she could win Gustave's love, she would live.

And she didn't need to keep his affection. She only needed to capture it long enough to regain her voice and break the transformation enchantment. Then she could return to the sea and live the rest of her life as a mermaid.

The thought made her feel a little guilty. Could she really make Gustave love her then abandon him? It seemed unfair.

Fiora pushed the guilt away. This was a matter of life and death. She had fought for love in the Princess Tests.

She could do it again.

Fiora closed her eyes so the silver vines on the ceiling would stop blurring with tears and she could pretend she wasn't crying.

It was hopeless. A tangled mess of feelings and identities unlikely to end well.

And her life depended on it.

Maybe it wouldn't be so bad to die.

Fiora wiped the tears from her eyes and glared at the ceiling as if it had personally made the suggestion. Whatever else happened, she was not giving up.

Fiora never gave up.

And she certainly didn't have time to follow the doctor's orders to rest. She needed to win Gustave's love, and she couldn't do that by staying in bed.

Fiora pulled herself to her feet. She ignored the pain and limped over to the wardrobe. The servants had likely been instructed to leave her alone so she could sleep. She couldn't risk asking for help and having them report her to Doctor Batiste.

She studied the gowns and selected the most elaborate one that she would be able to put on without help. It was light blue silk with decorative pearl buttons down the front.

Fiora slipped into it and fastened the tiny buttons with shaking hands. She breathed deeply, telling herself to calm down.

It was just like a Princess Test. She simply needed to be proper and play her part.

It had never worked before, but she had an advantage now. Gustave already liked her a little.

Hopefully that would be enough.

Fiora picked up a hairbrush and moved to the mirror. The blue dress matched her eyes. She smiled a little, enjoying the effect. Then she brushed the tangles out of her black hair and pulled it back into a demure braid.

There. She was looking more and more like a proper lady.

The dress had tiny golden flowers embroidered around the sleeves. It was beautiful work. An understated but masterful embellishment. If she studied the stitches long enough, perhaps she could recreate them.

If she lived long enough to embroider again.

Fiora pushed away the thought and looked at herself in the mirror. She was only missing one thing.

Shoes.

A proper lady would wear shoes.

Fiora checked the wardrobe and selected a pair of golden heels trimmed with tiny pearls. They were stylish and proper and complemented the dress perfectly.

And they would be torture to wear with her curse.

But if she wanted to win Gustave's affection and save her life, she needed to look her best.

She needed to actually try.

Fiora slipped her feet into the shoes and ignored the searing pain that accompanied walking in the stylish heels. She needed all the help she could get in this fight. She would show the King of Montaigne that she was a proper lady. Not some wild thing drawn from the sea.

She hobbled to the door, taking tiny steps that she hoped looked dainty rather than tortured, and peeked into the hallway.

Empty, thank goodness.

Fiora slipped out of her room and closed the door behind her as quietly as she could. Then she hurried towards the sewing room, using the art on the walls as her guide to navigate through the castle.

❧ 34 ❧

Gustave walked quickly through the hallways, trying to avoid people without looking like he was doing so. He wanted to catch Doctor Batiste after he finished examining Lady Mer, and he couldn't do that if he got caught up in a conversation with Marquis Corbeau.

Or Lady Annabelle.

Or Kara.

Or his grandmother.

Or Dale.

In fact, Elaine was probably the only person in the castle not hoping for a private audience with the King of Montaigne. Why had she even bothered to come if she found him so unappealing?

Perhaps her family had pushed her into coming. Still, it was rather unflattering to have someone who was supposed to be interested in you be so completely uninterested in you.

Gustave heard footsteps, peered around the corner, and saw Doctor Batiste walking down the hallway. Gustave hurried towards him.

"How is she?"

"Oh! Hello, Your Majesty."

The doctor kept walking. Gustave strode after him.

"Lady Mer. Was she hurt?"

"Your Majesty realizes I am supposed to keep the care of patients confidential?"

"She's my guest. I just want to make sure she wasn't seriously injured in the accident."

Doctor Batiste gave him a suspicious look, then sighed.

"Lady Mer is well except for a few minor bruises. She was very lucky."

"What about her feet? I've noticed her limping sometimes. Perhaps-"

"Her feet are fine, Your Majesty. Please excuse me. I have other patients to attend to."

The doctor bowed and hurried away. Gustave watched him go. Apparently he had been wrong. There were two people in the castle not eager to speak with him.

"Your Majesty?"

Gustave whirled around and relaxed when he saw it was a maid. He opened his mouth to dismiss her, then remembered his theory that perhaps the woman who rescued him worked in the castle. For all he knew, it was this woman. Someone always nearby but practically invisible. Gustave looked at the maid again, actually seeing her this time. She was a pretty sort of girl with dark hair and enormous brown eyes.

Blue eyes. He remembered blue eyes from that day at the beach.

Or was he thinking of the sky?

The maid shifted nervously, unsure what to do as he stared at her. Gustave shook himself out of his memories.

"My apologies. Did you need something?"

"Forgive me, Your Majesty, but the royal tailor needs to see you. There was an accident, and your suit for the gala was destroyed. He has selected another one, but it will need to be altered before tomorrow."

"An accident?"

Gustave didn't mean to sound harsh, but that was suspicious. The sewing staff in the castle were too careful to allow clothing to be destroyed by accident.

The maid swallowed and curtsied again.

"A bottle of ink spilled on it. I'm afraid it's beyond repair."

"I have duties to attend to. Guests are arriving today. Surely they can use the measurements from the last suit."

Not that he particularly wanted to fulfill his duties, but greeting royal guests would be better than being fit for a suit.

"Dowager Queen Bernadine said she would be happy to greet your guests and offer your apologies to them while you are with the tailors."

Oh, so his grandmother had a hand in this.

There was no escaping then. What was she up to?

Gustave hurried to the tailoring room and looked around it suspiciously as he entered. A team of tailors bustled around an old-fashioned blue suit spread over a table.

"What is that?"

"Your grandfather's suit, Sire. We're remaking it for you to replace the damaged one."

"This isn't a costume ball."

"Of course not, Your Majesty. That's why we're remaking it to suit modern tastes. Dowager Queen Bernadine thought this would be a nice way to honor your grandfather's legacy."

Gustave sighed. If his grandmother had decided he should wear this suit to the gala, there was little hope of changing her mind.

And apparently she had connections in the sewing room.

"I could wear one of my other suits. They're already modern."

The tailors looked at him as if that was the most ridiculous suggestion they had ever heard.

Gustave gave up and tried not to look impatient while they helped him into the suit and discussed how to best alter it. At least the fabric was nice. Light blue silk with embroidered borders of waves and starfish.

He hoped Lady Mer would like it. Maybe it would remind her of the sea.

Lady Mer.

Was she truly uninjured? Doctor Batiste had seemed sure of it, but Gustave couldn't shake the feeling that something was wrong. Sometimes her eyes looked so pained.

Probably because he kept making a mess of things. Accidentally insulting her and kissing her and being completely unhelpful.

He needed to do something nice for her. Apologize somehow.

"Do we have any seashells in the castle?" Gustave asked.

"Your Majesty?"

"I thought they might make good decorations. I- there's someone I know who likes them."

The tailor grinned knowingly.

"Flowers would be a more typical gift for a lady, Your Majesty. I hear Marquis Corbeau has ordered some rare lilies. Perhaps you could borrow a few."

"No, that's not it. I-"

Gustave looked to the ceiling to hide the flush creeping over his face. The last thing he needed was for rumors to spread that he was attached to someone. And he definitely didn't need Marquis Corbeau to hear those rumors.

Perhaps the tailors were right. Seashells were a stupid gift. They wouldn't help Lady Mer's injury or erase the fact that Gustave had kissed her at a completely inappropriate time.

Or that she had kissed him back.

Blast it all.

𝕩 35 𝕩

Fiora pushed open the door to the queen's sewing room without knocking, then silently scolded herself for doing so. A proper lady would knock. She needed to do better.

Kara and Lady Anabelle blinked at her as Fiora limped across the room and took a seat. Elaine was too engrossed in her book to notice.

Dowager Queen Bernadine's chair was empty, as was Princess Collette's. Fiora cast a questioning glance at Kara.

"They left to greet arriving guests. They should return shortly."

Kara turned her attention back to her knitting. She had finished the heel on the sock and was working her way up the ankle. Fiora watched her for a moment. Kara's needles clicked together with quiet efficiency.

Knitting wasn't one of the skills required for the Princess Test, so Fiora had never learned. Watching Kara, she wished she had. Perhaps she could have knit seaweed into clothing for herself instead of searching shipwrecks for fabric.

Kara looked up and gave Fiora a small smile. Fiora returned it with a scowl and pulled out the basket under her seat. She selected a dark red thread to add shading to the rose and began to sew.

Her breathing eased a little as she stabbed the fabric, stitching in a steady rhythm that calmed her racing thoughts.

"I see you finally found some suitable shoes," Lady Annabelle said.

Her own sewing project sat on her lap. Apparently she had only been working on it to impress Dowager Queen Bernadine, because she made no pretense of being interested in it now.

Fiora ignored the comment and stabbed her needle through the fabric again.

"And you even found a dress that matches your ring. I suppose when you only have one accessory, you must plan everything else around it. I would love to hear the story of where you managed to obtain a pearl ring when you can't even afford clothes. Won't you tell me?"

Fiora looked up just long enough to glare at Lady Annabelle, then stabbed her fabric again, pretending it was Lady Annabelle's face. That made the sewing even more stress relieving than normal. Her feet ached, and her resolve to be a proper lady was quickly fading. No one that mattered was here to notice, anyway.

Lady Annabelle took Fiora's frustration as encouragement.

"But of course you can't tell me, can you? That is a shame. Especially when King Gustave is looking for a wife who can sing. Fortunately, I've taken voice lessons for many years. Marquis Corbeau asked me to sing for everyone as entertainment after dinner. It will be a special treat for the gala guests who have arrived early."

"Stop it, Annabelle," Kara said. "You're making a fool of yourself."

"No, I'm making an effort. Anyone would think you don't care at all about King Gustave. You've hardly said a word to him the whole time you've been here. I'm the only one who has tried to engage him in conversation. Apparently I'm also the only one who is intelligent enough to question this woman's strange appearance and suspicious motivations."

"Annabelle! Lady Mer isn't suspicious!"

Kara set down her knitting and looked from Annabelle to Fiora in distress.

"It's Lady Annabelle. And is no one curious why she was in the library in the middle of the night in the first place?"

Kara and Lady Annabelle turned to Fiora. She shrugged.

"None of your business."

Of course they didn't understand the signs, but Fiora couldn't keep from replying any longer. Lady Annabelle's smile widened.

"Isn't it strange that she was rummaging through the gifts at night? Through the most valuable objects in the castle outside the treasury?"

Fiora desperately wanted to make a comment about the painting of Lady Annabelle. She wished Gustave was here so she could sign it to him. He would fight back laughter, trying to maintain his composure, but his eyes would crinkle in amusement.

"And then the pile of gifts fell, ruining the carefully organized stacks so no one would notice that anything was missing."

Kara gasped.

"The earthquake knocked them over. You shouldn't accuse people without proof!"

"Idiot," Elaine signed.

She had been reading her book and hadn't seemed to be paying attention to the conversation, so her response was a surprise. Fiora choked back laughter.

"You speak sign language?" she asked.

Elaine tucked the book into a hidden pocket in her skirt and shrugged.

"A little."

Then she winked at Fiora and waved her hands in an animated manner, signing nonsense while casting significant glances at Lady Annabelle.

"Stop it," Lady Annabelle said. "You shouldn't say things not everyone can understand."

"There go any hopes of intelligent conversation, then," Fiora signed.

Elaine shook her head a little to show she didn't understand, then laughed loudly as if she did. Kara looked from Elaine to Fiora, a small smile forming on her lips. Then she set down her knitting, timidly raised her hands, and began to sign the alphabet.

Fiora covered her hands with her mouth to hide her smile. She hadn't expected Kara to have that kind of spunk.

"I demand that you stop," Lady Annabelle said. "This behavior is most improper."

"T-h-a-n-k-s."

Fiora spelled the word out, hoping that Kara and Elaine would understand. They both nodded and grinned at her.

The door opened, and Princess Collette burst into the room.

"Oh, Lady Mer! I thought you were resting!"

"I couldn't sleep and thought some sewing would relax me."

"Please let the servants know if you need anything. I wish I could stay and sew with you all, but I have to review the budget with Marchioness Rouge before lunch. I just came to retrieve my notes."

"Is there anything I can do to help?" Kara asked. "I feel strange sitting idle while you are so busy."

"I'm afraid not. Just make sure you're rested for the reception tonight so you can help me entertain our guests. If everyone arrives on time, we'll have several princes and princesses in attendance."

Lady Annabelle brightened at the mention of princes.

"I'm going to sing for everyone's entertainment. Marquis Corbeau asked me to."

The tiniest flicker of annoyance flashed across Collette's face. Then she gathered her composure and smiled.

"I'm sure that will be lovely, Lady Annabelle. Please excuse me. I'll see you all at lunch."

Collette grabbed some papers from a table, curtsied, and hurried from the room.

"I wonder which countries have sent princes?" Lady Annabelle said.

Kara shrugged, and Elaine returned to reading her book. Fiora focused on sewing, adding dark red stitches to her rose until it began to resemble a real flower more than a mere outline.

"I've never met any foreign princes," Lady Annabelle said. "I've been invited to receptions for them before, but Father thought it best I not meet them in case I ever needed to participate in a Princess Test. Once Princess Collette is married, I'll be the most eligible noblewoman in Montaigne."

Fiora rolled her eyes. Lady Annabelle spoke as if she was guaranteed to win once she had the chance to participate in a Princess Test.

She had no idea.

And she wouldn't get very far with such terrible embroidery skills.

Fiora wished she could relay the comment to Gustave. But he wasn't here and saying such a thing would give away the fact that she was familiar with Princess Tests. Best to keep such knowledge to herself.

So she focused on her sewing, ignoring Lady Annabelle's ramblings until a servant came to fetch them for lunch.

The ladies moved slowly through the hallway, but it was still too fast for Fiora to walk comfortably in her shoes. Pain seared the bottom of her feet with each step she took.

"Lady Mer, are you well? Should I fetch the doctor?" Kara said.

Fiora scowled at her, angry that she hadn't been able to hide the pain well enough. Kara swallowed and looked away.

"I think we should hurry," Lady Annabelle said with a nasty gleam in her eyes. "We don't want to be late for lunch."

"But Lady Mer–"

Fiora gritted her teeth and forced herself to walk faster. She passed Lady Annabelle and led the way down the hall.

Being proper had never been this difficult. She wanted to tear the shoes off her feet and throw them out a window.

But she couldn't. She needed to prove she was worthy of a king's affection, and she only had a day and a half to do it.

A footman showed them into the dining room and seated them when they arrived. Dowager Queen Bernadine and Thomas sat at the head of the table. Marquis Corbeau, Marchioness Rouge, Princess Collette, Captain Whist, and Dale the merchant occupied the rest of the chairs. Gustave's seat was empty.

Marquis Corbeau scowled when he saw Fiora.

"I didn't expect to see you here. Doctor Batiste said you would need rest."

"Sorry to disappoint you."

The marquis looked to Thomas for a translation. The interpreter swallowed.

"Lady Mer said she feels perfectly well," Dowager Queen Bernadine said.

Fiora grinned, then remembered she was supposed to be acting like a proper lady. She smoothed her features into what she hoped was a serene expression.

"You may begin serving lunch," Dowager Queen Bernadine said to the staff. "Gustave had to have his suit altered at the last minute. I expect he'll be late."

The waiters nodded.

"I would like to talk to you later," Dowager Queen Bernadine signed to Fiora. *"We can do it while you're being fitted for your ball gown."*

Fiora blinked.

"I already have gowns-"

"You have a few spare dresses prepared on short notice. Nothing suitable for the gala."

Dowager Queen Bernadine's expression said she would not

take no for an answer, so Fiora nodded and turned her attention to her soup. A proper lady wouldn't argue with her hostess.

Besides, a better gown might help her catch Gustave's notice.

The lunch was awkward without him. She wanted to tease him about the soup. To dare him to make a comment on it to see how much Lady Annabelle would gush.

Instead, she sat with perfect posture and studied everyone around the table from the corner of her eye.

Elaine looked bored. She smiled when she caught Fiora's gaze then turned back to her food. Kara kept glancing nervously at the door. Wondering when Gustave would arrive?

"Has there been any signs of tidal waves, Captain?" Marchioness Rouge asked. "I know the earthquake puts us at risk."

"Nothing large enough to be dangerous," Captain Whist said. "I think we're clear."

Dale sighed.

"I had hoped a tidal wave might wash some of my goods ashore."

He picked up his fork and stared mournfully at it.

"Because a flood is no cause for concern if a shipment of silverware can be reclaimed," Dowager Queen Bernadine said.

The merchant flushed.

"Forgive me, Your Majesty. Of course I did not mean it that way. I am glad that those living near the shore are safe from disaster."

He looked ready to launch into another lament over his lost cargo. Collette interrupted before he could expound on his woes.

"Marchioness Rouge and I reevaluated the budget today."

"Did you?" Marquis Corbeau said. "I would be happy to offer any advice if needed."

"It is not needed," Marchioness Rouge said. "The princess has quite a head for numbers. She found several places where efficiency could be improved."

"Oh. Wonderful."

Marquis Corbeau did not sound enthusiastic.

"I thought we could use the surplus to help merchants affected by the kraken attacks," Collette said. "It isn't as if we need to spend the money on more jewels or parties."

Marquis Corbeau sniffed, as if to say this was exactly what surplus money in a royal budget should be spent on. Collette continued with a defensive edge to her voice.

"It would help Montaigne's economy to have the shipping routes active again. I know we normally don't assist private citizens, but this is a special case. If we all work together, we will rebuild faster. Of course the plan would need council approval. And we will need to see what Gustave thinks."

She looked around the table as if realizing for the first time that she was speaking out loud. Everyone stared at her, surprised by the passion in her speech as much as her ideas.

Collette shrank back in her chair as if trying to escape their stares. She reminded Fiora of an octopus folding in on itself to hide in a tight space.

Marquis Corbeau filled the silence by rambling about gala preparations. Something about flowers that matched the cake. Or maybe the flowers were on the cake? Or the cake was made of flowers? Fiora wasn't really paying attention. She watched across the table, waiting for Princess Collette to look up.

"It sounds like a good plan," she signed when she finally caught Collette's attention. *"I'm sure the merchants will be grateful, and it will do much more good for your country than a flower cake."*

Collette's eyes widened with surprise at the praise. Then she smiled and sat a little straighter.

"Thank you."

❧ 36 ❧

Gustave hurried through the hallway, late for lunch and hoping that his grandmother had expressed appropriate apologies to his guests when he wasn't there to greet them. It had taken longer than expected to tailor the suit, and then he had to get dressed and make himself presentable for the day.

He entered the dining room and found Marquis Corbeau rhapsodizing about the refreshments he had planned for the gala.

"Of course, it was difficult to secure the right kind of apples for the tarts. Normally we import them from Gaveron, but the kraken attacks made that difficult. Luckily I-"

The marquis stopped his story when Gustave sat down. The other diners looked grateful for the interruption. Gustave could only guess how long Marquis Corbeau had been rambling about the gala preparations.

He looked around the table and blinked with surprise when he saw Lady Mer.

"Doctor Batiste said you were resting."

"I'm fine."

She didn't look fine. A thin layer of sweat shone on her forehead, and her eyes were strained. Gustave agreed with Doctor

Batiste's evaluation that Lady Mer needed rest, but he suspected she was too stubborn to appreciate his saying so.

She looked different somehow. Her hair was pulled back, and she wore a more elaborate style of gown. As if she was trying to prove she was in good health by looking more polished than normal.

Gustave realized he was staring and looked down at his soup. First he kissed her, then he gawked at her. No wonder she was uncomfortable. It probably had more to do with his behavior than being buried in an avalanche of royal gifts.

He was tempted to comment on the soup to try to make Lady Mer smile, but the predatory gleam in Lady Annabelle's eyes kept him quiet.

"Has Your Majesty cleaned up after the earthquake? I'm sure you'll be sorting through the presents to make sure everything is accounted for."

Lady Annabelle gave Lady Mer a pointed look, and Lady Mer rolled her eyes. Gustave looked between them, trying to make sense of the tension.

"The servants and scribes are working to reorganize the library."

"I do hope that nothing is missing."

She seemed to be accusing Lady Mer of something, but Gustave had no idea what.

"Is everything ready for the guests arriving by sea, Captain?" Gustave asked.

Captain Whist nodded.

"There have been no signs of tidal waves, and I've posted extra guards and sent out some patrol boats just to be on the safe side."

Just in case another kraken attacked. He didn't say it, but Gustave knew that was what he meant.

"Will the patrol boats be on the watch for mermaids?" Dale asked. "If Your Majesty is planning another expedition, I would like to be on the ship."

"Out of the question," Marquis Corbeau said. "His Majesty will be too busy entertaining guests and preparing for the gala to search for mermaids."

Gustave sighed. As much as he wanted to continue the search for his father, he did have duties to attend to. Guests had already arrived, and he needed to be a good host. He hoped the visitors didn't include more eligible women, but that was probably wishful thinking. Knowing Marquis Corbeau, the list would only include eligible women.

"I'm afraid the search for my father will have to wait."

Gustave whispered "Find King Francois" to his ring and checked the light's direction with his compass.

It had not changed. Gustave glanced at Lady Mer and found her smiling sympathetically at him. He returned her smile and told himself that it was all right. He would focus on the search after the gala.

"It is strange," Captain Whist said. "I sent men to ask around and see how far the earthquake reached. It was weaker in the village. The stable boys said they heard a rumble but felt no shaking.

"Really?"

Gustave frowned. The stable sat just outside the castle grounds.

"You think the castle was the epicenter then?"

"Yes. Possibly the library, judging from the servant's reports.

"So the earthquake centered around Lady Mer?" Lady Annabelle said. "How very strange."

She gave a smug smile, as if she had just delivered a scathing accusation. Gustave frowned. He couldn't wait for Lady Annabelle to leave.

"Perhaps someone was targeting the castle?" Kara said.

"Don't be silly," Lady Annabelle said. "That isn't how earthquakes work."

"Could it have been caused by magic?" Lady Mer signed.

Thomas translated. Everyone stared at her.

"Magic? What a ridiculous thought," Lady Annabelle said.

Gustave shook his head.

"I saw a lot of magic in my recent visits to Aeonia and Santelle. It is certainly possible that it has come here. But how? And what can we do about it?"

"You have the most experience with such things, Gustave," Collette said. "You've researched magic while looking for Father."

Everyone turned to Gustave. He swallowed.

"I read what we have in the library about curses, which isn't much. And there was no mention of a curse ever causing an earthquake."

"That would be unlikely," Elaine said. "If this earthquake was something magical, it sounds more like the work of an enchanted object."

Everyone stared at her, jaws dropped in surprise.

Elaine took their surprise in stride, neither flustered nor embarrassed. She pulled a book from her skirt and waved it at them.

"Did you think I was reading romance novels this whole time? I accepted your invitation to the castle so I would have access to your library for my research. I've read everything we have at home about magic, but you have a much larger selection of texts."

"An enchanted object?" Gustave said when he finally found his voice.

"Yes, like your ring."

Gustave looked down at his ring and noticed Lady Mer did the same with hers.

Interesting. Was her pearl enchanted as well? What did it do?

Another question. When would he get answers?

"You think someone used an enchanted object to create an earthquake?" Dowager Queen Bernadine said after Thomas translated the conversation for her.

There was a little skepticism in her voice, but she seemed to take the idea seriously.

"It's certainly possible," Elaine said. "There is an enormous pile of gifts in your library. Perhaps some of them are magical."

"Then we'll search the gifts," Gustave said. "Elaine, could you help? I would be happy to loan you any of the books in our library as thanks."

"It would be an honor, Your Majesty. But I should warn you, I'm no expert in enchanted objects."

"Do you have any idea how to identify them?" Dowager Queen Bernadine asked.

"I know a few ways. I can't identify every type of magic, but I can find several."

"Then you're the best option we have. I'm glad to hear you have some use. I thought it was odd for Jeanine to have raised such a worthless granddaughter."

The guests around the table gasped, but Elaine simply laughed.

"I suppose I was so eager to make the most of my time with the books that I forgot to pay attention to the people. Forgive me, Your Majesty. I meant no offense."

"And I take none."

Gustave smiled with relief. Lady Mer raised an eyebrow at him.

"I'm glad she was simply distracted," Gustave signed. *"It's a little hard on your pride when someone who is supposed to be trying to marry you finds you that uninteresting. I was beginning to worry that I was horribly boring."*

"That's ridiculous. Of course you aren't boring."

Her smiled faded when she saw that Gustave was serious.

"Why would you think that?"

"It takes a lot of time to run a kingdom, and I spend every spare hour searching for my father. I've been working so much that I haven't even practiced dancing for the gala. I'll probably fall flat on my face tomorrow night."

"I'm out of practice as well," Lady Mer signed. *"The last time I was at a ball, no one asked me to dance."*

She frowned at Gustave's shocked expression.

"It's fine. I didn't mean-"

Gustave raised his hand to stop her.

"Lady Mer, I don't know who you associated with before, but they were fools if they could not see your worth."

To Gustave's horror, Lady Mer's eyes filled with tears. By the heavens, what abuse was she used to if such simple praise made her cry?

"What did you say to her?" Lady Annabelle said. "Why is Lady Mer crying?"

She sounded a bit too pleased by this turn of events.

"I'm sure she's just overwhelmed," Dowager Queen Bernadine said. "She has had a stressful day. Tomorrow will be better, dear."

Lady Mer's expression turned grim. Gustave couldn't stand the sorrow in her eyes another moment.

"Will you dance with me tonight, Lady Mer? I would like to practice before the gala."

He said it aloud instead of signing. He couldn't make up for what had happened at the last ball she attended, but he could make sure it didn't happen again. And he could make sure that everyone knew he found her a worthy companion.

But most of all, he wanted her to know. That seemed important somehow.

Lady Mer's eyes widened with surprise. Then she nodded and smiled at him. Lady Annabelle scowled.

"But I'm going to sing tonight."

"Perfect," Dowager Queen Bernadine said. "Thomas can accompany you. We'll need music so they can dance."

Lady Annabelle's expression was absolutely murderous. Gustave shared a look with Lady Mer, both of them doing their best not to laugh.

❦ 37 ❦

He wanted to dance with her. Fiora ducked her head, trying to hide both her blush and her concern at the thought of dancing. Her feet hurt so badly she could hardly stand.

But she would do it. She would do whatever she could to spend time with Gustave. She needed to.

And strangely, she wanted to.

No one had ever actually wanted to dance with her before. The men who had been forced to escort her for political reasons at various functions had always worn tight expressions and hurried away as soon as possible. They hadn't needed to say how unappealing they found her. Their silence spoke louder than words ever could.

But Gustave had just asked her to dance. Out loud. In front of everyone.

Fiora looked down at her ring. Was it her imagination, or had the bit of color grown wider?

She swallowed the spark of hope building in her chest. This was progress, but it wasn't enough. She would have to do better if Gustave was going to fall in love with her by tomorrow night.

She needed time alone with him. Or some kind of grand

gesture to catch his attention. This was more difficult than the Princess Tests. The competition wasn't official, and there was no schedule to follow. Even if he liked her, there was no deadline for him to decide that and declare his affection.

"Lady Mer?"

Fiora realized Gustave was speaking to her and frowned at herself. Ignoring him was not a good start. She looked up at him and smiled.

"Sorry. What did you say?"

"I asked if you would like to help Elaine and I search the gifts for enchanted objects this afternoon. I understand if you don't feel well enough, but-"

"I'd love to."

Fiora signed the words a little too quickly then scolded herself for appearing overeager. But this was her chance to spend time with Gustave, and she needed to make sure that he didn't spend time alone with Elaine. What if he discovered he liked the other girl better?

"Lady Mer is coming with me first," Dowager Queen Bernadine said. "She needs to be fit for her ball gown."

Fiora and Gustave shared a look, deciding if it was worth arguing with the dowager queen or not.

Gustave gave a small smile, and Fiora nodded. It would be easier for all concerned to give the dowager queen her way.

Besides, she did need a ball gown. And surely Gustave wouldn't fall in love with Elaine in the time it took to fit a dress.

At least, Fiora hoped not. She watched Gustave and Elaine hurry out of the dining room with a tightness in her throat.

"You'll join them soon enough, Lady Mer."

Fiora nodded and turned to follow the dowager queen. Making Gustave's grandmother angry wouldn't help matters. She would be as polite and charming as possible, and hopefully the fitting would not take long.

But Thomas seemed in no hurry as he pushed Dowager

Queen Bernadine's wheelchair through the castle. As much as Fiora wanted to get this over with, she was also grateful for the slower pace. She did her best not to limp, although more than once she glanced down to check if someone had lined the marble floor with knives.

It felt like they had. Fiora would not be surprised to see a trail of bloody footprints behind her, but when she looked back, she saw only pristine stone.

Thomas pushed Dowager Queen Bernadine back to the wing of the castle that held bedrooms. Fiora smiled at the portrait of young Gustave as they passed it. Her statue may be cracked and an ocean away, but the painting was fine.

As was the man the boy had grown to be.

Dowager Queen Bernadine noticed Fiora's interest.

"He's always been a sweet boy."

She waited for Fiora's answer, but Fiora didn't know what to say to that. She simply nodded and kept walking.

They reached Dowager Queen Bernadine's suite, and Fiora held the door while Thomas pushed the wheelchair through.

A beautiful gown the color of the moonlit sea hung in the middle of the room. Ruffles of gathered white lace formed waves on the full skirt, while diamonds and pearls on the bodice sparkled in the sunlight that streamed through the windows. A seamstress fluttered around the dress, adding a few finishing touches.

Fiora lifted her hands to say something, then let them drop again. What was there to say? It was the most beautiful gown she had ever seen. She walked closer to study the stitching. As seemed common for Montaigne dresses, the hems were decorated with embroidery rather than straight stitches. This gown had elegant gold patterns of waves and starfish.

Dowager Queen Bernadine smiled.

"This was mine a very long time ago. I had Marie rework it for you."

Fiora's eyes widened.

"Your Majesty, this is too generous. You can't-"

"Don't tell me what I can't do, girl. That's never worked for anyone before."

There was a gleam in Dowager Queen Bernadine's eyes. Almost as if she hoped that Fiora would try to refuse the gift so they could argue and see who had the strongest will.

Fiora laughed silently and shook her head in surrender. It would be much easier to win Gustave's heart in such a beautiful gown, and making an enemy of the dowager queen would not help her cause.

"Leave us, Thomas," Dowager Queen Bernadine said. "Lady Mer needs privacy to change."

Thomas left, and the seamstress helped Fiora into the dress. She darted in and out, marking places to alter, checking the overall effect, then adding more pins.

"What shoes will the lady wear?" Marie signed, more to Dowager Queen Bernadine than Fiora.

Fiora swallowed. A dress like this was meant to be worn with beautiful shoes. The skirt had been cut long to leave room for heels. It would make attending the ball agony, but she was managing so far.

"I will wear these," she said, pulling the skirt up a bit so they could see her feet.

"I thought you might like to wear flats," the dowager queen said.

She gave Fiora a searching look, and Fiora scowled. Apparently she was not hiding her pain as well as she hoped. She shook her head.

"I want to wear the heels."

She had limited weapons in this fight, and fashion was one of them. She couldn't afford to look anything less than perfect.

"I understand you suffered an injury in your accident and have pain in your feet," Dowager Queen Bernadine said. "I see no point in you making yourself miserable for the sake of fashion. Besides, the skirt is so full that no one will see your shoes."

Fiora looked at her reflection in the mirror. It was true. The dress was an old-fashioned style held out with multiple petticoats that would cover her feet completely. She could go barefoot if she wanted.

Still, it was the principle of the thing that mattered. Proper ladies wore proper shoes. Fiora shook her head and prepared for a fight. The dowager queen got that stubborn look in her eyes again, then shrugged.

"Very well, if you're sure. We'll still need to take the hem up a bit. Will you have time to adjust it by tomorrow night, Marie?"

The seamstress nodded and began to work. She circled Fiora, studying the drape of the skirt, then knelt and began to pin the hem.

Bernadine turned her attention to supervising the seamstress and offering her opinions on the ways to gather the new hem. Fiora watched for a while, then studied the room to distract herself from the pain of standing for so long in the heels.

Dowager Queen Bernadine's bedroom was as tastefully decorated as the rest of the castle, although a bit more cluttered than the other rooms. Mementos covered the tables, and portraits covered the walls. Fiora recognized young Gustave and Collette in many of them.

She stared at one that seemed familiar. It was a man with a curled beard. An older version of Gustave with streaks of gray at his temples. His eyes crinkled in a smile, and his expression was kind.

"My son, King Francois," Dowager Queen Bernadine said. "I had his most recent portrait moved from the hallway to my room when he disappeared. Perhaps I should have given it to Gustave or Collette instead. They do miss their father."

Something once again teased at Fiora's memory. She had seen this man before. Recently.

"Where was he last seen?"

"He was sailing to Gaveron, but his ship was blown off course and never recovered. We would have assumed it had been lost at sea if not for Gustave's ring."

"Gustave is determined to find him," Fiora signed.

"We all want to find him, but it has not been easy," Dowager Queen Bernadine said. "Francois would not want Gustave to risk his life searching for him. Or to put his life on hold. Although I think you have made him a little less reluctant to move forward. He's stopped acting stiff as a statue since you joined us."

"Your Highness, I-"

Fiora stopped mid-sign.

She remembered where she had seen King Francois.

He was the statue. The one that Leander had placed in the garden the day the kraken attacked. She recognized the beard.

She studied the painting, checking every detail. Yes, it was the same man. They must have commissioned the statue before King Francois disappeared. Perhaps it had been on one of the ships that was lost in the kraken attacks.

"Are you well, Lady Mer?" Dowager Queen Bernadine asked.

Fiora nodded, not willing or able to explain her revelation.

First a statue of Gustave, then one of his father. It seemed she was fated to run into this family even when she was under the ocean.

Fiora bit her lip. The painting of King Francois brought Dowager Queen Bernadine comfort. Perhaps the statue would do the same for Gustave.

It would also be a good way to catch his attention. Elaine could offer help finding enchanted objects, but Fiora could offer a gift.

Not to mention this family had been kind to her. She would like to do something for them in return.

She would give the statue to Gustave as a birthday gift. It

wouldn't be the same as having his father back, but it would be something. A comfort.

That and the beautiful gown were the only advantages she had at the moment. And in the fight for her life, Fiora needed all the help she could get.

Something crashed into the window. A seagull streaked with black. He landed on the ledge and tapped at the glass with the shell in his beak.

"That bird certainly seems fond of you, Lady Mer," Dowager Queen Bernadine said.

"Perhaps it was a mistake to feed him."

She tried to stay calm, but she couldn't help fidgeting as Spot continued to tap on the glass. The mermaids wanted to meet her. Perhaps they had found a way to break the enchantment, and she could stop worrying about being proper and winning Gustave's heart.

She refused to feel disappointed that finding a cure would mean leaving Gustave and the human world behind.

How long would the mermaids wait for her to come? How long would it take Marie to alter the gown?

"I've never seen a bird with markings quite like that," the dowager queen said. "He looks like he found a bottle of squid ink."

Fiora froze as Dowager Queen Bernadine cast a knowing look at her hair.

"I used squid ink for dye when my hair went gray. Unfortunately, that was a losing battle."

She gestured to her white hair with a playful gleam in her eyes.

Fiora took a deep breath and tried not to panic.

Bernadine knew. The dowager queen had somehow figured out that Fiora was in disguise and her hair had been dyed.

What else had she guessed? It seemed Bernadine had the sharpest eyes in the castle regardless of her age. Or perhaps because of it.

Whatever else she knew, the dowager queen didn't seem inclined to share it. Instead, she winked at Fiora.

"Dress fittings are rather dull, aren't they? Have you pinned enough to finish the hem, Marie? We can keep the shoes here to measure the height."

"Yes, Your Highness."

"Then let's help Lady Mer change and set her free."

✻ 38 ✻

"**Y**our Majesty, this is most inappropriate!"

Marquis Corbeau paced around the room as Gustave ripped the paper off packages and muttered a quick comment to the scribe, who scratched out as suitable a thank you note as he could manage under the circumstances.

"If there is an enchanted object here, we need to find it. Our safety is more important than propriety."

Marquis Corbeau waved his hands in the air in frustration and turned his attention to correcting thank you notes over the scribe's shoulder.

The door opened, and Gustave looked up. This would be a lot more fun with Lady Mer assisting, but it was Kara who entered the room.

"I thought I might be able to help?"

She looked hopefully at Gustave. He turned to Elaine, who nodded.

"We're pulling out all the smaller boxes first. They seem more likely to contain gemstones. If you bring packages to Gustave, I can focus on checking the items."

Kara nodded and walked over to the jumble of gifts. The

boxes had been pushed back against the bookshelves in haphazard piles. She searched the nearest stack, pulled out a small box, and brought it to Gustave.

"From Gaveron," she said with a shy smile. "The dwarfs there know magic, so this seems like a good place to start."

Gustave took the box. His fingers brushed against Kara's hand as he did so, and her face flushed. She looked quickly around the room, and Gustave followed her gaze. Marquis Corbeau was arguing with the scribe about the wording on a thank you note. Elaine was studying a pile of delicate purple glass that had probably been a vase before the accident.

No one was paying attention to them. Kara spoke rather quickly.

"Gustave, there's something I need to tell you while I have the chance."

Gustave hoped he didn't look as panicked as he felt. He motioned for Kara to continue. She swallowed before speaking.

"Thank you."

That seemed to be the extent of her speech. Gustave blinked at her. What was she thanking him for? And why did it leave her so flustered?

"When I was nine, I sprained my ankle in the garden while I was here visiting Collette. You carried me back to the castle. It was a hot day, and I know I was heavy. But you never complained. Never said a word. And I was too shy to thank you then. So I'm thanking you now."

"I don't remember."

He truly didn't. His head didn't ache from the golden fog or his injury. His mind was clear for once, letting him search his memories. And they didn't include Kara.

She ducked her head.

"It was nothing special for you. Of course not. That's just what you do, isn't it? Help people. That was just one incident in many."

"I'm sorry."

"There's no need to apologize."

Except there was, because Kara looked absolutely crushed. Gustave stammered a little, trying to think of something to say. Perhaps he should have lied and said he remembered.

But he had a feeling that would have caused an entirely different problem.

"Oh, is that from Gaveron? They're known for enchanted objects because of the dwarfs."

Elaine hurried over to examine the box. Kara smiled sadly at Gustave and moved away. He tried to ignore the disappointed slump in her shoulders as he opened the gift.

It contained a ruby brooch. The red gem and gold clasp glistened in the sunlight. Elaine let her breath out in a slow hiss.

"Enchanted?" Gustave asked.

Elaine tapped her finger against the stone as if checking to see if it were hot. When nothing happened, she picked it up and cradled it in her palm, then pulled it close to her mouth and whispered something that Gustave couldn't quite make out.

When she lowered the gem, it looked exactly as it had before.

"It doesn't seem enchanted," she said. "Just extremely generous."

"You're still suspicious?"

Elaine nodded.

"Gaveron must have some reason for giving you such a valuable present, but perhaps it has nothing to do with magic. I suppose we should keep looking."

Gustave sighed and turned his attention back to the mountain of gifts. Kara had disappeared.

"What would Your Majesty like to say about the brooch?" the scribe said.

Marquis Corbeau gave Gustave a look, as if daring him to make an inappropriate comment. Gustave stared at the glittering ruby, trying to organize his thoughts.

Why would Gaveron give him such a valuable gem? They were on decent terms with Montaigne, but had never been a close ally. Gustave wanted to say that the gift was as baffling as it was beautiful. If Lady Mer had been there, he would have signed it to her. She would have said something clever that would help him make sense of the situation.

But she wasn't there, and Gustave swallowed his words as he always had before he met her.

"Tell the King of Gaveron that I am truly grateful for such a generous gift," he said instead. "It has left me speechless."

❧ 39 ❧

"Squawk."

Spot flew circles around Fiora as she limped barefoot through the garden. She tossed the crust of bread she had grabbed for him into the air. The seagull dropped the shell and dove for the food. Fiora caught the shell, checked to confirm that it had Zoe's song carved into it, and walked through the garden towards their usual meeting place.

"Squawk."

Spot flew towards the beach instead. Towards the place where Fiora had taken Gustave when she rescued him after the kraken attack

She changed course and followed the bird, wishing that she had stopped to find shoes before leaving the castle. She had left the golden heels in Dowager Queen Bernadine's room and gone barefoot without thinking about it. Which meant everyone in the castle had seen her once again behaving improperly, and she now had to climb down the rocks without protection for her feet.

Blast it all.

Fiora walked carefully, trying to avoid sharp edges and balance her full skirt while she moved.

This climb had been easier without clothing.

She reached the sand and followed Spot to the enormous rocks at the end of the beach. They would provide a nice hiding place for a more private meeting

"Fiora!"

Zoe sang her name, sending a spray of mist and rainbows dancing in the ocean breeze. Fiora grinned in spite of everything and walked to the edge of the water. The waves washed over her toes, numbing the pain. Fiora waded until she was ankle deep, pulling her skirt up to keep it dry.

As the water danced against her skin, she could almost forget she was cursed. The roar of the wind and waves made her heart soar. For all that she had tried to escape it, the ocean was home. Whether she was on the coast or beneath the surface, it had always been there for her.

"Come around to the other side of the rock so we're hidden."

Fiora lifted her skirts and waded deeper until she was completely hidden behind the enormous boulder in the water. She sat on the driest stone she could find and dangled her feet in the ocean.

"Have they found a way to break the enchantment?"

"They're still working on it, but Althea isn't hopeful. She sent me to see how you're getting along with King Gustave."

Zoe nodded towards the pearl ring. Fiora held her hand forward to show her cousin.

"It's working!" Zoe said. "It's gleaming more than it was last time."

Fiora squinted at the pearl. It was difficult to tell in the bright sunlight, but the pearlescent streak did look a little wider.

"Althea said you should try singing the counter-charm every few hours. She's not sure how much love you will need before you regain your voice, but it might not take all of it."

That was a little comforting. Maybe giving Gustave the statue of his father would win enough of his heart to return her voice so she could return to the sea.

"I brought you some jewelry for the gala tomorrow. I overheard some humans on a ship talking about it. It sounds very fancy, and I know humans like to decorate themselves for fancy events."

"It will be fancy."

Zoe beamed.

"The humans said the king might choose a bride there."

"They're celebrating Gustave's birthday. Some of his advisers want him to choose a bride, but he doesn't want to."

"Of course he does!" Zoe said. "At least, he will once he sees you in all these jewels."

Fiora expected Zoe to produce something recovered from a shipwreck, but the mermaid pulled a simple strand of pearls and coral from her hair. Fiora ran it through her fingers before slipping it over her head.

"Thank you, Zoe. It's lovely."

"I made it myself to bring you luck. I've been trying to think of ways to help. Oh, speaking of help, I should probably warn you-"

Before Zoe finished her thought, Madam Isla burst through the water. She carried a soggy lump of something that Fiora eventually realized was fabric.

The mermaid stretched the fabric out, and Fiora laughed in silent surprise. It was a dress. A waterlogged dress retrieved from the bottom of the ocean. The fabric had probably been green once, but exposure to sunlight and saltwater had faded it to a sickly yellow. The thread was holding on as best it could, but it had disintegrated in places, leaving one of the sleeves dangling precariously from the shoulder

"It's the best I could find," Madame Isla said. "It should be dry by tomorrow night, but I'm not sure how the humans will react to it. Perhaps you would make a better impression if you followed mermaid custom and went in your natural skin decorated with oysters."

Fiora pressed her lips together, her eyes watering with silent laughter as she imagined attending a formal gala in the nude. Yes, that would certainly make an impression. Then Gustave could offer the Aeonian sweater to her instead of Annabelle.

"The humans have already loaned me a dress."

"Oh. Well, I hope it's suitable. It's a good thing I brought some other supplies."

Madame Isla tossed the dress against a rock, where it landed with a sickly squelch. Then she hauled up a fishing net overflowing with items.

"You may not realize this, Fiora, but human courtship rituals are long and complicated. They cannot usually be completed in a matter of days."

Fiora rolled her eyes. She did not need Madame Isla lecturing her on yet another aspect of being human. It was the forks all over again.

"But the king already loves her," Zoe said. "Look at the ring!"

Madame Isla looked and nodded in approval.

"He has some feelings for her, but not enough yet. That's why I'm here to help."

"How could you possibly help?"

Madame Isla pulled the fishing net onto a flat rock and sorted through the items inside it as she spoke.

"Human courtship rituals take a long time, but human seduction may be completed in a matter of hours. I am going to help you seduce King Gustave."

Fiora blinked.

"Seduce him?"

"Yes, seduce him. We are going to make you irresistible to this human man."

"Is that a dead fish?"

"There is a human saying. You get to a man's heart through his stomach. If you cook him food, he will be more likely to view you as a future mate. I wasn't sure if you knew how to cook, so I also had our chef prepare some things."

She set the fish down and pulled out a few lumps of mermaid food, which looked like greenish mud mixed with fish scales. Madame Isla set them beside the fish, where they slowly began to flatten out and ooze green liquid.

Fiora gagged. Spot noticed the dead fish and hopped closer to investigate. Madame Isla waved the seagull away and continued.

"We will build a fire and roast the fish. Then we will decorate your hair with gems and flowers so you sparkle and smell nice. Once the man sees you sparkling, smells you, and eats the food, he will be yours."

Fiora wasn't sure if she should laugh or cry.

"It's not that simple."

"Come closer so I can arrange your hair. We need to win him over before the gala so he doesn't have the chance to change his mind once he sees all the other girls."

Other girls. Gustave was with Elaine right now, and Fiora was sitting on the beach with delusional mermaids, a dead fish, and a hungry seagull.

She was doomed.

Madame Isla picked up a large fork and held it so it gleamed in the sunlight. Fiora swallowed and turned to Zoe. Maybe she could still salvage this situation.

"Zoe, there is a statue in our summer garden that is a likeness of Gustave's father. Could you bring it to shore so I can give it to him as a gift?"

"Ah, gifts," Madame Isla said knowingly. "It is more common for the man to offer them to the woman, but that's not a bad plan. Go fetch the statue, Zoe. You might be a little young to witness seduction, anyway."

"I am not seducing King Gustave, and I'm certainly not letting you help."

"You most certainly will. Or I'll go back and tell Queen Gallerus that you're stealing a statue from her garden."

Fiora glared at the mermaid. Madame Isla glared back. Finally, Fiora sighed. She wanted the statue, and hopefully she could undo whatever work Madame Isla did before anyone saw her. She shrugged to signal her defeat.

"Which statue is it?" Zoe asked.

One of the new ones placed close to the mirror garden. It has a very detailed beard.

Zoe dove under the water, splashing Fiora and Madame Isla as she disappeared. Spot took advantage of the distraction to swoop down and snatch the fish. He carried it to the beach and pecked furiously, eating as much as he could before the other seagulls noticed his prize. The globs of mermaid food had flattened into puddles of green liquid on the rock. Madame Isla scowled at them as if they had done it just to annoy her.

"Well, so much for the food. We'll have to hope the statue is an acceptable alternative. Now come here, child. You cannot seduce a man looking like that."

If she wasn't able to seduce a man naked, Fiora had little faith that she could do it once Madame Isla was finished with her. But she needed the statue, and she wouldn't put it past Madame Isla to use magic to hold her in place if necessary.

So she sighed and slid closer to the mermaid.

"Before I decorate your hair, we should remove all that nasty squid ink. I created a potion to remove the stains from your grandmother's hair. It should work for yours as well."

Madame Isla pulled a small green bottle from the net. Fiora snatched it away before the mermaid could open it.

No. My hair must stay as it is.

"Don't be difficult, Fiora. Changing the way you look is a very effective way to catch a human man's attention, and your red hair is much more attractive than this dull black."

The hair stays.

Fiora stuffed the bottle down the front of her dress. Not the most elegant hiding place, but it was the best she could do to keep it away from Madame Isla.

The mermaid scowled but did not push the matter further.

"Very well. I will simply add more decorations to your hair to make up for the lack of color."

She combed Fiora's hair with the fork, humming as she did. The song created a fine mist that swept over Fiora and dampened her hair. Fiora felt a weight on her head as Madame Isla secured the fork into a strand of hair and let it hang loose.

"Don't make it too heavy. Everything is heavier on land."

Madame Isla ignored Fiora and tied another fork into her hair.

Fiora sighed. Hopefully she would have time to take them out before she presented the statue to Gustave. Otherwise, she would catch his attention in all the wrong ways.

This was maddening.

"Most of my research has involved sailors, but Zoe and I recently discovered a human communication charm shaped like a golden sphere. It had many fascinating records of human formal events, and I will use what I have learned to aid your seduction.

"Stop saying that it is a seduction. Gustave has to fall in love with me. It's not the same thing at all. Besides, I'm not capable of seducing anyone."

Madame Isla's eyes gleamed.

"Perhaps not now, but you will be when I'm finished."

🦊 40 🦊

G ustave surveyed the wreckage strewn about the library.
Colorful paper and boxes covered the floor. Servants
waded through the mess, searching for places to store the
unwrapped gifts.

The ruby pin from Gaveron still sat on Gustave's desk. Even
though Elaine's test had found no evidence of magic, he couldn't
shake the feeling that the gift was more than it seemed.

"I did warn you that my tests weren't perfect," Elaine said.
"I've read a lot about magic, but I have very little practical experience. It's possible I missed something."

They both looked at the pile of unwrapped presents and
shook their heads. They hadn't found anything, but that didn't
mean there wasn't an enchanted object in the room responsible
for nearly killing Lady Mer.

"I still don't understand why would someone want to cause an
earthquake," Gustave said.

Elaine shrugged.

"Perhaps it was a natural phenomenon after all."

"I have never seen so many diplomatic gifts opened so quickly," Marquis Corbeau said. "I hope your travesties of thank you notes don't start any wars."

Gustave sighed and massaged his forehead. Somehow, he had managed to open half the gifts and think of polite things to say about them in a few hours. It was amazing what you could accomplish when properly motivated.

The door opened. Gustave looked up, hoping to see Lady Mer.

But it was only a servant.

"Please, Your Majesty, the Dowager Queen would like to see you."

Gustave looked back to the pile of gifts. What if the enchanted object was hidden in one of the unopened boxes? What if it caused another earthquake during the gala?

"Go," Marquis Corbeau said. "Your thank you notes are getting less and less coherent."

"I'll search the library for information about magical earthquakes while you're gone," Elaine said. "Maybe I can find another method for testing objects for magic."

Gustave nodded and left the room. He hoped his grandmother didn't want him to do anything too difficult. He didn't have the energy for another challenging task.

"May I have a word, Your Majesty?"

Gustave whirled around, prepared to flee for his life if the speaker was Lady Annabelle.

But it was Kara. She wore a travel gown, sensible hat, and determined expression.

"I- I was just going to visit my grandmother."

He must have sounded nervous because Kara laughed a little.

"I won't take much of your time, Your Majesty. I only wanted to say goodbye."

Gustave blinked.

"You aren't staying for the gala?"

"No. There's no point in that now."

He blinked again. He was missing something.

"It will be a good party. Marquis Corbeau is annoying, but he knows how to entertain."

Gustave thought the comment was funny enough to warrant a laugh, but Kara simply shook her head.

"I didn't travel halfway across the kingdom for a party, Your Majesty. I came here for you."

He stepped back, which made Kara laugh again.

"I thought I might as well be honest before I leave. King Gustave, I have had a crush on you since you carried me through the garden when we were children. You are charming and handsome and always kind. When I heard you were searching for a bride, I thought perhaps there was a chance for me. I convinced Collette to invite me to the castle a few days before the gala so I could get to know you better."

She paused, and Gustave felt he should say something. He opened his mouth, but no sound came out. He shut it again and gave Kara an apologetic look.

"It's all right," she said. "I knew I didn't have much of a chance. I'm not clever or beautiful or exciting. But I also know my worth, and I respect myself too much to trail after a man who barely knows I exist. Especially when I suspect he's in love with someone else."

Her soft tone and gentle smile took the sting out of the words. A wisp of golden fog in Gustave's head whispered that Kara was right. He was in love with another woman.

He swallowed.

"Kara, I am sorry if I hurt you. I don't plan to take a bride before I find my father. I have told my family that many times, but they don't seem to believe me."

"As I said, I simply wanted to give myself a chance. And now I won't spend my life wondering what might have happened. I hope you will be happy, King Gustave."

"You really should stay for the party."

"There will be enough young women there that my presence will not be missed. Besides, I received a letter from my brothers today asking if I could return at once. I am not needed here, but it seems I am needed at home."

She curtsied and walked away with her head held high. Much as Gustave hated to admit it, she was right. If she hadn't said goodbye to him, he probably would not have noticed her absence at the gala. Perhaps he should have made more of an effort to get to know her.

Or perhaps his family should have believed him when he said he was not looking for a bride.

"King Gustave! There you are. I found a book of duets in your music room. Would you like to sing one with me this evening?"

Lady Annabelle's eyes had that familiar predatory gleam, and she watched Kara retreat down the hallway with a little too much satisfaction. Gustave swallowed.

"I'm afraid I don't sing well. Please excuse me. I'm late to meet my grandmother."

He bowed and hurried away, relieved that Lady Annabelle didn't follow. But he slammed the door behind him and leaned against it when he reached his grandmother's room.

Just in case.

The dowager queen raised an eyebrow.

"Thomas, perhaps you should leave us for a moment. My grandson seems to be in some sort of crisis."

Thomas bowed and left the room. Bernadine fixed her sharp gaze on Gustave.

"Well? What is it?"

Gustave hesitated. He didn't want to admit that he had been running from Lady Annabelle. It was ungentlemanly.

Probably unmanly, period.

"Kara," he signed instead. *"She's decided not to stay for the gala."*

Dowager Queen Bernadine raised an eyebrow.

"I didn't think you knew that girl existed."

"I didn't. Well, not really. Not until she said goodbye and admitted that she's liked me since we were children."

"Well, I'm glad she found her voice at last. You said she's not staying for the gala?"

Gustave nodded.

"I didn't mean to hurt her, but I don't feel the same way. I'm not getting married until I rescue father. And I need to find the woman from the beach first. She's the one I love."

He added the last bit without meaning to. He had almost forgotten about the woman who rescued him. How could he have let her slip from his mind so easily when he loved her?

Dowager Queen Bernadine snorted.

"You'll drive yourself crazy thinking like that, Gustave. The girl from the beach is perfect in your memory because you don't know her, but a real woman will always be better than a dream."

Gustave turned away to hide his frustration and studied the portraits on Bernadine's wall. Normally he would focus on his father, but today the portrait of his grandfather claimed his attention.

"Are your memories of Grandfather perfect? You loved him."

Dowager Queen Bernadine laughed.

"In my memories, he is the perfect husband, but in reality, he drove me to distraction much of the time. It's tempting to look back and think everything was easy, but it wasn't. It never will be. If you wait for the right time to give your heart or the perfect person to give it to, you'll never love at all."

Gustave frowned.

"Are you saying I should have given Kara a chance?"

"I'm saying that you shouldn't wait for things to be perfect, because even true love never will be. Don't let your concern for your father or your daydream of a girl on the beach ruin your chance at something real."

"She's real. She saved my life."

"And she hasn't made any effort to contact you since. I've had all my spies out searching for a woman that matches your description. They haven't found her. Whoever she is, it seems she doesn't want to be found."

Gustave wasn't sure if he should ask for more information about the search for his rescuer or his grandmother's secret spy network.

"A real woman can't compete with your imagination, Gustave, and she shouldn't have to. When you find someone and are ready to settle down, I'll support you. Even if she isn't a traditional choice."

Dowager Queen Bernadine patted her grandson's hand. Gustave caught her fingers and raised them to his lips in a courtly kiss.

"*You are a gem, but I'm waiting until we find Father.*"

"Don't wait too long, Gustave. Some girls aren't willing to sit around forever. Not even for a king."

"*Are you referring to Kara or someone else?*"

His grandmother gave him a coy smile.

"As long as she's real, I'm talking about whoever captures your heart."

Gustave wished that Lady Mer's face didn't appear so quickly at his grandmother's words. There were too many mysteries around her, and he always managed to put his foot in his mouth whenever she was near. Besides, he couldn't afford distractions right now. He needed to focus on the search for his father.

"Find King Francois."

Gustave said this to his ring more out of habit than hope. He stared at the light that shone from the gem, not believing his eyes.

"It's moving," he breathed. "He's coming closer to shore."

"What was that?"

Gustave signed the words, and Dowager Queen Bernadine gasped as they watched the light track a path across the wall.

"It can't be," she whispered.

Gustave stood so quickly that he knocked his chair over. He ran from the room, bumping into Thomas in the hallway in his haste.

The light was moving. His father was moving.

"Summon a ship!" he yelled to no one in particular.

He heard a scuffle of activity behind him that hopefully meant he had been heard and obeyed. Gustave quickened his pace and raced through the garden as he followed the light.

❧ 41 ❧

Fiora's hair rattled when she stood. Madame Isla had tied five forks to the ends, as well as an assortment of shells and bits of glass. Things that would be considered trash if they washed up on the shore.

Madame Isla sang and smoothed out the water to create a smooth mirror on the surface. Fiora studied her reflection and tried not to grimace.

By mermaid standards, she looked very attractive. The effect would be better if her hair could float around in the water, but the decorations were nicely placed. They sparkled in the sun, casting glints of light on the nearby rocks.

By human standards, she looked like a garbage collector who stored everything she collected in her hair.

"It's-"

Thankfully Fiora was spared answering as Zoe burst through the waves with a cheerful song. The statue followed, flying through the air and landing in the sand with a soft thud. Zoe and Madame Isla sang together, creating a wave to wash it further up the shore and set it upright.

Fiora limped across the beach to study it. The statue had to be

King Francois. Why had she not noticed the resemblance to Gustave when she saw it before?

Probably because she had not known Gustave's face so well then.

"How will you summon the human man to be seduced?" Zoe asked. "Do you think he would follow the seagull?"

"I'm not seducing him, and sending a seagull as a messenger may be the most unromantic thing I've ever heard."

Madame Isla considered this.

"I suppose you'll have to go fetch him yourself and bring him back. That will give us time to find more fish and build a fire. You can offer him food after all!"

"No, please don't–"

But the mermaids were already gone.

Fiora sighed and stared at the statue. There was no way she could drag it up to the castle. It was taller than her and solid stone. She could barely hold her head upright from the weight of the forks and glass tied into it. She certainly wouldn't be able to move King Francois.

Madame Isla was right. Fiora would have to fetch Gustave and bring him to the gift instead. Maybe she could find him and get back before the mermaids covered the beach with dead fish in a misguided effort to help.

Seduction indeed.

Fiora winced, remembering how quickly Gustave had pulled back from kissing her. However bad Madame Isla's advice was, perhaps anything that distracted from her personality would be an improvement.

She looked at her ring. The stubborn streak of pink and blue still danced across the surface of the pearl.

Suddenly, Fiora felt too tired to stand. She slumped into the sand and leaned against the statue. If she had her voice, she would have talked to the stone king as she had talked to Gustave's statue when she was a child.

Instead, she leaned her head against King Francois's leg, careful not to stab herself with the many objects tied in her hair, and stared at the sea.

The waves rolled peacefully against the shore, never ending and never changing.

Why couldn't love be like that? Steady and reliable. Something that simply was. That you didn't earn and couldn't lose.

Was such a thing even possible?

A large wave washed halfway up the beach, leaving a streak of sea foam behind it. Fiora scowled at the water and stared at the sky instead.

One more day before the transformation charm ran out. She had one day to save her life by winning a king's love.

And the only thing she had to offer him was a statue pulled from the sea.

"Lady Mer?"

Fiora looked up, only mildly surprised to see Gustave running towards her. He seemed to find her wherever she went. She plucked a few bits of glass from her hair in a half-hearted attempt to make herself presentable.

"Lady Mer!"

Gustave's voice was urgent, and he sprinted across the sand as if his life depended on it. Fiora sat up a little straighter. What was wrong? Had something happened? He held his ring aloft, and the enchanted red light shone towards her.

No, it shone above her. Towards the statue.

"Lady Mer, you've found my father!"

❧ 42 ❧

Gustave raced across the beach. Sand flew behind his pounding feet as he gasped for air and followed the light towards Lady Mer and his father. She had found him! Somehow, Lady Mer had found him.

Then the sunlight shifted, and he realized she was sitting with a statue.

An impossibly realistic statue.

And the light from his ruby ring shone straight at it.

Surely that was impossible.

Gustave ran until he thought his heart would burst. He scattered a flock of seagulls pecking at a fish on the beach and slid to a halt in front of the statue.

Lady Mer stood and brushed sand from her skirt. Gustave wondered briefly why she had forks in her hair, but he was more curious about the statue of his father.

"Where did it come from?"

Lady Mer swallowed, looking more nervous than the mostly rhetorical question warranted. Gustave studied her while he waited for her response.

The bottom of her skirt was wet. It seemed she had been in

the water again. Her dark hair hung loose around her shoulders and was filled with an assortment of objects including forks, seashells, and bits of glass. The front of her dress was puckered. Had she stuffed something down it?

Gustave flushed and averted his eyes, realizing that he had accidentally been staring at her chest while trying to figure out what she had hidden in her gown. He turned his attention back to the statue.

"Find King Francois," he whispered to the ring.

The red light once again pointed to the statue.

Lady Mer's blue eyes widened.

"It's impossible," Gustave whispered.

But apparently it wasn't. This would explain how the mermaids kept his father alive underwater. King Francois had been imprisoned in stone.

"It's a statue of your father, isn't it?" Lady Mer signed.

"We never commissioned this. I think this statue *is* my father."

Lady Mer placed a trembling hand on the statue's arm, as if she hoped to sense the magic. She pulled it away, looking disappointed.

"How?"

"And why? And how do we free him?"

Lady Mer shook her head to say she didn't know. The forks in her hair bounced against her shoulders, reflecting light from the setting sun.

"Lady Mer, why are there forks in your hair?"

"What magic could have turned him into a statue?" she signed, avoiding the question.

"I've seen mermaid magic turn a man into a frog. Perhaps this is similar."

Gustave moved closer and kissed his father's cheek. He had seen one mermaid's curse broken with a kiss. Perhaps this one could be as well.

The stone was warm against his lips, but his father remained a statue.

"Mermaids didn't do this," Lady Mer signed.

A seagull streaked with black landed on the statue's head. Lady Mer waved her hands to shoo it away. Gustave turned to her.

"How do you know that mermaids aren't responsible?"

A shriek pierced the air. A cross between song and scream that made Gustave's scalp prickle. He knew that sound. He had heard it just before-

A giant tentacle shot out of the water, and Gustave groaned. He had heard it just before a kraken attacked Santelle. Apparently they were coming after Montaigne now.

"The mermaids were supposed to stop them."

As if that changed anything now. Gustave knew he should run, but he stood his ground, refusing to leave his father alone on the beach.

The song rang through the water again, and the tentacle swept towards shore. Lady Mer jumped in front of the statue and opened her mouth as if she meant to sing.

But no sound came out. She scowled and pulled two forks out of her hair instead. She brandished them at the tentacle as if they were swords.

"Look out!"

Gustave dove and pushed Lady Mer out of the way. The tentacle crashed onto the beach and sent sand flying over them. Lady Mer untangled herself from Gustave's arms and rushed back to the fight.

"Lady Mer, don't!"

She ignored him and stabbed the tentacle with the forks. Unsurprisingly, this had no effect. The tentacle ignored her and wrapped itself around the statue. Gustave sprang to his feet. This attack wasn't meant for them.

The mermaids wanted the statue back.

The song grew louder until it seemed to fill the entire ocean.

Rather than helping Lady Mer attack the tentacle, Gustave waded into the water. He plunged his head under the surface and squinted into the murky depths.

Yellow eyes stared back at him. Gustave resurfaced for air then ducked under the water again and stared back. He knew those eyes.

Leander.

Before Gustave could dive after the merman, a wave washed him back to the shore. He collided with Lady Mer, who offered him a fork. Gustave took it and stabbed the tentacle as hard as he could.

The fork bent in his hand as the kraken tentacle dragged King Francois towards the water.

A new song filled the air, and something silver rained from the sky. Gustave looked up in confusion. What was happening? One of the silver objects slapped his face, leaving behind a damp spot and a familiar smell.

Fish. Hundreds of fish rained onto the beach. Gustave slipped on them as he tried to reach the statue and fight the kraken. Lady Mer was having trouble walking as well. A second tentacle crawled up the beach and wrapped itself around her waist.

No. His father could survive underwater, but Lady Mer would drown.

Gustave turned away from the statue, slipped his way across the beach, and grabbed Lady Mer's hand. She clung to him, panic in her blue eyes as the kraken dragged her across the sand.

Another song filled the air, and the tentacle loosened. Gustave wrapped his arms around Lady Mer's waist and pulled, trying to free her from the kraken's grasp.

The song developed into a sort of battle. Gustave saw two mermaids floating in the shallow water singing together. He didn't recognize them. One looked young, and the other had flowing white hair. As their song intensified, the kraken tentacle around

Lady Mer loosened. She slumped into Gustave's arms as it slid back into the water.

The tentacle wrapped around the statue retreated as well. Gustave held Lady Mer tight as the kraken disappeared into the water. The white haired mermaid caught his gaze and winked. The young one giggled.

"Wait-"

But they had already disappeared into the sea.

Gustave helped Lady Mer sit on the beach and collapsed next to her. She clung to her fork and seemed to be having difficulty breathing. Gustave hoped the kraken hadn't cracked her ribs when it grabbed her.

He smoothed a strand of hair away from her face, then pulled his hand back. The action had been involuntary. Perhaps he shouldn't-

But she smiled at him and didn't seem to mind.

It felt right, somehow, being here with her on the beach. The only downside was the smell from all the fish, but Gustave forgot about the smell when Lady Mer leaned against him until their shoulders touched. He wondered if he should kiss her again. But maybe it was inappropriate to kiss her when she was still recovering from the attack. Should he ask? What if she said no?

Before he could decide what to do, the beach shook beneath them and rumbled with deep laughter. A tentacle wrapped around Gustave's ankle and pulled him into the ocean.

43

Fiora watched, too stunned to move, as a kraken tentacle pulled Gustave across the sand. He didn't have time to speak, but his eyes pleaded for help as he gasped for air and disappeared beneath the waves.

No. She wouldn't lose him.

Fiora jumped to her feet and ran across the beach. She wished that Madame Isla's misunderstandings of human fashion had involved knives rather than forks. Maybe those would have been more effective against a sea monster.

She waded until she was neck-deep, then took a deep breath and dove into the ocean. The salt water stung her human eyes, but she ignored the pain and searched for Gustave.

There. He was a few feet away, struggling to free his foot from the tentacle's grasp.

Fiora swam down and jabbed her fork into the kraken's suction cups, which seemed likely to be a weak point if the monster had one.

The tentacle did not react. It simply held Gustave below the surface. He kicked, but it did no good. Their eyes met, and Fiora read the panic in Gustave's expression. Her own lungs were burning, and he had been underwater longer than she had.

They didn't have much time left.

If only she had her voice! Her mermaid song might be able to control the kraken and make it loosen its grip.

Fiora stopped stabbing the tentacle and swam back a little to study the situation instead. Her hair floated around her, glittering with glass and shells. Her dress caught in a current and pulled her away from Gustave.

"Go back! Save yourself!"

Fiora ignored his signs and swam towards his leg. The tentacle was too large to wrap around something as small as a human leg effectively, and the suction cups were attached to Gustave's clothes, not his skin. She studied the seams of his trousers for a moment, then stabbed her fork through the fabric and pulled at the threads.

The fabric ripped at the seams and tore away. Fiora ignored the fire in her lungs and pulled off Gustave's shoe. Then she pushed down on the tentacle. As she had hoped, the suction cups stayed attached to the fabric. The kraken tentacle and torn cloth slid over Gustave's foot and sank into the water.

Fiora grabbed Gustave's shoulders and swam up. Her feet tangled in her voluminous skirt, slowing her ascent. Gustave kicked his legs and surged past her. He clutched her arm as he passed and dragged her through the water.

She gasped for air as her head broke through the waves. Gustave did the same, sputtering and coughing up water. Fiora continued to struggle with her dress as they limped through the ocean. Gustave kept a hand on her waist to help. They collapsed onto the sand and lay on their backs when they reached the shore. The statue of King Francois still sat on the beach. Madame Isla and Zoe had managed to drive the kraken away in time to save it.

Hopefully the mermaids could stop whatever was causing the

rumbling as well. Was it the same thing that had caused the earth-quake in the library?

There had been too many attacks to be a coincidence.

Gustave reached over and squeezed her hand, distracting Fiora from her musings. She smiled and squeezed back. He laced his fingers through hers and held tight. They lay together without speaking while they caught their breath. Seagulls and clouds floated in the blue sky over them.

"Thank you."

Gustave's voice was little more than a whisper. Fiora squeezed his hand again, grateful that he was still alive. If he had died-

She closed her eyes to hide the tears. There was no point thinking like that. He was alive. That was what mattered.

When she opened her eyes again, Gustave was sitting up and leaning over her with concern. The beach glittered silver around him. Beautiful until a breeze stirred up the scent of dead fish.

"Are you injured, Lady Mer?"

His hair and beard dripped water, and his eyes were filled with concern.

Concern for her.

"I'm fine."

"We should get you to a doctor."

"You're the one who needs a doctor."

Gustave sighed.

"Actually, my father is the one who needs a doctor. Or an enchanter. I'm not sure who would know how to break such a spell."

Fiora shook her head to show she didn't know either, and bits of glass rattled against her shoulders. She would ask her mermaid relatives about the king, of course. Althea seemed the most likely to know, and she could ask Zoe to search the library just in case. But the mermaids had never mentioned such an enchantment before.

Was Leander responsible? He was the only one Fiora could

imagine doing it, but what would he gain from capturing a human king? Why would he possibly want to drown Gustave?

She needed to speak with the mermaids as soon as possible. Something was going on here. Something strange that now involved her somehow.

"How do you think he washed up on the shore?"

Gustave gestured to the statue. Fiora swallowed. Telling him that she had found it and meant to give it to him as a birthday gift seemed impossible now. It would raise too many other questions after the kraken attack.

Honestly, it probably would have raised too many questions even without the kraken. This plan to catch his attention had been rather ill-conceived now that Fiora considered it further.

Then again, maybe it had worked out better than planned. Gustave took her hand again and held it tight. Fiora sat up and leaned her head against his shoulder. Gustave looked down at her and smiled.

"Your Majesty! There you are!"

Marquis Corbeau ran towards them. He slipped on a fish and stopped to stare at Gustave and Fiora. She couldn't blame him. Gustave's beard had dried into a frizzy mess. Her hair was full of forks and glass.

Not to mention there was a statue behind them that was really the King of Montaigne.

"We need to bring this statue back to the castle as quickly as possible," Gustave said. "It's my father."

"Obviously it's your father," Marquis Corbeau said. "But how? We never commissioned such a piece."

"I mean it's actually my father."

"Your Majesty!"

Captain Whist, Dale, and a group of soldiers ran down the beach. They also slipped on the fish, but fared better than Marquis Corbeau had.

"I heard the mermaid song," Captain Whist said. "Is there a kraken? What happened here?"

Gustave shook his head.

"It's gone now. Lady Mer fought it off with a fork."

Everyone stared at Fiora. She shrugged and waved the fork that she still held. Dale's eyes bulged.

"Lady Mer, where did you get that? I recognize the pattern. A custom design. It was on my ship that was lost."

Fiora didn't know what to say. She offered the fork to Dale, who clutched it like a lifeline. Now that she actually looked at it, the fork was rather unique. The handle was carved in the shape of a rose, and decorative vines crawled up it and curved around the tines.

"If this washed up, there may be more!"

Dale ran to the shoreline and searched the sand, kicking piles of fish aside in his quest for cutlery. Fiora and Gustave shared a look.

"Where exactly did you get that fork? And the rest of your, um, deco-rations?"

He let go of her hand to sign and gestured towards her hair. Fiora slumped into the sand. This had to be the least successful seduction in the history of romance. No matter how hard she tried, she just wasn't able to fit into the roles she was supposed to play.

"They're nice," Gustave quickly added. *"You look nice."*

Fiora gave him a look, and he laughed.

"I hope you'll tell me your story sometime, Lady Mer."

Then he stood, helped her to her feet, and walked over to direct the soldiers who were moving King Francois.

Fiora pulled bits of glass out of her hair and watched him place a hand on the stone to steady his father as the soldiers lifted him.

What would happen if she told Gustave her story?

Her heart pounded. If she told Gustave the truth, there was no going back. No pretending that she was not herself. No escape.

She pulled a fork from her hair. It was the same rose design as the one Dale held. She waved at the merchant and handed him the fork.

"Thank you, Lady Mer!"

Gustave looked back and smiled at her when he saw Fiora pull a third fork from her hair and hand it to Dale. Looking into Gustave's eyes, Fiora wasn't sure she wanted to escape. There was something there beyond his usual kindness and consideration. Something as steady as the waves.

She looked away, not sure she should trust the expression. Hearts were fickle. Men were fickle.

But this wasn't just any man. This was Gustave.

The soldiers hoisted King Francois onto their shoulders and carried him towards the castle, but Gustave stayed on the beach waiting for her. He smiled and offered his arm. He looked a little ridiculous with one trouser leg missing and his hair wild from the sea. But his gray eyes were steady and kind as always.

Fiora lifted her hands to tell him everything, then buried them in her skirt instead. She couldn't risk telling him the truth. Not when she needed his affection to save her life. Not when she had somehow managed to secure a bit of that affection through her disguise.

Gustave looked disappointed but didn't press her. He simply took her hand and helped her limp across the fish-covered beach. Seagulls scattered as they walked. The birds seemed unsure to do with their bounty. They hopped from fish to fish, fighting each other even though there was plenty to go around.

Fiora smiled as Spot stole a fish from another bird, and Gustave laughed with her. They walked hand in hand as they followed the soldiers and King Francois back to the castle.

❧ 44 ❧

"Y ou're saying this statue is my son?"

Dowager Queen Bernadine leaned back in her wheelchair, looking up at the statue with an expression that managed to be both calm and exasperated.

"But how?" Collette said. "How is this possible?"

She stared at King Francois and blinked back tears. Collette had already tried kissing the statue's cheek at Gustave's suggestion, as had Bernadine. Just in case.

It hadn't worked.

The conversation fragmented as everyone offered their theories and potential solutions. Gustave stepped back to examine the chaos from a different angle. Surely there was a way to fix this.

They had placed King Francois in the library. Dowager Queen Bernadine stared at him as if she could break the enchantment through intimidation alone. Collette walked slowly around the statue, studying it as if the answers were hidden somewhere in the stone. Marquis Corbeau and Marchioness Rouge argued about the implications this would have for the government and if the king's discovery should be announced publicly. Elaine searched the shelves for useful books.

Lady Mer and Dale stood near the window, seeming unsure if they belonged in this meeting or not. Dale was not so subtly eyeing the last fork in Lady Mer's hair. She noticed and untangled it with help from Princess Elspeth's mirror. The merchant took it gratefully and clutched the rose-inspired silverware to his chest in a strange bouquet.

Where had those forks come from? The whole incident on the beach had been bizarre, and Gustave had more questions for Lady Mer than he could keep track of.

As if she could hear his thoughts, Lady Mer turned and caught his gaze. Gustave swallowed. Whatever else had happened, she had saved his life. Not to mention she had found his father. Gustave couldn't shake the feeling that she was somehow responsible for bringing him back to Montaigne. Did she have some sort of connection to the mermaids who had kidnapped King Francois? How had she arranged for his release?

However she had done it, he was glad.

With a start, Gustave realized the room had gone quiet. Everyone had stopped arguing and turned to him for an answer.

Right. He was king. He was supposed to have all the answers.

"Obviously we don't know how to break the enchantment, and it may take some time to figure that out. Perhaps the most pressing question is what we do now. I propose we cancel the gala so we can focus our attention on Father."

"Cancel the gala?"

Marquis Corbeau's face turned a shade of outraged purple.

"Guests have already arrived," Collette said.

Her expression remained resolved when Gustave looked at her in disbelief.

"We can't do anything to help him right now, Gustave. Not unless Elaine has found something useful."

The group turned to look at Elaine, who had spread three books on a nearby table and seemed to be trying to read all of them at once. She looked up and frowned when Marquis Corbeau cleared his throat.

"I don't have anything yet, and I can't guarantee that you'll have anything in your library about this type of enchantment. Or that I'll be able to work the magic if we do find a spell."

Gustave looked to Lady Mer.

"You found the statue. Do you have any ideas?"

She shook her head. The bits of glass in her hair glistened like drops of water as she moved. Now that he was used to it, Gustave found the effect rather pretty. Marquis Corbeau, on the other hand, watched Lady Mer with the same expression he had worn when he saw the beach covered with fish.

"Your Majesty, we have royal guests! We missed greeting the Crown Prince of Eldria while you were off fighting kraken. The servants promised him that you would meet him for dinner tonight. We cannot cancel, and you cannot entertain a visiting monarch while you smell of fish and are missing half your trousers. We need to end this discussion and prepare for the reception."

Gustave looked down. He had forgotten that Lady Mer had cut off the leg of his trousers. That had been quick thinking, and she had saved his life while risking her own. He needed to thank her later. Maybe he could make her title official. Saving the king's life was surely worthy of a royal title.

But he couldn't do that or anything else that really mattered while he was entertaining guests.

"Perhaps if we told Prince Darian that we are having a family emergency–"

"Because the crown prince is renowned for his understanding and generous personality," Marchioness Rouge said. "Your Majesty, we should not offend him lightly. Trade with Eldria is very important to our economy."

"Gustave, as much as I hate to agree with him, Marquis Corbeau is right. We cannot ignore our guests, and we can't do anything for Father right now. We should prepare for dinner and smooth things over with Prince Darian."

Collette placed her hand on Gustave's shoulder. He shook his head.

"There must be something we can do. What about Lina? She knows a lot about magic."

Marquis Corbeau sniffed.

"Princess Evangelina is doubtless busy running her kingdom, Your Majesty. You should do the same. Starting with welcoming your guests at the reception tonight."

Gustave looked from the statue to the dowager queen.

"Grandmother-"

She shook her head.

"Gustave, there is nothing we can do for him tonight. But we can do something for Montaigne. We can celebrate your birthday and strengthen our relationship with Eldria. Your father would be proud of that."

Gustave looked away. He had been certain that at least his grandmother would support him. Why did everyone insist that a party was more important than freeing his father?

"They don't want to admit how confused they are," Lady Mer signed.

She stood behind the crowd, so her words were only for him.

"They don't know what to do, and that makes them feel helpless. Continuing with the gala will give them a way to keep busy while honoring your father."

Gustave considered this. Perhaps Lady Mer was right. He would do anything to help his father, but other than writing a letter to Lina, he had no idea what action to take. And the others weren't wrong about Prince Darian. Doubtless he was furious that he hadn't been properly greeted.

"You have him in the castle, at least. That's more than you had this morning."

Gustave nodded. He didn't know why his father had appeared

on the beach or why the mermaids had been there. Or why Leander had attacked them with a kraken to try to retrieve him. Or why Lady Mer had forks in her hair.

Or why fish had rained from the sky.

It had been a strange day that raised a lot of questions, and apparently he would not get any answers tonight.

Gustave looked at the statue of his father for guidance. King Francois's expression was sad but peaceful. Hopefully that meant the transformation hadn't been painful, and that he wasn't in pain now.

Because it seemed he would be a statue a while longer. Gustave took a deep breath and turned back to the crowd.

"We'll prepare for the reception," he said. "We'll greet Prince Darian and go on as if nothing has happened. But as soon as this gala is over and the guests have gone, I will focus my full attention on freeing Father from this curse."

❧ 45 ❧

Fiora watched the pile of glass and shells grow as the servants removed debris from her hair. They had taken one look at Fiora's tangled hair and one sniff of the fishy scent and declared there was no way they could have the lady ready in time for dinner. So they had summoned help and a tray of food so Fiora could eat while they worked.

She was grateful for the excuse to stay in her room. She closed her eyes, trying to push away the sinking feeling that had been building ever since Marquis Corbeau had mentioned that the Crown Prince of Eldria would join them for dinner.

Fiora had participated in a Princess Test and tried to win Prince Darian's affection last year. It had ended in a disaster almost as bad as the most recent one in Aeonia. After considering all the ladies present, Prince Darian had declared that none of them were fit to be his bride and ended the test without declaring a winner.

It was unprecedented and humiliating. Fiora could only hope that someone so arrogant had not been paying attention and wouldn't recognize her.

Or perhaps this was the perfect opportunity to reveal her true identity.

Fiora glanced at her pillow. She had hidden the dye removal potion underneath it. All she had to do was wash the squid ink out of her hair, and everyone would know.

"Are you alright, miss?"

She nodded and looked down at her ring. The pearly sheen had spread until it covered half the surface of the gem. Gustave loved her more now than he had that morning. Surely that was a good sign? And surely it would be far better to tell him herself than have an arrogant prince reveal her identity.

Then again, Prince Darian might not recognize her. He had considered her beneath him when she was a princess. He would likely think that even more when she met him as a mute commoner. Perhaps if she avoided him, she could remain in disguise.

But should she? Gustave half loved her. Perhaps if she told him the truth–

Someone knocked on the door, and Fiora rolled her eyes, annoyed to have her thoughts interrupted. The servants looked from the door to Fiora, unsure what to do. She waited a few moments, then shrugged her answer when the knocking didn't stop.

A servant opened the door and quickly dropped into a curtsy when she saw Princess Collette.

Fiora blinked. A visit from the princess was the last thing she expected.

"May I come in?" Collette said.

Fiora wanted to say no. If she'd had her voice, she would have done so at once. But it took extra time to form her thoughts into sign language, and somehow she found herself agreeing.

"You can leave us," Collette told the servants. "I'll finish helping Lady Mer prepare for the reception."

They curtsied and hurried away.

"If that's alright with you, that is," Collette added quickly.

Fiora shrugged her consent. Collette picked up a comb and worked it through Fiora's hair, removing the last few bits of glass. Fiora watched her work in the mirror and tried to guess what the princess wanted.

Collette swallowed a few times. She seemed to be working up the courage to say something.

Fiora waited. It wasn't like she had anything better to do. Finally, the princess won her internal battle and took a deep breath.

"Lady Mer, I've come to apologize. I've been rude to you since you arrived. I swore to use my position to help others, but I turned a blind eye to your need. I am sorry."

Fiora didn't know what to say. As far as she could remember, no one had ever apologized to her before she arrived in Montaigne. But the royal family seemed to do so as a matter of habit. Whether they had been unfriendly or a little too friendly.

Fiora scowled at the memory of Gustave's apology after the kiss. Collette flushed, thinking the expression was meant for her.

"I thought you were trying to trap my brother. The way you appeared and became inseparable from him seemed suspicious. Not to mention I had hopes of securing his affections for my friend."

Collette lowered her eyes and turned her attention back to Fiora's hair, twisting a few dark strands so they draped around her face.

"It seems so silly now, but you also reminded me of someone I've quarreled with in the past. I judged you by that person's actions instead of your own, which was a foolish thing to do."

Fiora's scowl deepened. She had a pretty good idea who that person was.

"But you're not her!" Collette said. "That's what I'm trying to say. She's awful, but you're not. It was a mistake, and I'm sorry."

Fiora sighed. Thank goodness she had dyed her hair. If the

normally kind Collette treated someone who reminded her of Fiora badly, how would she have treated Fiora herself?

And how would Gustave treat her if he knew?

This shook Fiora's confidence in the king's affections in spite of the pearl's glow. She was not a fool. She knew her reputation. She was so undesirable that her father had banished her to the sea to be rid of her.

Fiora looked at her pillow again. At the place she had hidden the potion that could wash away the squid ink and reveal her identity.

She couldn't tell him. Generous as he was, Gustave would not be capable of loving her as her true self. No doubt Collette had told him all the ways that Fiora had slighted her at the Princess Tests. And as king, Gustave would be familiar with other stories about Fiora and the royal family of Kell.

A tear slid down Fiora's cheek, and she brushed it away hastily. There was no point in regretting what couldn't be. Gustave's affection would crumble the moment she said her true name, so she wouldn't say it. Simple. Easy.

"Oh, Lady Mer, I've upset you further! Please forgive me!"

Was Collette apologizing for apologizing? The people of Montaigne really did take their manners too far sometimes.

"Please, don't trouble yourself. You are very considerate to apologize, but it is unnecessary."

"It is completely necessary! I may not have understood what my brother saw in you at first, but you risked your life to save him from a kraken this afternoon. Whatever misfortunes befell you in the past, you are brave and loyal. I would be honored if you would accept my apology and be my friend."

Collette held out her hand, and Fiora blinked at it. She had never had a woman offer friendship. Or a man either, for that matter. After a moment's hesitation, she reached out and clasped Collette's hand. The friendship was based on a lie as much as her relationship with Gustave was, but she would take whatever she could get.

"Would you like to get ready for the gala with me tomorrow?" Collette said. "The other princesses and honored guests will all get dressed together. I could use some backup against Lady Annabelle now that Kara has gone home."

Fiora smirked.

"You don't think you've misjudged her as you misjudged me?"

Collette sputtered for a moment before she realized Fiora was joking. Then she laughed.

"No, I certainly don't. That portrait–"

She giggled, and Fiora joined the princess in silent laughter.

"Oh, you've missed dinner as well," Fiora signed. *"Please, have some food."*

She gestured to her tray, but Collette shook her head.

"I had some paperwork to finish for the new budget proposal, so I ate in my room while I worked on it. It also gave me an excuse to gather my courage before facing the Crown Prince of Eldria. I've met him before at a Princess Test. I'm afraid he's rather insufferable."

If Fiora had her voice, she would have commented on Prince Darian at once and ruined her disguise. As it was, she raised her hands to agree and realized her mistake in time.

"We'll have to stick together at the reception, then. An arrogant prince can't be any worse than a kraken."

Collette tried not to smile, but she couldn't stop the corners of her mouth from twitching upwards.

❧ 46 ❧

Gustave hurried through the hallway. If he had to put his father's rescue aside to entertain guests, he would prefer to do it properly. Being late for dinner was not a good way to smooth things over with Prince Darian.

"Your Majesty!"

Dale ran towards Gustave and fell into step beside him. He was dressed for dinner but still carrying the forks Fiora had pulled from her hair. Gustave quickened his step, but the merchant matched his pace.

"I see we're both running late," Dale said. "I went back to the beach to look for more forks and regrettably ruined my clothes digging through fish."

"Did you find any?"

The merchant shook his head.

"It seems Lady Mer found all of them. I plan to return after the next tide to check again. Perhaps more will wash up."

"You're sure those are forks from your ship?"

"Of course. They're a custom design specially commissioned."

Dale handed a fork to Gustave, who studied it with interest. It truly was a unique piece of cutlery. The end was intricately carved into the shape of a rose. Delicate vines crawled up the handle and wrapped around the tines.

"It's not the most practical design, is it?"

"This is what my client wanted."

Dale took the fork back from Gustave and studied it with a frown.

"I'm afraid this confirms that my ship was lost at sea. These have been underwater. Look at the tarnish."

He pointed grimly to the spots on the silver. Gustave nodded. The forks had definitely spent some time in the sea.

So how had Lady Mer found them? Had they washed ashore? Had the mermaids brought them to her?

But why would mermaids bring her forks? And why would she tie them into her hair?

Gustave sighed. None of it made any sense.

Dale echoed his sigh.

"If there's no hope of retrieving my ship, I suppose I should sail back to Eldria. At least I'm not returning to my client completely empty-handed."

"Stay for the gala, at least," Gustave said.

"Your Majesty has been far kinder than I deserve, but I'm a humble merchant. I have no business socializing with royalty."

"I understand you want to return home, but it may take time to find a ship willing to take passengers after the kraken attacks. We can help you secure passage, and I hope you'll stay and enjoy the gala in the meantime."

Gustave was surprised to find that he meant it. Yes, Dale's inquiries had been annoying, but the man was simply trying to provide for his family. His persistence was understandable.

Dale smiled.

"I would like that, Your Majesty. It would give me at least one pleasant story to tell my family when I return. Your kindness is unprecedented."

Gustave shrugged, not sure what to say to that. The kindness had cost him very little.

They reached the dining room, and Gustave took a deep breath. It was time to be a king. He turned to the footman at the door.

"Have any of the guests arrived yet?"

"The crown prince is already inside. He insisted and said that he didn't mind waiting."

Not likely. Gustave squared his shoulders and prepared to face the arrogant prince.

"Very well. Please announce us."

The footman opened the door.

"His Royal Majesty King Gustave of Montaigne and Merchant Dale Mercer of Eldria."

Gustave held his head high as he entered the room and prepared for whatever insult Prince Darian threw at him.

But Darian wasn't in the room. A young man at the table quickly stood when Gustave entered. Gustave blinked, trying to remember where he had seen him before. What was his name?

"Crown Prince Edric at your service," the young man said, answering the question Gustave hadn't asked. "I believe we've been introduced once before, but that was several years ago. It is an honor to visit you in Montaigne, King Gustave."

He bowed low, raising a hand to hold his crown in place so it wouldn't fall off his head. It was a little too big, as if it had been made for someone else.

It probably had. Gustave thought back, trying to remember news of the Crown Prince of Eldria dying. He had been distracted while searching for his father, but surely not so distracted that he had missed or forgotten that announcement.

"Forgive me, but your brother-"

Gustave didn't finish the sentence. He wished he hadn't started it. Asking what had happened was basically admitting that he didn't know what had happened. Which was unbelievably rude. He had received condolences from every royal family in Myora when his father disappeared. If Prince Darian had died and Gustave had not sent condolences, that would be a horrible breach of etiquette.

But Prince Edric smiled.

"You have not missed a royal announcement, Your Majesty, and I apologize for not sending word ahead of my arrival. My older brother recently became unable to fulfill his royal duties and abdicated the throne to me. This is my first time attending a royal event as crown prince, and I do beg pardon in advance if I get anything wrong."

Prince Edric did not look particularly upset about whatever misfortune had caused his brother to be unsuitable for his duties. Either it was nothing serious, or he was rather pleased to have inherited the throne.

Possibly both.

Gustave looked around the room. The servants were waiting to put food on the table until the guests sat.

All three of them.

A footman entered the room and handed Gustave a note from Collette. She apologized for missing dinner and said she had paperwork to complete. For once, Gustave wished he was the one doing the paperwork. It would be better than trying to smooth over the awkwardness with Prince Edric.

The door burst open, and Thomas pushed Dowager Queen Bernadine into the dining room.

"I was afraid I was late, but apparently that was an unfounded concern."

She gave Prince Edric a questioning glance.

"Grandmother, this is Crown Prince Edric of Eldria," Gustave said.

She raised an eyebrow as she studied the prince.

"The younger son," Gustave signed. *"Apparently Darian is unable to carry out his duties and has abdicated."*

"Interesting."

Her expression said she found the whole thing suspicious. Marquis Corbeau burst into the room before the dowager queen could comment further.

"Your Majesty, please forgive my tardiness. I have just received word that another royal guest will be joining us tomorrow, and I-"

"Are you sure we have enough room?" Dowager Queen Bernadine said.

Marquis Corbeau glowered at her and shut his mouth with a snap. Lady Annabelle and Elaine entered with Marchioness Rouge. Lady Annabelle rushed over to Gustave.

"Oh, Your Majesty, I heard about your misfortune on the beach today. I am so glad you are well!"

"Misfortune?" Prince Edric said.

Lady Annabelle glanced at Prince Edric and smiled when she saw his crown.

"King Gustave has had the most interesting times on the beach lately. Would you believe he found a woman-"

"Shall we sit down to dinner?" Gustave said. "The food will get cold if we wait."

Lady Annabelle huffed a little, but brightened when Prince Edric offered his arm to escort her to the table. Since Lady Mer was absent, Gustave offered his to Elaine.

"I've had no luck," she whispered as they walked. "I only agreed to take a break because they refused to bring me a tray in the library. Something about the food damaging the books. I'll return to my research as soon as we finish dinner."

"Oh, Your Majesty, what are you whispering about over there?" Lady Annabelle said. "He is so terrible, Prince Edric. Always having private conversations and ignoring the rest of his guests."

"Well, perhaps we can show him how it feels to be left out," Prince Edric said.

He leaned over and whispered something to Lady Annabelle. She giggled.

Gustave raised an eyebrow. The former crown prince of Eldria had claimed that no woman was good enough for him. Apparently the new one was not so picky.

Why had they not notified him in advance? Eldria could hardly blame him for reacting with surprise when they swapped crown princes without warning. Whatever misfortune had befallen Prince Darian must have been very sudden indeed.

Gustave stared at the door, wishing Lady Mer would arrive so he could discuss it with her.

❦ 47 ❦

Fiora and Collette shared a look before entering the reception room. Collette seemed nearly as nervous as Fiora felt. Apparently Prince Darian had made a bad impression on everyone at his Princess Test.

But Collette was only nervous about a few minutes of unpleasant conversation. Fiora risked discovery if the prince recognized her.

She searched the parlor when she entered and breathed a sigh of relief.

He wasn't there.

Collette relaxed a little as well. She walked to the other side of the room, where Gustave was speaking with Lady Annabelle and a man with dark hair that Fiora didn't recognize.

Gustave smiled brightly when he saw Fiora. She smiled back and resisted the urge to look at her ring to see if she had completely won his heart yet.

It seemed the gift had worked. Not quite as intended, since the statue was apparently Gustave's father, but that was better in a way. She had caught his attention and given him something of value. If she could keep her identity a secret, she may be able to win his heart after all.

Now where was Prince Darian?

"Princess Collette, what a pleasure to see you again."

The young man beside Gustave bowed and reached up to keep his crown from falling off his head. Fiora hadn't noticed the crown before. Both she and Collette cast a questioning glance at Gustave.

"Please, allow me to introduce His Royal Highness Crown Prince Edric of Eldria."

"Oh."

Collette's small exclamation of surprise seemed involuntary. Fiora raised an eyebrow. Gustave seemed surprised by her surprise.

"Were you acquainted with Prince Darian?" he signed.

Fiora shook her head, cursing herself for reacting. Lady Mer should not know either prince of Eldria, much less which one was supposed to inherit the crown.

"He isn't the crown prince," Collette signed.

"Apparently he is now," Gustave answered. *"He said his older brother was suddenly incapacitated."*

"I see what you mean about secret conversations," Prince Edric said to Lady Annabelle. "I recognize Princess Collette, of course, but who is this lady?"

He turned his attention to Fiora. She felt her face flush under his scrutiny.

"That's Lady Mer," Lady Annabelle said. "It's a nickname, and she isn't really a lady. She's a mute that King Gustave found naked on the beach and adopted."

"How generous."

Prince Edric's searching gaze dropped lower as he studied Fiora from head to toe. Fiora wished she had her voice so she could tell him to go swim in a moat. She had to settle for glaring, but he was no longer looking at her face, so he didn't notice.

If he didn't stop looking at her like that, she might slap him to get his attention.

Gustave stepped between Fiora and Edric, cutting her off from his gaze.

"Lady Annabelle, didn't you agree to sing for us this evening?"

"Yes, of course! I believe Thomas is going to accompany me."

She waved to the translator. Thomas nodded and left the dowager queen to take his place at the piano in the corner.

"Charming," Prince Edric said. "I look forward to hearing you sing, Lady Annabelle. I have a great fondness for music."

And other things, apparently. Fiora rolled her eyes as Prince Edric followed Lady Annabelle across the room. At least she didn't have to worry about being recognized and exposed by the former crown prince. Prince Edric had not been involved in the Princess Test in Eldria and didn't know her. Her disguise remained safe for the time being.

"King Gustave is also very fond of music," Lady Annabelle said. "He has declared himself to be in love with a mysterious lady with a fine voice."

She nudged Prince Edric's shoulder and gave Gustave a meaningful look.

"She's trying to make you jealous," Fiora signed.

"They can have each other. Do you know Prince Darian? You seemed surprised to see Edric instead."

"No, I don't know him. I only noticed Collette's confusion."

Gustave turned to Collette for confirmation, but she had taken over translating for Dowager Queen Bernadine while Thomas played for Annabelle.

"I believe you promised me a dance?" Gustave said.

He offered his hand. Fiora took it, and Thomas began to play. Other couples followed the king's example and made their way to the dance floor.

Pain shot through Fiora's feet as she matched Gustave's steps. She ignored it and focused on his eyes instead. There was something in his gaze that she couldn't quite name. Something she hadn't seen when anyone looked at her before.

Lady Annabelle began to sing. Her voice was clear and sweet and didn't match her personality at all.

Fiora wanted to say this to Gustave, but she couldn't sign while they were dancing. She sighed in frustration and met his gaze instead, willing the words to communicate themselves to him.

"Dancing isn't the best place for conversation, is it?"

Fiora grinned in spite of her frustrations. How was it that he always seemed to understand her?

"I must admit, I have a lot of questions after today. But mostly, I want to say thank you. You saved me from the kraken. Also, I can't shake the feeling that you had a hand in bringing my father back to me."

It wasn't really a question, so Fiora didn't answer. Any conversation about the statue was bound to come around to mermaids and the sea, and she wasn't ready for that yet. Prince Darian's absence had bought her more time.

"I don't know when or how, but I hope someday you will trust me with your story."

Perhaps someday. She would have said that if she had her voice. Instead, she shrugged. That seemed to be enough for Gustave, and he didn't press further.

The song ended, and Lady Annabelle bowed as the assembled company clapped. She refused Prince Edric's request that she sing another song and set her gaze on Gustave. She wore a predatory smile as she stalked towards him.

There was no question about it. Lady Annabelle wanted a dance. Fiora loosened her grip on Gustave's hand and prepared to step back. He probably didn't want to dance with Lady Annabelle, but it would be impolite to refuse. And Gustave was always polite.

"Lady Mer, would you do me the honor of letting me escort you to the gala tomorrow?"

Fiora's eyes widened as Gustave kept hold of her hand and pulled her back towards him. He had spoken loud enough for the whole room to hear, and everyone fell silent and stared. She studied his face and found only steady regard in his eyes.

She nodded, not trusting her hands to be steady enough to answer with sign language.

Silent, secret conversations were one thing. A declaration this public was quite another. Lady Annabelle stood frozen in her tracks, too surprised to claim her dance.

Gustave smiled at Fiora, and something in her heart melted a little. Something buried so deep that she hadn't realized it was frozen.

The statue plan had worked better than anticipated. Gustave was well on his way to loving Lady Mer. The magical glow spread further over the pearl as they began another dance.

❧ 48 ❧

Gustave nodded to Thomas, who took his cue and began to play a slow waltz. Lady Mer fell into step with him again, watching him with her enormous blue eyes.

Gustave's heart beat faster than the slow dance justified. He hadn't planned to ask her to accompany him to the gala. The words had been as spontaneous as the kiss. A way to banish the insecurity that haunted her eyes.

But he didn't regret it. Being with Lady Mer felt right in a way that Gustave couldn't articulate. She was surrounded by mystery. He didn't even know her real name.

But he knew her.

Was that enough?

Lady Annabelle danced past in Prince Edric's arms. She laughed a little too loudly at whatever the prince said. Lady Mer rolled her eyes, and Gustave smiled.

No, he didn't regret it.

Lady Mer stumbled, and Gustave supported her weight while she caught her balance.

"You're injured."

She shook her head, looking fierce in spite of the tears welling in her eyes.

"Lady Mer, we can stop dancing. I would be happy to sit with you while you recover."

She shook her head again and pressed her lips together in a stubborn expression. Gustave placed a little more pressure on her waist, wishing he could hold her upright and heal whatever was hurting her.

"We'll have to open the gala with a dance while everyone watches. I'm sorry. I should have asked you in private first. I didn't mean to put you in a difficult position."

Lady Mer smirked, managing to look both amused and annoyed. Gustave had no doubt she would have plenty to say if she had a voice or use of her hands. But her expression seemed to say that it was fine, and he should stop apologizing.

At least, he hoped that was what she was saying.

"You don't mind?"

She shook her head. Gustave relaxed a little and focused on the dance. In spite of the pained look in her eyes, Lady Mer danced beautifully. Dowager Queen Bernadine nodded in approval from the side of the room. Even Collette looked pleased.

Marquis Corbeau looked annoyed, but that was nothing new.

The music ended far too soon. Lady Mer slid her hand off Gustave's shoulder and gave a wobbly curtsy. Gustave bowed low.

"My lady."

"My king."

She looked mischievous as she signed. Her attitude was nowhere near as respectful as her words. Gustave grinned.

"I think perhaps we should all save our energy for dancing at the gala," Marquis Corbeau said. "Tomorrow will be a full day, and today has been quite trying as well."

He glared at Gustave as if everything that had happened today was the king's fault. Gustave considered protesting. The reception had just started.

But he wouldn't mind ending it early. Lady Mer looked like she needed rest, and Gustave wanted to check on his father.

He turned to Dowager Queen Bernadine.

"Is it unspeakably rude to end things so soon?"

"Possibly, but I don't think anyone will mind."

Gustave turned to Prince Edric, who was still holding Lady Annabelle's hand even though the dance had ended.

"Do you mind an early night, Your Highness? We have all been rather busy with gala preparations. Marquis Corbeau may have a point."

"Not at all. I must confess, I am rather tired from my sea voyage."

The prince kissed Lady Annabelle's hand and crossed the room to say goodnight to the dowager queen. Collette excused herself from the conversation as soon as Thomas resumed his translating duties. She hurried over to Lady Mer.

"Would you like to walk with me back to our rooms, Lady Mer? I'm sure you must be exhausted after today."

Lady Mer looked to Gustave before nodding her head. Collette followed the gesture and signed to her brother.

"Don't stay up all night researching magic, Gustave. It took months to find Father. It may take as long to free him."

Gustave shrugged, not willing to promise anything. Collette raised an eyebrow but didn't press the matter. Gustave watched Collette and Lady Mer leave, then turned his attention to wishing everyone a good night so he could go to the library to check on the statue.

His father was just as they had left him. King Francois looked peaceful in the moonlight. Gustave stared at him as if wishful thinking alone could break the curse. Then he turned to the books Elaine had spread on the table.

She had already gone to bed, but had left notes highlighting pages that might be helpful. Gustave skimmed through them.

The book with the most notes was one about curses. He had read it after his father disappeared.

Elaine had marked information about curses that transformed humans into beasts or put people to sleep for a hundred years. Magic that could be triggered with words or enchanted objects.

On one page, she had lightly underlined a passage.

"The best way to break a curse is always connected to the casting of the curse. Some curses can best be dissolved by specific actions or objects that are woven into the design of the magic. Others bind the casting and the breaking together, so that only the same kind of magic that made the curse can reverse it."

Gustave wished he understood magic well enough to know exactly what that meant. The key to breaking Stefan's curse had been a kiss. A specific action. But a kiss had not freed his father.

So either King Francois's curse was designed to be broken by a different action, or it would require the same type of magic that had cast it. Which meant that even if Gustave could discover what magic had been used to turn his father into a statue, he would need to find someone who knew that particular kind of magic to undo it.

How many kinds of magic were there? Lina worked shadow magic, and Elaine had described enchanted objects. Was mermaid magic similar or something else entirely?

Gustave dropped his head into his hands, suddenly feeling very tired. He had thought finding his father would fix everything, but it had only brought more confusion.

He read the passages again, trying to make sense of the text. It was no good. He may be king, but he was completely useless here.

"Find King Francois."

Gustave studied the red light as it pointed at the statue. Without it, he might have assumed his father was dead and given up hope. But the ring only tracked people who were alive. So somehow, his father was still alive under that stone.

The light faded, and Gustave sighed. As much as he wanted to keep searching, he didn't know where to turn next. He needed sleep so he could be king tomorrow and stay awake for the gala. Perhaps rest would help him unravel the mystery.

Gustave walked slowly through the castle, realizing for the first time that the encounter with the kraken had left him with several large bruises on his legs. He didn't bother to change when he reached his room. He collapsed onto his bed fully clothed and let himself sink into oblivion.

❧ 49 ❧

Fiora awoke with the distinct feeling that something was wrong.

She lay still and took a few deep breaths to steady her nerves. Of course something was wrong. She was cursed and dying and need to flirt her way to survival.

But it was more than that. Moonlight streamed through her window, telling her that it was middle of the night.

A cool breeze washed over her, blowing wisps of hair across her face.

The window and curtains had been closed when she fell asleep.

Fiora sat up and froze.

There was someone in her room.

A woman. She wore a black cloak with the hood pulled over her face and hair. She was nearly invisible in the shadows, and she tensed when Fiora moved. Then she edged closer and reached for the conch shell.

Fiora tried to scream, but no sound came out. The woman laughed softly as she claimed the shell and put it in a satchel strapped around her waist.

Fiora jumped to her feet, ready to fight and retrieve the conch.

But pain shot through her legs when she stood. She collapsed back onto the bed.

The woman stayed still, watching. Fiora panted for air and tried to push away the agony. What did the intruder want? Would she be satisfied with the shell? Or was she here to do more than steal?

The woman seemed to be considering this as well. Fiora was an easy victim. Silent and helpless.

She took a step forward and reached into her satchel. For a weapon?

Fiora grabbed the nearest thing to her. The bell on her nightstand. She raised it, meaning to throw it at the intruder in defense. It made a loud clang, so Fiora shook the bell instead, ringing it and making as much sound as possible.

The woman sprinted out the door. Fiora dropped the bell and ran after her, fighting through the pain and forcing her shaking legs to keep moving. She needed that shell! Sweat beaded on her forehead as she pursued the thief through empty, moonlit hallways.

Fiora lost sight of her somewhere near the library. She leaned against a wall and gasped for air as tears ran down her face.

The curse was getting worse, and someone had just stolen the song she needed to break it.

A soft sound echoed through the hallway. Someone humming? Fiora limped towards it until she reached the library. Flickering light streamed under the door. Fiora pushed it open.

Elaine sat at a table reading and humming to herself as she worked. She flipped through pages and took notes with a quill pen. She had a streak of ink across her nose.

She didn't look up, and Fiora watched her in silence. Had Elaine stolen the conch? She had studied magic, so it was possible she recognized the mermaid charm and wanted it for her studies.

She would have had time to remove her cloak and hide it somewhere before Fiora came in.

But how could she have known the shell was in Fiora's room?

Fiora swallowed. If Elaine was responsible for the theft, she might be dangerous. But if she wasn't, she might have seen the person who was. Was it worth the risk?

At this point, Fiora had no choice but to take risks.

She knocked on the open door to get Elaine's attention. Elaine looked up and blinked in surprise as if waking from a trance.

"Oh, Lady Mer. What are you doing up so late?"

Fiora raised an eyebrow, reflecting the question back at Elaine. The girl made a face and scratched her nose, leaving another streak of ink across her skin.

"They kicked me out earlier, so I waited until everyone went to bed and sneaked back in. This is the most comprehensive book about curses I've ever read. There has to be an answer in here somewhere."

She didn't look guilty. Fiora might as well ask a few questions and see if she could gather any information.

"Did you see anyone run past?"

"I'm sorry. I didn't quite catch that. Could you spell it for me?"

Fiora hesitated a moment, then walked closer so Elaine could see her in the candlelight. If Elaine attacked her, Fiora wouldn't be able to run fast enough to escape. She would only make the other girl suspicious if she kept her distance.

Fiora repeated her question by slowly spelling out the words. Elaine shook her head.

"I haven't seen anyone. Why do you ask?"

Fiora considered how to answer. If Elaine had stolen the shell, she would doubtless deny seeing anyone. Then again, she was often so engrossed in her books that she failed to notice what was happening around her.

"I t-h-o-u-g-h-t I h-e-a-r-d s-o-m-e-o-n-e."

There was no point in explaining the robbery. If Elaine was responsible, she would deny everything. If she wasn't, mentioning the shell would raise questions that Fiora would rather not answer.

Questions like why a robber would take a seashell instead of a silver candlestick. The silver was far more valuable unless you knew the conch was etched with a magical song.

Fiora's heart sank. She hadn't memorized the song. She had almost won Gustave's love, but that wouldn't help her without the song. Even if she recovered her voice, she wouldn't be able to break the curse.

She massaged her forehead, trying to push back the headache and panic building in her skull. Surely one of the mermaids knew the notes for the transformation. If she did manage to recover her voice, they could copy the enchantment for her.

So why would someone steal it?

Elaine watched her with concern.

"Are you well, Lady Mer? Perhaps you should sit down."

Fiora sank into the chair Elaine offered. Losing the shell was bad but not the end. She would simply need to find a mermaid who knew the song after she won Gustave's heart. It would cut her precious time a little shorter.

More concerning was the fact that someone in the castle knew she was a mermaid.

And they wanted to keep her silent.

Were they working with Leander? Was this connected to the earthquakes and the kraken attacks?

Why were they so determined to sabotage her life?

Fiora looked to the statue of King Francois. The kraken had been trying to recover it. Maybe whoever wanted her quiet had also cursed the king.

Elaine followed Fiora's gaze and frowned at the statue.

"I've read everything in this book about breaking curses, but I haven't found anything useful. True love's kiss is a common method, but everyone with any connection to the king has already tried that."

True love's kiss. Fiora wished her enchantment could be broken so easily. Of course, that would still require her to win someone's love.

Elaine continued, talking to herself as much as Fiora.

"From what I understand, how to break a curse is usually woven into the way it is cast. So if we knew how King Francois was transformed, we would know how to free him."

Fiora raised an eyebrow. That seemed a difficult thing to discover. It wasn't as if King Francois could tell them. Elaine shrugged.

"I know. It seems hopeless. The other common way is exposure to the type of magic that cast the curse. For example, if mermaids cast this, mermaids would have to break it."

"I d-o-u-b-t i-t w-a-s m-e-r-m-a-i-d-s."

Elaine's eyes sparkled with interest.

"Oh? Do you have experience with mermaids, Lady Mer?"

Fiora glared at her and folded her hands into her lap. Elaine stared at her for a few moments, then shrugged and turned back to the books.

"It is also common for curses to bind their victim with a set of constraints. Things they can't talk about without severe consequences."

She said this casually, but her eyes glittered in the candlelight. Fiora fought to keep her face neutral.

"I-s t-h-a-t s-o?"

Her own situation was more complicated than that, but Elaine was less likely to ask inconvenient questions if she thought Fiora was unable to answer rather than refusing to do so.

"I've read that mermaids like to decorate their hair with bits of glass and shells. There are several accounts of sailors seeing them do it."

Fiora's eyes narrowed. Elaine was far too close to the mark for comfort. Likely the only thing keeping her from asking outright if Fiora was a mermaid was her belief that Fiora was bound by the constraints of a curse. Even if she hadn't stolen the shell, she was dangerous.

"G-o-o-d-n-i-g-h-t."

Fiora stood and left the library as quickly as she could without limping. She reached her room, closed her window, and pushed a chair in front of her door. Would that be enough to keep out intruders?

Maybe she should report the theft to the guards. She could at least tell Gustave.

But the story might make him suspicious, and she needed to keep her secrets until she won his love. She was so close now.

Fiora looked at her pearl ring. It shimmered in the moonlight. Only a tiny part of the surface was dull now.

Was it enough to break the enchantment?

She tried to sing the part of the song she remembered, but her voice remained out of reach.

❦ 50 ❦

Gustave awoke to the sound of singing. Not just any singing. It was *her*.

The song filled his head and twisted around his heart. Why had he been wasting time dancing with Lady Mer and looking for his father when the woman he loved was somewhere out there?

Not out there. She was here. Close enough that he could hear her song.

Gustave reached for a robe, remembered he was still dressed, and hurried through the hallway. The song grew louder, casting a golden haze over the moonlit stone. Everything was brighter when his love was near.

Her voice led him to the library. The melted remains of a candle sat on the table, but the room was empty. Gustave walked around the unopened gifts and past bookshelves searching for the source of the music. The statue of King Francois gleamed silver in the moonlight, but Gustave needed gold.

He caught a glimpse of light in the corner of his eye and turned towards it.

There. The mirror's golden frame sparkled in time with the song. Gustave walked towards it, letting the music and light fill his senses. They washed away memories of the past few days. Nothing mattered but his love. Nothing ever had.

Gustave stood in front of the mirror. Instead of his own reflection, he saw her. The girl he had been searching for since his accident. The golden mist made it difficult to see her face, but blue eyes shone through the gold. The blue that Gustave had been chasing since he woke up on the beach that day. For a moment he thought she was Lady Mer, but that wasn't quite right.

Golden hair with a hint of red brushed against her shoulders, moving in a breeze that swept through the library even though the windows were closed.

She smiled when she saw him but never stopped singing. Her voice consumed him. It was the thing he had been searching for. The part of him that was missing. It had been missing since that day on the beach.

The woman winked and reached her hand towards him. In the dimly lit room, it almost seemed that she was reaching through the glass. That if Gustave reached for her, he could touch her. Grab her hand and feel her warmth and finally know that she was real.

Gustave stretched his hand forward. The girl sang softer, drawing him in. He stepped towards the mirror, reaching for her and her song. She leaned forward, coming ever closer.

"Gustave?"

Collette's voice pierced the fog like a knife. Gustave blinked, and the woman disappeared. He stared at his reflection in confusion.

What had he been doing?

He turned and saw Collette standing beside the statue.

Why was he in the library? He must have been sleepwalking.

Strange. He had never sleepwalked before.

"Are you well?" Collette asked. "I know you're worried about Father, but you need to sleep."

"I could say the same to you."

"I don't have to deal with a ballroom of eligible young ladies tomorrow. Marquis Corbeau has a very full schedule planned for you."

"I suppose he expects me to become engaged by the end of the night now that I've found Father."

Collette made a face.

"Something like that. He's very excited about a royal guest who apparently agreed to come at the last minute."

"Who is it?"

"He's keeping her a secret, but I suspect she's his new favorite for your bride since Lady Annabelle has been such a disaster."

Gustave frowned. The last thing he needed was more surprises and marriage prospects.

"It's only one night, Gustave. It will be fine."

She hesitated, clearly having more to say. Gustave waited, knowing she would continue in her own time.

"Are you sure about escorting Lady Mer, Gustave? We don't know anything about her."

Gustave sighed.

"I know you don't like her-"

"No, it isn't that. I actually do like her now that I've given her a chance. I just- I don't understand why you prefer her to Kara. Someone you've known your whole life. Someone that we know is a good person who would make a good queen."

"Collette, nothing is official."

"Isn't it? Asking to escort her to the gala is rather official, and I've seen how you look at her. The whole court has. I just want you to be careful. Gustave, I don't want you to get hurt."

Gustave looked up at the statue of his father.

"There are no guarantees, Collette. There will always be something that can hurt you."

Collette leaned close to her brother and stared at the statue. Gustave wrapped his arm around her shoulders.

"We'll find a way to save him," he said. "There must be a way."

"I hope so."

"I heard Marchioness Rouge is impressed with your budgeting."

Gustave hoped the praise would cheer his sister, but instead she looked at him with concern in her eyes.

"I never meant to take your job, Gustave. As soon as the gala is over, I'll step into the background again. You don't have to implement my plan if you don't want to."

Gustave frowned.

"Is that how you see your role? As someone standing in the background?"

"You're the king, and I support you. Isn't that how it's meant to be? You'll take over the budgets, and I'll go back to tending the gardens."

The words were innocent enough, but the hurt in Collette's voice caught Gustave off guard.

"I thought you liked the gardens."

"I do like the gardens. It's just–"

She sighed in exasperation.

"Gustave, it's fine. Truly."

It clearly wasn't, but Collette was wearing a stubborn expression that said she was done discussing the matter, so Gustave let it drop. There would be time later to figure out what was bothering Collette and make it right.

They stood together with their father a few minutes longer before leaving the library and going back to their rooms.

This time Gustave changed into pajamas and settled in properly. He dreamed of his true love's voice and golden mist until the sun rose.

🌿 51 🌿

Fiora awoke to sunlight streaming through the window and birds singing in the garden. She lay in bed, listening for the fainter sounds of gulls and the ocean crashing against the shore. The song of the sea pulled at her heart, making her feel alone and out of place.

She tried to sing, but her voice remained as out of reach as ever. No matter since she didn't have the shell, but it would have been reassuring to have her magic back so she could run to the mermaids and ask for their help to recreate the song.

Fiora glanced at the door to make sure the chair still blocked the entrance. Then she checked her ring. The pearl glistened in the sunlight. Only a tiny streak across the side remained gray. If the ring was accurate, she was very close to winning Gustave's heart. It seemed impossible, but he had asked her to go with him to the gala. He hadn't admitted his feelings, but there was something in his eyes when he looked at her.

Or maybe she was imagining everything.

But he had asked her to the gala in front of everyone, and the pearl had regained its sheen.

So why hadn't her voice returned?

Fiora sighed and stared at the ring.

Perhaps it wasn't working because he didn't know who he actually loved. Perhaps a relationship based on deception didn't count.

Fiora pulled the bottle of dye removing potion out from under her pillow and held it up to the light. The glass glistened like a jewel, and the liquid inside rolled like ocean waves.

Should she tell Gustave the truth? She could wash away her disguise and attend the gala as Fiora instead of Lady Mer. She could explain everything.

Or not. She wouldn't have to tell him about the mermaids to reveal her human identity. Perhaps admitting her name would be enough.

Fiora closed her eyes and squeezed the bottle tight, trying to convince herself that Gustave's feelings wouldn't change if he knew who she truly was.

But instead of Gustave, she saw the face of every prince who had rejected her at the Princess Tests. She went through them in order, slowing down when she came to the two most recent.

Prince Darian, who had chosen no one and risked starting a war because he found her and every other woman completely inadequate.

Prince Alaric, who had ignored the rules and centuries of traditions to avoid choosing her in favor of a mysterious stranger.

She had won in Aeonia, and still she had lost.

And it wasn't just the princes. The royal women hated her as well. Princess Collette had been rude simply because Fiora reminded her of the Princess Tests. Lina and Carina had teamed up against her, as had countless others.

Her own father had found her so useless that he sent her back to the sea without even saying goodbye. Her stepmother had looked at her as little as possible and never had a kind word to say in the rare moments when she acknowledged that Fiora existed.

And Elspeth had pretended kindness only to turn a blind eye any time Fiora needed help.

Fiora shoved the bottle back under her pillow. She couldn't do it.

She couldn't tell Gustave and risk losing the one person who actually liked her. Even if that affection was based on a lie, it was all she had at the moment.

She stood, drawing breath in a sharp hiss when her feet touched the ground. How was it possible for the pain to keep getting worse?

She sat on the bed and blinked away tears. This was the last day of the enchantment. Things weren't going to get any better, but she couldn't afford to back down now.

She had come this far. She just needed to fight a little harder. Prove to Gustave that she was worthy of his heart.

If only she believed that herself.

Fiora looked to the window, hoping to see Spot waiting for her. Perhaps Althea would be able to fix this. Perhaps the mermaids would find a magical way to wipe away the curse and let her start again under the sea.

But the windowsill was empty.

Someone knocked on the door, and Fiora gritted her teeth. Time to battle.

She hoped it was a servant and not whoever had broken into her room last night. Now that she knew she had enemies in the castle, she needed to watch her back.

Fiora limped to the door, slid the chair to the side, and pulled it open. A servant curtsied and entered.

"The ladies are having breakfast in the garden this morning, miss. Would you like to join them?"

Fiora scowled. She had hoped to spend the morning with Gustave. How was she supposed to win his heart if she didn't spend time with him?

The servant backed away, intimidated by Fiora's fierce expression.

"It's a tradition on gala days. We can't use the dining room because they're decorating it for tonight. Princess Collette will entertain the ladies while King Gustave entertains the gentlemen."

Blast it all.

She would have to play along for now. Hopefully she could find a way to see Gustave before the gala. If she had to wait until evening, she would have only a few hours to win him over.

Fiora realized she was still scowling and forced herself to adopt a pleasant expression. She nodded to the wardrobe, signaling that she would like to get dressed.

The servant relaxed a little and pulled out a simple green gown.

"Will this be alright, Lady Mer? You don't need to dress formally because you'll begin preparing for the gala after you eat."

Fiora nodded again, and the servant helped her get dressed.

"I am sorry to rush you, but Princess Lenora arrived earlier than expected, so they're already in the garden. I'd hate for you to miss any of the fun."

Fiora frowned. She knew Princess Lenora from the Princess Tests. How many other royals would attend the gala? She had gotten lucky with Prince Edric, but would that luck continue?

She should have realized the guest list would include members of royal families from all over Myora. Of course it would.

And she would dance with Gustave in front of all of them to open the gala. She couldn't have drawn more attention to herself if she tried.

Perhaps she should have told Gustave the truth after all.

Fiora looked back at her window one last time.

No spotted seagull.

No help from the mermaids.

So she would have to do this on her own. Win Gustave's heart and save herself. She looked down at her ring. At the stubborn streak of gray.

Perhaps an evening of dancing would wash it away.

The servant smoothed Fiora's dark hair back into a simple twist and hesitated before pulling a pair of matching green slippers from the wardrobe.

"I know you sometimes prefer to go without shoes, miss, but-"

Fiora scowled and nodded to the ground. The servant quickly set the shoes down, and Fiora slipped her feet into them. The pain intensified as the shoes squeezed her feet, but Fiora smoothed her features and forced herself to smile.

She was a proper lady, and ladies wore shoes.

Fiora repeated that to herself to distract from the pain as she walked to the garden in search of the royal ladies.

Dowager Queen Bernadine, Princess Collette, Lady Annabelle, and Princess Lenora sat at a table in the center of the garden. Servants bustled around them, offering an assortment of juices, pastries, and fresh fruit. Thomas stood behind the dowager queen holding a large spyglass. Collette waved and gestured to an empty chair.

"Lady Mer, please join us! May I introduce Princess Lenora?"

Fiora curtsied, gritting her teeth at the pain that accompanied shifting her weight. Princess Lenora nodded her head in greeting.

Lenora looked much the same as Fiora remembered. Light gray eyes, dark brown hair, and a pleasant face. The main difference was her clothes.

When they participated in Princess Tests, all the girls wore matching outfits to obscure their true identities.

Now, Lenora wore an orange and yellow gown decorated with stripes and spots like a butterfly. The sleeves were long and full, creating the illusion of wings when the princess moved her arms.

Her hair was piled high and decorated with fresh flowers. Fiora raised an eyebrow as a butterfly landed on Lenora's head.

Apparently the princess of Darluna had a hobby. Or an unhealthy obsession. Difficult to say.

"It is a pleasure to meet you, Lady Mer."

Lenora sounded like she meant it, which was as good a sign as any that she hadn't recognized Fiora for who she really was.

Fiora swallowed a sigh of relief and tried not to stare as more butterflies landed on Lenora's head. They stayed there, sipping from the flowers and gently fluttering their wings.

The effect was strange but rather pretty.

Lady Annabelle cast sideways glances at Lenora, clearly trying to come up with a scathing insult but not sure where to start.

"Why does Thomas have a spyglass?"

The question was for Collette, but Lady Annabelle glared at Thomas, waiting for a translation.

"Lady Mer is wondering why I have a spyglass."

Annabelle's scowl deepened. She clearly didn't believe his translation was accurate.

"We're watching the harbor for arrivals," Princess Collette said. "Several other guests should be arriving by ship today."

Fiora nodded her thanks for the explanation and reached for a scone. She looked around the garden, still hoping that Spot would appear. She would happily give him every bit of food on the table in exchange for a message from the mermaids.

"Isn't the garden lovely?" Lenora said. "Princess Collette, you have outdone yourself with the landscaping this year."

"Thank you."

Lenora's compliment sounded genuine, but Collette's tone was strained. Lenora frowned and looked to Fiora for an explanation. Fiora shrugged. Even if she knew what was bothering Collette, she had no way to communicate it to Lenora.

"I oversee a small section of our garden back home, but nothing on this scale," Lenora said. "I would love to exchange seeds sometime. Our climates should be similar enough that the same plants would grow in both our gardens."

Collette nodded and pushed away whatever was bothering her. "Of course, that would be lovely."

"Is that a ship?" Lady Annabelle asked.

Fiora looked to the harbor. Yes, a ship was sailing into port.

It was the ugliest ship Fiora had ever seen. Surely no royal guests would arrive in such a vessel.

Thomas handed the spyglass to Dowager Queen Bernadine. She studied the harbor for a few moments, then passed the spyglass on to Collette.

"Santelle's delegation has arrived."

"Santelle?" Lenora said. "That ship can't be from Santelle."

Collette passed the spyglass to Fiora.

"Gustave did say that Santelle lost many ships in the kraken attack."

"More than we realized, apparently," Bernadine said.

Fiora looked through the spyglass and swallowed a burst of laughter. The ship looked even worse up close. It was short and fat and meandered lazily into the harbor, not in any hurry to reach its destination. The figurehead was a misshapen creature with a wide mouth that took up the entire bow of the ship. The boards were weathered and rotted in places and looked to be held together by barnacles and bad attitude.

Faded letters on the side declared that the vessel was called the *Sea Frog*.

Calling it a frog seemed generous. If anything, it was a toad.

Once Fiora recovered from her surprise at the ship's ugliness, she turned her attention to the crew. A stern woman in naval uniform stood at the helm. She wore her dark hair pulled back in a tight braid that only emphasized the severity of her expression.

Fiora didn't recognize her, but the woman's uniform was definitely from Santelle. Judging by the numerous pins on her jacket, she held a high rank in their navy.

A gangly boy sprinted across the deck. He moved like he had recently grown and wasn't accustomed to his new size yet. The woman gave him a sharp command. He saluted, ran back the other way, and disappeared below the decks.

He looked young enough to still be a cabin boy, but his uniform said otherwise. Perhaps he was one of the royal children? Fiora had heard that they began their naval careers early.

"Lady Mer, you must let everyone else take a turn," Lady Annabelle scolded.

Fiora rolled her eyes and handed over the spyglass. By everyone else, Annabelle clearly meant herself.

"Bring another chair," Dowager Queen Bernadine ordered the nearest servant. "Princess Serafina will be joining us shortly."

𝕊 52 𝕊

Gustave hurried to the library as soon as he woke, hoping to get there and do some research before the rest of the castle began preparing for the gala.

Elaine was already there. She shook her head at Gustave's hopeful look.

"I haven't found anything useful. I'm sorry."

"I read the passage you marked about breaking curses. Do you think it will help?"

"It would if we had any way of knowing what type of magic was used to cast the curse."

"Your Majesty!"

Marquis Corbeau burst into the library, calling out in triumph when he saw his king. Gustave sighed. So much for doing research first.

Elaine gave him a sympathetic look. Marquis Corbeau glared at her.

"The other ladies are having breakfast in the garden. I'm sure they would appreciate your company."

Elaine shrugged.

"They won't miss me. I'll join them when it's time to get ready."

Marquis Corbeau sniffed derisively, but what else could he do? Elaine was a guest. He had no way to force her to behave.

Gustave wished he could say the same for himself, but he couldn't avoid his royal duties. Not today.

"Prince Leonardo has already arrived," Marquis Corbeau said. "He and Prince Edric are waiting for you in the stables."

"The stables?"

"I've arranged for you to go on a morning ride with them. You'll find a snack in your saddlebags, and breakfast will be served in your study when you return."

"Is the ride necessary?"

Marquis Corbeau narrowed his eyes.

"It is a tradition to provide amusement for your guests, Your Majesty. So yes, it is necessary. Not everyone finds sitting inside and reading books all day enjoyable."

He cast a pointed look at Elaine, who ignored the marquis and gave Gustave a sympathetic smile.

"Think of it as an opportunity, Your Majesty. Aeonia and Santelle have dealt with magical attacks recently. Perhaps other countries have as well. Or perhaps they have resources in their libraries that we could borrow."

Gustave considered this. It was a good suggestion. Edric and Leonardo were both crown princes. They would have access to information that others didn't. Although Edric might not have been crown prince long enough to be well-informed.

"Do not bore your guests with talk of magic," Marquis Corbeau said.

"And what are we supposed to talk about instead?" Gustave asked.

It was meant to be a hypothetical question, and he walked out the door without expecting an answer.

Marquis Corbeau followed him.

"You could inquire if Princess Lenora is attached to anyone. I had not considered her because she has a reputation for being rather eccentric. But at this point, our options are so limited that she could be worth pursuing."

"You want me to ask Prince Leonardo if his twin sister is available for marriage?"

"Yes, exactly!"

Gustave quickened his pace. Taking a ride and getting away from the castle suddenly seemed like a very good idea.

The grooms had already saddled his horse and two others when he arrived. Prince Leonardo looked from Gustave to Edric with a questioning glance, obviously trying to ask Gustave what had happened to Crown Prince Darian.

Gustave shrugged to say he didn't know. He raised his hands to sign further comments, then dropped them again. Leonardo didn't know sign language. There was no way to communicate secretly with him as Gustave did with Lady Mer.

He hoped Lady Mer was having a better time this morning than he was. There was no telling what his grandmother would do in the name of entertaining the ladies.

He wished he could skip this whole ordeal and spend time with Lady Mer instead. They could walk along the beach and look for mermaids. He could find more shells for her.

Prince Edric's crown slipped down over his forehead as he mounted his horse. He took it off, fixed his hair, and replaced it. Leonardo and Gustave shared a look. Neither of them wore their crowns. It was typical to wear them for ceremonies and official appearances, but while riding?

Definitely not.

Once Edric had adjusted the crown to his liking, Gustave nudged his horse and rode ahead to show the way. He picked a path that led up towards the mountains. There was an open stretch on it that would give them an opportunity to gallop if they wanted, and it would be less crowded than the beach.

Once they reached the plateau, Gustave slowed so the princes could catch up and ride beside him. Edric reached into his saddlebag, pulled out an apple, and began to eat.

So much for galloping. Gustave shared another look with Leonardo, then shrugged and pulled food from his saddlebag as well.

The horses walked at a leisurely pace while the men ate. Gustave stared ahead, considering Elaine's advice. It was possible that either Edric or Leonardo had information about magic, but how could he ask them about it without raising suspicion about why he was asking? It didn't seem wise to tell people he didn't trust know about his father's condition.

But maybe he was being overly paranoid. The only way the kingdoms could help each other was if they worked together.

He would need to discuss that with his council first.

In the meantime, how could he bring up magic casually? It wasn't exactly a common topic of conversation.

"I heard you had trouble with magic in Santelle," Prince Leonardo said.

Then again, maybe it was.

"Yes, we were attacked by kraken and mermaids."

"What? When?"

Apparently news of the incident had not yet reached across the sea to Eldria. Prince Edric dropped his apple in surprise. He watched it roll away, shrugged, and pulled a piece of ham from his saddlebag.

Prince Edric was occupied with his ham, so Gustave turned back to Leonardo. He seemed to be the better informed of the two princes.

"There was an incident in Aeonia as well. I expect your father told you about it."

"Yes. There seems to be a trend of dark creatures attacking, especially in coastal cities. Do you think the mermaids are angry with humans for some reason?"

Gustave hadn't considered that most of the attacks had happened in countries by the sea.

"It's possible. You haven't seen anything unusual in Darluna?"

"No, thank goodness. I'm sure you've got your hands full rebuilding after losing the ships to the kraken."

"Yes, although we weren't hit as hard as Santelle."

"If the mermaids are mobilizing kraken, that is a cause for great concern. We may need to call an emergency Council of Kings."

"If the mermaids are attacking, I don't think they are all in agreement about it. Some of them seem to be trying to stop the kraken. One of them saved my life."

"Then why have they not come forward and offered friendship? Why is there no treaty?"

This conversation wasn't exactly going how Gustave had imagined. Before he could answer, the ground shook beneath them. The horses pranced nervously, and Gustave swallowed.

"What was that?" Edric said.

"An earthquake. I think. Perhaps we should ride back."

Prince Leonardo nodded, and they turned back towards the castle. Gustave pressed his horse into a trot. Perhaps that was a normal earthquake. Not a seemingly magical one like the one that had buried Lady Mer in books and boxes.

But he wasn't willing to assume anything at this point. His pulse raced. He did his best to appear calm, but he wouldn't be at ease until he knew that Lady Mer was safe.

"So you don't think the mermaids are unified in their attacks?" Prince Leonardo said.

"I wish I had better information for you, but I only had a few conversations with them. The mermaid I spoke to seemed capricious. Helping one moment and threatening to kidnap humans the next."

"You actually spoke to mermaids?" Edric asked.

Gustave had almost forgotten that Edric was riding with

them. He turned to the prince, who had a strange expression on his face.

"Yes, I spoke to mermaids."

Edric swallowed and looked nervous.

Interesting.

"Has Eldria experienced any magical attacks recently?" Prince Leonardo asked. "You're on the coast and share a border with Aeonia."

"A small border," Edric said quickly.

He adjusted his crown, then realized they were waiting for him to answer the question.

"No, we haven't experienced any magical attacks. Perhaps whatever attacked in Aeonia has moved to your side of the sea."

"Lina said a goblin attacked in Aeonia," Gustave said. "There haven't been any goblins here."

"Just kraken," Prince Leonardo said. "I don't know enough about magic to know how different goblins and kraken are. Besides the obvious differences in size and shape, of course. Do you think they could be working together? Perhaps coordinating with the mermaids?"

Gustave hadn't considered this.

"I don't know enough about them to say. Lina might."

"Yes, the mysterious Evangelina Shadow-Storm does seem to know something about all this. You believe her story?"

"He offered evidence for her in the Council of Kings," Prince Edric said. "I should hope that he does."

It sounded almost like an accusation.

"I have no reason not to believe her."

Gustave couldn't help sounding defensive. He bristled at the implication that he would promote lies to the Council.

"My father thinks it was an excuse," Edric said. "A way for Prince Alaric to marry the commoner he loved but still maintain his claim to the throne.

Gustave laughed. He couldn't help it. That preposterous

theory reminded him of the King of Santelle, who had refused to believe in magic or kraken until he saw them firsthand.

"The older generation does seem strangely resistant to the idea of magic," Prince Leonardo said. "But is it really that far-fetched? What about the witch who enchanted King Noam? Or all the historical accounts of powerful magicians? Or even enchanted objects like your ring, King Gustave? Magic may be increasingly rare, but it certainly does exist."

"Increasingly common may be a better description," Gustave said. "Do you have historical accounts of magic in your library? We have a few texts, but nothing that has proved useful in dealing with mermaids or kraken or curses."

He added the bit about curses hoping to lead the conversation away from mermaids to magic in general.

"We might," Leonardo said. "Perhaps an exchange of information would be helpful. If these magical attacks spread inland, I want Darluna to be as prepared as possible. What about you, Prince Edric?"

"What's that?"

"Does Eldria have any magical texts in their library that they would be willing to share in an exchange of information?"

Prince Edric stiffened.

"I don't know. I haven't spent much time in the library."

They reached the castle and dismounted. Gustave pulled a groom aside and asked him to check on Lady Mer and report back, then led the princes to his study.

A table spread with breakfast food had been set by the window. A boy dressed in a naval uniform sat at the table. He had piled his plate high with food and already worked his way through half of it.

"Oh good, you're back!"

He stood and gave a crisp salute. Then he seemed to remember he wasn't on a ship and bowed as well.

Gustave, Leonardo, and Edric stared at him.

"Let's eat!" the boy said.

He sat down and bit into a strip of bacon.

After a moment of blinking at him in surprise, Gustave sat as well.

"King Gustave of Montaigne at your service," he said, trying to stay polite and hoping this wasn't one of Marquis Corbeau's ridiculous schemes.

The boy swallowed his bacon and grinned.

"Prince Massimo of Santelle at yours. Sorry I started eating without you. Marquis Corbeau said you would be riding for a few hours and told me to wait here. Our ship arrived a few minutes ago."

"Prince Leonardo of Darluna at your service. Who else came from Santelle?"

"My sister Serafina and our crew. King Gustave, why is there a wedding dress in your study?"

Massimo gestured to the mannequin in the wedding dress, which still stood where Marquis Corbeau had placed it. Gustave grimaced. With everything else that had happened, he had forgotten about Marquis Corbeau's ridiculous scheme to prepare everything for his wedding in advance.

"You've found a bride?" Prince Edric said. "I had not heard that news. Congratulations."

"I have not found a bride. Marquis Corbeau just wants to be very ready when I do."

"Is it because he planned for you to marry Carina?" Massimo asked.

Gustave pressed his lips together. Weren't the royal children of Santelle supposed to be disciplined and tight-lipped? Serafina certainly was.

Apparently Massimo was more similar to Carina than his eldest sister.

"You had an understanding with Carina?" Edric asked.

Massimo chimed in before Gustave could answer.

"No, Carina fell in love with a frog and moved to Aeonia. Well, she was technically banished, but I think she would have gone with him anyway."

Prince Leonardo dropped his bacon and stared at Massimo. The young prince beamed.

"Serafina said I might find my time here boring, but you all aren't boring at all."

"There was a curse," Gustave said.

This was as good an opportunity as any to bring up curses and gather information.

"Prince Stefan of Aeonia was cursed and became a frog. Princess Carina saved him. Have you all heard of anything similar? I've been reading as much as I can about the subject in case it happens again."

"Turned into a frog? How is that possible?" Leonardo asked.

He sounded more curious than disbelieving, but he didn't sound like a promising source of information.

Prince Edric was so surprised by the story that he choked on his juice. He coughed, trying to regain his composure. His face had gone pale.

So much for promising sources of information. The only person at the table who knew more about curses than Gustave wasn't old enough to shave.

A servant entered the room and bowed.

"Your Majesty will be happy to know that Lady Mer is perfectly well and has suffered no ill effects from the earthquake."

Massimo grinned.

"Who's Lady Mer? Is she the reason you didn't want to marry Carina?"

Gustave closed his eyes and wished it was acceptable for a king to hide under the table. Suddenly, he couldn't wait for the gala.

❧ 53 ❧

"Oh, Lady Mer. You look beautiful!"

Fiora blinked at her reflection. Collette stood beside her and grinned in the mirror. Fiora hesitated only a moment before smiling back.

Because she did look beautiful. Dowager Queen Bernadine's dress suited her perfectly. The seamstress had tailored the gown to fit her figure and shortened the hem so the golden heels peeked out from beneath the skirt when Fiora moved.

"Let me see."

Fiora turned in a slow circle so the dowager queen could study her from every angle. Bernadine's eyes twinkled with approval.

"Excellent. Now what should we do with your hair?"

Fiora's heart skipped a beat. It was a perfectly innocent question, but Bernadine's tone seemed to carry extra meaning. Fortunately, the dowager queen did not comment on squid ink dye again.

"I could braid it if you want," Princess Serafina offered.

The crown princess of Santelle studied Fiora with eyes every bit as intense as Bernadine's. Fiora swallowed. She had never met

Serafina before today. There was no reason for the princess to recognize her or be suspicious.

So why did Fiora feel like Serafina was sizing her up and looking for weaknesses?

"Um, I'm not sure a braid would complement the dress?" Fiora signed to Collette.

She didn't want to get on Serafina's bad side, but the tightly pulled back hairstyle that Serafina called her "dress braid" was too severe for a formal event. She needed to look her best so she could win Gustave's heart.

"That's very generous, Princess Serafina, but we have a hair-dresser on staff that will see to Lady Mer's hair," Collette said. "You should focus on getting ready yourself first."

"I am ready."

Fiora and Collette blinked at Serafina, who met their surprise with a steady gaze. The crown princess of Santelle wore a naval uniform. Granted it was clean and perfectly starched, but it was still a uniform.

"This is my dress uniform. I wear it to all formal events."

"Oh, of course," Collette said. "Forgive me. It's just that Carina never wore a uniform, so I didn't think-"

"Carina isn't in the navy."

"Yes, of course."

Fiora wished she could sign something to Collette that showed she was surprised as well. Carina and Serafina were about as unalike as sisters could be. Even more so than Fiora and Elspeth.

But Lady Mer didn't know Carina, so Fiora kept the thought to herself. So far, her luck was holding. She couldn't let a careless comment ruin her disguise.

"It seems you all still have a lot to do before the gala," Serafina said. "Would you mind if I slipped away? There's something I'd like to discuss with King Gustave."

"Not at all," Collette said.

Fiora tried not to let her concern show on her face. The question hadn't been addressed to her, and she had no reason to worry.

But what if Serafina and Gustave had formed an attachment while he was in Santelle? What if–

Fiora took a deep breath and pushed the thought away. Serafina was unlikely to complicate her status as crown princess by marrying a king from another country.

And if he liked her, Gustave would have asked to escort Serafina to the gala.

Instead, he had asked Lady Mer.

Fiora looked back to her reflection. Beauty was far from the most important factor in a relationship, but looking this good certainly couldn't hurt matters. Perhaps seeing how beautiful she was would further convince Gustave of her worth and capture the rest of his heart.

Someone knocked, and a maid opened the door. Princess Lenora, Elaine, and Lady Annabelle entered.

"Oh, Lady Mer, you look beautiful!" Elaine said.

Princess Lenora nodded her agreement. Lady Annabelle looked like she wanted to murder Fiora, which was as close to a compliment as she was likely to get.

"Our maids said it would be easier for the hairdresser if we all came to your chambers, Dowager Queen," Princess Lenora said. "I hope that was correct?"

"Certainly. Please, make yourselves at home."

Princess Lenora took the queen at her word and placed an enormous bouquet of flowers on a nearby table.

"For my hair," she said, answering Fiora's questioning look.

She wore another butterfly inspired gown. This one had a long lace train embroidered with a butterfly motif.

"Please ask Princess Lenora if I may take a closer look at the embroidery on her gown," Fiora signed to Thomas.

The translator repeated the question, and Princess Lenora nodded.

"Of course! I didn't do the stitching, but I did help design it. It's based on my sketches of all the butterfly species that live in our garden."

She held up the train for Fiora to inspect.

"I don't know enough about butterflies to know the different species, but the needlework is exquisite."

Lenora beamed after Thomas translated.

"I'm glad to hear it! I appreciate good sewing, but I'm hopeless with a needle myself. It's always my weakest skill at the Princess Tests."

Fiora raised her hands to sign that embroidery was her favorite skill at the Princess Tests, but remembered just in time that she was Lady Mer. And a lady pulled from the sea shouldn't know anything about Princess Tests.

"I'm sure it's not so bad," she signed instead.

"Oh, I'm sure it is! Would you like some flowers for your hair, Lady Mer? The hyacinth would match your dress beautifully."

Fiora blinked in surprise. Was Princess Lenora really offering to share flowers with her? She looked to Collette, who was considering the offer and studying the bouquet.

"We'll ask the hairdresser what she thinks, but I believe it would look nice. Plus the blue would complement her eyes."

"Of course you may have some as well if you want, Princess Collette. I brought enough to share. Perhaps the camellias?"

Fiora shared a look of amusement with Dowager Queen Bernadine.

"We'll all be covered in flowers and butterflies by the end of the evening," Fiora signed.

The dowager queen winked.

Fiora joined the ladies at the table while they sorted through the flowers and picked out their favorites. Everyone laughed and chatted, and Collette translated whenever Fiora had anything to say.

A huff behind her interrupted Fiora's thoughts. She turned

and saw Lady Annabelle standing in the corner of the room with her arms crossed.

It was such a familiar scene that it made Fiora's heart ache. How often had she stood in a similar position, either alone or with other bitter girls gathered around her? When you viewed every woman in the room as competition, it was impossible to see them as friends.

Was that how she saw these women now?

She was still trying to win Gustave's heart, but Fiora's perspective had shifted. Somehow, she had become friends with the ladies gathered around the table. They had become like human sisters.

With surprise, Fiora realized that she had been enjoying herself for the past few hours. Not pretending. Not competing. Simply having fun with friends.

She looked back to Lady Annabelle, who met her gaze with a haughty glare. Fiora tapped Collette on the shoulder.

"Perhaps we should offer flowers to Annabelle?"

Collette glanced at Annabelle, who stiffened when she realized they were talking about her.

"Are you sure?"

Fiora nodded. She knew how it felt to stand in the corner, but perhaps it was unnecessary. Perhaps they could all get along.

"Would you like some flowers for your hair, Lady Annabelle?" Collette said.

Annabelle's eyes widened with surprise. Then they narrowed with suspicion.

"Certainly not."

Collette gave Fiora a look that said "I told you so" and returned to sorting the flowers. Fiora looked at Lady Annabelle, who had moved to a mirror across the room and was brushing imaginary wrinkles out of her skirt.

Perhaps getting along with everyone was too much to hope for.

"Tired of your guests already, Your Majesty?"

Gustave quickly looked away from the statue and bowed to Princess Serafina. He had thought he could escape for a few moments alone while everyone prepared for the gala, but apparently that wasn't the case.

Serafina winked.

"I don't blame you for hiding. Massimo has that effect on people."

"No, he's been fine."

Her mouth quirked into a smile that said she didn't believe him. Gustave laughed.

"He's simply young and overeager."

"Something like that."

"Shouldn't you be getting ready for the gala?"

Serafina gave him a look, and Gustave's face burned. What had possessed him to ask such a question? The last thing he needed was to insult the Crown Princess of Santelle. His time with Lady Mer had loosened his tongue, but that wasn't always a good thing when you were a king.

He opened his mouth to apologize, but Serafina spoke before he could.

"Military dress takes a lot less effort than civilian formal wear. I can get ready quickly and make better use of my time."

She gestured to her clean-cut uniform, and Gustave nodded. He didn't know much about lady's fashion, but her outfit looked easier to manage than the elaborate gowns most women wore.

"I heard you had another encounter with a kraken."

Of course news of that incident had traveled to Santelle already. Gustave wouldn't be surprised if the neighboring country had planted spies somewhere in Montaigne.

"Two, actually. It seems giving the Kraken Heart to the mermaids didn't solve all our problems after all."

"That's a shame. I'd hate to think Carina was banished for nothing."

A hint of bitterness crept into Serafina's normally stoic voice. Gustave hurried to reassure her.

"I'm sure the Aeonians will take good care of her."

"Oh, Carina can take care of herself. I'm more worried about the kraken. May I be frank, Your Majesty?"

Gustave nodded, not sure what else he could do under the circumstances.

"Carina trusted you, so I'm going to trust you as well. My father would probably consider this treason, but he won't always be king. I have to think of our future, and one day we will be neighboring monarchs."

She seemed to expect some kind of response, so Gustave nodded again. Serafina continued.

"I think we're missing something. Dark magic is waking up across Myora, and the methods that worked to stop it in the past are no longer effective. There must be a cause."

"You think this is part of a larger plot?"

"It would be foolish not to consider the possibility."

"Prince Leonardo suggested something similar. He thinks the

mermaids are responsible because only coastal cities have been attacked."

"And what do you think? You have more experience with mermaids than I do."

"Not much more, and I still find them confusing. In the latest kraken attack, one tried to kill me and two tried to save me. I have no idea what they hope to accomplish."

"It's certainly possible that mermaids are responsible, although I have reason to believe humans are involved as well."

She paused a moment, studying Gustave with a stern expression before continuing in a hushed voice.

"I've been sent on a mission to hunt pirates. They're taking our ships, and even our most experienced captains can't stop them. Father is still reluctant to admit magical interference, but at this point no other explanation makes sense."

"You're chasing magical pirates in that ship?"

Serafina scowled, and Gustave mentally kicked himself for speaking so freely. He had noticed the *Sea Frog* docked in the harbor while riding back to the castle. It was the ugliest ship he had ever seen, but that didn't mean he should insult it to its captain's face.

"This statue is my father."

He blurted it out, trying to distract the princess from his blunder. Serafina raised an eyebrow, as if to say she knew what he was doing, but played along and turned her attention to the statue.

"Is it a good likeness?"

"No, I mean this statue is literally my father. Find King Francois."

The light from his ring shone at the statue. Serafina's eyes widened.

"You found him then. But how is this possible? Where was he?"

"On the bottom of the ocean, I suspect. He washed up on

shore and Lady Mer found him. A kraken tried to drag him back, but mermaids stopped it and then disappeared."

Serafina studied the statue for a moment. Gustave appreciated that she believed him without question.

"What do you think of Lady Mer?" she asked.

Gustave blushed, then realized she was asking from a strategic perspective. She wasn't interested in their relationship.

"What do you mean?"

He couldn't help sounding a little defensive. Serafina grinned.

"It just seems a bit coincidental that a young lady would appear in the sea just as all this magic washes in. And that she would find a statue of your father. Are you sure she's what she seems?"

"I suspect she may be cursed. She won't say anything about her past."

Serafina considered this.

"Prince Stefan's curse came with similar restrictions. Perhaps I can gather some useful information from her. I don't have Carina's skills for subterfuge, but I am rather good at getting what I want."

Gustave swallowed. He wouldn't want to stand in Princess Serafina's way when she set her mind to something. Her expression was quite fierce.

She noticed his discomfort and winked at him.

"Don't worry, Your Majesty, I won't hurt your lady. I should join the others before my absence becomes too obvious. My condolences on your father's curse. If I find any useful information in my travels, I will send it your way."

She hesitated, and Gustave waited. He knew the look of a woman who had more to say and had learned the best strategy was to wait and listen.

Finally, Serafina pulled an envelope from her jacket pocket.

"Could you send this to Carina? I'm not technically allowed to correspond with her, but I think she'll find this useful."

"It would be my pleasure."

He took the envelope, and Serafina gave him a crisp military bow.

"Thank you, Your Majesty. Save me a dance tonight?"

It sounded far less like a question than a command. Gustave nodded and tucked the envelope into his pocket while Serafina strode out of the room.

He returned to staring at his father. He really should go back to his guests, but he couldn't bring himself to do it just yet. Besides, it was almost time for the gala. Everyone except Serafina would be busy getting ready.

He should get ready as well, but it wouldn't take that long to dress in the reworked suit. He could spare a few more minutes.

A flash of light caught his attention, and he turned. The golden mirror gleamed in the light of the setting sun.

Gustave walked over to it and stared at his reflection. A memory tugged at the back of his mind. A song and a girl. She was out there somewhere. She was real.

But thinking about her was driving him crazy. Maybe Grandmother was right. Maybe she didn't want to be found. Maybe he had built a dream around her that could never come true.

Gustave turned from the mirror and looked at King Francois again.

He had been so certain that finding his father would fix everything. Just as it seemed that everything would fall into place if he could only find the woman from the beach.

But maybe life wasn't that simple. Maybe no one thing could ever solve all your problems.

Maybe it wasn't possible to know all the answers.

Gustave thought of Lady Mer and smiled. She had caused more problems than she had solved, but somehow that just made him like her more.

Dreams had done him no good. Perhaps he should give reality a chance.

Gustave walked closer to his father. He felt a little silly talking to a statue, but maybe King Francois could hear him somehow. And there was a conversation Gustave desperately wanted to have.

"I've met someone," he whispered, looking around the room to make sure he was alone before he continued. "A girl. Well, a woman. She's not at all what I expected to find. She surprises me constantly. It's only been three days, but I-"

He stopped, not sure if he should say the words out loud. Even if he was only speaking to a statue, voicing that thought would make it real.

"I'm going to give this a chance," he said instead. "I swore that I would wait until I found you and made things right, but I'm not sure that's even possible now. I don't know how to break your curse, and I'm not sure she'll wait until I do. So I'm going to give this a chance."

❧ 55 ❧

Fiora breathed deeply and stepped into the hallway. Her skirt rustled around her as she took tiny steps that sent pain coursing through her legs. The pain in her feet just kept getting worse, and the beautiful golden heels enhanced the torture.

She exhaled slowly. She only needed to endure this for a few hours. Just long enough to convince Gustave that she was a proper lady worthy of his attention. Just long enough to win his love and recover her voice.

Then she would run to the ocean and hope that she could find a mermaid who had the transformation song memorized.

And that whoever had stolen the shell didn't try to stop her.

Fiora swallowed.

She felt nervous, but perhaps not as much as the situation warranted. She had performed under pressure before, and she had been alone then. Now, thanks to her disguise, she was surrounded by friends. Collette, Elaine, and Lenora walked beside her, chatting and laughing as the group made their way to the ballroom. They were too distracted by the excitement of the moment to notice her discomfort.

Thomas and Dowager Queen Bernadine followed behind

them. Lady Annabelle walked behind the dowager queen, still sulking. Princess Serafina joined them in the hallway and fell into step beside the queen. She nodded to Fiora when their eyes met. The gesture wasn't exactly friendly, but then again, nothing about the crown princess of Santelle was friendly.

Fiora had never attended a formal event with friends before. Their presence was more comforting than she could have imagined. She looked down at her ring and smiled when she saw that the tiny streak of gray was even smaller now. Surely it would be gone by the end of the evening. The pain would disappear, and Gustave would love her.

Well, he would love Lady Mer.

That would have to be enough.

Gustave and the other royal gentlemen met them at the top of the stairs that led to the ballroom. Gustave stared at Fiora in surprise, then blinked a few times and grinned at her. Her heart fluttered at his undisguised admiration.

She knew she looked beautiful. The princesses and Montaigne's castle staff had made sure of that. But Gustave's expression removed any trace of doubt.

No one had ever looked at her like that before.

Fiora grinned back when she realized she was staring at him just as openly. The King of Montaigne looked even more handsome than usual. He wore a crown and a rather unique blue suit made of the same fabric as Fiora's gown.

How was that possible?

She moved closer to get a better look at Gustave's outfit. Yes, the fabric was the same as her gown, and the hems were decorated with the same embroidered pattern of waves and starfish.

Both Gustave and Fiora turned to Dowager Queen Bernadine. She shrugged, but the twinkle in her eyes didn't match her innocent expression.

"This explains a lot," Gustave signed.

Fiora smiled and offered him the hyacinth boutonniere that

Princess Lenora had helped her make. It matched the flowers nestled in her hair. Gustave bowed as he took it, and his fingers brushed over hers. He pinned it carefully to his suit while Fiora watched.

A wave of sadness washed over her. Whatever happened tonight, she would have to leave him at the end of it. These would be their last few hours together.

Gustave finished pinning the boutonniere and frowned when he saw her expression. He raised his hands to sign a question, and Fiora shook her head. She couldn't explain, and she couldn't answer questions. She was running out of time.

He bowed and held out his hand. Fiora curtsied. Pain shot through her feet, and she grimaced.

"You're hurt."

"I'm fine."

"No, you're not."

Fiora's face flushed as everyone stared at them. She couldn't afford for anything to go wrong. She needed this evening to be perfect so she could win Gustave's love!

She attempted another curtsy, and tears filled her eyes as pain washed over her. Fiora wiped the tears away and stared at the ceiling, hoping Gustave wouldn't see.

Blast it all!

The King of Montaigne stepped away from her, and Fiora closed her eyes to hide her disappointment. She had been a complete fool to think she could keep his interest. Gustave had his choice of women to escort to the ball. Princesses and ladies and brilliant scholars. He didn't even know her name, and she was so damaged she could barely stand. It was only to be expected that he would back away and choose someone else.

But when she opened her eyes, Gustave once again stood beside her. Fiora blinked at him through her tears. He looked different somehow. What had changed?

He was holding something. His shoes.

Fiora gasped and looked down at his feet. Gustave wasn't wearing shoes. He wiggled his toes through the silk stockings and handed his shoes to a footman.

"It seems a shame that our outfits should match in every other way, Lady Mer. Will you honor me by removing your shoes?"

"You can't attend your birthday gala without shoes!"

"I most certainly can. As can you."

Then he simply waited with a calm expression on his face.

"Gustave, it's not the same. My skirt covers my feet, but everyone will see if you go barefoot."

"Why are you torturing yourself if your skirt covers your feet?"

Because she needed to be a proper lady to be worthy of his love.

Only, that didn't seem to matter. Gustave's expression was calm, but there was a stubborn glint in his eyes that made Fiora think he might take after his grandmother more than anyone realized.

She shook her head in defeat and stepped out of her shoes. The cold marble floor soothed her skin and sent waves of relief up her legs. It didn't remove the pain completely, but Fiora was no longer in agony.

Gustave picked up her golden heels set them next to his shoes on a nearby bench.

"They make a fine couple," Gustave said.

Then he turned red, as if realizing that his words could be taken to mean more than the shoes.

"They do."

Fiora's eyes twinkled with amusement as Gustave smiled and offered his arm. She held on a little too tightly and looked back to see what the others thought of Gustave's lack of footwear. Princess Collette and Elaine didn't seem to care. Princess Serafina simply raised an eyebrow. Dowager Queen Bernadine seemed rather pleased.

Fiora suddenly felt suspicious again. Her gown had been hemmed slightly too short for the heels, which meant it was the perfect length now that she was barefoot. She gave the dowager queen a questioning look, but Bernadine shrugged as if she had no idea what Fiora wanted from her.

Lady Annabelle and Marquis Corbeau looked completely scandalized, which made Fiora forget about Bernadine's schemes and smile even wider.

❧ 56 ❧

Gustave bit back a smile at Marquis Corbeau's scandalized expression. That alone would make removing his shoes worthwhile.

But the relief in Lady Mer's eyes when she stood barefoot made it doubly so. Why had she suddenly decided shoes were necessary? They obviously aggravated whatever condition caused her pain.

Gustave wished he could offer more assistance and find a way to cure her permanently.

Perhaps he could. There were other doctors in Montaigne who could offer opinions. He would do whatever was necessary to help her.

She clung to his arm as they entered the ballroom and brilliant light washed over them. Gustave descended the stairs slowly to make sure she could keep up. He glanced over to make sure she was well. She smiled and took his breath away all over again.

Gustave's stockinged foot slid across a marble step, and he turned his attention back to walking. The last thing he needed was to fall down the stairs at his birthday gala because he was distracted by a pretty girl.

She was beautiful.

Gustave studied the room to help him resist the temptation to stare at Lady Mer. The ballroom was a dazzling display of white and gold. Marquis Corbeau had filled the room with white flowers arranged with intricate golden filigree ribbons. Hundreds of candles added a soft glow. It was luxurious without being gaudy.

Much as Gustave hated to admit it, Marquis Corbeau had outdone himself.

If the decorations were muted, then the guests provided the color. Their bright gowns and suits filled the dance floor like a field of wildflowers. They applauded when Gustave reached the bottom of the stairs, and the orchestra played a fanfare to announce his arrival.

Collette and the rest of the royal guests followed behind him. Then four soldiers carried Dowager Queen Bernadine down the stairs in her wheelchair while Thomas walked beside her.

When everyone was settled, Gustave turned to address his guests.

"I thank you all for taking the time to attend my birthday gala. The past year has been difficult for Montaigne. My father-"

He stopped and looked to Collette. He was tempted to explain everything and hope someone in the crowd had answers.

Collette's lips twitched into a frown, and Gustave nodded. There were friends here, but also potential enemies. Best to keep King Francois's condition a secret for the time being.

"My father would be proud to see that Montaigne thrives. He would be proud that we have come through the kraken attacks and still have cause to celebrate. He would be proud to see friends and allies gathered together."

Gustave nodded to the group of foreign royalty standing behind him. Prince Leonardo, Princess Lenora, Prince Edric, Princess Serafina, and Prince Massimo nodded back. Well, Massimo bounced more than he nodded, but the sentiment was there. Edric's crown slipped over his forehead. Lady Annabelle reached up to straighten it.

Lady Mer snorted at the gesture, and Lady Annabelle gave her a nasty smile. Elaine looked amused by the whole thing.

Gustave would be so glad when this evening was over. He had been worried that Lady Annabelle might try to stay after the gala and keep pursuing him, but she seemed to have transferred her attention to Edric. She stayed close to the Eldrian prince, watching him with a gleam in her eyes that said anyone who wanted to dance with him would have to go through her first.

Good luck to both of them.

Gustave shook himself out of his musings and realized he had not finished his speech.

"And of course, Father would be proud of our family and the loyal council members who continually serve Montaigne. I would like to give a special thanks to Marquis Corbeau for arranging this evening's festivities."

Marquis Corbeau bowed as everyone applauded enthusiastically. His face glowed with triumph. Gustave shared an amused look with Lady Mer.

"Are you ready to dance?" he whispered.

She nodded and followed him to the center of the dance floor. Was she nervous? Or was there another reason for the tension in her eyes?

Whatever it was, he would find the cause and fix it. Gustave put his hand on Lady Mer's waist and pulled her close. As soon as this gala was over, he would take all the time he needed to win her heart.

❧ 57 ❧

The scent of flowers mixed with the fresh sea air that blew through the ballroom. Open doors led to balconies with views of the ocean. Fiora could just see the glint of moonlight on the water. Barely hear the waves.

Then the orchestra began to play, and Gustave's hand was on her waist, and they were floating across the dance floor.

Fiora rested her hand gently on his shoulder, determined not to show how much her feet still hurt. Being barefoot made standing tolerable, but dancing was another matter entirely.

But she would do whatever it took. This was her last chance.

It felt like the ballroom floor was made of knives, but Fiora ignored the pain and kept smiling. The crowd whispered around them, doubtless wondering why the king was not wearing shoes.

"Are you well?" Gustave whispered.

She nodded, suddenly wishing very much that she had her voice and could tell him everything.

Because this man deserved the truth. It was the one thing of value that she could offer him, and it seemed far too little after all that he had done for her.

Gustave led her across the floor, spinning her until she felt like she was back in the ocean floating weightless in the waves. Fiora knew she should feel nervous, but she didn't. The crowd didn't matter. Not when Gustave looked at her like that. Not when he smiled.

Not when he slipped in his socks, and for once, she was the one helping him to keep his balance. He laughed out loud, finding the slip more amusing than embarrassing. Fiora grinned and laughed silently with him.

As soon as the dance ended and she had free use of her hands, Fiora would ask if they could slip away so she could tell him the truth. It would be difficult. Where to even start?

But she knew he would wait patiently until she found the right words.

She would take him to one of those moonlit balconies overlooking the sea, and she would tell him everything.

And she would pray that the light in his eyes didn't dim when he learned her true name. When he learned that she had to leave him.

She didn't want to leave him.

The music began to slow, signaling the end of the dance. Fiora swallowed a lump in her throat. This wouldn't be easy.

One by one, the instruments dropped out until only a solo flute played. The melody twisted and twirled as Fiora and Gustave circled each other. The dance was slowing, but Fiora's pulse quickened. This was it. As soon as the music ended, she would make her confession.

But the music didn't end. A woman's voice joined the flute, transforming the solo melody into a sensuous duet.

Gustave slipped again, and Fiora caught him. She wished she could ask if this was part of the plan. She glanced at the orchestra, but couldn't see the singer. The musicians looked puzzled.

Should she keep dancing?

The confused flutist finally stopped playing, but the singing continued. The woman's voice grew until it filled the entire ballroom. What language was she singing in? The sound echoed too much for Fiora to make out the words.

Gustave stopped dancing, and Fiora crashed into him. He held her close, his arm around her waist to keep her from falling as he looked for the singer. Everyone in the ballroom did the same. The voice seemed to come from everywhere at once.

Then the doors at the top of the staircase opened, and a young woman in a golden gown stepped into the room. She glittered in the candlelight as she descended the staircase, her appearance almost as enchanting as her song.

Gustave's arm dropped from Fiora's waist. She reached for his hand, but he shook her off and walked slowly towards the singer, leaving Fiora alone on the dance floor. The woman smiled at him and kept singing. The candles seemed to move in time with her music, glowing golden around her.

She reached the bottom of the stairs and reached for Gustave. Her smile was bright and innocent, as if she were completely unaware of the commotion she had caused. When she stopped singing, the silence in the ballroom was almost as captivating as her song. Fiora's breath caught in her throat. She knew that smile. She would know it anywhere.

Elspeth.

Her sister's red-gold hair gleamed as she stood hand in hand with Gustave. Her green eyes glittered.

Gustave stood still as a statue, staring at Elspeth like a man entranced. Collette waved, trying to get her brother's attention and sign something to him, but he didn't notice.

"Your Majesty. Please forgive me for being late."

Elspeth's sweet voice rang through the ballroom. Her smile was pure sunlight. The space around Fiora seemed to darken as Elspeth glowed in her golden splendor.

"I suppose I can forgive you since you saved my life. Where have you been? I have been searching for you since that day."

Everyone in the ballroom gasped. This was the mysterious girl who had saved Gustave on the beach?

Fiora shook her head. That was impossible. She hadn't seen the woman's face that night because of the cloak, but how could it have been Elspeth? Why would her half-sister have been on a beach in Montaigne? She was supposed to be in Kell.

Fiora looked to the royal family. Princess Collette and Dowager Queen Bernadine seemed just as surprised as she was. Perhaps even more so. Princess Serafina stood beside the dowager queen and watched Elspeth with fierce eyes. Elaine's gaze was questioning as she looked from Gustave to Fiora.

Marquis Corbeau looked absolutely delighted at this turn of events.

Elspeth ducked her head in the shy, maidenly way that Fiora had seen many times before.

"Forgive me for hiding, Your Majesty. I was not sure if you felt the same way I did, and I could not bear to face your rejection. But the longer I waited, the more I could not stand to be apart from you. I decided the invitation to the gala was my best chance to meet you."

The marquis puffed out his chest with pride and shot a meaningful look at Dowager Queen Bernadine. The queen looked from Fiora to Elspeth with a scowl.

"Please, what is your name?"

Gustave sounded so eager to know. Fiora swallowed her hurt, desperate not to cry. A chill spread through her chest as her body slowly went numb. Gustave seemed to have forgotten she existed.

How could he abandon her so easily?

"I am Princess Elspeth of Kell."

It sounded like a song, the way she said it in her lilting accent. The guests gasped again. King Gustave's mysterious savior was a princess? What could be more perfect?

"Princess Elspeth, will you do me the honor of accompanying me for the first dance?"

Elspeth nodded, and Gustave beamed at her. There was a bright light in his eyes. A light Fiora recognized.

A light she had thought was reserved only for her.

She had been a fool.

Fiora did cry now. Silent tears ran down her cheeks as Gustave took Elspeth's hand and led her to the dance floor.

He had asked Elspeth to accompany him for the first dance. Had he completely forgotten that he had already danced with Fiora? Did that not count now that he had found someone else?

Almost with realizing it, Fiora stepped back to make room for the couple. Elspeth took her eyes off Gustave for a moment and looked at Fiora with a triumphant smile.

And just like that, it was all over. Fiora might fool strangers by changing her hair color, but not her sister. Elspeth winked, and there was no missing the recognition in her expression.

Elspeth knew.

Fiora kept walking backwards, too numb to do anything but retreat. The front row of guests parted, making a path for her so she could disappear into the crowd. Fiora pushed her way past them, suddenly desperate for fresh air.

Music began. The orchestra played the same song, as if it truly was the first dance.

As if Fiora didn't exist. As if she didn't matter now that Elspeth had come.

Fiora tried to push to the edge of the ballroom so she could escape through one of the doors and disappear into the garden, but the guests pressed forward, eager for a look at the mysterious newcomer. The ocean glinted just out of Fiora's reach as the crowd swept her away.

❧ 58 ❧

A million questions raced through Gustave's head, but a golden fog swallowed them and swept them away. It swept everything away until he was only aware of the beautiful girl in his arms. Her smile was everything he had been searching for his entire life. It washed his doubts away until he knew only one thing for sure.

She was his love. His destiny.

"Marry me, Elspeth."

"Of course."

She said the words in a soft, lilting accent that was more song than speech. It thickened the golden haze in Gustave's mind and steadied his resolve.

"Marry me tonight."

Something flashed through her eyes. Triumph? If she hadn't been his one true love and the light of his life, Gustave might have thought she looked a little vicious.

"Of course, Gustave. We'll be married tonight. Now be quiet and dance with me."

The music swelled, and Gustave spun Elspeth into his arms and dipped her towards the ground. He met his grandmother's

368

gaze as he did so. Dowager Queen Bernadine looked furious about something.

Why was she angry?

Gustave tried to remember the events leading up to his dancing with Elspeth. Had something happened to anger his grandmother before the gala started? He couldn't shake the feeling that he had forgotten something important.

Had she asked him to do something for her?

He lifted Elspeth and stared into her brilliant blue-green eyes. She smiled at him and hummed along with the music. Her voice filled Gustave's senses and his worry disappeared. He had been trying to remember something, but there was no use thinking when Elspeth looked at him like that.

He didn't even remember getting dressed that morning.

Gustave looked down at his clothes, suddenly not sure that he actually had gotten dressed. He sighed in relief when he saw that he was wearing a light blue suit.

Why had he chosen that color? This wasn't the suit he had planned to wear to the gala.

And why was he wearing a boutonniere?

Elspeth noticed him looking at the flower. She pulled the bloom from Gustave's collar and dropped it on the ground. Then she stepped on it, grinding it under her delicate shoe without missing a step in the dance.

Shoes.

Gustave wasn't wearing any shoes.

How could he have forgotten to put on shoes?

He was dancing with the love of his life, and he wasn't wearing shoes.

It was rather embarrassing. Thank goodness Elspeth didn't seem to mind.

"You may propose to me publicly when the dance ends, King Gustave."

He nodded, suddenly eager for the dance to finish.

❧ 59 ❧

The crowd jostled Fiora, pushing her through the room like the waves on a stormy sea. She gave up fighting and let it carry her. As long as she was moving, she had a chance to escape.

But somehow the mass of people pushed her to the front again. Gustave and Elspeth were still dancing. Still staring at each other like a couple in love.

Fiora gritted her teeth.

If she couldn't push through the crowd to the balconies, then the only exit was the staircase to the main hallway. Everyone would see her as she ran up it, but Fiora didn't care. She just needed to get out of here. Her vision was blurry from tears, and she wasn't sure if they were caused by the pain in her feet or the ache in her heart.

Perhaps losing Gustave's affection had worsened the effect of the curse.

Fiora looked down at her ring, expecting to once again see a dull, gray orb. Instead, the pearl still shimmered. Streaks of pink and blue danced in the candlelight.

A streak of gold had replaced the gray.

What did that mean?

Fiora wiped away the tears that were blurring her vision and stared at the gem, trying to make sense of the swirls of pearl and gold.

Maybe the magic was broken. How could Gustave love her when he had abandoned her for Elspeth?

Or perhaps Gustave had never been the one who loved her. Perhaps someone else secretly cared, and Fiora had been too distracted by Gustave to notice.

That seemed unlikely. What were the odds that Fiora would manage to catch two men when years of effort had failed to catch one?

Maybe Dale had fallen in love with her after she retrieved some of his precious forks.

Fiora snorted in spite of everything. That would be just her luck.

"Lady Mer!"

Fiora jumped as Collette's voice cut through the music.

"Please, come join us."

Collette gestured to the small group of royals standing beside her. Princess Serafina and Elaine were studying the dancing couple with suspicion. Dowager Queen Bernadine looked fierce, but her expression softened when she caught Fiora's gaze. She raised her hands to sign something, then dropped them with a frustrated shrug.

Fiora understood. What was there to say?

She eyed the staircase. It was freedom. She could run up and-

And do what, exactly? Swim out to sea and hope the mermaids found her? At this rate, her legs would give out before she made it out of the castle, and she still didn't have her voice.

Collette grew tired of waiting, walked over, and grabbed Fiora's hand. She pulled the reluctant princess over to their group.

"I'm sure he was just surprised to find the girl who rescued him," Collette signed. *"He'll come to his senses in a moment."*

Fiora shook her head.

"It's fine."

"It's not! He invited you to the gala then abandoned you. Gustave is usually more considerate than that. I am so sorry, Lady Mer."

Fiora blinked, surprised at the apology.

"It isn't like Gustave to get carried away like this," Dowager Queen Bernadine said. *"I'll speak with him as soon as this dance ends."*

"You don't have to do that. He doesn't owe me anything. We're not-"

Fiora stopped. She had been going to sign that she and Gustave weren't engaged, but that was rather obvious. They weren't even officially a couple. Apparently she had simply been a convenient companion until someone better came along.

"Stop it," Collette said. "Whatever you're thinking, just stop it. He was surprised and wanted to thank her for saving his life. As soon as the dance is over, he'll come to his senses, and we can talk about this."

Fiora took a deep breath and tried to relax. Maybe Collette was right. The pearl still glowed with magic.

"Or perhaps it is love at first sight," Marquis Corbeau said. "And with a princess!"

Everyone glared at him, but the marquis's smile didn't waver.

"You may not care about such things, but I have been trying very hard to find someone suitable for Gustave to marry. I find this turn of events quite fortuitous."

He gave Fiora a significant glance. She rolled her eyes. Before Collette or Dowager Queen Bernadine could comment, the music ended. Gustave kept one hand on Elspeth's waist and waved the other to get everyone's attention. Collette and Bernadine tensed, ready to rush out to the dance floor and intercept Gustave as soon as they could.

"Ladies and Gentlemen, my apologies. I know you came here to celebrate my birthday, but plans have changed."

Fiora shared a nervous look with Collette. This didn't sound good.

Then Gustave took Elspeth's hand and knelt in front of her.

"Princess Elspeth of Kell, will you marry me?"

"Yes, of course."

Fiora's heart sank even further as her breath caught in her throat. He was proposing?

How could she have been so very wrong about his feelings?

Collette let out a little gasp and covered her mouth with her hand. She looked to her grandmother. Dowager Queen Bernadine was signing furiously to Thomas, ordering him to wheel her across the room so she could stop this nonsense.

Thomas was signing back just as quickly, trying to reason with her.

"We'll be married tonight," Gustave said.

"Out of the question," Bernadine said.

But the crowd's cheers drowned her words. The guests all seemed to think they were witnessing a great love story.

Perhaps they were.

Suddenly, even standing was too much effort for Fiora. She had trusted Gustave and been very wrong.

And now she was out of time.

She slumped towards the floor, but someone caught her and wrapped an arm around her waist to hold her upright.

"Do you know her?" Princess Serafina asked.

She held Fiora upright with a firm grip and studied her with a look that said she already suspected the answer. Fiora shook her head anyway, denying everything.

"I should go."

"Sorry, I don't know sign language."

Serafina didn't sound sorry at all. Fiora looked to Collette and Bernadine, but they were staring at Gustave as he brought Elspeth over to meet them.

Fiora's half-sister looked angelic in the candlelight. Her eyes glowed. Possibly with love, but Fiora thought it looked more like triumph.

But she might be a little biased.

Fiora tried to pull away from Serafina, but her legs wouldn't hold her. She stumbled, and the princess of Santelle tightened her grip.

"You aren't well, Lady Mer. Massimo, help me support her."

Prince Massimo came over and tucked himself under Fiora's spare arm.

"Do I still have to dance if there's a wedding?" he asked, sounding rather cheerful.

"There won't be a wedding," Serafina said. "There's no way they can prepare for a royal wedding in one night."

"Blast."

Marquis Corbeau hurried forward to meet the couple.

"Your Majesty, let me be the first to offer my congratulations! If the young lady will come with me, I have a wedding gown that will suit her quite nicely. We can be ready for the ceremony within the hour."

Elspeth curtsied.

"That is most kind, Marquis. I will also need a wedding attendant."

"I'm sure Collette would be delighted," Gustave said.

Collette was too stunned to do more than blink in response. Elspeth nodded at her.

"Yes, of course your sister should attend me. As should mine."

She turned to Fiora with a serene smile.

"Lady Mer?" Collette said.

Elspeth laughed.

"Is that the name she's been using? Your Highness, surely you recognize my older sister, Princess Fiora of Kell?"

60

Gustave kept his arm wrapped around Elspeth's waist. The touch helped convince him that she was real. This was not simply a pleasant dream or imagined song.

"Princess Fiora?" Collette said.

She took a step back and stared at the dark-haired woman. Gustave supposed that Fiora resembled Elspeth a little. Mostly in the eyes.

But why was everyone so shocked by his love's announcement? There were plenty of royal guests at the gala. What was one more?

"Princess Fiora, would you be willing to serve as my bride's wedding attendant?"

It seemed a reasonable question, but everyone stared at Gustave as if he had something very shocking. Even Prince Leonardo and Princess Lenora looked surprised. Grandmother still looked furious. Why was she so angry?

"Please, Fiora?" Elspeth said.

Fiora gave Elspeth a long look, then met Gustave's gaze.

Her eyes made Gustave's breath catch in his throat. Even

filled with tears, they were beautiful and teased at a memory buried in the back of his mind. Why did she look so heartbroken?

Elspeth hummed a tune under her breath, and golden rain washed away Gustave's concern for Princess Fiora.

He should be more concerned with making his true love happy than placating the feelings of a stranger.

"We would be honored to have you in our wedding party, Princess Fiora," he said.

The princess closed her eyes for a moment, and tears spilled down her cheeks. Then she met Gustave's gaze and nodded. Elspeth grinned.

"Wonderful. Now, Marquis, I believe you said something about a wedding gown?"

"Gustave, this is ridiculous," Dowager Queen Bernadine said. "You can't actually mean to marry this girl tonight."

"He's the king," Marquis Corbeau said. "And she is a most suitable young lady. He can marry her whenever he likes. Everything is ready. If we delay, he may ruin things like he did with Princess Carina."

"But you don't know her," Collette said. "Gustave-"

Her voice trailed off. Gustave swallowed, trying to understand why everyone was so upset. He had expected them to be happy, but Marquis Corbeau was the only person who looked pleased.

"You all want me to get married," he said. "You've been pushing me to get married for months."

"Yes," Bernadine said. "But we didn't mean to rush you quite this much. You could at least wait until tomorrow. Or next week."

Elspeth squeezed his hand, and Gustave shook his head.

"Even one night is too long to spend away from my true love."

"Gustave, you're being absolutely ridiculous."

Dowager Queen Bernadine's expression was rather terrifying. Under other circumstances, it would have made Gustave want to run and hide.

But with his true love standing next to him, he wasn't afraid of anything. Besides, the law was on his side in this matter. There was nothing they could do to stop the wedding.

So he ignored his grandmother and turned to the marquis.

"Marquis Corbeau, please take Elspeth to be fitted for her gown. Fiora and Collette will attend to her. I trust you can have the rest of the preparations ready within the hour?"

"Of course, Your Majesty! This is everything I have been hoping for!"

Gustave had never seen Marquis Corbeau look so happy. Something in the back of his mind said that wasn't a good thing. Anything that made Marquis Corbeau happy usually meant trouble for those around him.

Then Elspeth stood on her tiptoes and kissed his cheek, and Gustave forgot everything else.

"This is the most ridiculous thing I've ever heard," Dowager Queen Bernadine said. "You can't just waltz in here and drag my grandson to the altar."

His grandmother's voice pierced through the fog, and Gustave's head began to ache. He looked from Elspeth to his grandmother. What did she have against his bride?

Elspeth squeezed his hand tighter and hummed again. She kept doing that. It must be a nervous habit.

Suddenly, Gustave was very annoyed that his family kept making his love nervous.

"You said you would respect my choice," Gustave said. "You said even if it wasn't traditional, you would respect my choice."

"We don't know her, Gustave," Collette said. "You don't know her."

Her voice was soft. Reasonable. That annoyed Gustave even more than his grandmother's anger.

"We do know her," Marquis Corbeau said. "This is Princess Elspeth of Kell. A most eligible match."

"But she's a stranger," Lady Annabelle said.

She looked nearly as outraged as his grandmother and sister.

"Gustave and I have met before," Elspeth said. "We spoke at a state function several years ago and have exchanged letters since then. I hoped to meet him again at a Princess Test, but my older sister was sent instead."

She nodded to Princess Fiora as she said this. Fiora's face was pale, and she leaned on Princess Serafina and Prince Massimo for support.

"Gustave, why didn't you mention this before?" Collette asked. "Why did you let us keep suggesting potential brides if you were already in love with someone? Why did you-"

Her voice trailed off, and for some reason she looked at Princess Fiora.

"Why indeed?" Dowager Queen Bernadine said. "You've never been one to keep secrets from us, Gustave."

"I-"

Gustave couldn't quite form the thoughts he needed to answer. He tried to remember meeting Elspeth and writing the letters. The golden fog in his mind assured him it had happened.

Then why had he kept it secret?

"We weren't sure my father would approve," Elspeth said. "He wanted Fiora to marry first, but she kept proving unsuccessful in the Princess Tests. Finally, I convinced him to let me attend Gustave's birthday gala. We were sailing here when I discovered Gustave after his shipwreck. It seemed like fate that I saved his life on the beach that day. Isn't that right, Gustave?"

Gustave remembered the beach in a vague sort of way, but not meeting Elspeth or writing her letters. He had not been in the habit of speaking to princesses when he was supposed to be nego-tiating with their fathers. Had he ever even negotiated with the King of Kell?

"Tell them, Gustave."

Her voice was musical and pleading. A golden haze swallowed the memories and told him that it didn't matter if he remem-bered. If his love said it happened, then surely it had happened.

Gustave nodded his agreement.

"Princess Elspeth and I have been acquainted for several years."

The words floated from his mouth as if someone else had put them there. But that was ridiculous. They were his own thoughts.

No one looked convinced. Elspeth pulled him close and whispered in his ear.

"You're the king, Gustave. Don't let them keep us apart."

Her lips brushed against his ear, and the music in her voice filled his head. Gustave straightened and glared at the crowd gathered around him.

"Elspeth and I will be married tonight. There is no reason to delay. The guests are already here, and Marquis Corbeau has everything prepared. Captain Whist will perform the ceremony."

"And we'll leave on our honeymoon right away," Elspeth said. "My ship and crew are ready for us."

"Is it wise to sail right now?" Collette said. "Kraken have attacked recently."

Elspeth gave her a condescending smile.

"I sailed here from Kell without a problem. My charm to repel dark creatures is apparently more effective than whatever you are using. I will be happy to share it with your navy when I return from my honeymoon and take my place as Queen of Montaigne."

Dowager Queen Bernadine snorted in disbelief and gave Gustave a look that made him feel he was five years old and had been caught sneaking cookies from the pantry. Something buried deep inside told him that Grandmother was right. All of this was unreasonable.

He looked away from his grandmother to avoid finishing the thought and met Princess Fiora's gaze.

The heartbreak in her deep blue eyes cleared the fog for a moment. She had wrapped her arms around herself as if she were trying to hide from the world. Gustave couldn't shake the feeling that her sadness was his fault.

He had promised her something. Had meant to do something with her tonight. To ask her something.

What had it been? Apparently something important. Something that mattered to her very much.

Elspeth tightened her grip on his arm. He looked down and met her eyes. His regret at disappointing Fiora disappeared in a wave of golden joy. Elspeth hummed another tune, and Gustave's heart beat in time with it. Whatever else happened, this was right. Elspeth was right.

"Go prepare for the wedding," Elspeth said. "I'll see you soon."

Then she pulled his head down and kissed him.

Gustave stood frozen for a moment. It was hardly appropriate for her to kiss him in front of everyone like that. They had just met. What was she doing?

Then a song rang through his head and Gustave wrapped his arms around Elspeth's waist and kissed her back. He felt her grin before she pulled away. She winked at him, grabbed Fiora's hand, and ordered Marquis Corbeau to show her to a chamber where they could prepare for the ceremony. Fiora stumbled as they walked away.

Gustave watched them go in a daze. His head cleared a little when Elspeth left the room, and he realized that everyone in the ballroom was staring at him.

"Please, dance and enjoy yourselves while we prepare for the wedding," he said. "It would be a shame to waste this party."

"Gustave, I would like a word in private."

Dowager Queen Bernadine was positively bristling. Without Elspeth to give him confidence, Gustave shuddered. Whatever his grandmother was angry about, he didn't have time to deal with it right now. Not if he was going to be married within the hour.

"It's best not to keep my bride waiting."

He ran up the stairs before anyone could stop him. The song filled his head as he left the room, and joy flooded his heart. At last, something had gone right. He had found his love, and they would rule Montaigne together.

The memory of the betrayed expression in Fiora's eyes made him miss a step, and his stockinged feet slipped on the smooth marble floor. Gustave leaned against the wall to catch his balance and rubbed his head. Something was wrong. Things were mixed up somehow.

Then a golden haze washed away the memory of those sad eyes.

Nothing was wrong.

For once in his life, everything was just right.

Or at least, it would be once he found his shoes.

❧ 61 ❧

"Why didn't you tell us you were Princess Fiora?"
Collette looked angry, but was it because of the
deception or Gustave's sudden infatuation with Elspeth?

Probably both.

"I'm sorry."

It wasn't an answer, but it was all Fiora felt she could say.

*"Did you know that Gustave was in love with Elspeth? Was your
coming here all part of some game?"*

"What? No!"

Fiora glared at Collette. The princess of Montaigne returned
the expression. Her face looked strained, as if her features weren't
used to arranging themselves in anything but a gentle smile.

"Ladies, you shouldn't have conversations that Princess
Elspeth can't understand," Marquis Corbeau said. "You are her
wedding attendants. It is rude to ignore her."

Collette bit her lip, clearly trying to refrain from yelling at the
marquis.

*"It is beyond rude to crash a birthday party and turn it into your
wedding,"* Fiora signed.

Her friendship with Collette was ruined, and Gustave had lost interest in her the moment he saw Elspeth. Fiora had nothing left to lose but her life, and that would happen soon enough. She might as well just be herself.

To Fiora's surprise, Collette's lips quirked up in a small smile before returning to a scowl.

"What did my sister say?" Elspeth asked.

Her sweet smile never wavered. Surely she knew that Princess Collette was upset, but she acted as if everything was fine.

Collette glanced at Fiora.

"Princess Fiora was reminding me to ask Marchioness Rouge about commissioning a crown for you. The expense will have to be approved by the council immediately if we want it to be ready by the time you get back from your honeymoon."

"Oh, how thoughtful."

Elspeth looked to Marquis Corbeau for confirmation. He nodded.

"Princess Collette and Marchioness Rouge have been overseeing the budget while King Gustave took care of gala matters. But I can speak to Marchioness Rouge for you. There is no need to neglect your duties as Princess Elspeth's wedding attendant."

"Oh, but both of us must sign the paper to make it official. Surely you don't want Princess Elspeth to wear an old crown for her coronation?"

Marquis Corbeau considered this.

"And I know you have a lot to do to prepare for the wedding," Collette continued. "I would hate to take you away from your duties and risk delaying the ceremony."

"Oh, we shouldn't delay," Elspeth said. "Please, go, Princess Collette. My sister can assist me."

"Very well," Marquis Corbeau said. "But make sure you commission something worthy of our new queen. Perhaps you could use the surplus budget you were going to spend on assisting merchants to buy new jewels."

"Yes, of course," Collette said.

She curtsied to Marquis Corbeau, then turned to Fiora.

"Stall her. I'll summon the council and find a way to stop this."

Fiora blinked in surprise. Collette looked rather fierce. The princess of Montaigne raised her eyebrow in a question, and Fiora nodded. Gustave seemed to have made up his mind about the matter, but she owed it to Collette to help however she could.

Princess Collette rushed out the door before Elspeth or Marquis Corbeau could demand a translation of their conversation. The seamstress bustled into the room, carrying a gorgeous white dress trimmed with pearls and embroidered seashells. Her assistant followed with an armful of white shoes.

Marquis Corbeau bowed to Elspeth.

"Send word if you need anything else, Your Highness. I will go take care of the other preparations."

"Thank you, Marquis. I look forward to working with you as your queen."

Marquis Corbeau beamed, bowed again, and hurried from the room.

Fiora sank into a chair, taking the weight off her feet as the seamstress helped Elspeth into the gown and marked the places to alter.

There weren't many. The dress looked as if it were made for the princess.

"I'll take this back to the sewing room and have it ready for you soon," the seamstress promised. "Would you prefer to wait here or accompany me?"

"We'll wait here," Elspeth said. "I would like a few moments alone with my sister before the ceremony."

The seamstress nodded and carried the dress out of the room. Elspeth turned to Fiora.

"Well, you have managed to get into quite a mess."

Fiora glared and crossed her arms over her chest.

"Have you really lost your voice?"

"Of course I have. What are you doing here, Elspeth? Why didn't you ever mention that you were writing letters to King Gustave?"

Elspeth shook her head.

"I'm sure you're trying to explain yourself, but it's no good. I don't understand sign language."

Fiora snorted. If this conversation was going to be one-sided, why was Elspeth so determined to have it?

Perhaps *because* it was going to be one-sided. Because Elspeth had won, and now she could gloat without worrying about being interrupted.

"I know Father is difficult, Fiora, but is he really so bad that you had to run away from home?"

Fiora raised an eyebrow, and Elspeth laughed.

"Perhaps he is. I know I'll be happy to be married and out from under his roof. It will be nice to be the one making the rules for a change."

Fiora desperately wanted to respond. To yell. To fight back somehow.

But her voice was gone and her heart was broken. Not to mention her feet hurt so badly she couldn't walk, and she was almost out of time.

The only question now was, would the transformation enchantment kill her first? Or would she turn into sea foam when Gustave married Elspeth?

Fiora glared at her ring. At the enchanted gem that dared to glisten as if she still had some hope of surviving the night.

At that mysterious wisp of gold curling around the surface. What did it mean?

"I know someone who could help you," Elspeth said.

Fiora narrowed her eyes. Help with what?

"You're clearly in some kind of distress. Your voice is gone. You're hiding from your family. Are you under some sort of curse?"

Fiora shrugged. Her very existence felt like a curse at this point.

"I have a friend who knows magic, and I think she could help."

Elspeth hesitated, and Fiora waited. It wasn't like she had anything better to do.

"Come with us," Elspeth said finally. "You can serve as my lady-in-waiting when Gustave and I leave on our honeymoon. There's plenty of room for you on our ship. We'll sail to visit my friend and see if she can help you."

Fiora swallowed. The last thing she wanted to do was see Gustave and Elspeth together any more than necessary. Accompanying them on their honeymoon would be torture. The way he looked at her—

Fiora closed her eyes and pushed the image away. Whatever she had thought Gustave felt towards her, she had been wrong. The ring was wrong. He loved Elspeth.

"I'm family, Fiora. I know we haven't always gotten along, but I'd like to help you. I doubt the royal family of Montaigne will want you to stay here since you lied to them. Come with us and let me help you."

Fiora swallowed. Elspeth had never helped her. Not once in ten years.

But maybe she had been trying. Maybe Fiora herself had been the problem.

This castle would be unbearable without Gustave.

Although Collette had asked her to stall the ceremony. Was it a gesture of friendship? Or simply desperation?

Elspeth waited for an answer. Her face looked angelic. She glowed like a woman in love.

It wasn't Elspeth's fault that Gustave loved her. That Fiora was unlovable. That her entire relationship with the king had been based on lies that had crumbled like a sandcastle.

Fiora sighed. Even if Elspeth's friend couldn't help her, getting on a ship would bring her closer to the mermaids. They seemed her best chance at survival now.

It was better than staying in Montaigne and waiting to die at sunrise.

She nodded, and Elspeth smiled brightly.

"Oh, I'm so glad, Fiora. It will be so nice to spend some time together, and I know Gustave will be pleased as well. He seems to value your friendship."

Friendship.

The word stabbed through Fiora like a knife. It was hard to tell exactly what caused the pain. The curse or Gustave's betrayal or Elspeth's misplaced kindness.

The rest of the time before the ceremony passed in a blur. The seamstress returned and helped Elspeth into the wedding gown. Marquis Corbeau bustled in and out, checking on the bride and commanding an army of servants.

Fiora did what she could to slow things down, but Marquis Corbeau was too efficient to allow many delays.

And then it was time. Collette joined them outside the door to the ballroom. The princess looked exhausted, as if she had been sprinting around the castle since she left them. She probably had been. Collette met Fiora's gaze and shook her head.

Apparently her attempt to stop the wedding had not been successful.

Marquis Corbeau whispered to a few servants, checking on last-minute details, then nodded to the footmen to open the doors.

Soft music played as the princesses descended the stairs. Fiora leaned against the railing, trying desperately not to show how much pain she was in as she walked into a candlelit nightmare.

₰ 62 ₰

Somehow, in the space of an hour, Marquis Corbeau had transformed the already beautiful ballroom into a candlelit dream. The elegant floral arrangements from the gala had been swept away and replaced with cascading bouquets of lilies. A majestic cake and an assortment of matching pastries sat in the corner. Even the musicians had changed clothes to match the new decorations.

Gustave stood with Captain Whist on a white dais etched with golden swirls that matched the gentle curve of the lilies. The captain wore his dress uniform and a hat that was only slightly larger than the standard issue. In spite of the elegant clothing, he looked more somber than usual. Gustave wondered why. Shouldn't his friend should be happy on such an occasion?

He studied the crowd behind him, searching for answers to the questions that his mind wouldn't quite let him ask. His grandmother still looked furious. The assembled royal guests looked either excited or confused. A few were missing. Princess Serafina and Elaine were not in the crowd.

Where had they gone?

No matter. What they did was their business.

Except they were here as his guests. What could they possibly be doing that was more important than attending his wedding?

Music began to play, and the candlelight seemed to grow more golden. The doors at the top of the stairs opened, and Gustave forgot everything but Elspeth.

She looked like a dream in the wedding gown that Marquis Corbeau had commissioned. A vision of white and gold that made everything else in his life feel insignificant.

People walked behind her, but Gustave did no more than register that Elspeth wasn't alone. His bride was all that mattered tonight.

She seemed to float across the floor. She smiled at him, and Gustave's heart beat faster. By the time she stepped onto the dais and took his hand, he could hardly breathe.

She was perfect. An angel. The thing he had been searching for all his life.

Elspeth's smile said she felt the same way. At least, Gustave hoped it did. How was it possible that such a perfect woman would love him?

Truly, how was it possible? How had they met? How had Gustave managed to win her heart?

His eyebrows knit together. It was important that he remember. Such things mattered to women. How could he be worthy of Elspeth and make her happy if he couldn't even remember the first time they met?

Captain Whist began to speak the words of the ceremony. Gustave was distracted for a moment by Elspeth's attendants adjusting her gown. Collette and Fiora.

Collette's hair was in disarray, and her gown was wrinkled. What would possibly cause her to come to his wedding in such a state?

Fiora was very pale and refused to look at Gustave. She stared out the window instead, as if she were searching for something.

Gustave followed her gaze, wondering what could be more

fascinating than his bride. All he could see through the windows were gardens and the ocean. Elspeth was infinitely more charming than either.

Elspeth cleared her throat, and Gustave quickly looked back to her face. He moved his hands to sign an apology, then remembered that Elspeth didn't know sign language.

Why had it been his first instinct to sign to her?

"Squawk!"

Gustave flinched as a seagull streaked with black flew into the ballroom. Elspeth shrieked as the bird dove towards her. Gustave stepped in front of his bride to intercept the attack, but the gull swooped up and circled over them instead.

It dropped something, and Princess Fiora let go of Elspeth's train to catch it. Whatever it was, Fiora looked relieved to see it. She held it in the palm of her hand, studying it for a moment before she slipped it down the front of her dress and picked up Elspeth's train as if nothing had happened.

The seagull squawked again. The harsh sound cleared Gustave's head a little, and he blinked at Fiora. Why had she just received a message from a bird?

"Get out of here!"

Marquis Corbeau shooed the bird away from the dais. It flew to the side of the room and landed on the cake. The marquis shrieked with rage and ran after it. The gull hopped off the cake and pecked at an apple tart instead. Finally it grabbed the largest tart on the tray and flew out of the room.

Marquis Corbeau stared mournfully at the ruined cake and pastries. Then he turned and glared at Fiora as if she had somehow caused the chaos.

"Please, may we continue?" Elspeth asked with a soft smile.

Captain Whist looked to Gustave, who nodded. Elspeth hummed softly to herself as the captain asked Gustave to repeat his vows. He did so in a blur, not quite sure what he was saying and hoping he didn't make a horrible blunder of the ceremony.

And then Elspeth was confessing her love. Promising to cherish him for the rest of their lives. Her voice, though soft, seemed to fill the ballroom. Gustave stared at her in wonder. How had he convinced such perfection to love him? How had he courted her?

No truly, how had he done it? The memories had disappeared in a golden haze. He only knew that somehow he had. The evidence in front of him was overwhelming.

He would ask Elspeth later and hope she wasn't offended by the question. Maybe the kraken hitting him on the head had made him forget.

That seemed as likely as anything.

"I now pronounce you man and wife, king and queen of Montaigne. May your reign be long and prosperous."

Why didn't Captain Whist sound more excited about this announcement? It was good news, wasn't it? Gustave was fully king now. Montaigne could function as it should.

And they had the perfect queen.

"Perhaps we should skip the reception," Elspeth said. "That seagull made quite a mess of it."

It was true. One bird had succeeded in ruining Marquis Corbeau's perfectly prepared banquet. Gustave laughed.

"Yes, perhaps we should."

"Gustave, you need to-"

His grandmother was saying something, but Gustave had eyes only for Elspeth. If she wanted to skip the reception and go straight to their honeymoon, he had no objections.

"My sister will come with us to serve as my lady-in-waiting," Elspeth said.

Gustave looked to Princess Fiora, who still refused to meet his gaze. It was a little strange to bring your sister-in-law along on your honeymoon, but who was he to refuse Elspeth anything?

"Whatever you like. Lead the way to your ship, my bride."

❧ 63 ❧

The crowd of guests chased after Gustave and Elspeth as they left the ballroom. They threw rose petals that floated in the sea breeze and scented the air.

Fiora gritted her teeth and quickened her pace to keep up with the procession. If her pain got much worse, turning to sea foam would be a mercy.

They walked through the city until they reached the docks. Sailors and merchants stared at them as they passed. The gala guests' bright clothes and jewels glittered in the torchlight.

"The king has found a bride!" Marquis Corbeau shouted. "Long live the queen!"

After a few confused moments, the sailors nearest him took up the cheer. It spread through the docks and into the town.

"Long live the queen!"

Their voices filled the night and drowned out the sound of the sea. Fiora breathed deeply, taking in the salt-scented air. She searched the shoreline for signs of the mermaids. Spot had brought a shell from Althea. Hopefully that meant her aunt had found a way to break the enchantment.

But the mermaids couldn't approach her when the docks were overflowing with wedding guests and sailors. Fiora could either run down the shore to search for them or board Elspeth's ship.

The shore was likely to stay crowded as everyone watched the royal couple sail away. And Fiora wasn't sure she could make it to the usual meeting place before her feet gave out entirely. So she took a sailor's hand and let him help her up the gangplank. Then she leaned against the railing and studied the crowd while the sailors prepared to depart.

Dowager Queen Bernadine and Princess Collette were having a frantic discussion with Marchioness Rouge and Elaine. Elaine kept gesturing to the *Sea Frog*, where Princess Serafina and her crew were also preparing to set sail.

Prince Leonardo and Princess Lenora stood beside Prince Edric and Lady Annabelle. They seemed surprised by this turn of events, but not as shocked as Gustave's family.

The rest of the guests were cheerful. They had come for a gala and witnessed a royal wedding. What luck!

Fiora sighed and turned her attention to the water. She watched the dark waves lap against the ship and hoped she wasn't making a huge mistake in sailing away with Elspeth and Gustave. What if the mermaids were waiting for her down the coast, and she missed them?

She checked her ring. The blasted pearl still shone with magic, but the golden streak across it had grown wider.

Fiora looked at the night sky filled with glittering stars. How much longer did she have until sunrise?

"You must be tired," Elspeth said. "Let me show you to your room?"

Fiora shrugged. The mermaids wouldn't be able to contact her until the ship was further away from the harbor. Maybe not until everyone else was asleep. So she limped behind Elspeth as her sister led her to a small cabin above the deck.

"Gustave and I are staying in the captain's cabin across the ship. If you need anything, just ask one of the crew members. We won't want anyone disturbing us tonight."

Elspeth winked, and Fiora felt like she might throw up. She suddenly wished she had turned down Elspeth's offer and stayed in Montaigne. Collette and Bernadine were angry at her deception, but surely they would help if they knew her situation.

At the least they would arrange for someone to help Fiora get to the beach to say goodbye to her family.

"We'll reach my friend's house sometime tomorrow," Elspeth said. "The one who can help you."

Tomorrow would be too late.

The ship lurched as it moved away from the dock. Fiora tried to sign to Elspeth that she had changed her mind, but her sister had already left and closed the door behind her. Fiora limped across the room and pushed on the handle.

It was locked.

She pounded on the door, but no one paid any attention to the noise. Fiora watched through a knot in the wood as the crew lowered the sails and the ship floated out of the harbor.

Blast it all. She was trapped.

Fiora frowned and pulled Althea's shell from her dress. She limped over to a porthole and studied the shell's carvings in the moonlight. The shell didn't contain any special messages. Just Althea's signature.

What had her aunt found? Had she summoned Fiora to offer her a cure?

Or to say goodbye?

Fiora slumped into a chair and watched the moonlight glisten on the waves. How had everything gone so very wrong?

She would give anything to be a mermaid again. She might not fit in under the sea, but at least merfolk were honest. They didn't act like they loved her then toss her aside like garbage.

However complicated their love was, at least it was real.

Tears rolled down Fiora's cheeks. It was dark now. The sun would rise soon, and she was spending her last few hours of life locked in this room. Her tears felt pathetic, but what else could she do?

"Crying won't do any good."

Fiora gasped and leaned her head out the window. Althea, Kathelin, and Zoe floated in the water beneath her.

"You found me!"

Zoe smiled.

"Of course we did! We wouldn't abandon our sister."

"Did you win the love of a human man?" Althea asked.

"Someone stole the shell. I won't be able to transform unless you have the song memorized."

Althea scowled.

"Leander and Madame Isla know the song by heart, but Madame Isla is back in the summer city and Leander has disappeared. Still, if someone loves you, we will have time to fetch Madame Isla."

"I didn't win his love. At least, I don't think so."

Fiora pulled off her pearl ring and tossed it down to her aunt. The mermaid studied it with a troubled expression before throwing it back to Fiora.

"I don't know what that means. But if your voice has not returned, I'm afraid you didn't win his love."

Fiora tried to sing but made no sound. Her scowl deepened. So much for her aunts having answers.

"I think it means I was a fool to think anyone would want me."

"There is still time before sunset," Zoe said. "Perhaps you can still win his heart."

"But Gustave married another tonight. My human sister Elspeth."

Zoe gasped, and Althea's face grew grim. She shared a look with Kathelin.

"We'll have to do it, then?" Kathelin said.

A.G. MARSHALL

"He's left us no choice. Zoe, stay with Fiora while Kathelin and I complete the enchantment."

The two sisters dove beneath the waves. Fiora turned to her cousin.

"So you have found a way to heal me?"

Zoe nodded, but didn't look happy about it. Fiora's heartbeat quickened.

"Zoe, what's wrong?"

The serious expression looked out of place on Zoe's normally cheerful face. The young mermaid shook her head and forced a smile.

"They found a way to save you, Fiora. That's all that matters."

Somehow, Fiora doubted it was that simple.

It was never that simple.

A soft duet rippled through the waves as Kathelin and Althea resurfaced. They pulled strands of silver from the air as they sang, weaving them into a long, thin shape. The water glowed white around them as something luminescent rose from the ocean floor. The light grew brighter and combined with the silver until the strands united to form a gleaming pearl dagger.

It hovered in the air for a moment, then fell into the ocean with a splash.

Althea grabbed it before it sank and cut off her hair in one swift motion. The dagger's light darkened as it absorbed the hair into a liquid that swirled around the surface.

Before Fiora could process what had happened, Kathelin took the dagger and did the same.

Then Zoe cut her hair as well.

"I feel naked," Zoe whispered.

She looked naked without her long hair wrapped around her like a cloak. The strands reached just past her chin now and waved wildly in the wind.

"What are you doing?" Fiora signed.

"This is forbidden magic, Fiora. It requires that the enchanters use part of themselves to create it."

Fiora stared at her mermaid family. They had sacrificed their hair to save her. They had created something forbidden to protect her.

And their faces said that the magic didn't stop there.

Althea held the dagger towards Fiora with grim resolve.

"Fiora, this will allow you to break the curse and return to the sea as a mermaid. It will remove the pain from your feet and restore your voice."

Fiora reached for the knife, but the porthole was too high. Althea hummed, creating a small geyser of glowing white water that carried the dagger to Fiora's hand.

She closed her fingers around it. The knife felt cold to the touch and sent a shiver down her spine.

The pain in her feet did not go away. She gave Althea a questioning look, and her aunt met her gaze with an expression as cold as moonlight. Zoe and Kathelin looked down at the water.

"The pearl ring was designed to keep you human by allowing a human to share his soul with you," Althea said. "Nyssa was convinced the human man loved her and would love her forever. But she was wrong. Human hearts are fickle and untrustworthy. We cannot trust the ring to save you."

Fiora nodded. Her father had taught her that, and Gustave had confirmed it.

But that fact alone did not explain her aunt's severe expression.

"You must have a human life to save yourself, Fiora. If he is not willing to give it, then you must take it."

Fiora flinched. Surely she didn't mean-

But Althea nodded slowly.

"The human man proved unworthy of your love and unwilling to share his life, but this dagger will let you take it. You must stab King Gustave with the dagger and kill him. It will absorb his life and transfer it to you. You can then use that magic to save yourself and return to the sea."

Fiora raised her hands to say something, but they were shaking too badly to sign.

Besides, what was there to say?

"I know this is hard," Althea said. "But the human betrayed you and married another. I will not lose another sister to a human's infidelity. King Fergal took Nyssa away from us. I will not let King Gustave take you."

Tears glittered in Althea's eyes. She hummed softly, and a kraken tentacle pushed her out of the water and up to the porthole. Fiora reached down and clasped her aunt's hand. The mermaid squeezed tightly as if she might never let go.

"We love you, Fiora," Kathelin said.

"We will do anything for you," Zoe added fiercely.

Even forbidden magic. Even murder.

Fiora swallowed.

"You must use the dagger by dawn," Althea said. "If you don't, you will turn into sea foam and be lost to us forever."

Fiora set the dagger on a nearby chair. It gleamed dangerously in the moonlight.

"I'm locked in this room."

Kathelin sang quietly. A stream of water climbed the ship and crawled across the floor. It crept up the door and filled the lock. Something clicked, and the door opened slightly.

"Wait until everyone has gone to bed," Kathelin said. "Then we will create a diversion to distract anyone who is still awake."

"They might stay up late," Zoe said. "They are celebrating a marriage, after all."

Althea shook her head.

"The bride and groom will want time alone. I expect everyone will go to bed within the hour."

Fiora closed her eyes to hide the tears that welled up at the thought of Gustave and Elspeth's wedding night. She reached for the dagger and squeezed it tightly. The smooth surface was cold and unyielding in her hand.

"Wait for our signal," Althea said. "I'm sorry, Fiora, but this is the only way."

Fiora nodded. She didn't like it, but Althea was right.

If she didn't want to die, this was the only way.

🎄 64 🎄

Gustave leaned against the railing, watching twinkling lights of the city disappear on the horizon. He blinked as a wave crashed against the ship and splashed his face.

He blinked again and saw his surroundings as if he had just woken up from a deep sleep. He stood on the deck of a ship sailing in the open water. Montaigne was a smudge of light on the horizon.

Gustave felt pressure on his fingertips and realized he was holding hands with someone. He followed the hand upward, examining a delicate arm and elegant shoulder before reaching the woman's face.

She was pretty, although he couldn't quite place her. It wasn't that he knew her, but rather that she reminded him of someone else that he knew very well. Those eyes were achingly familiar, although not quite blue enough. And her hair seemed too light. Too golden.

She wore a wedding gown. The wedding gown Marquis Corbeau had commissioned. It suited her, but somehow also looked out of place. Gustave preferred it on the mannequin.

Or Lady Mer.

Gustave's hand went limp as he remembered the events that had led him here. He had abandoned Lady Mer on the dance floor. The look of betrayal in her eyes should have melted stone, but he had simply walked away.

Why had he walked away?

Because there had been a song. A voice. The voice he had been looking for since the shipwreck.

He tried to pull his hand away, but the woman tightened her grip and pulled him towards her.

"Is everything alright, Gustave?" she whispered.

That voice. Gustave knew that voice. It curled around his thoughts like a snake, filling every crevice and covering the memories of Lady Mer and his family until there was only her.

Only Elspeth.

She squeezed his hand again and smiled. That smile drove any doubts out of Gustave's head. He was happy now that he had her.

Elspeth was all that mattered.

"Come to bed with me?"

Her voice was a song that filled Gustave's senses. With a start, he remembered they were married. That was why Elspeth was wearing a wedding gown. This was their wedding night.

No, that wasn't right. Gustave looked to the sea again, trying to make sense of the evening and take control of his thoughts. He hadn't meant to marry anyone tonight. Elspeth hummed, pulling his attention back to her face. To her lips.

Golden fog filled Gustave's head, and he bent over to kiss his bride. The fog intensified as his lips met hers, and he wrapped his hands around her waist to pull her closer. Elspeth clung to him, returning the kiss until they were both gasping for breath.

The world had never felt so right.

Elspeth leaned close and sang softly in his ear. That tune. That voice. It was everything.

She took his hand and pulled him across the ship to the captain's cabin.

"Alone at last," Elspeth sang.

She reached up and ran her fingers through Gustave's hair.

It was a warm room. Maybe a little too warm, all wood and flickering candles reflected in an ornate mirror in the corner. Moonlight streamed through a large picture window, illuminating an enormous bed in the center.

Gustave's pulse raced when he saw the bed. A warning tried to ring out in his head, but the golden fog swallowed it. He was excited about his wedding night. That was all.

He turned to his bride, who smiled sweetly at him.

"Perhaps some wine first, my love?"

She poured a glass and offered it to him. The ruby liquid glistened against the crystal. Gustave took the glass and watched the wine ripple in the cup while Elspeth poured another glass for herself.

The longer he looked at it, the more it reminded him of blood.

"To true love," Elspeth said.

She raised her glass to clink against Gustave's, then took a sip.

Gustave did the same. The taste was darker than he expected. Bitter.

His already foggy thoughts blurred further. He stumbled, spilling most of the wine onto the floor. Elspeth took the glass from him and held it to his lips.

"Take another drink, Gustave. Just one more sip. For me."

Her face was a beautiful blur. A smear of gold and white in the darkness. Gustave tried to obey her and take another drink, but the wine sloshed onto his beard instead. Elspeth sighed.

"I suppose that's the best you can do. Come to bed now, Your Majesty."

She set their glasses down on a nearby table and guided him across the room. Gustave followed clumsily. Bed. That was where he should be. It was his wedding night, and he was supposed to be in bed.

Gustave collapsed face first onto the covers and rolled over, searching the darkness for Elspeth. He should tell her that he loved her. He should apologize for falling asleep so quickly. This was their wedding night, but he was so very tired. He just needed a short nap, then he could give her the attention she deserved.

His love deserved everything.

But Elspeth had disappeared, and Gustave could no longer keep his eyes open. Darkness swept away the golden fog as he fell into a deep sleep.

❧ 65 ❧

Fiora sat in the darkness and stared at the dagger. It was as elegant as it was deadly. The blade and handle were carved from a single pearl and decorated with symbols like the ones used to carve songs into seashells.

But this enchantment was not created with a song. It drew power from hair and blood. From the body itself.

Forbidden magic.

The knife gleamed in the moonlight, swirls of red and black that had once been the mermaids' hair trapped in its luminescent surface. They danced around each other as if they were alive.

Fiora closed her eyes, but the colors remained, dancing through black instead of white.

The sun would rise soon. She could feel it. The pain had spread from her legs to her stomach and settled there in knots that refused to uncurl.

Would it hurt to turn to sea foam? Or would it come as a relief to fade into the waves and gently wash to shore?

Fiora bit her lip, wishing she could scream in frustration. She didn't want to die.

And she didn't want to kill.

She set the pearl knife on a nearby table and stared at the moon until Althea's signal came. Her aunt's soft song made the dagger flicker like candlelight, as if it could sense the magic in the mermaid's voice. Fiora pushed off the chair and gasped in pain as her feet hit the floor. She gathered up the full skirt of Dowager Queen Bernadine's gown and looked down at her legs.

Dark bruises had spread across her skin. They traced the patterns of her veins and crawled up her ankles. Fiora took a shuddering breath and picked up the knife. There was only one way to stop this.

And it must be stopped.

The ship's deck was empty. Fiora heard a noise in the distance and squinted at the horizon. Althea's distraction had apparently involved luring the entire crew into a lifeboat and sending them back to shore. The boat floated towards Montaigne and disappeared into the darkness.

So long as Gustave and Elspeth stayed asleep, no one could stop her.

Fiora limped across the deck, stumbling as waves rocked the ship. She tried to hurry as she felt the curse's magic growing, but it was no good. She couldn't walk any faster than her current pace.

The rough wood of the ship's deck stabbed her feet, aggravating her skin rather than soothing it as the cool marble had. If she had been walking on knives before, she was walking on broken glass now.

Fiora kept her gaze on the cabin door as she moved. She needed to focus on her goal. The knife warmed in her hand as if agreeing with her.

When she finally reached the other side of the ship, Fiora leaned against the wood to rest for a moment. She pressed her ear against the door and listened.

She heard only soft, rhythmic breathing.

The newlyweds were asleep.

Fiora turned the latch and pushed. The door opened without a sound.

The candles had sputtered out, but the moon shone through the window brightly enough to illuminate the room.

Gustave lay asleep in the bed. Elspeth's side was empty. It seemed the new bride had gone elsewhere after her groom fell asleep.

Fiora pushed the door closed and locked it. Then she swallowed and turned back to the bed.

Gustave still wore his suit from the gala. The one that matched Fiora's gown. At some point he had put on shoes, and he hadn't bothered to take them off before going to sleep.

He lay on top of the covers in a wrinkled mess. His hair was tousled, and something sticky stained his beard.

His right hand stretched across the bed towards the place where Elspeth should have been. Fiora stared at his hand for a moment. It looked lonely, lying empty on the bed by itself like that.

If they were truly in love, shouldn't they be snuggled together? Where had the bride gone?

Fiora shook her head. It was a good thing that Elspeth was gone. She needed to hurry and finish this before her sister returned.

Pain rippled from her stomach to her chest, and Fiora doubled over in agony. She was running out of time.

She leaned against the wall, using it to keep herself upright as she limped towards Gustave.

Why did it have to be Gustave? Why couldn't she have stabbed a random crew member?

Or Elspeth. Would the dagger work if she killed Elspeth instead?

There was no time to ask Althea, and Fiora shook the thought away. As much as she hated her half-sister, she didn't want to kill her. Elspeth was family.

And Gustave was–

Fiora paused, studying Gustave's peaceful face.

What was Gustave to her?

A friend, certainly. Also the man who had betrayed her. The one who had offered hope then ripped it away.

Fiora pushed away from the wall and raised the knife. It was simple enough. Plunge the dagger into his heart. Spill his blood and save her life.

She stood for a long moment with the knife raised. Gustave's chest rose and fell as he breathed peacefully.

Stop that breathing and save yourself. Silence his gentle voice forever.

The dagger glowed brighter, filling the cabin with an ethereal glow. It seemed eager to fulfill its purpose. As if it could sense what she was about to do.

The life she was about to take.

Gustave's face blurred as Fiora's eyes filled with tears. She lowered the knife.

She couldn't do it.

Call it weakness. Call it crazy. But no matter how he had betrayed her, Fiora could not kill this man.

She loved him too much.

The realization washed over her in waves almost as painful as the curse. She dropped to her knees and gasped for air as silent sobs shook her body. She loved Gustave.

He did not return her love. He never would. But that changed nothing.

Love was a thing freely given. Not a prize to be earned.

And she would give it. She would pay for it with her life.

Fiora set the knife on the floor and raised shaking hands.

"I love you. I know you can't see me. You wouldn't hear me even if I could speak. But I love you, and I hope you'll be happy."

Fiora crawled forward, smoothed Gustave's tangled hair, and kissed him softly on the forehead.

He stirred, and Fiora stiffened. What would she do if he woke up now? How on earth would she explain what she was doing in his bedroom on his wedding night?

But Gustave only smiled and sighed in his sleep. He was probably dreaming of Elspeth.

Fiora didn't have the strength to stand. She grabbed the knife and crawled across the floor. She unlocked the door, pulled herself over the ship's deck, and leaned against the railing.

Althea, Kathelin, and Zoe floated in the ocean below. They looked at her with hopeful expressions that quickly turned to horror.

"No," Althea said. "Fiora, he's not worth it!"

Fiora stared at them a moment longer, silently apologizing.

Then she lifted the dagger and threw it as far as she could.

The pearl knife hit the water with a hiss and disappeared beneath the waves.

❦ 66 ❦

Black and gold swirled together in Gustave's dreams. He had the vague feeling that he should be resting, but instead his heart pounded as he fought something he couldn't quite name. Pressure built in his forehead, and he wished he could sleep and forget it all.

If he slept more, maybe he could remember whatever was pressing at the back of his mind. The faint sense of urgency that he was missing something important.

Something soft and warm pressed against his forehead. The gold mist shone brighter for a moment, then disappeared into darkness. His headache vanished.

Gustave tried to open his eyes, but he couldn't move his eyelids. He couldn't move anything. His body refused to cooperate.

But his mind was finally clear. The thing he had been trying to remember flooded back to him.

It was a face. A woman. She sat beside him on a beach. Her red hair gleamed in the moonlight, and her blue eyes sparkled. She sang to him. A song of healing that washed away the pain.

And finally, Gustave recognized her.

Princess Fiora.

She had saved him somehow. Found him at sea and brought him to safety.

Why hadn't he remembered that before?

Another face appeared in the memory. This woman was similar to Fiora, but her hair was less red and her eyes less blue. She sang as well, but instead of healing Gustave, the song imprisoned him, wrapping around his thoughts and filling his mind with confusion.

He had been cursed! Elspeth had used a song to ensnare him and make him forget Fiora!

Gustave tried to sit up, but his body still refused to move.

The events of the past few hours rushed back to him. Elspeth appearing at the gala and luring him away from Lady Mer with her song.

Lady Mer was Princess Fiora. Why hadn't he seen that before?

Had he actually married Elspeth? Gustave groaned as scenes from the evening flickered through his mind. No wonder his grandmother had been furious. Collette had probably been working like mad to find a way to stop him. What else could explain her disheveled state at the ceremony?

But Gustave was king, and he had insisted. And Marquis Corbeau had been prepared for anything.

The mattress rocked beneath him, and Gustave remembered that he was on a boat.

On his honeymoon.

Blast it all. He was on a honeymoon with Elspeth. He searched his memory, trying to remember what exactly had happened once they left Montaigne. His stomach churned as he remembered his lips on hers. His hands on her waist. Had it gone further than that?

He didn't think so, but why couldn't he remember?

There had been wine. A strange bitter taste.

That witch had drugged him!

Gustave fought the drowsiness that held him captive. It didn't feel magical. Not like the golden fog that Elspeth had spun with her song. This was likely caused by whatever she had slipped into his wine.

Something had made the fog disappear. Why had it suddenly released him?

According to Elaine's research, it was likely true love's kiss or exposure to the same kind of magic that had created it.

Elspeth had cursed him with a song. Gustave didn't remember hearing anyone else sing when the golden mist faded.

Had someone kissed him then? Was that what the soft touch on his forehead had been?

Gustave opened his eyes and found himself alone in the moonlit cabin. Whoever had kissed him was gone.

As was his bride.

Gustave pushed himself up and stood. He swayed and waited for the dizziness to pass.

He needed to get out of here. He needed to escape and find Lady Mer and apologize.

"Lady Mer is Princess Fiora."

On one hand, that seemed unbelievable. It would take some getting used to.

On the other, it seemed obvious. Why hadn't he realized it before? Fiora's bright blue eyes had stayed with him since that day on the docks in Aeonia. Why hadn't he realized they were the same as Lady Mer's?

Because of the curse, although that felt like a thin excuse. He should have been stronger. Should have realized what was happening and fought it. Should have resisted Elspeth somehow.

He hoped Fiora would forgive him. He hoped he could explain.

He had been so convinced that she was under a spell, but he had been the one cursed all along.

But Princess Fiora wasn't mute, and she had sung for him that day on the beach.

Why had she remained silent as Lady Mer?

Gustave stumbled as a wave of dizziness swept over him. He crashed into the table, knocking over the poisoned wine as he scrambled to catch his balance and stay upright. The ruby liquid ran over the wood, soaking a stack of papers held in place by a large conch shell.

He rubbed his head, trying to push away the last of the dizziness, and stumbled out of the cabin. He tripped on something outside the door and cried out in alarm when he saw what it was.

Princess Fiora lay sprawled unconscious on the ship's deck.

❧ 67 ❧

Fiora groaned as someone lifted her into the air. Her whole body ached as she moved, then settled onto something soft. A bed?

She opened her eyes. Pain blurred her vision, and she breathed deeply until her head cleared enough for her to see the person sitting next to her.

It was Gustave.

He studied her with concern and gently took her hand.

"Lady Mer- I mean, Princess Fiora, I am so sorry. I know there is no excuse for this. I-"

He looked away from her, studying the room with an anguished expression.

"Gustave?"

Fiora gasped and clamped her hands over her mouth. Had she just spoken out loud? That was impossible. Unless...

She looked down at her ring. The mysterious streak of gold on the pearl had disappeared. The gem glowed softly in the candlelight. Brighter than it ever had when her father's love had powered the charm. The color looked different. A little warmer somehow. It had a coppery hue that was a similar color to her hair.

"I love you, Fiora."

Gustave said the words in a rush as he grabbed her hands again.

"I know. I-"

Fiora meant to say more, but a spasm of pain took her breath away. Gustave's eyes grew wide with concern as she gasped for air.

"Fiora, what's wrong?"

"Why didn't it work?"

Fiora's voice carried a hint of magic that made the spilled wine tremble on the table. Why was she still in pain? Gustave loved her. His love had restored the pearl, which had restored her voice

But she had yet to break the mermaid's enchantment.

"Why didn't what work? What do you need?"

The shell. She needed the conch shell carved with the transformation song.

Fiora glanced around the room as if mere wishing could bring it back.

She blinked and stared at the table across the room.

A large conch shell sat in a pile of dark red liquid. Fiora sat up to reach for it, but her body trembled and she fell back to the bed in a wave of pain.

"The shell," she whimpered.

Gustave looked from her to the shell, taking a moment to realize what she wanted. Then he stood to retrieve it for her.

"Oh, I don't think that's a good idea."

Gustave and Fiora looked around the room, searching for the source of Elspeth's voice. Then they saw her.

She was in the mirror. Not reflected in it. Actually in it. Something large and gray floated behind her. With a start, Fiora realized it wasn't floating. It was being carried by massive hands that blended into the darkness.

Elspeth walked closer and slowly came into focus, as did the objects behind her. The gray thing was the statue of King Francois. The hands belonged to a hulking shape made of stone and shadow. It had stocky legs and massive arms that held the statue as if it weighed nothing at all. A horned head peeked from behind the stone as it walked.

"What is that smell?" Fiora asked.

She was in agony, and the smell wasn't helping. Gustave wrinkled his nose in disgust.

"It will fade," Elspeth said.

Then she stepped out of the mirror. Huge, clawed hands reached out after her and set the statue of King Francois into the cabin. Then the hulking shape pulled back and disappeared. A fresh sea breeze blew the stench away, but Fiora still tasted it in her mouth.

"Gustave, what are you doing in bed with another woman on our wedding night?"

Elspeth smiled and sang softly, her voice laced with magic. Fiora tensed and looked at Gustave. The spell was meant for him. Had Elspeth enchanted him somehow? Was that why he had abandoned her in the ballroom?

Gustave took Fiora's hand and glared at Elspeth. Whatever hold the song had once had over him, it seemed powerless now. Elspeth scowled.

"Abandoning your bride so soon? What a shame."

"What are you doing with my father?"

"I suppose I should have kept a closer eye on you, Fiora, but I honestly didn't expect you to escape and kiss him. I was hoping you'd stab him like your aunt suggested. It would have made everything so much simpler."

"You kissed me?"

Fiora laughed, amused that Gustave was more interested in the kissing than the stabbing. The laugh turned into a cough that sent spasms through her body. There wasn't much time left before sunrise.

"The shell. Please."

Her voice was little more than a whisper, but Gustave heard. He always heard. He reached for the shell, but Elspeth grabbed it and shook her head.

"I suppose I shouldn't have left that lying around. Now then-"

Gustave lunged towards her and ripped the shell from her hands. Elspeth flung herself at him and clawed up his arm. Gustave sidestepped and pushed her away. Elspeth crashed to the floor in a tangle of bright hair and white silk.

Gustave handed the shell to Fiora then bowed to Elspeth.

"Apologies, my lady."

"You! How dare you?"

While Elspeth struggled to untangle herself from her voluminous skirt, Fiora quickly read through the notes on the conch shell to make sure she knew how to sing the enchantment.

"You really should have stayed asleep, Your Majesty."

Elspeth crawled across the floor and placed her palm against the mirror.

"Leander, are you there?"

"Of course, princess. What do you need?"

Fiora didn't wait to see what Leander and Elspeth had planned. She removed her ring so it wouldn't interfere with the song and tied it into a strand of her hair. Then she took a deep breath and began to sing. The magic of her voice filled the room as she followed the notes on the shell. Gustave watched in alarm as her singing turned into more of a desperate scream.

The pain in Fiora's chest eased as magic coursed through her veins. Relief spread through her skin, then traveled deeper into her body. Her legs knit together, and her feet flattened into fins. Her formal gown covered most of her fin, but not the gills that appeared on her neck or the scales that appeared on her arms.

"Fiora?"

Gustave stared at her with wide eyes.

"I'm so sorry," Fiora said. "I didn't know how to tell you."

She sat up and flipped her tail over the edge of the bed. The sea beckoned to her through the window, sparkling with moonlight and the stars overhead. Her shimmering fin peeked out from under the gown. Gustave noticed it and swallowed. He seemed speechless.

Fiora's heart sank. She would have preferred to explain everything to him first, but there hadn't been time.

And now she had to leave him.

But how exactly was she going to get into the water?

Before Fiora could decide the answer to that question, Elspeth began to sing. Leander's voice rang through the mirror, joining her in a slow duet. Their voices blended together in perfect harmony, weaving human and mermaid song into a single spell.

But what spell were they weaving?

Fiora looked to Gustave to see if he knew.

But he wasn't looking at her or Elspeth. He was staring at his feet.

Fiora followed his gaze and gasped.

Gustave's feet had turned to stone. The spell climbed up his ankles, draining the color from his clothes as they transformed. Gustave tried to run. His knees jerked from side to side and his arms waved, but his feet stayed frozen in place.

"Gustave!"

Fiora tried to stand to help him and crashed to the floor. Blast it all, she had forgotten that she was a mermaid again. She flopped awkwardly, pulling herself towards him.

The ship lurched, and she rolled against Gustave's legs.

They were solid stone. The enchantment spread to his knees, locking them in place, and continued to crawl up his thighs.

"I'll stop her," Fiora said.

She pushed with her tail, trying to crawl towards Elspeth. Her scales slid against her smooth silk skirt, and she stayed exactly where she was. Fiora gave up on that and grabbed the bedpost so she could pull herself instead.

Strong hands wrapped around her waist and lifted her into the air. Fiora found herself in Gustave's arms, hugged against his chest. He smiled sadly at her, and his gray eyes shone with love.

"Good idea," Fiora said. "Throw me at her so I can shut her up."

She placed her hands on Gustave's chest, ready to push off for extra momentum so she could launch herself at Elspeth and wipe that smug smile off her sister's face.

Gustave shook his head.

"Run, Fiora."

Before she could protest, King Gustave twisted as far as he could and threw Fiora out the window.

❧ 68 ❧

Fiora flew through the window in a cascade of shattered glass and fluttering silk. Gustave swallowed as she hit the ocean and sank out of view. He hoped crashing through the window didn't hurt her, but it had been the only way to get her away from Elspeth.

"Brave, Your Majesty, but we'll find her."

"Leave her alone."

Gustave tried to stay calm and not to look down. Tried not to track the progress of the curse by the numbness spreading up his body. It had reached his waist now. Soon his lungs would turn to stone, and he wouldn't be able to breathe.

He looked at his father. According to the enchanted ruby, King Francois was still alive even though he had been turned to stone.

Hopefully Elspeth was using the same enchantment on him. This wasn't the end. He wasn't dying.

Gustave closed his eyes and took one last breath before the numbness crept over his lungs.

He hoped he wasn't dying.

He hoped Fiora swam away as fast as she could and didn't look back.

Elspeth winked at him as the numbness reached his neck. She couldn't say anything to gloat while she was singing, but she didn't need to. She had won.

His mouth had turned to stone, so Gustave couldn't say anything in return. He turned towards the shattered window, not wanting Elspeth's smug face to be the last thing he saw before the curse took him completely.

Moonlight sparkled like diamonds on the ocean waves. Gustave studied the water, desperately trying to think of anything but the cold sensation crawling up his nose.

He loved Princess Fiora of Kell.

She was a mermaid.

Gustave didn't know how that was possible, but he hoped she could swim fast enough to escape before Elspeth came after her.

Something flickered under the surface of the water. Fiora? Another mermaid? A kraken?

Gustave's vision went dark.

❦ 69 ❦

F iora barely had time to cover her face before she hit the window. The impact knocked her breath away and left tiny cuts all over her skin.

She flew through the air and crashed into the water. The force of her landing sent her sprawling out of control beneath the waves. Her dress tangled around her tail and made swimming impossible. Shards of glass sank into the water around her, sparkling like a shower of shooting stars.

"Fiora!"

Zoe sang her name and created a current that slowed Fiora's descent and helped her regain her equilibrium. Fiora's dark hair wrapped around her, and she brushed it away in a desperate attempt to untangle herself.

"We have to save him!"

She kicked her tail, trying to return to the surface.

To Gustave.

"Absolutely not," Althea said. "You have already sacrificed enough for that human."

Her aunt's short hair made her look more severe than ever. Fiora pulled water through her gills, trying to calm herself. She pushed down the enormous skirt billowing around her, but it floated back up and obscured her view.

So this was why mermaids didn't wear clothes.

"Elspeth and Leander turned Gustave into a statue. We have to save him!"

"What's this about Leander?" Kathelin asked.

She flipped her short hair out of her face. It floated away from her head, framing her face in a sort of halo.

"He's helping Elspeth. I'm not leaving Gustave."

Fiora kicked her tail and darted towards the surface. The skirt streamed behind her. Althea sang and created a current to drag her back. Fiora countered it with her own song. Her magic wasn't as strong as her aunt's. Not even close. But between the singing and swimming as fast as she could, she managed to keep Althea from pulling her deeper.

Then another song filled the water, and something large and round glowed beneath them. Deep laughter rippled through the waves as a kraken tentacle wrapped around Althea.

The mermaid's song ended abruptly as the kraken squeezed her and cut off her air. The current holding Fiora disappeared, and she shot towards the surface. She broke through with a splash and wiped away the hair that plastered her face.

A song rang out from Elspeth's shattered window. Fiora swam closer. Gustave looked down at her, and for a moment she thought that he had escaped the curse.

Then he glinted in the moonlight, and Fiora's heart sank. Gustave was made of stone. He had been looking out to sea when he was transformed.

Looking for her?

A scream rippled through the water, and Fiora swallowed. The mermaids were in trouble.

"I'm so sorry."

She didn't know if Gustave could hear her. She hoped he couldn't see her abandoning him as she dove beneath the waves.

Kraken tentacles had wrapped around Althea, Kathelin, and Zoe. The mermaids wriggled and sang, but the enormous creature ignored them. Fiora swam deeper, dodging wayward tentacles as she moved.

Leander floated near the kraken's head, silhouetted against its enormous glowing eye. He held a small mirror that reflected the light. As he sang, another voice accompanied him in a duet.

Fiora listened for a moment and recognized the voice as Elspeth's.

Why was her sister working with Leander?

"Well, the little mermaid returns," Leander said.

He stopped singing, but Elspeth's song continued to echo through the mirror. The kraken tightened its grip on the three mermaids.

"What are you doing, Leander?"

He shrugged.

"All part of the plan. I-"

"For the love of everything, don't explain the plan!" a new voice said through the mirror.

It was a woman's voice, shrill with frustration. She sounded like the same woman who had spoken to Leander in the gardens, but it was difficult to say for sure. Perhaps she had been speaking to him through one of the mirrors in the mirror garden.

"Who are you?" Fiora asked.

"A friend."

The woman sounded like she was trying very hard to keep herself calm. The kraken shifted, and Leander resumed his song to hold it in place.

"I can help you, Fiora," the woman in the mirror continued.

"How do you know who I am?"

"I can help you find a place to belong. Help you understand your magic."

"Like you helped Elspeth and Leander?"

"Yes, exactly. Go back to the ship, and Elspeth can explain everything."

"Let my family go and then we'll talk."

"Oh no, dear. They've interfered too much. Besides, they're not special. Not like you are."

"Why am I special?"

The voice didn't answer.

Zoe whimpered in pain, and Fiora turned to look at the mermaids. The kraken tentacles had wrapped around them, constricting like large snakes and squeezing their life away. Kathelin looked concerned, and Althea looked angry. Zoe's face was twisted in agony and panic as she tried to shake herself loose. She met Fiora's gaze, a silent plea for help in her eyes.

Fiora gritted her teeth. She had to do something!

But what?

Zoe shrieked as the tentacle tightened again. The kraken seemed to have picked her as the easiest prey.

Leander and Elspeth's song swelled through the water. How often had they practiced together? Their magic intertwined until it seemed that they sang with one voice.

One voice. Both mermaid and human.

Fiora's eyes widened. What had Elaine said about breaking curses?

Sometimes, you had to break them with the same kind of magic that caused them.

Althea and Kathelin let out a desperate burst of song, trying to free Zoe. It was filled with powerful magic, but the kraken ignored them. The mermaids slumped in defeat, as if they had put their last bit of strength into the music.

Their mermaid magic couldn't stop the kraken, because Leander was singing with Elspeth. A human.

Fiora's eyes widened as everything came into focus. Even the power of the Kraken Heart and an entire mermaid choir hadn't been enough to stop the kraken when it awoke and attacked Gustave's ship before.

But she had. Her voice had halted the attack.

Was this why Elspeth and the others had been so determined to silence her? Why they had stolen the shell and tried to kill her?

"What's happening down there, Leander?" the voice in the mirror said. "Is she going to join us?"

"I doubt it. She doesn't look very cooperative."

"Then take care of her," the voice said with a sigh. "Take her alive if you can."

Leander grinned. The gleam in his eyes said he wasn't going to try too hard to follow that order.

He altered his song, Elspeth followed his lead. A kraken tentacle shot towards Fiora.

She countered with a melody of her own. The tentacle swerved and just missed her. It created a current in the water that caught her skirt like a sail and pushed her back.

Fiora regained her balance and began to sing.

Her voice rang through the water. Her strange, unique voice. Neither mermaid nor human.

For the first time in her life, Fiora let herself be both. She didn't worry what she sounded like or if it was right. She simply let her full voice ring through the water exactly as it was.

The kraken loosened its grip on the mermaids.

Althea pushed free first. She shrieked with rage and launched herself at Leander. His song ended in a muffled grunt as she crashed into him. The mirror dropped from his hand and drifted to the ocean floor.

Elspeth's voice faded as the mirror sank. Kathelin shook free and turned her attention to helping Zoe. The young mermaid's face was pale, and she floated limply in her mother's arms.

Kathelin gave Fiora an anguished look, then carried Zoe away, singing a song of healing as she sped through the water.

That left Fiora alone with the kraken.

The creature studied her with its enormous glowing eyes. Fiora glared back at it. Her hair and dress floated around her, making her look bigger than she actually was, but she was still tiny compared to the monster.

The kraken blinked, as if waking from a deep sleep, then leaned its enormous head forward. Fiora tensed, readying for an attack, but the kraken simply straightened back up and continued to stare at her.

Fiora blinked. Had the creature just bowed?

It seemed to be waiting for something. For her?

Fiora pulled water through her gills and began to sing. Not sure what else to do, she sang the song of healing. Her voice lilted through the water, and the kraken began to sway.

Was it dancing?

Fiora grinned and swam closer. The kraken swirled its tentacles around her in graceful, flowing motions. Fiora spun in the currents it created and poured more magic into her song. The dance continued, and the kraken spun her ever closer, guiding her with waving tentacles until she floated just in front of its enormous eye.

She stared into it, mesmerized by the warm glow. The kraken stared back, unblinking, and lowered its tentacles softly into the sand.

Then a deep rumble shook the ground, and the kraken's eye narrowed. It shot out a tentacle and knocked Fiora away. Before she could recover from the impact, Leander's scream rang through the water. He darted towards the surface with Althea close behind him.

The scream grew into a high-pitched song, and Althea flew away as a burst of magic hit her. Leander sang a different tune, and the underwater world began to spin.

The whirlpool caught Althea and pulled her further away from the merman. Fiora's dress rippled in the current and wrapped around her as she tried to hold her position.

The kraken was too large to be pushed around so easily, but it was still agitated from the earthquake. Leander's whirlpool pulled debris from the bottom of the ocean and flung it into the kraken's eye. The creature shrieked in protest and waved its tentacles, trying to push the objects away.

Leander dodged and swam towards a bright spot on the ocean floor.

The mirror.

Althea dove after him, dodging tentacles and shards of glass as she sped towards the merman.

Fiora gathered her skirts and prepared to follow. Then the kraken reached a tentacle up towards the surface, and the loud crack of splintering wood rippled through the water.

The angry kraken had finally found something to lash out at.

Elspeth's ship.

"Teuthida somnum statim!"

Fiora sang as loud as she could, trying to calm the kraken and put it to sleep.

The kraken blinked at her for a moment, then resumed its attack.

Fiora pushed the human qualities out of her voice and sang as a mermaid. Then she sang as a human. Then she mixed everything together.

She sang every song she knew, desperate to stop the rampage.

It did no good. Her unique magic was able to break the curse cast by Leander and Elspeth, but this attack was not the result of an enchantment. This was an angry creature lashing out at the first available target.

And she wasn't strong enough to calm it.

The kraken slammed another tentacle into the ship. Broken wood flew out from the impact and floated on the waves, littering the ocean surface.

Fiora dodged the tentacles and swam up until she broke through the waves. The kraken had knocked a massive hole in the side of the ship, and water lapped hungrily at the gap. The vessel wouldn't hold together much longer.

Fiora switched tactics and sang a song of movement, trying to create a current to pull the ship to safety. But Leander's raging whirlpool held it in place.

Someone screamed.

Elspeth.

Deep laughter shook the water around Fiora. The kraken raised a single tentacle high into the air and brought it crashing down. The ship splintered down the middle. Both halves leaned against each other so the decks sloped steeply towards the center.

The kraken swiped another tentacle against the mast, snapping the wood and toppling it into the water.

Fiora gritted her teeth. If the kraken kept this up, it would turn the ship to kindling. She needed to save Gustave and his father before a stray tentacle smashed them into gravel.

And in spite of all her half-sister had done, she should probably save Elspeth as well.

Blast it all. She had been in Montaigne too long. Their tendency to help everyone had rubbed off on her.

F iora dodged bits of wood as she worked her way towards the ship. A board snagged on her skirt, and she pulled it off, ripping the fabric in the process. The kraken smashed the ship again and sent debris flying towards her. Fiora dove below the surface and stayed underwater until she reached the ship.

What was left of the vessel tilted dangerously in the water. The sides sloped, steep and jagged and impossible to climb.

Fiora turned to the broken mast. It leaned into the water, creating a sort of ramp. She could climb it.

But not as a mermaid.

She untied the pearl ring from her hair and held it flat in her palm. The gem still shone with that strange mix of pearl and copper magic. Hopefully that meant Gustave was still alive somewhere underneath the stone.

Fiora flicked her tail as she studied the ring. She shouldn't use it. She knew that. Loving a human man had killed her mother, and it might prove just as fatal for her if she attempted this rescue.

If the forbidden magic didn't kill her, the enraged kraken would.

Blast it all.

Fiora slid the ring onto her finger and grabbed the mast. The pearl's magic ran over her skin, splitting her tail and closing her gills.

While the transformation song had been agony, this magic simply felt warm, like sunlight on her skin.

Fiora gripped the mast tighter and kicked her legs as the transformation finished. Her voluminous gown dragged her towards the ocean. The elegant petticoats were now heavy and a very real hazard.

She dug her fingernails into the wood and pulled herself onto the mast. Her feet connected, and she wrapped her legs around it to stabilize her position.

Fiora clung to the mast and stared at the ship above her. She tried to pull herself up but gained only a few inches.

She would never reach Gustave in time at this rate. The wood was slick and full of splinters. The waterlogged evening gown weighed her down. Fiora tried to walk up the steep slope, but the skirt clung to her legs, wrapping them together until she might as well have been a mermaid.

With a silent apology to Dowager Queen Bernadine for ruining the gown, Fiora plucked at the intricate embroidery on the skirt's seam until she pulled a thread loose. She unraveled the stitching, apologizing to the original seamstress as well. The skirt was stitched together beautifully.

Which just made it that much harder to take apart. This was taking too long.

Fiora changed tactics and found a nail sticking out of the wood. She stabbed the top three layers of fabric through the nail and let go of the mast, using her body weight to tear the skirt away as she fell. Then she climbed back up and repeated the process. Fiora shrugged out of the loose layers, peeled the wet fabric off her legs, and threw the skirt into the ocean.

She still wore a few petticoats, but removing the outer layers had reduced her weight considerably. Fiora pressed her feet into the wood, gripped the sides of the mast, and began to climb.

She had never been particularly athletic, but she felt strong and light now that the curse was lifted and she wasn't in pain. The whole ship swayed and creaked as waves pushed against it. Fiora used the rhythm of the ocean to her advantage, pulling herself up in time with the sea. The kraken pummeled the ship again, and she wrapped her arms as far around the mast as she could to keep from falling into the water.

When the ship stopped shaking, she tucked her feet in and climbed again, ignoring the splinters that pierced her skin. When the next wave lifted the mast, Fiora jumped.

She hit the deck less gracefully than she would have liked. Most of her weight landed on her right ankle, which collapsed under her as she toppled to the floor. She stood, and it buckled underneath her.

Perfect. It seemed she was destined to have trouble walking wherever she went.

Fiora hopped across the deck, gritting her teeth as the motion jarred her injured ankle. The ship looked like it would sink at any moment, but a song still echoed from Elspeth's cabin. A song Fiora meant to end as quickly as possible.

Elspeth looked surprised when Fiora burst into the cabin, but only for a moment. Then she winked and resumed her singing. Fiora hopped towards her, but another kraken blow rocked the ship and tilted the floor even further. Fiora stumbled backward and crashed into the statue of Gustave as her ankle gave way. She wrapped her arms around his waist to hold herself upright. The stone was solid and unyielding beneath her grip.

Elspeth grinned.

"You just can't stay away from my husband, can you?"

"Shut your mouth."

Fiora had thought recovering her voice would make her feel better, but words seemed completely inadequate at the moment.

She just wanted to punch Elspeth in the face and be done with it.

Elspeth's grin said she knew it. And that she also knew Fiora was injured and would fall over if she let go of Gustave.

"I don't know what you're so happy about. Your ship is sinking."

Elspeth shrugged.

"It happens. I can still save you if you want. My friend is rather interested in you for some reason."

"And to think I climbed up here to save you from the sinking ship and attacking kraken. Obviously I need your help instead."

"Please. We both know you're here for him."

The ship shook as deep laughter rumbled through it. Loose boards rattled. It wouldn't hold together much longer.

"Last chance," Elspeth said. "Come with me?"

She held out her hand. Fiora glared at her.

"I don't want anything to do with you."

"Are you ready, song wench?" a deep voice said.

It came from nowhere and everywhere all at once. Fiora clung to Gustave as the floor beneath them rumbled and bits of ceiling fell around her.

"Yes, Nog, I'm ready."

The hulking shadow appeared in the mirror, and a disgusting smell filled the room. Fiora could see the shape better now that it wasn't hidden behind the statue. Whatever the creature was, it was enormous and powerfully built. Its horned head looked at Elspeth with an impatient expression.

"Last chance, Fiora."

"Elspeth, what's going on?"

Another kraken blow rocked the ship. King Francois toppled onto the bed, and Gustave slide across the deck as the floor tilted. Fiora tightened her grip on him, but it was a losing battle. Inch by inch, Gustave slid closer to the shattered window. He was too heavy for her to hold.

"Hurry up, human."

Nog's voice rattled the ship, and Fiora felt it vibrating through the stone as she tried to hold Gustave in place.

A clawed hand reached through the mirror and rested on Elspeth's shoulder. Fiora gagged as the stench grew stronger.

"Get your hands off me. I'm coming."

Elspeth winked at Fiora and stepped into the mirror. It rippled like water as she passed through it, then hardened back into a smooth surface.

The stench disappeared as Elspeth and Nog walked into the distance and out of view. The mirror shimmered a little, then stilled until it once again reflected the room.

Before Fiora could do anything more than blink in surprise, a kraken tentacle crashed through the cabin walls. It swept away the ceiling and knocked the mirror into King Francois. The mirror cracked in half from the impact and toppled into the ocean.

Then another tentacle took out the bottom of the ship, and the floor fell out from under them. The statues landed in the ocean with an enormous splash and disappeared beneath the surface.

Fiora toppled after them. She landed in the ocean and gagged as she swallowed salt water. She gasped in surprise and swallowed even more. Her lungs screamed for air, but what was left of the skirt tangled around her legs and kept her from swimming back to the surface. Panic filled her chest.

Fiora pulled the ring off her finger. A gentle warmth swept over her skin, and Fiora was a mermaid again. She sputtered and took a few deep breaths through her gills. Then she tied the ring into her hair and searched the water for the statues.

They had disappeared into the depths, the stone sinking far faster than she did. The first rays of the rising sun tinted everything red. Fiora swam down, blinking as her eyes adjusted to the dim light of the underwater world.

There.

Leander's whirlpool still raged, and it was pulling the statues towards the kraken. The creature waved its tentacles, searching for a new target to lash out at since it had destroyed the ship.

Its enormous eye saw the falling statues and narrowed in anger. It pulled its tentacles back, preparing to attack.

Fiora let out a burst of song and dove towards Gustave.

❧ 71 ❧

There was a voice.

Her voice.

A kraken had attacked, and Gustave was sinking in the ocean again. This all felt strangely familiar.

But this time he couldn't move, and she was the one in danger.

Blast it all. How could he save her if he couldn't move?

Gustave struggled against the numbness that held him prisoner, but her voice faded into silence before he could break free.

72

The kraken swiped at Fiora as she swam. She dodged, but the fabric of her dress dragged in the water and slowed her down. The tentacle connected with her tail and sent her tumbling through the ocean. Fiora reached behind her as she floated, pulling at the buttons on the back of the gown.

She needed her full speed to save Gustave, and this gown was getting in the way.

"I've always found human clothing to be overly complicated."

Fiora whirled around and found Madame Isla floating behind her. The mermaid smiled.

"Fortunately, I've made a study of it. My research on buttons alone has-"

The kraken swiped at them again, forcing both mermaids to retreat.

"Just get me out of this," Fiora said.

She pulled her hair up so the mermaid could access the back of the dress. True to her word, Madame Isla was quite capable at unfastening buttons. Fiora wondered if she had practiced on sunken gowns as part of her research.

As soon as the bodice loosened, Fiora wriggled out of the gown and dove towards the kraken. Madame Isla dove after her.

"Fiora, what are you doing?"

"I have to save them!"

Fiora swam towards the statues, which had landed beside the kraken. They were out of the creature's sight, but still in danger of being smashed by tentacles.

"Fiora, those are statues!"

Before Fiora could explain, the kraken roared and lunged at them. Madame Isla let out a single high note that pierced the water. It seemed to surprise the kraken more than anything.

"Sing with me," Madame Isla signed.

Fiora pulled water through her gills and matched Madame Isla's pitch. It was aggressive. An attack rather than a lullaby.

And it worked. The kraken pulled its tentacles back, giving Fiora space to dive towards Gustave.

The water pulsed with blue light, and a soothing song filled the air. Fiora shared a glance with Madame Isla and quickly changed her song to join the choir.

"Teuthida somnum statim."

The kraken's eyes began to close. It slumped to the ground and lowered its tentacles. The light grew brighter, silhouetting a group of merfolk swimming over the horizon.

Help had arrived.

Then the ground shook with deep laughter, and the kraken blinked. Fiora searched the ocean floor for the source of the sound and saw a pale reflection of the blue light glistening in the sand. A shadow hovered over it.

Leander and the mirror.

It was cracked, but that only made the glass look more sinister as it reflected the light of the Kraken Heart.

"Did your research include magic mirrors, Madame Isla?"

"Mirrors can contain magic?"

Apparently not.

"We need to destroy that one."

Fiora swam towards Leander with more anger than a plan. The merman grinned when he saw her.

"*I already defeated your sisters. What can you possibly do, little mermaid?*"

Fiora had no idea, but she didn't slow down. Leander and Elspeth had endangered everyone she loved, and she wouldn't let them get away with it. Elspeth may have escaped, but Leander was still within reach.

Leander's smug smile slipped as the blue light grew brighter. Fiora didn't look back. She didn't need to. She saw the approaching mermaids reflected in the mirror.

Althea and Kathelin swam at the front of the choir. Zoe carried the Kraken Heart and looked fully prepared to use it.

"*Teuthida somnum statim.*"

The Kraken Heart pulsed in time with the music, and the kraken's eye closed again. The merfolk sang a final chord and sustained it until the kraken fell asleep and crashed into the ocean floor. The ground shook, and the statues of Gustave and Francois slid across the sand towards Fiora.

Leander scowled and stopped singing.

"I guess that's my cue to leave."

"You're giving up so easily, fish boy?"

The deep voice echoed from the mirror and shook the ground.

"Do you want to come out here and fight an entire civilization?"

"At least finish her off first."

Leander turned back to Fiora. He screamed, and his eyes glowed yellow. Half of the broken mirror lifted off the sand and flew towards her.

Fiora countered with her own song, deflecting the mirror so it sliced open her tail instead of her neck. She screamed in pain. The mirror shuddered and turned black as her blood spilled over it.

Without waiting to see the result of his attack, Leander swam into the other half of the broken mirror. The surface rippled as he slipped through it.

Once he disappeared, the deep rumbling continued. The kraken shuddered and opened its eye again.

Fiora pressed her hand against her tail to slow the bleeding and glared at the remaining piece of the mirror. Whatever was in there, she needed to keep it from getting out.

She picked up the glass and slammed it against the ground. It sank into the sand, and the deep voice continued to reverberate through the ocean.

Fiora looked around. She needed something solid. A piece of coral. A rock.

Or a statue.

Gustave stood nearby, his head still turned to look out the window for her.

The mirror shook as the deep voice laughed. The hulking silhouette appeared, reflected in the distance but getting closer.

Fiora swung the mirror at Gustave, singing to add force to her blow.

It smashed against his head and shattered in slow motion. Shards of glass floated around him, glowing like stars in the Kraken Heart's blue light.

Gustave looked uninjured, thank goodness. The deep, rumbling laughter disappeared. Peace descended on the ocean as the mermaid's lullaby filled the waves. The Kraken Heart settled into a gentle heartbeat pulse as the kraken slept.

Fiora shuddered. That had been close.

"Fiora, are you well?"

Kathelin swam over, her eyes wide with concern. She looked from the shards of mirror to the statue to Fiora's bleeding tail.

"Please, will you help me carry that statue to the surface?"

Fiora signed to keep from interrupting the mermaid choir's song. Kathelin shook her head.

"Can you swim? I'll heal you, but we need to put some distance between us and the choir first."

"Fine, but bring the statue."

Fiora nodded to King Francois. Kathelin's eyebrows knit together, but she didn't protest. She wrapped her arms around the statue and kicked her tail.

Fiora did the same with Gustave. He was heavy. Solid stone, and bigger than her. Pain shot through her tail as she swam, and she left a trail of blood in the ocean.

Fiora pulled of water through her gills and forced herself to keep swimming through the pain. Whatever else happened, she had to save Gustave.

And since Leander and Elspeth had worked together to curse him, her magic was the only way to set him free.

That or a kiss.

They reached the surface, and Kathelin listened for a moment to make sure they were too far away to hear the choir. Then she sang the song of healing, knitting the gash in Fiora's tail back together.

Fiora kissed Gustave's stone cheek, just in case that was the way to break the curse.

Nothing happened.

So she sang.

She tried to remember Elspeth's song. The words had been foreign, but the tune was easy enough. Fiora started with that. When she came to a place in the melody she couldn't remember, she made something up. She let her voice resonate softly, both human and mermaid. Both parts of her working together.

That combination of magic had turned Gustave to stone. It should be able to break the enchantment as well.

When nothing happened, Fiora kept singing. This had to work. She didn't know what else to do. If she was mistaken-

Then Gustave shuddered, and his stone chest heaved with a silent gasp. He grew soft in Fiora's arms, turning from cold stone to warm flesh.

Kathelin let out an alarmed shriek as King Francois did the same.

"Fiora, these statues are turning into people!"

Fiora smiled and kept singing. Gustave blinked and turned his head from side to side, staring into the distance in confusion.

Finally his gaze settled on Fiora. She kept singing. The curse was broken, but she didn't know what to say. She was a mermaid. And herself, not Lady Mer.

There was so much to explain, and she didn't know where to start. So she sang instead.

Gustave wrapped his arms around her and held her tight.

※ 73 ※

His hearing came back first. That voice. It was always that voice.

Then air rushed into his lungs, and Gustave realized he was cold.

And wet.

What on earth had happened?

The voice kept singing. Gustave opened his eyes and stared at the horizon. Why was the ground moving around him?

Someone shrieked.

"Fiora, these statues are turning into people!"

Gustave looked from side to side, searching for whoever had screamed.

As he looked, he realized the moving ground was water. It stretched as far as he could see in every direction.

He was in the middle of the ocean.

His leg brushed against something solid, and he realized someone was holding him.

He probably should have noticed that first.

Gustave stared at her. She was so close that her face was out of focus, but he would know her anywhere. This beautiful woman with brilliant blue eyes.

And gills.

Those were new, but Gustave didn't have time to process that. More memories flooded back. The gala. Dancing barefoot together.

Leaving her for Elspeth.

Gustave's heart sank. He didn't deserve Fiora. Not after what he had done.

She kept singing. There was something unique about her voice. Gustave couldn't place what was different about it, but it sounded like it belonged here amidst the sounds of the sea.

She stared into his eyes, relief and uncertainty filling her gaze.

Gustave wrapped his arms around her and held her tight. She stopped singing, surprised by the sudden movement.

The gentle rhythm of waves and wind filled the silence.

"Fiora, I am so sorry."

His voice broke. There was more to say, but he couldn't find the words.

She shrugged out of his grasp and held him at arm's length so she could glare at him.

"Don't you dare apologize for being cursed."

Then she pulled him close and pressed her forehead against his. Gustave relaxed a little, and Fiora tilted her head and softly kissed his cheek. Gustave hesitated only a moment before leaning in and meeting her lips. Fiora tightened her grip and kissed him fiercely.

"You see, Zoe? That's the proper way to seduce a human man."

Fiora tensed and broke the kiss. She was glaring at him again. No, at something behind him. Gustave wrapped his arm around her shoulder and turned so he could see.

A group of mermaids floated nearby. An older one with long white hair pointed at Gustave as if he were a specimen on display. A younger one with short hair watched with an enthusiastic grin.

A.G. MARSHALL

Behind them, Althea rolled her eyes. She had cut off her long hair since he last saw her. It only made her look more intimidating. Gustave leaned a little closer to Fiora.

Kathelin floated beside Althea. She held something in her arms. Someone.

"Father?"

Gustave turned further in Fiora's arms, trying to get a better look. The man lifted his head.

"Gustave?"

"Stay still, Your Majesty," Kathelin said. "You're still very weak."

The mermaid cradled the king to her chest like a child. He looked from her to his son.

"Gustave, where are we? Who are these people?"

"Mermaids. We're in the ocean."

His father's eyes widened in alarm, and Gustave wished he had made up a comforting lie instead. King Francois did not look well.

Kathelin began to sing. Gustave recognized the melody as the same one Fiora had sung for him that day at the beach.

King Francois's face relaxed, and he fell asleep. Gustave looked to Fiora.

"It's a song of healing," she said. "He'll awake refreshed."

"We should take them back to land," Althea said.

"No need," Zoe said. "There's a ship!"

Fiora turned to look, and Gustave turned with her. The approaching ship formed a squat silhouette against the sunrise. An ugly rescue, but a rescue nonetheless.

"It's the *Sea Frog*," Gustave said. "But what is Princess Serafina doing out here?"

"Is she a friend?" Althea asked.

"Unless you're smashing her city with a kraken."

Althea ignored sarcasm in his voice. She hummed a tune, and their group floated towards the ship. Or maybe the ship was floating towards them. Gustave found it difficult to say for sure.

444

"Mermaids, ho!" Massimo screamed from the ship's deck.

The young prince of Santelle sounded like he was having a good time. At least someone was enjoying themselves tonight.

Although, Gustave wasn't going to complain too much about being held in Fiora's arms. Had he told her he loved her yet? He had a vague sense that he had, but his memory hadn't exactly been reliable for the past few days.

"I love you," he whispered into her hair, just in case he hadn't.

She stilled, and for a moment Gustave was afraid he had made a terrible mistake. That he had misremembered their relationship and-

"I love you too."

She whispered it softly, her Kellish accent becoming thick with emotion.

Why did she sound so sad?

A strand of dark hair blew against Fiora's face and stuck to her skin. Gustave reached up and gently brushed it away. He left his hand against her cheek, caressing her skin and catching her tears. Why was she crying?

"Fiora, I never meant to hurt you. I was under an enchantment. I know that's no excuse, but-"

"Gustave, I told you not to apologize for that. I-"

"Permission to send humans aboard, Captain?"

The mermaid's shout swallowed whatever Fiora had been about to say.

"Um, granted?"

Serafina's usually commanding voice sounded confused.

Before Gustave could quite process what was happening, a rush of water swept him out of Fiora's arms and pushed him towards the ship. She reached for him. Their fingers brushed against each other for a moment, then a new song rang through the air. Fiora sank into the water with a small gasp.

"Fiora!"

Gustave tried to swim towards her, but he was helpless against

445

the current. The song crescendoed, and he floated up to the ship's deck on a wave of water and magic.

Serafina pulled him over the railing before he could protest. King Francois floated up on a second wave, and Collette shrieked with joy as she helped her father onto the ship.

Princess Serafina looked into the water for a moment, then shrugged.

"Set a course for Montaigne," she ordered the man at the wheel.

The man was hidden in shadows, but he looked more like a pirate than a naval officer. He spun the wheel with one hand and gave a roguish salute with the other.

Serafina rolled her eyes and turned back to Gustave.

"What happened to your ship? To Elspeth?"

"Gone, I think. Kraken."

That was all a bit blurry, obscured by poison and magic. Serafina's expression grew serious.

"And Fiora?"

"She's a mermaid."

Gustave crawled to the railing and looked down at the water.

The mermaids had disappeared and taken Fiora with them. The ocean stretched empty for as far as he could see.

"What do you mean Fiora is a mermaid?" Serafina said. "Are you saying that Princess Fiora of Kell is a mermaid?"

"How is that possible?" Collette said.

Gustave shrugged. He had no idea. He was more concerned with how to get her back.

"Father won't wake up," Collette said.

Gustave tore his gaze from the water, remembering that other people needed him. Collette's eyes were tense with worry.

"The mermaids put him into an enchanted sleep so he could heal. He was weak from being cursed for so long."

Collette's tight shoulders relaxed. She gathered part of her enormous skirt into a pillow and gently placed it under her father's head.

Gustave watched him sleep for a few moments, then turned his attention back to the water as the *Sea Frog* sailed towards Montaigne.

Towards home, although he wasn't sure what that meant any more. He had found his father and lost his love. The ocean stretched around them, vast and empty.

There had to be a way to find her. He had survived multiple kraken attacks and been turned to stone. He would face worse to be with the woman he loved.

As if answering his thought, something splashed near the ship.

"Fiora?"

Gustave leaned over the railing and almost collided with a tentacle emerging from the ocean.

Althea sat on the tentacle and watched Gustave through narrowed eyes. Another splash broke the stillness, and Kathelin bobbed up on a second tentacle. She smiled brightly at Gustave as if she were stopping in for tea.

"Where's Fiora?"

Althea glared so fiercely at the question that Gustave's heart sank. Had something gone wrong?

"You ladies have control of those kraken?" the man at the wheel called.

He even sounded like a pirate. Definitely too roguish to be in Santelle's navy.

"We have perfect control now that Leander is gone. He was sabotaging our enchantments with mixed magic," Kathelin called back.

The man seemed satisfied with that explanation, as did Serafina. She raised an eyebrow at the two mermaids, then shrugged and left Gustave to deal with them. She had a ship to sail.

"Where is Fiora?" Gustave repeated.

"Home, for now," Althea said. "She was injured and needed to heal."

"She's hurt?"

Gustave fought back panic. Why hadn't Fiora told him she was hurt? Was it serious?

"Getting thrown out of a window and cut with an enchanted mirror takes a lot out of you. We put her to sleep with a healing enchantment. She'll be fine by morning."

Gustave relaxed a little. Althea did not.

"Fiora is the reason we're here," she said.

It sounded more like an accusation than anything.

"You love her," Kathelin said.

She held up a ring. Fiora's ring. The pearl glistened in the morning light, flickering with bits of copper as if it were reflecting a fire. That gem was definitely enchanted, but what did it do?

"Yes, I love her."

"See, Althea? He loves her."

Kathelin waved the ring at her sister as if it proved her point. Althea didn't look convinced.

"Truly-" Gustave began.

Althea raised her hand to silence him.

"It isn't your love I question. It's your lineage."

She gestured to where King Francois lay on the deck.

"What's wrong with my lineage?"

"It's royal. You're a king."

The mermaid spit out the words as if saying them physically pained her. Gustave swallowed.

"Yes. Well, I suppose I'm a prince again now that my father has returned. It's all a bit confusing."

Kathelin nodded sympathetically, but Althea's scowl didn't waver.

"Did you know that Fiora was a mermaid when you fell in love with her?"

"I didn't even know she was Fiora. I called her Lady Mer."

"See, Kathelin, it's just like last time."

"Althea, that's unfair."

But a small wrinkle of worry creased Kathelin's brow.

Gustave rubbed his forehead, trying to erase the headache he felt building.

"Begging your pardon, but I don't understand."

"Of course you don't," Althea said. "And I'm not sure you can. But Fiora loves you enough to sacrifice her life for yours, so I'm going to try to explain."

She gestured to the ring as if it explained everything. Gustave studied it, desperate to understand whatever the mermaids were trying to tell him. The longer he stared, the more the copper swirling across the surface of the pearl looked like strands of Fiora's hair.

"We're going to tell you a story," Kathelin said. "The story of Fiora's parents. And then you're going to make a choice."

"Does this have anything to do with the shell you gave me?"

Gustave pulled it out of his pocket, a little surprised that it was still there after everything that had happened. Kathelin's eyes widened.

"Why do you have that? It was for Carina. Well, I suppose it could work in this situation as well."

Althea smirked at Gustave's confusion.

"That shell contains the notes to a magical song that will turn a man into a frog. I believe Kathelin was giving Carina a way to turn Prince Stefan into a frog again if she so desired."

"But we could turn you into a frog instead if you like," Kathelin said. "You could join Fiora under the water then. It would be a little strange, but I'm sure you could make it work."

"What?"

"Focus, Kathelin. Remember why we're here."

"Right. To tell Gustave the story of Nyssa and Fergal."

Gustave blinked. King Fergal of Kell was Fiora's father.

"Who's Nyssa?"

"Fiora's mother. Our sister. She died because a king betrayed her. We're here to make sure you don't do the same."

Gustave swallowed.

"I would never–"

"You wouldn't mean to," Althea said, "But as I said, you don't understand. That's why we're here to explain. To make sure that what happened to Nyssa doesn't happen again."

🍂 74 🍂

F iora woke up feeling better than she had in days.
　　And worse.

As much as she had wished to return to the ocean, it felt strange to be back.

She stared at the shifting blue light dancing against the coral reefs and sighed. A stream of bubbles danced towards the surface, sparkling like diamonds in the morning sun.

Fiora pushed off the bed and floated through the water. Her hair swirled around her, a dark cloud since it was still dyed with squid ink.

"Fiora! You're awake!"

Zoe zipped towards her cousin but stopped just short of tackling her.

"Do you feel better?"

Fiora nodded and frowned at the dark bruises on Zoe's torso. "How do you feel? Why haven't they healed you?"

Zoe shrugged.

"They did, but it will take time for the marks to fade because they were so deep. You've got a new scar as well!"

Fiora glanced down at the thin, silver scar across her tail. Apparently the mirror had cut deeper than she realized.

"Is everything alright? The kraken are under control?"

Zoe nodded.

"And the choirs are searching for Leander."

"He disappeared into a mirror. I doubt they'll find him."

Fiora couldn't begin to understand how that enchantment worked. Perhaps she and Gustave could figure it out together.

Gustave. Was he well? Had he suffered any injuries from being transformed into a statue?

Fiora combed through her hair, searching for the pearl ring. She knew she shouldn't use it. The forbidden magic was dangerous and unpredictable.

But surely one more day wouldn't hurt? She would go to Montaigne and explain everything. Explain why she had to leave him.

Or maybe, if he still wanted her, she would stay. The magic was risky, but so were a lot of things in life.

Fiora's hands combed through her hair and found nothing. She twisted her hair together and pulled it around so she could see the ends.

The ring wasn't there. It must have come loose and fallen out during the fight. Her heart sank.

"Fiora, are you alright?"

Fiora shook her head. Without the pearl, she had no way to be with Gustave. Well, no way that lasted more than three days at a time. Not to mention the enchantment would take her voice and cause her pain.

How much was she willing to sacrifice to return to the shore?

Zoe noticed Fiora's distress and wrapped her in a hug. Fiora returned it. Maybe she could find the ring someday. It was probably buried in sand by now, but she could dig. Maybe she would find more of Dale's forks while she was at it.

"Everyone is meeting in the throne room," Zoe said. "They're

waiting for you to wake up before they decide anything important. Race you there?"

Mischief gleamed in the young mermaid's eyes. Fiora
grinned in spite of everything and flicked her tail to claim a
head start.

It was fun, racing Zoe through the summer city. Moving was
easier underwater. Like flying. Fiora turned a somersault even
though she knew it would give Zoe time to catch up.

Zoe grabbed her hands and spun her around. Fiora's hair
streamed behind her. Zoe's short hair stuck out from her head in
all directions. The sight sobered Fiora's mood.

Much had been sacrificed last night. For her.

"I'm sorry about your hair, Zoe."

The mermaid shook her head, sending her short hair flying
through the water.

"It's fun, although I feel a bit naked."

Fiora laughed, and they continued towards the castle. They
swam up the sides of the building and darted through an opening
in the ceiling.

Trays of food floated throughout the room. Fiora grimaced.
Some things never changed. The disgusting blobs that passed as
food underwater were apparently one of them.

"Fiora! Are you feeling well?"

Kathelin beamed as Fiora swam into the room. Althea looked
angry.

But then, she always looked angry.

Behind them, Queen Gallerus beckoned for Fiora to come
closer. Madame Isla floated beside the queen. The mermaid held a
fishing net full of lumps of cloth that had probably been dresses
once. Fiora hoped Madame Isla wasn't preparing for another
seduction.

There was no point without the ring.

She swam to her grandmother and touched her tail to her
forehead in a bow.

"I understand you helped in the defeat of Leander and the kraken," Queen Gallerus said.

Fiora nodded.

"He was working with a human. Combining magic. My magic is already combined since I'm half-human, so I was able to counter his charms."

Queen Gallerus nodded. Doubtless she already knew all this information, but she still looked pleased.

"If one merman working with humans caused so much chaos, it seems wise for us to seek out human allies who could help us understand their ways and prevent further disasters. The royal family of Montaigne seems trustworthy. Do you agree?"

Fiora nodded, too surprised to speak.

"Tell me about them," Queen Gallerus said.

"They were kind to me. They're kind to everyone. And honorable. And-"

She stopped because her grandmother was looking rather amused.

"Princess Fiora may be biased about the humans of Montaigne, but I believe she is also correct," Madame Isla said.

"And they know sign language," Kathelin said. "A most useful quality for human allies."

Queen Gallerus looked to Althea. The mermaid gave a sharp nod but said nothing.

"You gave him the message?" the queen signed.

"And he agreed," Althea signed back.

Fiora raised an eyebrow. Everyone in the chamber understood the signs, so the private conversation was hardly private.

Although she still had no idea what they meant.

"Very well," Queen Gallerus said. "We will proceed as planned. You all will go to the royal humans in Montaigne and begin negotiations for a treaty. Madame Isla has secured clothing for you."

Madame Isla waved the fishing net full of fabric with one hand and lifted a familiar conch shell with the other.

Fiora blinked when she realized that she was being included in the group.

"Is it safe for me to use the transformation song again?"

"You don't need to," Kathelin said. "You can use this."

She held up the ring. The pearl gleamed in the shifting underwater light. Fiora laughed with relief.

"You found it!"

She grabbed the gem and held it close to her heart.

"Are you sure this charm is safe to use?" Queen Gallerus said. "This magic is forbidden for a reason."

"We've taken precautions," Althea said. "And we will take further measures if he doesn't keep his word."

"That won't help her if she's dead."

"But it will make us feel better."

Fiora raised an eyebrow. Was her aunt making a joke?

That would be a first, but it was difficult to tell for sure.

What on earth were they talking about?

"Let's go!" Zoe said. "We're going to see the humans!"

She grabbed a golden ball from beside the queen's throne, tossed it up, and caught it as it slowly descended in the water.

Queen Gallerus nodded.

"That human charm will be quite useful. Capture everything you see, Zoe."

"Of course!"

And that seemed to settle the matter. Fiora, Kathelin, Althea, Zoe, and Madame Isla swam towards shore. Althea and Kathelin took turns singing to create currents that pulled the mermaids quickly through the water. They swam towards the docks, but Fiora directed them to the empty shoreline by the castle instead. Five mermaids emerging naked from the water in the middle of a shipyard would cause chaos for multiple reasons.

They hid behind a rock while Madame Isla pulled the gowns out of the fishing net and laid them out to dry. They were in varying states of decay and looked like they had come from a variety of countries at various points throughout history.

Spot landed nearby and studied the mermaids hopefully. Fiora hummed a tune, pulled a fish out of the water, and threw it to him. The gull squawked and flew away with his prize.

Fiora lifted her ring, preparing to transform into a human.

"Wait."

Madame Isla offered Fiora a small vial of liquid.

"Would you like to remove the squid ink from your hair first? I still think changing your appearance is a good way to catch the attention of a human man."

Fiora laughed. Madame Isla didn't give up easily.

But she took the bottle. She had spent enough time hiding. This time when she returned to the human world, Fiora would do so as herself.

G ustave hurried to the dining room, silently scolding himself for sleeping so late. He had intended to get up early and have a private conversation with Father, Grandmother, and Collette.

Instead, he was late for breakfast and hadn't had a chance to warn anyone about what would happen today.

And a lot would happen today.

Gustave stopped to gather his thoughts before he entered the room. He needed his composure for this. He needed to be king.

He swallowed when he saw how full the dining room was. It made sense for the royal gala guests to attend the meal, but Gustave had forgotten about them after everything that had happened last night.

When he had pictured the scene, he had only imagined his family.

They were there, of course. Collette, King Francois, and Dowager Queen Bernadine sat at the head of the table. Thomas hovered beside Bernadine, translating the numerous conversations happening as best he could. Prince Leonardo, Princess

Lenora, Prince Edric, Lady Annabelle, and Elaine sat on Collette's side of the table.

Princess Serafina and Prince Massimo were absent. Serafina had announced last night that they would rise early and sail with the tide. Unlike Gustave, it appeared that she had followed through with her intentions and woke up on time.

Marquis Corbeau, Marchioness Rouge, and several other council members sat on the king's side. Captain Whist and Dale the merchant sat with them.

The chair at the other end of the table was empty. Waiting for him.

Gustave took it and gestured for the head waiter.

"Have five extra places ready to set if necessary," he whispered. "I'm expecting a few more guests. I'm not sure when they will arrive, but they may be here before the meal ends."

The waiter nodded and hurried away to make the preparations.

"I apologize for my tardiness," Gustave said.

"It is quite understandable, Your Majesty," Prince Leonardo said. "You had an eventful evening last night."

Gustave waited for more questions, but no one asked. He looked to Collette.

"I've already told everyone what happened," she signed. *"And slipped the important details to the most gossipy servants, so the whole castle should know by now. I thought it would be awkward if everyone kept asking about your bride."*

Yes, that would be excessively awkward. With everything else that had happened, Gustave had almost forgotten about his wedding.

Granted, he couldn't remember much of it even when he tried. Just a golden fog and blissful happiness.

And dull regret that he couldn't shake no matter how many times he told himself that he had been cursed. That what happened with Elspeth had not been his fault.

"We've annulled the marriage on grounds of magical coercion," Dowager Queen Bernadine signed. *"Believe it or not, there is a precedent for that."*

Gustave believed it. He nodded his thanks and looked out the window to the sea. It stretched to the horizon, gray and empty.

Please let them come. Let the mermaids keep their word and come.

"You look well, Father," Gustave said, forcing his attention back to the dining room.

King Francois smiled at his son.

"I feel well, although I have a lot to catch up on. I apologize to those present if I am a little behind in matters of state. Spending a year as a statue will do that to you."

He cast a curious look at Prince Edric but said nothing further.

"The growing frequency of magical attacks is rather alarming," Prince Leonardo said. "I'm going to urge my father to work with Montaigne and Aeonia to find the cause. Perhaps with a free exchange of information we can better understand what is happening."

"We don't have much information to exchange," Elaine said.

"That may be true, but you seem to have a knack for finding what is available. My library is at your disposal if you wish to use it for your research."

"Oh. Thank you!"

Elaine's eyes glittered with excitement at the prospect of exploring a new library.

"The royal family of Montaigne would be happy to share-"

Gustave didn't get the chance to finish his offer. The doors burst open, and five women walked into the dining room.

Everyone gasped. The women did make quite a spectacle. Their hair was tangled and tousled from the wind. Their clothes were damp and wrinkled and clung to their skin. The women dripped on the floor, creating five sizable puddles around their bare feet as they stood in the doorway.

Gustave shook off his surprise and looked closer at each of his guests.

Madame Isla wore an ornate gown that was probably red at one point, but had faded an unappealing shade of pink. The bodice was too small and strained at the seams, while the large puffed sleeves drooped around her arms like soggy pastries. Her white hair was pinned up with a number of forks.

Dale leaned forward in his seat and studied the forks with interest.

Althea and Kathelin wore matching green dresses that were far too big for them and hung awkwardly around their bodies. If anything, the matching outfits only highlighted their differences. Althea looked displeased with everyone and everything in the room, while Kathelin looked delighted.

Zoe's dress was bright yellow and in worse shape than the rest. Its fabric was so threadbare that the sleeves had difficulty supporting the garment. The seams had already torn in several places, and the whole thing looked like it might disintegrate at any moment. The color might have been flattering before it was exposed to sea water, but Gustave doubted it. Nevertheless, the young mermaid beamed as if she was dressed to the heights of fashion.

Then Gustave saw Fiora and forgot everything else in the room. She wore a wrinkled blue dress and held her chin high, as if daring anyone to criticize her appearance. The skirt was too short and showed her bare feet and ankles. As far as he could tell, her feet were no longer in pain.

Her hair was red again and hung loose around her shoulders. Gustave had forgotten how bright and brilliant it was. How it complimented her blue eyes.

She took his breath away.

Then she looked at him, and Gustave forgot how to breathe altogether.

Her eyes were sad, and it broke Gustave's heart. Did she still feel unsure of him because of what had happened with Elspeth?

Or did the sadness have something to do with her past? With the story Althea and Kathelin had told him last night?

Madame Isla signed something too quickly for Gustave to catch. Fiora nodded.

"On behalf of Her Majesty Queen Gallerus of the Ocean, we royal sisters have come to negotiate a treaty of peace with the humans of Montaigne."

Her voice was so rich and confident and perfect that it took Gustave a moment to process what she had actually said. Her Kellish accent only added to the allure.

The rest of the diners reacted slowly as well. But her words caused a stir once they sank in. Everyone at the table turned to their neighbors in surprise.

Then they turned to Gustave.

He looked to his father. Surely King Francois would prefer to handle this? After all, he was king now.

But his father shook his head and nodded at Gustave. Gustave swallowed.

"It is an honor, ladies. Please, join us for breakfast."

He nodded to the waiters, who hurried to add the extra chairs to the table and set extra places. The spacious table was suddenly rather crowded.

And rather more exciting.

Zoe tossed a golden ball into the air a few times, then stuffed a croissant into her mouth.

Gustave stared. Was that Carina's golden ball? Where had the mermaid found it?

"This food is amazing!" Zoe signed. *"Try some, Fiora."*

She reached across the table for another croissant. Her sleeves tore as she moved, leaving the bodice supported by only a few threads.

Zoe seemed completely unconcerned with her dress disintegrating, but Fiora and Gustave shared a wary look.

"I wonder if the royal household of Montaigne would like to provide more durable clothing for my cousin as a gesture of goodwill?" Fiora signed. *"Perhaps a certain sweater?"*

Gustave choked back a laugh. Fiora's expression remained calm, but her eyes twinkled with amusement.

He summoned the head waiter again, whispered a few words, then picked up his fork and took a bite of scrambled eggs. Madame Isla stared at him with her jaw dropped. He nodded politely at her and took another bite.

The white-haired mermaid watched his every move. Then she pulled a fork from her hair and carefully took a bite from her own plate. Gustave tried to keep eating, but it was difficult to enjoy the food with a mermaid mirroring him.

He set down the fork, feeling too self-conscious to eat anything else. Madame Isla started copying Marquis Corbeau instead. He glared at her, and she smiled back.

"Are you well?" Gustave signed to Fiora.

She nodded, and her brilliant red hair shimmered in the sunlight as she moved.

"Is he trying to seduce her?" Zoe signed to Madame Isla.

Madame Isla didn't answer. She had switched her attention to Lady Annabelle, who was eating soup with a spoon. The mermaid picked up a spoon and tried to mimic Annabelle's movements. She spilled most of the soup on her dress, but seemed content with the small amount she managed to get into her mouth.

Lady Annabelle turned her attention to Prince Edric, trying very hard to ignore Madame Isla. The mermaid didn't seem to mind.

"Perhaps we could stop speaking in signs and have conversations that everyone can understand?" Marquis Corbeau said.

"The enchantment that allows mermaids to become human also takes their voice," Fiora said. "I'm here to translate as necessary."

"But they understand speech?" Dale asked.

When Fiora nodded, he turned to the mermaid closest to him. Unfortunately, that mermaid was Althea.

"My Lady, I wonder if I could trouble you to help me find something I lost at the bottom of the ocean? You see, a kraken attacked my ship, and-"

Althea gave him a look so fierce that Dale grew pale and turned away.

"Were you able to subdue the kraken?" Gustave signed to Fiora.

It wasn't what he actually wanted to ask her, but there were too many people at the table who knew sign language for their conversation to be truly private.

Not to mention Zoe was recording his every move with that blasted golden ball.

Fiora gave him a small smile, and Gustave had the feeling that she understood his hesitation.

"Perhaps we should begin the negotiations now, Your Majesty," Madame Isla signed. *"This enchantment takes a lot of magic to sustain, and our queen will be eager to hear the results."*

Thomas spoke her words out loud for everyone.

The head waiter returned with a parcel and handed it to Gustave with a bow.

"First, a gesture of goodwill," Gustave said. "I would like to give you a present."

He bowed to Zoe and handed her the box. Her eyes widened with delight as she pulled the sweater out. The colors were even brighter than Gustave remembered, and the jeweled seagulls were unbelievably gaudy in the sunlight.

"You wear it," Fiora said. "Like this."

She helped Zoe slip the sweater over her head and arms.

"Magnificent," Madame Isla signed.

"It's so soft!" Zoe signed.

The mermaids stared at the garish stripes with delight. The humans gathered around the table looked both relieved that Zoe was covered and horrified by the sweater.

"But- You can't-" Marquis Corbeau stammered.

"He already has," Dowager Queen Bernadine said. "It looks lovely on you, dear."

She seemed delighted by the chaos that had descended over breakfast.

"I believe King Gustave has something to say," Althea signed.

She glared at Thomas, who quickly spoke her message out loud.

Everyone turned to Gustave.

He took a deep breath and pushed away his nerves. He had planned to make this announcement privately first. To discuss it with his family and make sure they understood his reasons. But he had already made up his mind. Perhaps it would be better simply to proceed and see what happened.

He stood and nodded at everyone assembled at the table.

"Please forgive me for interrupting your meal, but I have an announcement I must make before negotiations begin. It will only take a moment."

He signed the words as well. Thomas was an excellent translator, but Gustave didn't want his grandmother to hear this from a secondhand source.

She gave him a piercing look, and Gustave had the strange feeling that she already knew what he was going to say.

But that was impossible, wasn't it? He himself hardly knew where to begin.

"As you all may have noticed, I-"

He stopped. That wasn't quite the right place to start.

Then again, he had to start somewhere.

"As you all may have noticed, I got married last night under magical coercion. I normally would not do something so important in such haste. Especially not when my heart belongs to another."

He looked at Fiora, who met his gaze with wide blue eyes.

"I knew her first as Lady Mer, and I still feel like a fool for not recognizing her true identity sooner. Princess Fiora came to us under a curse, but to me that curse was a blessing because it gave me a chance to know her."

"Do you think this infatuation is the result of further magical coercion?" Marquis Corbeau whispered to Marchioness Rouge. "Perhaps the skill runs in the family."

"You're the one who helped him get married so quickly last night," she replied. "They're too polite to say it, but that wedding was largely your fault."

Marquis Corbeau turned red and stood to his feet.

"The marchioness makes an excellent point. In my haste to see King Gustave suitably married, I ignored the signs that something was wrong. I most humbly apologize for that."

He sounded genuinely sorry. Gustave couldn't remember the marquis ever apologizing before.

"That's quite alright–"

"And I think there is a lesson to be learned from last night. No matter how strong your feelings, it does no good to be hasty when making decisions. Especially about matters of the heart."

He cast a significant look at Fiora, who returned it with a scowl.

Gustave sighed. He had been trying to build a solid case and explain his reasons. But perhaps in this instance, it was best to be blunt and simply say what he meant.

"I am abdicating the throne to be with Fiora. Madame Isla and the other mermaids will negotiate with my sister Collette and my father to arrange the treaty."

Lady Anabelle let out an enraged squeak. Everyone else stared at him in stunned silence. Their expressions varied. His grandmother looked a little surprised, but Gustave guessed it was more from his bold manner of speaking than the content of his announcement. Leonardo, Lenora, and Edric looked bewildered. As did his council members.

Collette jumped to her feet.

"Gustave, that isn't necessary. Fiora is a princess. You can marry her and still be king."

"What did I just say about being hasty?" Marquis Corbeau said. "You were hasty last night and look where that got you!"

"You're sure, Gustave?" Bernadine signed.

"I'm sure."

"I know I missed a lot," King Francois said, "But apparently I missed even more than I realized. Gustave, what is this about?"

Gustave looked at Fiora. She seemed almost as confused as everyone else in the room. Blast, he was not handling this as well as he had hoped.

"Princess Fiora is half mermaid," Gustave began.

He paused, searching for the right words.

"Fiora's mother was a mermaid who fell in love with King Fergal of Kell. Her sisters made her a ring that would let her use the love of a human man to share his life and transform herself into a human. But when his brother died, Fergal's responsibilities as king pulled him away from Nyssa. He chose his duties to his kingdom over his love, and that caused Nyssa's death.

"Fiora still has the ring, and it will allow her to remain human through my love. But she must have me completely. I must value her above my other responsibilities, and I cannot do that if I am serving as king. Not to mention this country deserves better than a conflicted monarch. That is why I must abdicate. As much as I love Montaigne, I cannot risk Fiora's life for my country. Besides, Collette will make an excellent queen. After only a few days, she has already-"

Gustave had been so caught up in his speech that he didn't realize Fiora had moved until she threw her arms around him and kissed him.

❧ 76 ❧

F iora kissed Gustave thoroughly before pulling away. After all her time without her voice, she had realized that sometimes actions were more efficient than words.

"Are you sure?" she whispered. "I didn't ask this of you."

"You didn't have to."

He wrapped his arm around her waist, and they faced the table together.

Fiora met Dowager Queen Bernadine's gaze first. The queen looked rather pleased with this turn of events.

"You knew," Fiora signed.

"I guessed."

Fiora didn't ask how. Bernadine probably wouldn't explain anyway.

"Your Majesty, your abdication is completely unnecessary," Marquis Corbeau said. "Princess Fiora may be a bit brash, but Kell has a respectable lineage. There is no reason she couldn't make a suitable queen with a proper education. And many monarchs maintain a balance between ruling and loving their family."

"He's already abdicated," Fiora said. "He doesn't have to listen to you anymore."

"I liked you better when you couldn't speak."

"No, you didn't."

The marquis shrugged in agreement.

"Gustave, I-" Collette's voice failed her.

"I don't know what to say," she signed. *"I never planned to rule this country. I'm not sure I can."*

"Of course you can," Gustave said. "And you won't be alone."

"I still don't think this is necessary."

"There is more to the story," Althea signed.

Fiora looked at her in surprise. Thomas translated, and the conversations around the table quieted.

"When Fiora sacrificed herself to save Gustave last night, she changed the enchantment by sharing her life with him. They are bound to each other through that ring."

Fiora looked at the ring with surprise.

"Is that why there are strands of copper in the pearl?"

Her aunt nodded.

"You hold Gustave's life as much as he holds yours. If you abandon him for another, he will die as Nyssa did."

Fiora swallowed as a strange weight of responsibility settled over her.

"I'm sorry," she whispered, squeezing Gustave's arm. "I didn't mean to."

"Don't you dare apologize for saving my life."

He winked at her, and Fiora laughed.

"But even that doesn't mean that Gustave needs to abdicate," Collette said. "They can rule together. Gustave, you've prepared your whole life for this. I-"

"You're capable and strong," Fiora said. "And you're not alone."

She gestured to everyone at the table. To Dowager Queen Bernadine and King Francois. To Marquis Corbeau and Marchioness Rouge.

"You are more than capable, my dear," King Francois said. "And I'm here to help now. If Gustave truly wants to do this, then I support him."

"You'll be an excellent queen," Dowager Queen Bernadine said. "I'll teach you everything I know."

"And I'll teach you everything that you actually need to know," Marchioness Rouge said.

Dowager Queen Bernadine turned to Thomas for a translation. He swallowed nervously before signing the words, but Bernadine just laughed.

"I'll still be available to answer questions if you need me," Gustave said.

"Yes, we'll help as we can," Fiora said, surprising herself. "You're my friend. I won't abandon you so easily."

She had definitely spent too much time in Montaigne.

But perhaps that wasn't a bad thing.

"Tell them the rest, Gustave," Althea signed.

He nodded.

"Last night, the merfolk offered me a position as a liaison between them and the human world, and I accepted."

"And as a royal sister, Fiora will serve as an ambassador for the mermaids on land," Madame Isla signed. *"As a princess of mermaids and humans, she is uniquely qualified to bridge the gap between us."*

Fiora blinked, too surprised to speak. Thomas spoke the words out loud so for everyone.

"We recommended this to Queen Gallerus last night, and she agreed with us," Kathelin signed. *"This responsibility is different than ruling a country and should not interfere with the enchantment. Of course this means you'll have to visit often. Turn Gustave into a frog, and he can come with you."*

Fiora felt Gustave shudder. She interlaced her fingers with his.

"Perhaps it would be fun to be a frog?"

He laughed and squeezed her hand.

"So you've abdicated your throne and become engaged to a

mermaid princess serving as an ambassador for the queen of the sea." Marchioness Rouge said. "This may actually be a very strategic match. An alliance with the ocean will be very beneficial for Montaigne."

She shared a look with Marquis Corbeau, who nodded reluctantly.

"Given the events of the past few weeks, improving relations with the merfolk does seem wise."

"Engaged? I- That is-" Gustave stammered.

Fiora nudged him with her shoulder and winked at him. He was adorable when he was flustered, but there was no need to rush. They had time now. All the time they needed.

"I hope the merfolk will consider an offer of friendship from Darluna as well," Prince Leonardo said. "We would be honored to form an alliance with our friends in the sea."

He smiled at Fiora and each of the mermaids in turn.

"And you must come visit us when you are able, Fiora," Princess Lenora said. "I would be honored to give you a tour of our gardens."

A butterfly flew through an open window and landed on her head.

Fiora blinked in surprise. After everything that had happened, Lenora still wanted to be friends?

"Eldria would also like to be part of any treaty negotiations," Prince Edric said.

He sounded more like he was reciting a memorized speech for a school assignment than genuinely offering friendship.

"We are only authorized to negotiate with the humans of Montaigne, but we will bring your good wishes to our queen," Madame Isla signed.

Lady Annabelle sniffed in disgust, and Fiora fought the urge to laugh.

"I'd like to know more about mixed magic," Elaine said. "I've never heard of such a thing, but perhaps it was a common practice when magic was more prevalent."

She looked, not to Fiora, but to Madame Isla.

"I've read that mermaids can live to be three hundred years old. Is that true?"

Everyone looked from Elaine to Madame Isla with wide eyes. Fiora waited for the mermaid to deny it, but instead she merely looked thoughtful.

"We'll talk later," Madame Isla signed to Elaine. *"For now, I agree that we should discover more about mixed magic. It has never been practiced amongst mermaids, and I haven't encountered it in my research. Is there a human who would know the answer to such things?"*

Thomas translated out loud, and Fiora and Gustave shared a look.

"Please, no," Fiora signed. *"Not her."*

"Lina might know," Collette said when no one else answered. "We should ask her."

Fiora's heart sank. Lina was the last person on earth she wanted to talk to.

"How would you feel about trying out that frog enchantment sooner rather than later?" Fiora signed to Gustave. *"We could hide in the ocean."*

She expected Gustave to reject the idea, but he seemed to be considering it.

"Visiting Lina will mean visiting Aeonia," he whispered. "Stefan and Carina."

He shuddered a little, and Fiora laughed.

"So we hide?"

"I have a feeling your aunts would find us rather quickly. Perhaps it won't be so bad if we're together.

Fiora smiled. That would help a little.

A very little.

"If that's settled, perhaps we should finish eating," Dowager Queen Bernadine said. "I believe some of our guests are planning to leave after breakfast. I wouldn't want to delay them."

She cast a significant look at Prince Edric. The prince bowed.

"Yes, I'm afraid I must be going soon. In fact, I think I should leave now since this meal has gone on rather longer than planned. Merchant Dale, are you still interested in sailing to Eldria with me?"

Dale looked from the prince to the mermaids, clearly torn between his desire to return home and his desire to retrieve his forks from the bottom of the ocean.

Althea glared at him again, and that settled the matter.

"I would be honored, Your Highness. I should return to my daughters as soon as possible."

"Then please excuse us. It has been an honor."

Prince Edric bowed. His gaze lingered on Lady Annabelle for a few moments before he turned and walked away. Dale expressed his fervent thanks to the royal family and hurried after the prince.

"Good riddance," Dowager Queen Bernadine signed to Fiora.

Fiora laughed out loud, not caring that her voice filled the room. Gustave smiled at her.

"Will you join me for breakfast, Princess Fiora?"

"Of course, King Gustave."

"Just Gustave now."

Fiora smirked.

"You'll be a prince of merfolk when we're married."

Gustave flushed, and Fiora winked at him.

"There's plenty of time to work all that out."

"So we agree that Gustave and Fiora should go to Aeonia and see what Lina knows about mixed magic?" Collette asked Madame Isla.

The mermaid nodded.

"I don't know this Lina, but if she is knowledgeable about magic, then Fiora must speak with her."

"Sit by me," Gustave whispered, pulling a chair next to his.

Fiora sat and stared at her plate. It looked delicious, as the food in Montaigne always did, but she felt too nervous about trav-

eling to Aeonia to eat anything. It might as well have been
mermaid mush.

"And what about Princess Elspeth?" Dowager Queen Bernadine said. "Should we send a message to Kell to inform King
Fergal what happened? Do you think he was involved?"

Everyone looked to Fiora.

"I have no idea," she said. "Kell has had some problems lately,
but my father never told me about them in detail. He only
stressed that it was essential that I marry a prince so Kell could
have an ally."

That seemed a world and a lifetime ago.

"That does seem curious," Prince Leonardo said.

"The sudden demise of Prince Darian of Eldria also seems
suspicious," Bernadine said.

"Demise? He isn't dead," Collette said.

"But he doesn't seem the sort to give up the throne easily,"
Gustave said. "I wonder what happened."

"I'm sure it was nothing untoward," Lady Annabelle said.

Everyone ignored her.

"I don't know anything of this Darian either," Madame Isla signed.
"What happened to him?"

"It seems I have missed even more than I thought," King
Francois said. "I agree we should discuss these matters, but
perhaps we should negotiate with the mermaids while they are
here since their time on shore is limited."

"Finally, someone with sense," Althea signed. *"Your Majesty, before
we begin the negotiations, I would be interested to know what you
remember about your enchantment."*

"Not much," Francois admitted. "But I'm happy to answer
your questions as best I can."

Althea took that as an invitation to launch into a series of
rapid questions in sign language. King Francois answered her in
sign language, taking his time as he tried to remember details.

Across the table, Madame Isla signed with Collette and Bernadine, asking them about the finer points of using silverware. Zoe tossed her golden ball into the air, capturing the conversations so that Queen Gallerus could see them later.

Leonardo and Lenora chatted with Elaine, describing their library and planning the details of her visit. Lady Annabelle fluttered her eyelashes at Leonardo, trying and failing to catch his notice.

Kathelin kept her attention on Fiora and Gustave. She winked when she noticed Fiora's questioning gaze. The mermaid looked even happier than usual. Fiora smiled at her aunt and twisted the pearl ring around her finger.

Gustave bent over and kissed her cheek, and for the first time in her life, Fiora felt that she belonged. She had two families now, and both loved her. Gustave loved her enough to step away from his country and join her in the strange place she occupied between sea and land. They would make their own way together.

It seemed that even when you were part of two worlds, both could feel like home.

EPILOGUE

"*G* *ustave, she won't be happy to see me.*" Fiora signed so the servant leading them wouldn't overhear. Walking through the halls of the Aeonian castle brought back unpleasant memories of the Princess Test. Her desperate attempts to win Alaric and get Lina disqualified.

Her humiliation when she had won and still not been chosen.

Fiora took a deep breath and gritted her teeth. She regretted everything about that time, but the experience had led her to Gustave. She didn't regret that.

And if Lina had answers, then Fiora needed to face her.

"*I'm sure it will be fine.*"

"*What will we do if they kick us out?*"

Gustave raised an eyebrow.

"What exactly happened between you and Lina at the Princess Test?"

The servant looked back at them. Fiora glared and gestured for him to keep walking.

She didn't exactly expect them to kick her out. She wouldn't let them when so much hung in the balance.

But she wouldn't be surprised if they tried.

The servant led them to a door that Fiora recognized as the way to the throne room. It was closed.

"It seems that Princess Evangelina is already in council. If you'll wait here, the footman will open the door and fetch you when she is finished."

Fiora nodded, and the servant hurried away. Gustave waited patiently, leaning against the wall and studying the ceiling.

"I think those tiles were in a different pattern the last time I was here."

Fiora glanced up at the ceiling, but didn't comment. She had been too focused on Alaric when she was here to notice the ceiling.

She clasped her hands together. Then unclasped them and paced in front of the door, trying to burn off the nervous energy coursing through her veins.

They shouldn't keep her waiting.

To be fair, they didn't know she was waiting.

Or maybe they did. Maybe Lina had decided not to see Fiora. Maybe she meant to send her away just like her father had.

"Fiora, look at me."

Fiora looked. Gustave's eyes were as warm and steady as always. He took her hands and smiled.

"It will be fine."

He sounded so sure that she almost believed him. Fiora studied his face, basking in the affection in his expression. She fought the urge to glance at her pearl ring to confirm that he still loved her. She didn't need magical confirmation of Gustave's feelings now.

Muffled voices on the other side of the door interrupted the moment. Fiora stared at the doorknob, suddenly very tempted to eavesdrop. Gustave met her gaze, and Fiora knew he was having similar thoughts.

He was just too polite to do anything about them.

"Keep watch."

Gustave stepped back so he could watch the hallway for anyone coming their way. Fiora leaned her ear against the door.

"I just want to make sure you understand the serious nature of this mission," Prince Alaric said. "We have heard reports of dark magic in Eldria, but Prince Darian has not answered any of my letters regarding the matter. I'm sending you to investigate, but there will be serious consequences if you're discovered."

Fiora raised an eyebrow and signed a translation for Gustave. He looked intrigued. Apparently they weren't the only ones to notice something strange happening in Eldria.

"Investigate? We're simply sneaking away to see the mountain scenery and spend some time together."

That was Princess Carina, and Fiora could practically hear the smirk in her voice.

But who was going with her?

"Honestly, brother. You don't think we can handle a simple intelligence-gathering mission to a neighboring kingdom? You're talking to Santelle's greatest spy and the man who is her equal in cleverness."

Apparently Prince Stefan, the second oldest prince, had been chosen as backup on the mission.

Interesting. He had seemed quite useless at the Princess Test. As had Carina.

Fiora realized Gustave was waiting and quickly summarized the conversation for him. She kept her ear pressed against the door so she didn't miss any additional comments.

"Carina and Stefan are in there?"

Now Gustave was the one who looked nervous. He eyed the hallway as if he was considering making a run for it.

Fiora was too busy laughing at his expression to notice the approaching footsteps on the other side of the door. It opened, and Fiora fell inside, sprawling onto Queen Marta. The queen caught her and helped her regain her balance.

"Oh! Hello, dear."

Fiora smoothed her dress and stepped back. The Aeonian queen looked just as Fiora remembered from the Princess Test. Short and stout with frizzy brown hair and a friendly face. More goat herder than queen, even after years on the throne.

"Queen Marta, please forgive us," Gustave said. "We were told to wait here until your council finished."

He bowed low. Marta smiled at him.

"Oh, hello, Your Majesty. I'm sorry you were kept waiting. We didn't receive word that you were planning to visit."

"Well, we didn't exactly plan it," Gustave said.

He paused, seeming unsure how to continue.

"There was a kraken attack in Montaigne, and some unusual magic was used," Fiora said. "We thought Lina might be able to help us understand it."

"Oh. Well, in that case, you'd better go in at once."

Queen Marta gestured towards the hallway that led to the throne room.

"Oh, we can wait until she's done speaking with Stefan and Carina," Gustave said. "We wouldn't want to disturb them."

Marta raised an eyebrow, as if to remind him that she had just caught Fiora eavesdropping on that very same council.

"Thank you," Fiora said.

She hurried down the hallway, leaving Gustave and Queen Marta behind to sort through the necessary formalities. She wanted to see whatever was happening in the throne room for herself.

"Just be careful," Lina said. "You never know-"

Fiora had intended to hide in the shadows and eavesdrop, but the throne room's ceiling had disappeared, leaving the room more brightly lit than she expected. Sunlight glinted off her red hair as she rounded the corner. Lina scowled.

"What are you doing here?"

Fiora wasn't quite sure how to answer that question, so she glared instead, her shoulders tense and her head held high.

Lina glared back. The shadow warrior wore an elegant black dress and a headband covered with a multitude of jewels. Her green eyes narrowed with suspicion at Fiora.

Prince Alaric's eyes were wide with alarm. He wore a military uniform, which was much less stylish than anything he had worn at the Princess Test, but his long blond hair was still curled and hung loose down his shoulders.

Fiora smirked a little. Thank goodness he hadn't chosen her as his bride. He was handsome in his way, but she much preferred Gustave.

Prince Stefan looked just as Fiora remembered. Spiky brown hair and a mischievous expression that promised trouble. Princess Carina stood beside him with her hand resting on his shoulder. Her curly blond hair hung loose down her back, and she wore the most ridiculous frilly pink gown Fiora had ever seen.

Carina studied Fiora for a moment, then curtsied and pulled Stefan towards the door.

"We'll just be going then," she said.

"Yes, I'm sure you all have a lot to talk about!" Stefan said.

He and Carina sprinted out of the room while Prince Alaric sputtered something about giving them further instructions.

"They weren't listening anyway," Lina said. "Warnings to be careful are wasted on those two."

She glared at Fiora again and put her hand possessively on Alaric's shoulder.

"I'm here for you, not him," Fiora said.

Lina and Alaric gaped at her, and Fiora wished she hadn't said anything at all. In some ways, not having a voice had been rather convenient.

She felt a hand rest supportively against her back and didn't need to look to know that Gustave had joined her. She leaned against him, wishing that they were back in Montaigne and didn't have to deal with Lina and magic and everything else in the world.

"King Gustave? This is a pleasant surprise."

Prince Alaric sounded far more surprised than pleased. Lina relaxed a little.

"It's good to see you again, King Gustave."

"It's just Gustave now, Your Majesty."

"Oh?"

Both Lina and Alaric looked intrigued.

"A lot has happened," Fiora said.

Her voice lilted, as it always did when her emotions ran away with her. Gustave wrapped an arm around her waist and pulled her closer.

Lina raised an eyebrow.

"Apparently it has. Should we clear our schedule for the day, Alaric? I have a feeling this will take a while."

Alaric nodded. Lina fixed her gaze on Fiora, looking more curious than hostile now. Fiora sighed. It was going to be a long day.

"It will be fine," Gustave signed. *"We'll figure this out together."*

Fiora looked into his calm gray eyes, and suddenly, she believed him. As long as they were together, they could face anything.

She wrapped her arms around him and kissed him. Gustave kissed her back, ignoring the fact that this was definitely not a proper place for such things.

"Maybe I should learn sign language," Prince Alaric said thoughtfully.

Lina laughed and kissed her husband on the cheek. He pulled her close, and for a moment, both couples forgot their troubles.

ABOUT THE AUTHOR

A.G. Marshall loves fairy tales and has been writing stories since she could hold a pencil. She is a professional pianist and perfected her storytelling by writing college papers about music (which is more similar to magic than you might think).

Want more stories? Find deleted scenes, blog posts, coloring pages, and writing playlists at my website! Sign up for my newsletter while you're there to get an exclusive short story for free!

www.AngelaGMarshall.com

angelagmarshall@outlook.com

ACKNOWLEDGMENTS

I know this is the part most readers skip, but I can't go on without saying thank you to some people who helped make this book possible.

Writing is a solitary pursuit, but living isn't. I have to thank so many people for encouraging me through this book. My mom was always ready to talk writing and stories. She read several extremely rough drafts and assured me that there were good moments there. The rest of my family and friends also provided incredible support and encouragement.

My beta reader team gave great feedback and helped me keep everything consistent with the past few books. A huge thanks to Erika Everest for spotting several potential problems and helping me solve them! My mom and Aunt Cindy provided great insight and encouragement as always.

Thanks to Lucy Tempest for providing accountability through writing sprints and kraken memes. Between dancing Squidward GIFs and white shoes, we made it through.

Thanks to Davis for listening to endless rants about mermaids and the logistics of magic and always telling me I could do it when I started to doubt if I could.

Thanks to Kristin Stecklein for her encouragement and helping me figure out the logistics of mermaid cuisine and cooking underwater.

Thanks to Olivia Ellis for proofreading and catching those last few typos.

Thanks to Alex Taussig for her invaluable health coaching and encouragement. She helped me push myself past my limitations and reach the next level.

Thanks to Jakob Tanner for providing great accountability and encouragement.

And thank you to the design team at Moor Books for the beautiful covers for this series!

I wrote a portion of this novel at the 20Books Edinburgh conference, and I can't say thank you enough to the organizers for putting so much of their time into making that event happen. Writing in a Scottish castle helped me channel my inner Fiora and power through the rough draft. And meeting all the wonderful writers there gave me inspiration to keep writing long after I left Scotland.

Lastly, thank you to all the wonderful readers who waited patiently for this book and were so wonderful and encouraging throughout the process. You all make this possible.

Made in the USA
Middletown, DE
24 December 2019